What readers are saying about
K A R E N   K I N G S B U R Y ' S
books

"This is one of the most absorbing series I have read in many years. There are many spiritual lessons to be learned from the stories."
—**Helen**

"*Forever* was a wonderful, inspiring, and heartwarming ending to the Firstborn series and I enjoyed the book the entire way! I can't wait to read the Sunrise series!"
—**Theresa**

"This book is awesome! Like the other books in Karen Kingsbury's series, this book refreshes your soul! I think *Forever* may very well be my favorite so far. I have already read it several times, finding something new to think about each time."
—**Sharon**

"I found myself with tears rolling down my face in several parts of this book. I have read the Redemption series and all the previous books in the Firstborn series but this is definitely my favorite so far."
—**K.S.**

"The Firstborn series is excellent. I enjoy this author so much and am looking forward to her Redemption series. These are hard books to put down and the messages they contain are inspiring."
—**Linda**

"Wow! I can't wait for the next series. Karen Kingsbury is incredible! I highly recommend the Redemption and Firstborn series to everyone I meet! What an inspiration the Baxter family is."
—**Beverly**

"Karen Kingsbury has the ability to grab my heart and emotions and also to make her characters real to me. The Firstborn series stresses family and relationship. You'll want to read all of this series and won't want it to end."　　　　　　　　**—Elaine**

"A story of love and forgiveness and a reminder of what marriage is supposed to be about. The ending was perfect and gave me warm fuzzies. I can't wait for the first book in the Sunrise series— I feel like a part of the Baxter family myself!"　　　　　**—Renee**

"Karen Kingsbury's books are filled with the unshakable, remarkable, miraculous fact that God's grace is greater than our suffering. There are no words for Ms. Kingsbury's writing."　　**—Wendie**

"Thank you, Karen, for writing so well and delivering a God-given and God-centered story with 'real' people who make mistakes."　　　　　　　　　　　　　　　　**—Tony**

"I dearly LOVED this series. I couldn't put any of the books down for more than a moment. I loaned these books, one at a time, to a friend who came back every day or two for the next one."　　　　　　　　　　　　　　　　　　**—Anita**

"Karen's books are addictive. I see a new one and need to order it, and once they arrive, I cannot rest until I complete it. Thank You, Lord, for the beautiful writing gift given to Karen for the benefit of her readers."　　　　　　　　　　　　**—Dee**

FOREVER

Karen
KINGSBURY

NEW YORK TIMES
BEST-SELLING AUTHOR

BAXTER FAMILY DRAMA™~FIRSTBORN SERIES #5

Tyndale House Publishers, Inc.
Carol Stream, Illinois

Visit Tyndale online at www.tyndale.com.

Visit Karen Kingsbury's Web site and learn more about her Life-Changing Fiction at www.KarenKingsbury.com.

TYNDALE and Tyndale's quill logo are registered trademarks of Tyndale House Publishers, Inc.

BAXTER FAMILY DRAMA is a trademark of Tyndale House Publishers, Inc.

Forever

Copyright © 2007 by Karen Kingsbury. All rights reserved.

Logo illustration copyright © 2003 by David Henderson. All rights reserved.

Cover photograph of woman copyright © by Rebecca Nathan/Trevillion. All rights reserved.

Cover photograph of tall grass copyright © by David Engelhardt/Tetra/Getty. All rights reserved.

Cover photograph of red dress copyright © by HBSS/Corbis. All rights reserved.

Author photograph copyright © 2008 by Dan Davis Photography at dandavisphotography.com. All rights reserved.

Designed by Jennifer Ghionzoli

Edited by Lorie Popp

Published in association with the literary agency of Alive Communications, Inc., 7680 Goddard Street, Suite 200, Colorado Springs, CO 80920.

Text about the five love languages (Chapter 23) inspired by The Five Love Languages © 1992 by Gary Chapman. Published by Northfield Publishing, Chicago, Illinois.

Scripture quotations are taken from the Holy Bible, New International Version,® NIV.® Copyright © 1973, 1978, 1984 by Biblica, Inc.™ Used by permission of Zondervan. All rights reserved worldwide. www.zondervan.com.

Library of Congress Cataloging-in-Publication Data

Kingsbury, Karen.
  Forever / Karen Kingsbury.
    p. cm.
  ISBN 978-1-4143-0764-0 (pbk. : alk. paper)
  I. Title
  PS3561.I4873F66 2007
  813'.54—dc22   2006035370

Repackage first published in 2011 under ISBN 978-1-4143-4980-0.

Printed in the United States of America

17   16   15   14   13   12   11
7   6   5   4   3   2   1

To Donald, my Prince Charming

We've reached a new year, another season in life, and still I cannot imagine this ride without you. Our kids are flourishing, and so much of that is because of you, because of your commitment to me and to them. You are the spiritual leader, the man of my dreams who makes this whole crazy, wonderful adventure possible. I thank God for you every day. I am amazed at the way you blend love and laughter, tenderness and tough standards to bring out the best in our boys. Thanks for loving me, for being my best friend, and for finding "date moments" amid even the most maniacal or mundane times. My favorite times are with you by my side. I love you always, forever.

To Kelsey, my precious daughter

You are seventeen, and somehow that sounds more serious than the other ages. As if we jumped four years over the past twelve months. Seventeen brings with it the screeching of brakes on a childhood that has gone along full speed until now. Seventeen? Seventeen years since I held you in the nursery, feeling a sort of love I'd never felt before. Seventeen sounds like bunches of lasts all lined up ready to take the stage and college counselors making plans to take my little girl from here and home into a brand-new big world. Seventeen tells me it won't be much longer. Especially as you near the end of your junior year. Sometimes I find myself barely able to exhale. The ride is so fast at this point that I can only try not to blink so I won't miss a minute of it. Like the most beautiful springtime flower, I see you growing and unfolding, becoming interested in current events and formulating godly viewpoints that are yours alone. The same is true in dance, where you are simply breathtaking onstage. I believe in you, honey. Keep your eyes on Jesus and the path will be easy to follow. Don't ever stop dancing. I love you.

To Tyler, my beautiful song

Can it be that you are fourteen and helping me bring down the dishes from the top shelf? Just yesterday people would call and confuse you with Kelsey. Now they confuse you with your dad—in more ways than one. You are on the bridge, dear son, making the transition between Neverland and Tomorrowland and becoming a strong, godly young man in the process. Keep giving Jesus your very best, and always remember that you're in a battle. In today's world, Ty, you need His armor every day, every minute. Don't forget . . . when you're up there onstage, no matter how bright the lights, I'll be watching from the front row, cheering you on. I love you.

To Sean, my wonder boy

Your sweet nature continues to be a bright light in our home. It seems a lifetime ago that we first brought you—our precious son—home from Haiti. It's been my great joy to watch you grow and develop this past year, learning more about reading and writing and, of course, animals. You're a walking encyclopedia of animal facts, and that, too, brings a smile to my face. Recently a cold passed through the family, and you handled it better than any of us. Smiling through your fever, eyes shining even when you felt your worst. Sometimes I try to imagine if everyone everywhere had your outlook—what a sunny place the world would be. Your hugs are something I look forward to, Sean.

Keep close to Jesus. I love you.

To Josh, my tender tough guy

You continue to excel at everything you do, but my favorite time is late at night when I poke my head into your room and see that—once again—your nose is buried in your Bible. You really get it, Josh. I loved hearing you talk about baptism the other day, how you feel ready to make that decision, that commitment to Jesus. At almost twelve, I can only say that every choice you make for Christ will take you closer to the plans He has for your life. That by being strong in the Lord, first and foremost, you'll be strong at everything else. Keep winning for Him, dear son.

You make me so proud. I love you.

To EJ, my chosen one

You amaze me, Emmanuel Jean! The other day you told me that you pray often, and I asked you what about. "I thank God a lot," you told me. "I thank Him for my health and my life and my home." Your normally dancing eyes grew serious. "And for letting me be adopted into the right family." I still feel the sting of tears when I imagine you praying that way. I'm glad God let you be adopted into the right family too. One of my secret pleasures is watching you and Daddy becoming so close. I'll glance over at the family room during a play-off basketball game on TV, and there you'll be, snuggled up close to him, his arm around your shoulders. As long as Daddy's your hero, you have nothing to worry about. You couldn't have a better role model. I know that Jesus is leading the way and that you are excited to learn the plans He has for you.

But for you, this year will always stand out as a turning point.

Congratulations, honey! I love you.

To Austin, my miracle child

Can my little boy be nine years old? Even when you're twenty-nine you'll be my youngest, my baby. I guess that's how it is with the last child, but there's no denying what my eyes tell me. You're not little anymore. Even so, I love that—once in a while—you wake up and scurry down the hall to our room so you can sleep in the middle. Sound asleep I still see the blond-haired infant who lay in intensive care, barely breathing, awaiting emergency heart surgery. I'm grateful for your health, precious son, grateful God gave you back to us at the end of that long-ago day. Your heart remains the most amazing part of you, not only physically, miraculously, but because you have such kindness and compassion for people. One minute tough boy hunting frogs and snakes out back, pretending you're an Army Ranger, then getting teary-eyed when Horton the Elephant nearly loses his dust speck full of little Who people.

Be safe, baby boy. I love you.

And to God Almighty, the Author of life,

who has—for now—blessed me with these.

ACKNOWLEDGMENTS

This book couldn't have come together without the help of many people. First, a special thanks to my friends at Tyndale, who have believed in this series and worked with me to get this fifth book to my readers sooner than any of us dreamed possible. Thank you!

Also thanks to my amazing agent, Rick Christian, president of Alive Communications. I am amazed more as every day passes at your sincere integrity, your brilliant talent, and your commitment to the Lord and to getting my Life-Changing Fiction out to readers all over the world. You are a strong man of God, Rick. You care for my career as if you were personally responsible for the souls God touches through these books. Thank you for looking out for my personal time—the hours I have with my husband and kids most of all. I couldn't do this without you.

As always, this book wouldn't be possible without the help of my husband and kids, who will eat just about anything when I'm on deadline and who understand and love me anyway. I thank God that I'm still able to spend more time with you than with my pretend people, as Austin calls them. Thanks for understanding the sometimes-crazy life I lead and for always being my greatest support.

Thanks to my mother and assistant, Anne Kingsbury, for your great sensitivity and love for my readers. You are a reflection of my own heart, Mom, or maybe I'm a reflection of yours. Either way, we are a great team, and I appreciate you more than you know. I'm grateful also for my dad, Ted Kingsbury, who is and always has been my greatest encourager. I remember when I was a little girl, Dad, and you would say, "One day, honey, everyone will read your books and know what a wonderful writer you are." Thank you for believing in me long before anyone else ever did. Thanks also to my sisters Tricia and Susan and Lynne, who help out with my business when the workload is too large to see around. I appreciate you!

And to Olga Kalachik, whose hard work helping me prepare for events allows me to operate a significant part of my business from my home. The personal touch you bring to my ministry is precious to me, priceless to me. . . . Thank you with all my heart.

And thanks to my friends and family, especially my sister Sue, who is a new addition to my staff, and to my niece Melissa Kane, who helped me with a major project this past year. Thanks to Ann and Sylvia and all of you who pray for me and my family. We couldn't do this without you. Thanks to all of you who continue to surround me with love and prayer and support. I could list you by name, but you know who you are. Thank you for believing in me and for seeing who I really am. A true friend stands by through the changing seasons of life and cheers you on not for your successes but for staying true to what matters most. You are the ones who know me that way, and I'm grateful for every one of you.

Of course, the greatest thanks go to God Almighty, the most wonderful Author of all—the Author of life. The gift is Yours. I pray I might have the incredible opportunity and responsibility to use it for You all the days of my life.

FOREVER IN FICTION

A SPECIAL THANKS to Heidi Jones, who won the Forever in Fiction auction at the Veritas Classical Christian School in Oregon. Heidi chose to give the gift to her friend Susan Johnson, who chose to honor her sister, Cynthia Crivellone Deming, by naming her Forever in Fiction.

Cindy Deming died in a car accident at age thirty-seven. She was pregnant with her first child and survived by her husband, Sean. Cindy was passionate about animals, and at the time of her death she had eight cats, three dogs, two ferrets, and a rabbit. She was a very giving person, quiet by nature, and a good listener. She was petite with long, naturally curly brown hair, and she had just one sibling, Susan Johnson. She was also survived by her parents, Leonard Murphy and Barbara Murphy, who died seven months after Cindy.

Cindy enjoyed scuba diving and hiking the Oregon mountains, because she was always up for a challenge. She once went to Europe with friends and stayed at hostels, figuring out transportation as they traveled from one place to another. Even so, her favorite vacation spot was easily Hawaii. Cindy was a dedicated sister and daughter and granddaughter and would go out of her way to spend time with family. She was looking forward to being a mother.

In *Forever*, I chose to make Cindy a neurosurgeon so her character could take part in saving the life of someone who had also been in a terrible car accident. Heidi and Susan, I pray that Cindy is honored by her placement in *Forever* and that you will always remember her with a smile when you see her name in the pages of this novel, where she will be Forever in Fiction.

For those of you who are not familiar with Forever in Fiction, it is my way of involving you, the readers, in my stories while raising money for charities. To date this item has raised more than $200,000 at charity auctions across the country. If you are interested in having a Forever in Fiction package donated to your auction, contact my assistant, Tricia Kingsbury, at office@KarenKingsbury.com. Please write *Forever in Fiction* in the subject line. Please note that I am able to donate only a limited number of these each year. For that reason I have set a fairly high minimum bid on this package. That way the maximum funds are raised for charities.

CHAPTER ONE

THERE WERE MOMENTS when the sun shone so brightly on her life that Katy Hart could barely stand beneath it. Moments when she would be getting ready for a day of Christian Kids Theater rehearsals or folding laundry or filling her tank with gas and she'd have to check her ring finger. Just to be sure it had really happened.

Dayne Matthews had asked her to marry him.

She opened the door to her apartment, stepped inside, and exhaled. She'd spent the afternoon and evening with the Flanigans, first shopping with Jenny and then having dinner and watching a movie with the family. Now she wanted to be upstairs when Dayne called, the way he called every night around this time. She closed the door behind her and leaned against it for a minute.

Overnight God had taken her life from foggy uncertainty to crystal clear panoramas. She and Dayne wanted a simple wedding on the shore of Lake Monroe. He had already met with a wedding planner in Hollywood, a woman known for her brilliance at pulling off secret ceremonies, events the paparazzi never figured out until they were over.

The job would be a tough one, and Katy had resigned herself to the possibility that the press might find out, that helicopters could circle overhead and cameramen could infiltrate the trees along the lake to get a picture. Whatever. They'd already dragged her name across the cover of the tabloids.

She was marrying Dayne Matthews. Soon the whole world would know anyway.

They hadn't picked a date, but spring seemed perfect. Bloomington was beautiful in April and May. Dayne would have time to film one more movie by then, and it would allow enough time to find a wedding dress and figure out the reception, time to fly to Chicago and talk to her parents about the plans. Dayne had told her they didn't have a budget, but Katy wanted something simple and elegant, something she could find in Indianapolis as easily as in New York City.

It was the third week of July, which meant they had eight or nine months. Not much time considering how busy they would be in their separate lives over the next few months. Dayne was working six-day weeks filming his current movie in Los Angeles, the romance film with Academy Award–winning actress Randi Wells. And Katy needed to sort through the scripts for the lineup of plays slated for CKT's coming year. Sometimes she felt dizzy with everything that had happened in the last two weeks.

Katy sighed. Yes, the sun was shining brighter than ever in her life.

She changed into her pajamas and brushed her teeth. As she headed for bed, the phone rang. She darted across the room, grabbed the receiver, and bounced onto the mattress. The caller ID told her what she already knew. It was Dayne. She hit the Talk button. "Hey."

"Mmmm." He sounded tired, lonely, but even so she could practically see his eyes dancing. "Do you know how good that feels?"

"What?" An intimacy filled her voice, one that was reserved for him alone.

"Hearing you, knowing you're at the other end of the line." He drew a slow breath. "I look forward to this minute all day long."

She smiled. "Me too."

They talked about his day, and eventually that led to Dayne's recent conversation with his missionary friend Bob Asher. "God's making it all so clear—the future and how it's supposed to play out."

Katy thought about the weeks and months when the future had seemed anything but clear. During Dayne's involvement with Kabbalah or his time with Kelly Parker. "There were days I didn't think we'd ever be here."

"I know." He was quiet for a moment. "I thank God every night, Katy. Every night."

The topic shifted again, and he told her about the movie he was making. The director still believed they had a major hit on their hands, and a buzz had started that maybe this was the film that would earn Dayne his first Academy Award. That led to talk about the paparazzi and how a reporter for *Celebrity Life* magazine was getting closer to the truth about the identity of Dayne's birth family.

"It doesn't matter." Katy leaned back against her headboard. "They'll find out one day anyway."

"Not now, though. Not before the wedding."

They talked about the Baxters, how Ashley had accepted the role of assistant director for CKT's coming season and how the other Baxters were excited about Thanksgiving, when the whole family would be together for the first time.

Dayne steered the conversation back to the two of them. "Have you found it?" His voice held depth and tenderness, a tone that told her how much he missed her.

"What?" She glanced at a photo of them on her nightstand.

"Our house. I keep thinking you'll call and tell me you found it."

Katy sat up and crossed her legs. "You're serious?"

"Of course." An easy laugh came from him. "If you like it, I'll like it."

"But . . ." She ran her fingers through her hair. "Shouldn't you be here?"

"You find it and I'll fly out and take a look. How's that?"

"I don't know." If he were any other guy, she'd ask him about their price range. But that wouldn't be an issue with Dayne—something else that would take adjusting to. "I know we talked about it before, but really, Dayne, you should be here. You said near the lake, but do you want acreage or a smaller place closer to town?"

"Not near the lake." He chuckled. "*On* the lake. A big yard and a sweeping porch."

She grinned. "I told you . . . lakefront property is almost non-existent. Something *near* the lake, maybe. But *on* it?"

"I can dream, can't I?" He laughed again. "Okay. Eventually I want to be on the lake, but for now it doesn't matter. As long as I'm with you we can pitch a tent in the Baxters' backyard. Which we might have to do if you don't start looking."

"All right, I get it. I'll look." She gazed at her ring and adjusted her left hand so the diamond sparkled in the light. "I'll start tomorrow. I have a CKT meeting at Ashley's house; then I'll drive around the lake and see what's for sale." The task ahead still felt daunting, but if Dayne trusted her, that was all that mattered.

"No pressure, Katy. As long as we're in Bloomington . . ." She could almost see his smile over the phone line. "Although . . . I have this props job I'm interested in, so I should probably be pretty close to the theater."

She giggled. Gone were the sad, drawn-out conversations between them. Instead they were always laughing, always playing. She tried to sound more official. "If the director hires you, you mean."

"True." He paused. "But see, I know her. Got her wrapped around my finger."

"Is that right?" She held the phone closer. If only they didn't have so long to wait until they were together again.

"Yep." His tone changed just enough to let her know this next part was serious. "But not nearly like I'm wrapped around hers." He hesitated. "By the way, my director says I'm more convincing than ever." Dayne's voice filled with tenderness. It felt like he was sitting beside her. "Can you believe that?"

"Must be Randi Wells." Katy was teasing. Dayne obviously wasn't interested in his costar, though at first the tabloids questioned an offscreen romance. He had kept things so platonic that after a few weeks of filming, the gossip rags did an about-face and hinted at feuding between the two.

"You know what it is, right?"

"What?"

"It's you." His tone changed, and she could almost hear his beating heart. "I've never been in love before . . . so how could I have been convincing?"

She sighed. "How am I going to survive until I see you again?"

"If you figure it out, let me know."

Katy opened her mouth. She was about to suggest that maybe she could come out for a weekend, stay at a local hotel, and at least share a few days with him between weeks of filming. But the last time she'd been in Los Angeles the paparazzi had chased them and nearly caused a major collision. Dayne had made it clear: until they were married, they needed to do their visiting in Bloomington. She would've suggested he break away for a visit, but during filming there was often weekend work. They'd have to wait until his film wrapped up.

They talked for another half hour, dreaming out loud about their wedding and the days ahead.

When the call ended, Katy turned off the light and lay back on her pillow. For a long time she stared into the dark, replaying the conversation and missing Dayne. Maybe she would fly to Los Angeles anyway. Show up on his set and surprise him. If they didn't run from the paparazzi, maybe they could avoid a chase. She was still thinking about the possibility when she fell asleep.

The next morning Katy woke up later than she'd intended and hurried through her morning routine. As she raced out of the house, she checked her watch. Thirty minutes until the nine o'clock meeting at Ashley's house, and she still wanted to pick up coffee for the group. Ashley was thrilled about her new position with the theater kids. A week ago CKT coordinator Bethany Allen had asked Ashley to join the theater group's artistic team. She would oversee sets and work with Rhonda Sanders as an assistant director. All of which was wonderful, since Katy would be busy planning a wedding.

This morning the team wanted to come up with a list of props and sets needed for the three upcoming productions. But that wasn't all they would talk about. Ashley was about to become Katy's sister-in-law. By now, all Ashley's siblings knew that Dayne was their brother. It was why they'd made plans for a Thanksgiving celebration.

Katy yawned and focused on the road. Never mind the thunder-clouds on the distant horizon; she felt like squinting. The future looked that bright. Yes, they still had some details to work out: How often Katy would visit Dayne during his filming once they were married or whether he'd do all the traveling so their visits could be more private. They needed to figure out a plan for the paparazzi so they wouldn't always be running.

But none of that felt insurmountable. Now that Dayne had decided to live in Bloomington, every aspect of their future felt possible. And one day—maybe not too far down the road—they might even live as normal people. Because Bloomington was the kind of town that treated people like friends and family. Fame had no place in the circles Katy ran in. Bloomington would embrace them and protect them, and they would virtually disappear from the media landscape.

She checked the digital clock on her dashboard and thought about the coffee. As she looked up, a sign ten yards ahead caught her eye: Estate Home—For Sale by Owner. The stoplight turned red and Katy slowed her car. When she was close enough, she scanned the sign. Most of it was illegible, but she could make out one very distinct word: *lakefront.* The sign pointed right. Katy bit her lip and hesitated. Ashley's house was left.

Dayne's words from the night before filled her senses. *"Not near the lake. On the lake. A big yard and a sweeping porch."*

Before she could analyze her options, she made a right turn. She flipped open her cell phone and dialed Ashley's number. "I'll be a few minutes late." She didn't want to say that she was following a For Sale sign on a whim.

"I was just going to call you." Ashley sounded out of breath. "Bethany just called. She can't be here till nine thirty, and the kids are running me ragged. Take your time."

Katy smiled. "Okay. See ya." She hung up just as she saw the next sign. Sure enough, it directed her toward a secluded part of the lake. Her heart beat a little faster. She followed the signs another few miles, through a series of turns and onto a two-lane road that ran along the perimeter of the lake. She was familiar with the area, and suddenly she remembered something. There was a house out this way—more of a landmark really—that had been written about in the newspaper recently. Could that be where she was headed?

She rounded a bend in time to see a larger sign posted close to the road, right in front of the house she'd read about. Katy pulled over and stared at the place. The article had been in last Sunday's paper. The rustic, cabin-style structure had belonged to Carol and Elmer Nichols for sixty-two years. Elmer had built the house, and for six decades it was a place of love and laughter and much activity. But several years back, both Carol and Elmer had grown ill and been placed in a local nursing home. Their kids lived out of state with their own children and grandchildren, and the grand old place had slowly fallen apart. Even so, the family hadn't wanted to sell.

But a year ago Carol died, and last month Elmer followed. Their deaths made the house part of an inheritance, and that was the subject of the newspaper article. The kids had taken a vote and decided that they would sell the house only if no one in the family was able to restore it. The article had quoted the oldest Nichols daughter as saying, "The last thing we want to do is let the place go to someone outside the family."

Apparently things hadn't worked out, because here it was, definitely for sale. Katy pulled into the driveway and realized how large the property was. There were several acres of overgrown grass that made up the distance from the road to the house. Katy's heart beat a little faster. Even in disrepair the house was unlike any other in Bloomington.

The place was big enough to be a lodge, and if Katy hadn't read the recent article she would've assumed it was. It was situated at the far end of the field on a bluff overlooking the most beautiful part of the lake. Wrapped around the exterior was a full-size porch, and from what she could see, an oversize deck came off the back of the house.

Katy parked and got out of her car. The building looked empty, and as she walked closer she could see the house better. The old place had certainly fallen apart. The decks and railings sagged, and in some places they were broken in half. Two of the windows were cracked, and an old screen door hung from one hinge. The exterior of the house needed painting, and the roof looked damaged in some spots. Katy narrowed her eyes, trying to imagine the place fixed up. It would be spectacular, a house even Dayne couldn't have dreamed she'd find in so short a time.

She jogged to the For Sale sign and pulled a flyer from the box. *Six-bedroom, four-bath, lodge-style home in as-is condition.*

The price was seven figures, but the property alone had to be worth that. She looked around the field. The house sat on at least ten private acres bordered by huge maple trees on two sides and a worn-out, split-rail fence near the road. Nothing blocked the view on the lakeside.

Suddenly Katy had to see. Since the house appeared abandoned, it couldn't matter if she peeked at the backyard. She hurried toward the edge of the bluff and angled closer to the house. The backyard was a mess—a broken hammock; an overturned wheelbarrow; a rusty swing set; old, dilapidated furniture scattered about. Beyond that was a damaged staircase leading down to a private dock.

Again she felt her heart soar. She could picture the yard cleared out and cleaned up, with new decking and railings. She took in the lake view and felt dizzy with the possibilities. The setting was perfect. She could almost see the future playing out before her, hear the voices and laughter from family and friends who would come here for a barbecue or a birthday party. She could see it all—and Dayne by her side, the two of them living out a dream.

Katy turned and studied the abandoned house. What a shame the Nichols family had let it fall apart this way.

Katy folded the flyer and headed back to her car. She could hardly wait to talk to Dayne. She dialed his number on the way to Ashley's, and though she couldn't talk long, she told him she'd found it. Their dream house. She would fill him in on the details later when he was off work.

For now she had to focus on the meeting at Ashley's, get the work done so she could tell Ashley about the house. All her life Katy had wanted a sister, someone to share her heart with, someone who would have another viewpoint on family matters and relationships. She had Rhonda and Jenny, but a sister would be more than a confidante and a friend. A sister was family.

She leaned back in the driver's seat as she made her way to Ashley's house. As the meeting finished and she finally had the chance to tell Ashley all about the house, Katy thanked God. This was just one more way He had blessed her through Dayne's love. Ashley was already a friend.

One day soon she would be a sister.

CHAPTER TWO

ASHLEY BAXTER BLAKE hung up the kitchen phone and grinned at her husband. "I did it. He's coming. I knew he would." She raised her eyebrows. "But not a word to Katy."

"What if it's not the right house?" Landon held a fussy Devin in his arms, and he reached for the pacifier on the kitchen counter. The baby was three months old now, and already he looked so much like Cole.

"It is. Katy said so." Ashley couldn't have been happier. Ever since Katy told her about the house, she'd been dreaming up this plan—talking Dayne into coming to Bloomington and surprising Katy.

Landon looked worried. "Shouldn't you have let her tell him first?"

"She did. She told him as soon as she found it." She flashed him a look meant to show her innocence. "I didn't say anything she hadn't already said. I just told him Katy needed him. That's all it took."

Devin started crying.

Landon kissed him on the forehead. "Colic, I think." He handed the baby to Ashley and kissed her at the same time. "This is fun for you, isn't it?"

"Colic?" Ashley pulled Devin close to her and rocked him.

"Besides that." Landon gave her a silly look. He crossed his arms and stood against the wall. "Knowing Dayne, being involved with him and Katy."

"Are you kidding?" She held the pacifier snug against the roof of Devin's mouth, and the baby quieted. A quick laugh filled her throat. "Finally knowing my older brother, being able to pick up the phone when I want to and fill him in on his fiancée, who's one of my closest friends." She could feel the way her smile took up her face. "Yes, I'm having fun. Between that and colic—" she smiled and reached for Landon's hand—"and having you and Cole beside me, life doesn't get much better."

Devin spit out the pacifier. His cries grew louder, and he flailed his little arms.

"Well—" Landon looked at the baby—"there's nothing mild about our son's behavior. Not this afternoon."

Ashley rocked him and moved out of the kitchen into the living room. She sat in the old armchair, the one that seemed to swallow her up. This was her favorite spot to feed Devin, not only because the chair was comfortable but because it backed up to the front window, and in the daytime—no matter the weather—she could always count on a soft infusion of light to fall over her baby's face, just enough so she could marvel over every detail of him, the miracle he was in their lives.

Devin was quiet almost instantly, and Ashley could hear Landon in the kitchen. She waited until he returned with iced tea for her and a cup of coffee for himself. "Hey—" she met his eyes—"thanks for watching the boys. The meeting went great."

"Good." He settled into the sofa nearest her. "I love this."

"What?" Their conversation was easy, relaxed.

"Watching you, the way being a mother comes so easily."

His compliment touched her more than she would've guessed. Maybe because the first time around she'd been a single mom, dependent on her parents for survival and certain she was among the handful of worst mothers ever. She felt wistful and nostalgic. "I wish Cole would've had me like this."

They heard the patio slider and the sound of his feet. Cole was about to enter third grade, and the combination of that and his role as big brother had aged him quickly since summer began. Where once there had been only silliness and make-believe, now there were conversations between Cole and her and Landon that always surprised her. But one thing hadn't changed—he still loved exploring outdoors, finding whatever the backyard allowed.

His latest experiment was with tadpoles. Cole had caught some from his grandfather's fishpond a few weeks ago and brought them home. It was late in the summer, and most frog eggs had already hatched, the tadpoles already frogs. But a batch of them had shown up late, and Ashley's dad had helped Cole catch them a day or so after they appeared.

They had bought a baby wading pool at the local Wal-Mart, and her dad and Landon had filled it with sand and dirt on one side that slanted down to pond water and rocks on the other.

"You know why we have to use pond water, right, Mommy?" Cole had asked her that day. "Because that's their natural habicat."

"*Habitat.*" She smiled at him. "It's *habitat.*"

"I know." He giggled at himself. "I think *habicat's* a better word 'cause most cats live outside."

That was something else that had changed about him. He was always looking for a way to make her laugh—just like Landon. The mistakes he made in grammar or word choices weren't a precious matter of fact any longer; they were intentional—meant to be funny.

Ashley listened to Cole grabbing something from the cupboard and running across the kitchen toward her and Landon. The wading-pool experiment had been perfect. They'd watched the tadpoles grow little legs and eventually lose their tails. Landon had told him that once that happened, they could walk onto land and hop around—tiny baby frogs, the tadpole stage over. Cole had practically kept an hour-by-hour vigil waiting for the moment.

"Mom!" he called now as he ran. "Daddy . . . look! It happened!" He turned the corner, carrying one of their better drinking glasses, his hand over the top.

Ashley winced at the thought of drinking iced tea from the glass again, but she hid her concerns and allowed only a look of wide-eyed excitement. "Baby frogs? Are you serious?"

"Let's take a look." Landon and Ashley moved next to Cole and stooped down so they could see inside the glass.

Sure enough, there at the bottom Ashley saw three tiny frogs. "I've never seen frogs so small."

"They grow fast." Landon put his finger to the glass. "When they finish the tadpole stage they still have to be very careful. They feel independent, but they can get in trouble pretty quick if they go too far from the edge of the water."

Cole gave a serious nod and peered into the glass. "I like the light green one. He's the big brother."

"Oh." Ashley swapped a look with Landon but hid her smile. "I'll bet that spotted one's the little brother."

Cole looked closer still. "Yeah." He lifted his eyes to hers. "How'd you know?"

"See that?" She pointed to the frogs. "The light green one never stops looking at the spotted one. Because he would never let anything happen to his little brother."

"Yep." Cole puffed out his chest just enough to notice. "That's how big brothers are."

"That's sure how you are, Coley." Landon messed up their son's blond hair. "How about you go put 'em back so they don't get too scared."

"Yeah, I was just thinking that." He raised the glass and looked through the bottom. "They have the cutest feet, Mommy." He lowered the container, leaned close, and kissed Devin on the cheek. "Just like baby Devin." Then he was off, racing through the house and out the patio door.

When the door closed, Landon sat on the edge of the chair arm and chuckled. "That boy and his frogs. There's nothing better in all the world to him."

"Except having a brother." Ashley turned her attention to Devin and dabbed a soft rag against the corners of his mouth. She lifted him onto her shoulder and patted his back. "He loves having a brother."

"He does." Landon stroked the back of Devin's fuzzy head. Then he ran his fingers through Ashley's hair. "What I was saying earlier . . ."

Ashley thought. "About independent frogs?"

"No." Landon laughed. "About watching you be a mother." His look went deeper, beyond the light and easy surface.

"Oh." She pressed her cheek to Devin's. "Right."

"And you said you wish Cole could've had you like this." Landon's tone was kind.

"I do." It was her one regret about Cole's early years.

"But here's the truth." He touched her cheek. "He does have you like that. Cole . . . when he's older . . . will have nothing but amazing memories of you, Ashley. You're the best mom." He came closer and kissed her. "I loved you when we were in high school, but after I saw you with Cole—" Landon looked toward the backyard, where Cole had run off to, then at her again—"that's when I knew I wasn't stopping until you were mine."

It was another one of those moments, the ones Ashley noticed all the time now. When she would have to draw a breath and hold it just to feel the pressure in her lungs, just to know that she was alive and awake and not dreaming. Landon really was here, and they were raising two amazing little boys. Times like this she was sure she wouldn't have survived the past few years without him.

But then, that had been God's gift to her, allowing Landon and her to be together despite all the odds they'd faced. Despite her pride and doubts, despite the threat of death and distance and disease, here they were. She put her hand alongside his face. "Thanks for chasing me, Landon."

He stood and stuck out his chest, much like Cole had done a few minutes earlier. "Yeah, well . . . deep down I knew it was really the other way around. That you were chasing me."

She giggled. "Was I that obvious?"

"Honestly? I'm not sure." His teasing faded, and he kissed her longer this time. "Because you're right. I was too busy running after you."

"Oh, okay." She flashed him a flirty look. "The truth comes out."

He straightened and held his hands up in mock surrender. "You got me." He looked at his watch and did a dramatic gasp. "You almost made me forget! It's Saturday!" He hurried out of view toward the patio door. She heard the sound of it opening, and he shouted, "Cole . . . ten minutes, buddy. Almost time for the lake."

"Fishing!" His high-pitched squeal followed. "Can I bring the baby frogs?"

Ashley laughed. The two of them were wonderful together, Landon and Cole. She glanced at Devin sleeping in her arms and was overwhelmed by God's goodness. *I was almost too proud to let Landon in.* She shuddered, imagining the cold dull grays life would've been without him. *Thank You, God, for changing my heart. Me, Cole, Devin . . . all of it is only because You brought Landon into our lives.*

Her husband darted back through the living room and down the hallway. "The fish are calling," he yelled as he ran. "Your dad won't beat me in another contest, Ashley. You know that, right?"

She couldn't answer him without startling Devin, so she only smiled. It was good that Landon kept this date with Cole every Saturday in summer. The fire station had been kind, giving him every Saturday off, even though he sometimes had to make up for it by working a double shift. The years were zipping by at warp speed already, and soon enough Cole would have baseball practice or soccer clinics or driver's training to keep him busy on the weekends.

For now, though, he was still a tadpole, swimming around in the waters of boyhood, his tail still in sight. And the days Landon and Cole shared, the hours of fishing sitting atop an old red ice chest on the shores of Lake Monroe, were precious—every one. They allowed Ashley the chance to appreciate everything about her life—but especially Landon. His wisdom and love and tenderness and courage.

He flashed back into the room wearing a baseball cap Cole had given him for Father's Day—one with a satin, multicolored fish tail sticking out the back. He held up his tackle box. "Ready!"

Ashley smiled. She loved all those things and something else—something that would always mark these most tender, precious, fleeting days. The way he made her laugh.

The way he always made her laugh.

CHAPTER THREE

DAYNE STRETCHED his legs out on the leather sofa and stared out the window of the private Gulfstream jet. They were flying around 43,000 feet, higher than most commercial jets, and he felt like he could see much of the Midwest from his vantage point. He would be in Bloomington in half an hour.

Five days had passed since Dayne talked to Ashley, and he'd worked things out with his director to take this time off. The editors needed a look at the footage they had to make sure they were headed in the right direction. There were technical shots and a few stunt scenes to film, so a day off was necessary anyway.

His director, Riley S. Rosvold, was the movie industry's magic man of the moment. He was in his late thirties, and everyone in Hollywood knew him simply as Ross. He was a smart man, and no matter how badly he hinted that Dayne should be spending time with Randi Wells, his costar, Ross knew the truth. Everyone close to Dayne did. When Dayne asked for time off, Ross had only given him a resigned look. "Going to Indiana?"

"Taking the private jet." Dayne grinned. With the arrangements in place, he could already smell the clean summer air that breezed around the edges of Lake Monroe. His shoulders lifted in an easy shrug. "A few hours there early tomorrow, a few hours back later that night. Can't think of a better way to spend a day off."

Ross had looked pensive for a moment. "Mitch Henry told me about her, told me she read for him for the part in *Dream On*. Rumor around town is that she's the real deal, Dayne. She can act. You should get her out here. If she has that much talent, she's wasting it out in Podunk, Indiana."

Dayne pictured Katy, the way she looked surrounded by kids onstage at the Bloomington Community Theater and then as she lay sprawled out beneath a fallen artificial Christmas tree minutes before he proposed to her. He saw her sitting in her favorite box seat, teary-eyed as the girl who played Orphan Annie belted out "Tomorrow" in a way that took the breath of everyone in the theater.

"No . . . I don't think she's wasting it, but I'll tell her what you said." He winked at Ross. "Between you and me, I'd still love a chance to star opposite her in a film. One of these days I might even get brave enough to tell her."

Ross chuckled and started to walk away. "Fine, Matthews. Enjoy your day in the sticks."

"I will. Hey . . ." Dayne lowered his voice to a mock whisper. "I'm at home if the paparazzi ask about me. The trip's a secret."

After that, the hours had passed slowly through the afternoon and into the evening. Filming was almost finished, and so far Ross had been ecstatic with the footage they'd captured.

The movie was a romance with a well-known cast. Ross firmly believed the film would surpass its competition and succeed well beyond box-office expectations. "It's got Academy Award written all over it, folks," he told them every few days. "We're making it happen here, people. Keep pushing."

Dayne had to agree. His emotions had never been more transparent, his ability to convey feelings for the camera never more convincing. It was Katy, of course. He didn't have to struggle to find his emotions anymore. Every one of them was wrapped up in her.

The jet engines rumbled quietly in the background. Dayne turned away from the window and looked around the small plane. It was set up like an intimate living room: plush leather sofas along either side, tables and pillows at every convenient location, and a big-screen television built into the wall. A catalog of DVDs was available in a magazine pocket on the wall, and the cabin had state-of-the-art surround sound. The floor was even covered with thick, soft carpeting. Not surprising when the price was twenty times that of a commercial flight. Dayne studied a patch of storm clouds below. Never mind the cost. He would've chartered a space shuttle if it meant getting to Katy on his day off. He missed her that much.

Private air travel was a must from now on. He'd made that decision after his last flight to Indiana. Between the Baxters and his upcoming wedding, he didn't want anyone knowing when he visited Bloomington.

He made the arrangements through a private airline that catered to celebrities and dignitaries. Yesterday Dayne asked for an open account with the company. A simple call, a credit-card number, and he had a personal flight arranged for six in the morning. Show up fifteen minutes before departure and enter through a private terminal, then show his ID and avoid the entire airport scene. Just a simple, nonstop ride straight to his destination.

The takeoff had been smooth, but the captain had warned him there'd be turbulence landing in Bloomington. Thunderstorms were forecast for the day. Dayne felt a flicker of anxiety; he'd seen firsthand the strength of an Indiana thunderstorm. But at least they were landing in Bloomington. There'd be no hour-long drive to town. Just a rental car ready for him when he landed and an hour later he'd meet Ashley at the old house—the one Katy had told him about.

The plane jolted hard to the left and then to the right. Dayne tightened his grip on the armrest.

From the cockpit, the flight attendant appeared. She was a woman in her late fifties. She smiled at him. "Your seat belt's on?"

Dayne gave his seat belt a tug. "Nice and tight." He hated this, his fear of small planes. But it was understandable. He had been eighteen when his adoptive parents died in a small-plane crash over an Indonesian jungle. The story hadn't even made the papers back in the U.S. Dayne always joked with his costars that he'd rather travel commercial. That way if something happened, at least it'd make banner headlines across the country.

The plane started its descent, heading for the towering thunderheads. The cabin shuddered and jerked for a few seconds before the plane found smooth air again.

Dayne swallowed and looked out the window. *Okay, God . . . I'm okay with this. But please put Your arms around this plane. Get us onto the ground safely. Thanks, Lord.*

Nothing audible sounded in his heart, but there was an assurance that came with talking to the Creator of the universe. Even here, nothing would happen that could possibly take God by surprise.

Dayne exhaled and settled back into his seat. His thoughts drifted to Ashley's phone call. It had come a few hours after Katy's quick call that morning about the lake house. Ashley had explained that Katy had been over for a CKT meeting, and she'd been very excited about a house she'd found on the lake.

"She told me."

"Good. Well, we finished our meeting, and Katy just left, so I had to reach you." Her tone had been full of excitement. "She misses you so much, Dayne."

"I miss her too."

"That's why I have an idea."

Later, after Katy explained the house more fully, Dayne talked to Ashley again. He was dizzy trying to keep up with her. He loved

Ashley, loved her spunk and spontaneity. He could only wonder what it would've been like to grow up with her. Ashley's plan was that he fly out on his first available day, and she would hold a CKT meeting that same morning or find another reason to meet with Katy. Then, sometime before noon, she would ask Katy to take her to the old house out on the lake for a look around. When they got there, Dayne would be in the backyard waiting for them.

"Katy won't believe it. She'll think it's Christmas in July." Ashley sounded like a kid. "Come on, Dayne. . . . Can you do it?"

The idea was impulsive, but it had worked so far.

Dayne sucked in a slow breath. The thunderheads were right below them now, and as the pilot maneuvered around them, again the plane shook and pitched.

"There's some water next to your seat—in the built-in ice chest." The flight attendant was warm, motherly, and for the most part she kept to herself. The company was used to flying high-profile clients. Celebrities were commonplace to the crew.

Dayne reached for a cold bottle and twisted off the cap. "Thanks."

The clouds surrounded them, and for the next ten minutes the jet bounced around like a raft on stormy seas. But in the final seconds, the plane leveled off and came in for a smooth landing. The pilot steered the plane across the tarmac and up to the private terminal. Once they stopped, the men climbed out of the cockpit, and one of them motioned for someone to drive up Dayne's rental car.

This was another benefit. On a one-day trip, he had no luggage. Dayne grabbed a small backpack, thanked the crew, and jogged down a flight of stairs to the ground. Ten feet away his rental was waiting for him, the driver's-side door open. He had already tipped the crew, so he gave them a quick wave and drove off.

As soon as he was out of the airport and onto the streets, he exhaled. It was just after eleven in the morning. He had almost an hour to locate the house and wait for Katy and Ashley.

He had found directions on Google, and now he headed for

the lake. As he drove, the conversation with Katy about the house came back again. Dayne had been home after a long day on the set, eating a sandwich on the deck of his Malibu house.

"It's amazing, Dayne. I never thought I'd find anything like it." There was a sliver of doubt in her voice. "One problem, though."

On the other end, Dayne had smiled. What problem could possibly matter? Like he'd told her, they could live in a tent and they'd have no problems now that Katy had agreed to marry him, now that he'd taken time to face the rest of his life and make a list about what mattered most. God, then Katy, then his family. No questions whatsoever. And that placed him in Bloomington—the sooner the better. As long as the place had a roof and walls, they'd make it a home. "One problem?"

"Yes." A single nervous laugh filled the phone line. "The place needs a little work."

"Okay, so we fix it up." He took a bite of his sandwich, chewed it, and waited.

"Well . . . it sort of needs a new roof and windows . . . and the decks in the front and back are pretty much ruined. And in a few places—not everywhere but here and there—I can see straight through the walls into the house."

Dayne chuckled and swallowed his bite. "You mean you've fallen in love with a pile of rotten wood?"

"Maybe." She sounded sheepish. "You have to be here. It has so much potential; I don't see it the way it is." Her tone gained confidence. "I see it how it could be."

He had leaned his head back and pictured her, wishing he were with her. "Hey, Katy, if you get tired of your day job, you'd make a great Realtor."

"Thanks." She laughed. "Seriously . . . the place is amazing. There's nothing like it along the entire shore."

Katy told him the price, and he had to set down his sandwich. "That's all? You couldn't buy a waterfront storage space in Southern California for that."

They decided Katy would contact the seller, since she lived there and since it was for sale by owner. At this point they didn't want to involve Dayne. He could transfer funds into her account so the offer could come from her alone. They would ask for sixty days' escrow so they could have the house and grounds inspected. Wood rot or termites could present a bigger problem than the need to replace a wall or a window. That would take them until the end of September. In the meantime, Dayne would set up an account so that once the title was in her name, Katy could start hiring contractors to do the work. If things went well, he planned to move to Bloomington Thanksgiving weekend, in time for the big dinner at the Baxter house. By then he would've wrapped all filming on his current project, and he wouldn't start another one until mid-February.

May, they had decided, would be best for the wedding. He would be on another break, and when they returned from their honeymoon they would have time alone together, time for long walks and quiet talks, time to draw closer and enjoy their first few months of being married before he was needed back in Hollywood.

Everything was coming together perfectly.

But even after talking about it that day, Katy had doubts. "I can't believe you'd let me make an offer on a house without seeing it."

"I trust you." Real-estate transactions weren't that big a deal for him. He'd invested in commercial and oceanfront property for the past decade. His manager handled finding the places and working out the transactions, and Dayne was merely the person giving approval. But Katy had never bought a house before. He forced himself to see the purchase through her eyes. "If you like it that much, I'm sure it'll be perfect."

"But maybe we could wait. . . . You'll get a break in the next few weeks, right?"

"With real estate, if you're sure you want it, you should jump." He loved that she was careful. He would never have to wonder if she'd fallen for him because of his money or his fame or any of the other things that the world saw in him. She loved who he was on the inside. "If it's that great, if you like it that much, make the offer."

"I just hate making the decision without you." Katy's voice still held doubt.

When he hung up that night, he knew Ashley was right. Katy would be thrilled that he'd found a way to come see the house before the purchase agreement could be worked out. This way they could look around it and maybe even inside it—like any normal couple.

He stopped at a Wendy's drive-thru for lunch, careful to keep his baseball cap low over his brow. Less than an hour after leaving the airport he pulled up in front of the house. From the two-lane road, it looked better than he'd imagined—bigger, grander. Katy was right; the place was beautiful. The property was expansive, and once someone started taking care of it, the acreage would stretch into a sea of manicured green. Beyond it was the prettiest view of Lake Monroe he'd ever seen.

He turned onto the gravel driveway. As he drove closer to the house he could see what Katy was talking about. Damaged decks and walls and windows, a sagging roof, and debris gathered around the front and back. It would take a lot of work to have the place ready by Thanksgiving.

Dayne parked his car in the back so it was hidden from the road. The clock on the dashboard said it was almost noon. Ashley would be with Katy—probably at Ashley's house—and right about now she'd be asking Katy for a look at the lake house.

Excitement welled inside him. Because of the house, yes, but also because in less than half an hour he would have Katy in his arms again. Hear her voice in person and feel her hands in his. Then they could do what Ashley had suggested.

They really could celebrate Christmas in July.

CHAPTER FOUR

ANOTHER CKT MEETING was over, and Katy was glad. She loved her artistic team, and she was thrilled with the upcoming plays and the direction she planned to take them, but this was the tiresome part of the job. One meeting after the next. The weeks of working with the kids—that was what she loved most.

Al and Nancy Helmes and Bethany and Rhonda were gone, and Katy was packing her bag with loose copies of the scripts and notes they'd made after going over scenes for the fall show.

Ashley came up, carrying keys in her hand. "You said you had errands, right?"

"Right." Katy grimaced and looked out the window. Thunderstorms had been rolling through since late morning. "At least I'm not wasting a sunny day."

Katy needed to hit Sam's Club for Jenny Flanigan, and she wanted to stop by the garden shop for a bag of fertilizer. She and the Flanigan boys had planted a summer garden, but only the zucchini was thriving. They'd have bushels of the stuff before summer was over, for sure. But the tomatoes and corn were seriously struggling.

"I have errands too." Ashley looked a little too peppy at the idea. "How about I follow you, and we start with a look at your new house?"

Katy felt her eyes light up. She'd asked Ashley to come see it twice since Saturday, but each time her future sister-in-law had been busy. She glanced at Devin and Cole sitting on a blanket nearby. Cole was showing his little brother a plastic alligator. "What about your kids?"

"They can come." She jingled her keys. "Landon's working a twenty-four, and all of us need a reason to get out. I'll probably go by the station after we see the house."

"Yeah, Mommy! Let's do that!" Cole was on his feet. "Daddy said I can sit in the driver's seat of the fire engine next time."

Ashley reached out and poked her son in the ribs. "Just don't start the engine."

"I won't." He laughed and looked from Devin back to Ashley. "You're funny, Mommy."

She tickled him once more. "I know. I am funny."

"Yep, you are and I am too." He began running in small circles around Devin. "See me, Devin? . . . See how funny I am?"

Devin cooed and stretched out his arms.

Cole yelled again, louder this time, "See how funny I am?"

Ashley looked at Katy. "Yes, we definitely could use a reason to get out."

Katy laughed. "Follow me in your van. That way we can go our own ways after we take a look."

"Perfect." Ashley scooped up Devin and pointed for Cole to get his shoes on. "We'll be right behind you."

Ashley could hardly wait for the surprise that lay ahead. She had the kids buckled in, and she was just pulling her van in line behind Katy's car when her cell phone rang. She picked it up off the console and glanced at the caller ID. It was her brother Luke calling from New York.

She opened the phone and held it to her ear. "Luke, you won't believe this!"

He hesitated. "Hello to you too."

"Right . . . hi. Sorry." She kept her eyes on Katy's car. "It's just, you won't believe this."

"Okay, fine. I'm still dazed and confused after taking the bar, but what?" He sounded mildly frustrated. "Let me guess. You've found *another* brother out there and he's governor of California."

Ashley frowned. This wasn't the first time she'd sensed an attitude from Luke. So far she hadn't questioned him about it. "You took the bar exam?"

"Remember?" His tone let up a little. "I asked you to pray."

Ashley slapped her hand against the steering wheel. "I completely forgot. I'm sorry." She glanced over her shoulder at the boys in the backseat. Cole was explaining tadpoles to Devin. Ashley pursed her lips. "How did it go?"

"Great." He sounded relieved. "A lot of people don't pass it on the first try, but I think I did okay."

"Good. That's great, Luke. Really." She switched lanes to stay behind Katy. "I can't believe I forgot. You've only been waiting to take the bar since you were in high school."

"Don't worry about it. So what's the big news?"

"I'm following Katy Hart out to this gorgeous house she found right on the shore of Lake Monroe. And guess who's meeting us there?"

"Let me think . . . our big brother." This time there was no denying the subtle sarcasm in his voice.

Ashley felt her shoulders sag. "How'd you know?"

"It wasn't hard. Lately every time you're excited it's about Dayne Matthews."

"Luke! Is that what you think?" She decided not to tell him that they were all having dinner tonight at the Baxter house.

"It's true." Luke's tone became a strained-sounding calm. "We find out Dayne's our brother, and every time I talk to you or Kari or Erin or Brooke it's 'Dayne this' and 'Dayne that.'" He laughed, but it fell flat. "No big deal. I'm getting used to it."

Understanding came over Ashley, and her heart hurt. "You're jealous? Is that it?"

"Of course not." He sounded angry at the suggestion. "Never mind, Ash. I have to go. Just thought you'd like to know I did okay on the bar."

She had more questions, but she needed an hour. Uninterrupted. "Congratulations." Her mind raced. "I'll call you tonight and we can talk longer, okay?"

He hesitated. "Sure. Reagan falls asleep by nine anyway."

Ashley made a mental note not to forget the call. "Okay . . . well, we can talk more then, all right?"

"Yep. Have fun with Dayne and Katy."

Their good-byes were short. After Ashley snapped her phone shut, she realized that Luke hadn't asked her to tell Dayne hello. Just a clipped line about having fun with Dayne and Katy. Was it tension from taking the bar? Or was his mood entirely caused by the mention of Dayne? Ashley set her phone down. She would find out tonight. Since September 11, she and Luke had been closer than ever. Nothing would come between them now. She wouldn't let it.

She stayed behind Katy, turning right at the next light.

"Was that Uncle Luke?" Cole grabbed the edge of her seat and leaned forward.

"It was." She gave him a quick smile.

"Is he mad?"

"I'm not sure." Ashley reached behind and patted her son's hand. He was always so perceptive.

"Maybe he's feeling a little bit left out because of Uncle Dayne." Cole and all the Baxter grandchildren knew about him now. They hadn't gotten to really know him yet, but they knew he was moving to Bloomington. "Last year that happened to me. Remember?"

Ashley dreaded what was coming. "Because of Devin?"

"No, not him." Cole slid back in his seat. "I love that little guy."

"Good." She didn't need something else to worry about. "At school, you mean?"

"Yeah. Avery and me were best friends, and then Skyler came to school. Right away Skyler got all the attention, and the guys wanted him on their team for kickball. Even Avery." Cole's tone changed. "I was sad for a little while after that."

"Oh." Ashley pulled into the left-turn lane behind Katy. "And you think maybe that's how Uncle Luke is feeling?"

"Maybe."

Ashley checked the rearview mirror in time to see a grin spread across Cole's face.

"But pretty soon everything was good again because Avery remembered about me. Me and Avery are still best friends."

"Like Uncle Luke and me?"

"Right." Cole leaned forward again. "Just make sure you remember him."

Ashley nodded. Sound counseling from an eight-year-old. "I'll do that."

They turned onto the two-lane road, and she checked her watch. By now Dayne would be parked behind the house waiting for them. Katy had no idea, and Ashley could barely stand it. Ever since her last conversation with Dayne she'd been looking forward to this moment, to seeing the surprise in Katy's eyes.

Ashley replayed that thought. Or was she really more anxious to see Dayne, to connect with the brother she'd missed out on knowing all her life? Maybe Luke was right. Was she so excited about finding Dayne's connection to them that she'd ignored Luke?

No, that wasn't why she was feeling this way. She was happy for Katy; that's all. And if the surprise gave her another chance to connect with her older brother, then so what?

They finally reached the house, and she followed Katy into the driveway. Katy parked near the front of the house, and Ashley pulled up beside her.

Katy was out of the car and waiting for Ashley by the time she unsnapped Devin's baby carrier. He was asleep, so she was careful not to wake him as she slipped the handle over her arm. She was adjusting the pacifier in Devin's mouth when Cole took his place next to her.

He looked up at the building. "Wow . . . that's the biggest house I've ever seen."

"Me too." Katy laughed and looked at the front door. "This is it." Her eyes sparkled, and she made a squealing sound. "What do you think?"

Ashley let her gaze wash over the wooden house. "Katy . . . it's perfect." She took a few steps to the side so she could see the entire front. "I have to include it in a painting after you fix it up."

"You think Dayne'll like it?"

Dayne! The house was so amazing that Ashley had almost forgotten. "Uh . . . yes. I definitely think so." She set off toward the left side of the house, forcing herself to take slow steps. "Show me the backyard."

"That's the best part!" Katy took the lead, and they walked to the front corner of the house.

As they did, the lake came into view, and Ashley noticed how special the place really was. "There's no view like this anywhere on the lake."

"I know." Katy was beaming. "That's what I thought."

They walked along the side of the house, and as they rounded the corner, there on the edge of the dilapidated deck was Dayne. He wore khaki shorts and a casual, long-sleeved, white button-down with a T-shirt underneath. For a single moment Ashley was sure she was looking at Luke. They were that similar. And only then did she realize Luke was right. Because in that moment she wasn't thinking about Katy's reaction or how the two of them must be feeling. Rather she was thinking about herself and how right it was to be in the same place as her older brother.

Even for just a few minutes.

CHAPTER FIVE

KATY WAS PICTURING the backyard the way it would look when it was renovated, imagining Dayne beside her on the back porch watching the sun set over Lake Monroe, when she turned the corner and saw him.

At first she thought she was seeing things. But her imagination couldn't account for the way Dayne stood and held her eyes, the way his face lit up as she came closer. And that could mean only one thing: he was really here; he'd flown in to surprise her. And now she couldn't breathe or talk or move.

Dayne winked at Ashley and Cole, but he came to Katy first. "You wanted me to see the house, right?"

Katy grabbed a quick breath and fell into his arms. "You're here." She breathed the words against his chest. "I can't believe you're here."

He held her, but only for a few seconds. "It was Ashley's idea." He moved from Katy to his sister and pulled her into a hug. "Nice work."

Ashley grinned at Dayne, then at Katy. "Very nice, I'd say."

Cole took a small step toward Dayne. He seemed more shy than usual. "Hi."

"Hey, Cole." Dayne patted his nephew's shoulder. He peered into the baby carrier. "Wow . . . Devin's bigger in just a few weeks."

"I know." Cole smiled, more relaxed. "He's growing like a weed."

Dayne chuckled. "No question about that."

Ashley turned her attention to Katy. "So are you surprised?"

Katy looped her arm through Dayne's. "My heart's finally beating again, if that's what you mean."

They all laughed, and Ashley seemed to take the moment as a cue. "Your house is beautiful." She caught Cole's hand and moved back a few steps. "Early dinner tonight at the Baxter house, like we talked about?"

"Can't wait," Dayne said.

Ashley took another step. "Okay, you two. Have fun." She pointed to the back door. "Just don't walk across any broken floorboards."

"We won't." Katy waved. "See you later."

"Bye!" Cole turned and started jogging toward the van.

Ashley fell in behind him. But not until she was gone around the corner, not until Cole's cheerful voice faded did the moment finally begin to feel real to Katy.

She turned and took hold of Dayne's hands. "Every time you do this it feels more like a dream."

"Get used to it." Dayne's eyes danced. "I took a private plane." He worked his arms around her waist. "If it's this easy, I might come once a week."

"Dayne . . ." She closed her eyes and pressed her head to his chest again. It was true—having him show up unannounced felt like a dream. But sometimes so did everything else about their relationship. As if maybe she'd only created the story in her head: Hollywood heartthrob Dayne Matthews stumbles onto a small-town Indiana theater, steps inside and watches fifteen minutes of a play, falls in love with its director, finds the faith he'd lost somewhere along the way, and asks the director to marry him.

But having him here like this, his arms around her . . . there was no doubt the story was real. Because Katy could feel his heartbeat against the side of her face, feel him breathing into her hair. She held on a little longer, then eased back. "When you're here like this I have no choice but to believe."

Dayne touched his lips to hers. "Believe what?"

"This." She held out her left hand and looked at the ring. "That it's all really happening."

"The house is unbelievable," he whispered against her face. His breath smelled faintly like peppermint.

"Thanks." They were still standing where they'd been when Ashley left them. This time Katy took the lead, kissing him shyly at first and then with a depth that made her pull away and catch her breath.

"It feels so good to be here. I don't know how I've stayed away this long." He brought his fingers to her face and kissed her longer this time, a kiss that told her more than his words could say about how much he'd missed her. When he withdrew, a smoldering passion shone in his eyes. "We could stand here like this—" he kissed her again—"until my plane leaves, and it wouldn't be long enough."

There were no words to describe how wonderful it felt being here with him. Kissing him gave her only a glimmer of what lay ahead after the wedding. "Then let's."

This time when their lips met, the feelings between them grew more intense. Dayne seemed to realize it first. He took a step back and gently put his hands on her shoulders. "Okay . . . about this house you picked out." He was breathless, the desire in his eyes deeper than before. He took her hand and turned to face the back of the house. "Why don't you give me the tour?"

Katy exhaled, steadying herself. "Good idea." This was one more thing she loved about her fiancé. He had a colorful past, but he treated her like a princess. He respected her completely. They'd drawn the line on safe ground, so there was never any question about things getting out of control.

They walked into the house through the back door, and Katy saw the place through Dayne's eyes. The door led to a great room, but the space was dark with only two small windows. Mold grew on one of the walls from the floor to the ceiling, and cobwebs hung from every corner.

Dayne pressed her fingers between his and gave a lighthearted laugh. "You weren't kidding. It definitely needs work."

"And maybe a few windows." Katy noticed that the linoleum was peeling in places. "And a new floor."

"Yes." He put his arm around her shoulders. "But I can see it, Katy." He turned and looked out the sliding door to the deck. "Once it's fixed up, it'll be gorgeous."

"You think so?"

"Definitely." He gazed at her, and for a moment they were lost in each other's eyes. "But never as gorgeous as you."

Katy felt like she was walking on cotton candy as they moved from the great room through the kitchen and down a hallway into a laundry room. When they were finished with the downstairs, they went up, careful to step over the two broken stairs. "Lots to do, huh?" She gave him a sheepish grin.

"It doesn't matter." He followed her toward one of the bed-rooms. "If it isn't ready by Thanksgiving, I can stay with John. He already offered."

"Good." She stopped him just before the bedroom door. She circled her arms around his waist and looked into his eyes. "As long as it's ready after the wedding."

He looked like he wanted to kiss her, but instead he retreated a step. "What's in here?"

The joy in her heart was so strong it made her dizzy. Her voice fell a notch, and she heard the shyness in her tone. "Our room."

They walked in together, and she heard Dayne take a deep

breath. He stopped and put his arm around her waist. The former owners had skimped on windows downstairs but not here. An entire wall was made up of a series of three enormous sheets of glass, giving the master bedroom an expansive view of the lake. At one end of the room was a sliding door and beyond it a balcony that was sagging on one side.

Dayne released his hold on Katy's waist and took her hand. "Bob said this would happen."

"What?" Katy loved hearing about Dayne's missionary friend. He and his wife and kids would be coming to the wedding, and she could hardly wait to meet them.

"He told me God wanted to give me the desires of my heart—as long as those desires were lined up with His. That's why on my list of what mattered most I had God first. He's already done enough for me." He shrugged. "I guess now I want to leave this part—the desires of my heart—up to Him."

Katy touched his face. "And look what He's given us."

"More than I could've imagined."

They finished touring the house, and when they found their way to the backyard again, Dayne looked at the house and nodded slowly. "It's possible, Katy. It could be ready by Thanksgiving." He took her hand and brought it to his lips. "Let's wait for the inspection, but if the contractors here are anything like the ones in LA, you can make it worth their while to move quickly."

"I'll make some calls next week."

He led her toward the edge of the bluff. "The stairs down to the water don't look real safe."

"But there's a path." She had dreamed of this moment, known that when he came it would happen exactly like this. The two of them walking through the house, imagining what it might be one day, what it needed to make the transformation complete. And then they would take a walk to the shore. She'd found the path two visits ago. It wound down the hillside, and though it was overgrown with weeds, she'd made it to the bottom without a problem.

Dayne led the way. "Out here, it doesn't even feel like Hollywood exists." He was careful not to move too far ahead of her. "Not Hollywood or the paparazzi or the gossip of Tinseltown." He breathed deep. "Out here I'm just a guy in love counting the days till his wedding."

And that's the way he came across the rest of the afternoon as they reached the water, took off their shoes, and walked barefoot along the beach for a mile, stepping over the occasional rock or piece of driftwood. They talked about the wedding plans and the press and his new movie. Katy told Dayne about the script for *Cinderella*. Everything was coming together for the fall performance.

Before they climbed back up the hill, he let go of her hand and waded into knee-deep water. "Wow. It's a lot warmer than the ocean."

And more private. But she didn't say so. She wanted to forget how careful they had to be on the beach behind his Malibu home. All those days were behind them now. She moved toward him, and as she did, he leaned close to the surface of the lake and flicked a few drops of water at her.

"Oh no. Not this time." She made a move, intent on splashing him back.

But before she could get him wet, he started to run. "Okay, okay." He held up his hands. "You're right."

She gave him an innocent look. "Don't worry, Dayne." She took slow steps toward him, her eyes never leaving his. "I won't get you wet. No paybacks from me—no sir." But just as she reached him, just as she went to push him, he lost his balance and slipped backward into the shallow water. With nothing to catch her, she fell forward and landed on top of him.

Katy gasped as the water splashed her face and drenched her clothes. At the same time, Dayne propped himself up on one elbow and wiped his eyes so he could see. Katy tried to scramble free, but she couldn't get a footing and she fell on him again.

"Hmm." He grinned at her. "This could be interesting."

"Dayne!" Katy braced herself and pulled her knees up. She spit a mouthful of lake water at him, and they both laughed. "Help me!"

With a single motion, he smoothly flipped her onto her back, soaking the only parts of her that were still dry. He was on top now, though he used his arms to keep some space between them. He brushed his nose against hers. "It's easier to get up from this position."

"Is that right?" She splashed him with both hands, but before she could squirm free, she realized that they'd never been this way, this close before. And even though it was an accident, she could understand how people with the best intentions could fall into temptation in a matter of seconds. The feeling was heady and different from anything she'd ever experienced.

He must've sensed it, because his expression changed. "I want to kiss you so bad."

"Me too." She swallowed and, without meaning to, eased her hand around his waist, against the small of his back. Suddenly, in a terrifying and scintillating rush, she wanted to forget every promise she'd ever made about staying pure. Every inch of her wanted him to draw closer. "Dayne . . ."

Under the gentle pressure of her hand, he lowered himself a fraction of an inch, then another fraction. But just when it seemed like they might both tumble toward a point of no return, Dayne closed his eyes. From the depths of him he groaned, but it came out as a single whispered word: "No." Then in a decision that looked like it took everything he had, he pushed himself up and away from her.

With his knees still in the sand, he sat back against his heels and reached for her hand. His sides were heaving from everything he must've been feeling. "I can't, Katy. I . . ." He rubbed the back of his neck, then found her eyes. "I gave myself a line." He clenched his jaw and stared at the sky above. There were blue patches now, the storm clouds breaking up. "No matter what I want, I promised God I wouldn't cross it."

Katy sat up and picked a piece of lake moss from her shirt. Her body screamed for more—more of him, more of his nearness, more of his kisses—but at the same time her heart pounded from how close they'd been. How close they'd come to turning a corner from which there would be no backtracking. *God . . . I'm sorry. . . . I never want to be this close again.* Shame made her cheeks hot. "It'd be so easy."

"Yeah." He surveyed their surroundings. The lake formed a private cove at the base of the hill. There were no people or boats or houses in sight. He leaned over and gave her a single tender kiss. "I have a feeling we'll spend a lot of time down here." He helped her to her feet. "Just not right now."

Katy was more than impressed. Resisting the pull of the moment had taken all her resolve. But what about him? Staying pure was something new for Dayne Matthews. His determination to honor her was further proof of the depth of his love, his commitment. More than that, it was proof that he intended to live out his faith in every area of his life. Regardless of his past, he was telling her the truth when he said that he'd never loved like this.

She had no doubts.

They stood in knee-deep water, facing each other, the air around them silent except for the gentle lapping of the water against the shore. She hung her head. "I always felt . . . I don't know, better than other girls." She lifted her eyes to him. The guilt in her heart was so strong she was sure he could see it. "When I was in high school I made a decision to wait until I was married. A lot of my friends did too, but . . . over time, one by one, most of them gave in."

He framed her face with his hands. "But not you."

"No." A breeze came off the lake and made a chill run down her spine. She wanted to take a step closer to him, but she didn't dare. "I always thought it was only a matter of will. Make a promise and keep it. That sort of thing." She studied him. "But just then . . . something came over me, Dayne. A part of me wanted to forget I ever made that promise at all."

"I know." He ran his thumb along her brow. "I felt the same way." He hugged her, but after a few seconds he reached for her hand and took a step toward the shore. A tender smile played on the corners of his lips. "That's why we're going back up the hill."

And that's exactly what they did, not looking back even for a moment. Katy was grateful too. Grateful to Dayne and to God most of all. Because if Dayne had turned around, if he had swept her into his arms and back down to the shore, she was no longer sure about one thing.

Whether she'd have the strength to tell him no.

CHAPTER SIX

DAYNE LED THE WAY, and they reached the top of the hill in less than five minutes. He was still catching his breath from the scene down in the water.

Relief flooded him. Distance was a good thing. Only by God's strength had they avoided doing something they both would've regretted. Now that he was thinking clearly, now that his brain had the upper hand again, he had no intention of leading Katy astray. Even if she did look irresistible with the sun in her hair.

Dayne pointed to a patch of grass washed in sunshine. "Let's sit there." He wrung out the cuff of his shorts and gave her a wry look. "We can't go to the Baxters' looking like this."

She followed him and sat a few feet away. "How long do we have?"

"An hour. Dinner's at four." He put his hands behind him and leaned back. He loved the privacy they had here, loved being with her, talking to her without the threat of paparazzi or any of the craziness that came with his life. He studied the backyard and imagined it with a new deck and porch. "I see what you mean, how you can picture us here a year from now. Five years." He met her eyes. "Twenty years."

"Mmm. It's the perfect retreat, like the rest of the world doesn't exist."

He was quiet for a minute before he drew a slow breath. The sound of a passing car faded in the distance, and a gentle wind stirred the maples that lined the property. If they were going to share everything, then he needed to tell her what he'd been feeling. "Hey . . . I need to talk to you."

A ripple of concern showed in her eyes.

"Don't look like that." He reached for her hand. "It's not about us."

"Oh. I didn't think so, but . . ."

"Katy, you're perfect. This—" he waved his hand to encompass the lake and the house—"all of it is perfect." A sigh rattled loose from somewhere deep inside him. "It's about my job."

A smile tugged at her lips. "Your job?"

"Yeah, is that funny?"

"I guess so. Hearing you talk about it like that." Katy laughed, and the sound mixed with the breeze. "Like you're an engineer or a salesman and not, you know, *the* Dayne Matthews."

He made a face. "It's still a job, whatever way you look at it." He pulled his knees up and leaned on one of them so he could see her better. "Anyway, it's bugging me lately."

She waited for him to explain.

"The love scenes." He released her hand and stared at the expanse of water. He'd been thinking about this since that day in the canyon—the scene with Randi and her comment about wishing they could've done multiple takes. Now that he loved Katy, he was uncomfortable kissing anyone else. Even if it was all pretend. He sensed something change in Katy. "What are you feeling?"

She looked at the line of trees. When she spoke, uncertainty hung in her voice. "I don't know. I always figured the love scenes came with the territory."

"And until a month ago you figured the two of us were finished."

"Right. I haven't had time to think about it." She shaded her eyes. "What brought it up? You and Randi Wells?"

"Me and her. Me and whoever they cast me with." He could hear the frustration in his voice. "My films always have love scenes. Some more than others."

Katy looked like she didn't want to ask, but now that he'd brought it up, she did. "How much in this film?"

"Not as much as some." He frowned and looked out at the water. "No bedroom scenes. But still . . ."

Katy was quiet. She plucked a blade of grass and turned it over in her fingers. "Makes me glad I've been here trying to get ready for *Cinderella*."

"And now all you can picture is Randi and me, right?" He knew the topic would be touchy. But there was no way around it. He had to tell her how he was feeling. "One love scene after another."

"I guess. It's not something I want to think about." She tucked her legs beneath her. "I can see where it would bug you."

"It does. A lot." He pictured the canyon scene. "I'm standing there in front of fifty people kissing another woman, and for the first time in my life it feels all wrong. Completely wrong."

She studied the ground next to her. "The Hollywood answer is obvious. Whatever happens on a set is simply acting, nothing more." She looked up. "But if that's true, then why do so many leads fall for each other during the course of filming?"

"Exactly." He raked his fingers through his hair. "I have no feelings for Randi. But I wake up every day missing you like crazy, and I spend the afternoons in the arms of a stranger. I don't like it."

A pair of eagles caught their attention at the same time, and they watched them dipping and soaring in wide, graceful circles. Dayne knew Katy wouldn't have asked him to change for her, wouldn't have brought up the topic. But it was eating at him more than he'd realized until now. Until he looked at it not only from his perspective but from hers.

"You're the star, but do you really have any control?"

"Not for a script I've already approved. Not for this film." He nodded slowly. "But for the next one, you know? And all the others after that."

"What could you say? I mean, look at you." The smoky depth he'd seen in her eyes earlier down at the lake was back. "The film industry will expect you to have a leading lady, and that means love scenes." She lifted one shoulder. "Maybe there's no way around it."

"I could ask for a clause saying no between-the-sheets scenes. That's what some people do." He raised his brows. "Most of them don't work for long, but I guess that wouldn't be an issue for me."

"No." Katy smiled. "I don't think so."

He sighed. "There's always going to be some of it, Katy. Until I move to the other side of the camera."

"Directing?"

"Yeah. Someday. Maybe after my contract's fulfilled." He'd been thinking more about it. An actor could only lend so much creativity to a film. A director could make or break it.

She looked like she didn't want to say much. "It's your career, Dayne. Your decision." She put her hand on his shoulder. "I don't question your loyalty for a minute."

"I can think of one way around the problem." His tone lightened.

"How?"

"You, Katy." He took hold of her fingers. Memories flooded his mind. Paparazzi chasing them through the parking lot at Malibu Beach and later down Pacific Coast Highway. The insane fan rushing from the bushes intent on killing Katy. But couldn't they figure out a way to work together even still? "We missed the chance before, but maybe you could be my costar." The idea was appealing. Especially since everyone would know by then that they were married.

She laughed quietly. "We'll have to see."

"At least you didn't say no." He tilted his face toward the sun. "My director says he'd love a chance to work with you."

"Really?" Katy looked surprised. She'd appeared in only one movie, after all. A television special that never amounted to anything. "How does he know about me?"

"The audition film on you was amazing. Mitch Henry told every casting director in town."

"Wow." Her cheeks darkened. "I had no idea."

"So think about it, okay?" The possibility was already taking root. He and Katy in a film together? Their love for each other would make their on-screen chemistry far better than it had been when she auditioned the first time. He leaned back and stared at the distant clouds. Hadn't Katy told him she'd always dreamed of starring in a movie? Her privacy wasn't at stake anymore; she was already a familiar face in the tabs. Working with Katy would be magical, a chance for her to share his world and show Hollywood what she was capable of.

Katy slid a little closer to him. "It could be fun."

"Really?"

"Really."

"Good." He released her hand and stood. "Down the road a few months, I might have to remind you of that." He felt the cuff of his shorts. "Well . . . I'm getting drier."

She ran her fingers over her shorts. "Me too."

He helped her up and pulled her close. "We won't have a lot of alone time later." He gave her a shy grin. "Which could be a good thing."

"Yes." The color returned to her cheeks.

"No time for long good-byes."

She put her arms around his neck. "Or swims in shallow water."

"Or that." He smiled, but after a few seconds his expression grew serious. "Hey, Katy . . . thanks for understanding."

"About your job?"

"Yeah. You never complain. That means a lot."

"I understand. And I feel better now that we talked about it."

He removed one hand from her waist and brushed a piece of her hair behind her ear. "I love the house." He ran his fingers along her jaw and slowly brought his lips to hers, then breathed the next words close to her ear. "But I love you more."

They kissed again, but this time the restraint that had always kept them in line was back in place.

After a few seconds, Dayne turned and studied the house one last time. "Take pictures before they start the work. One day we won't believe it ever looked like this."

Katy smiled and he felt it reach to the farthest places in his soul. The sun beat down on them, all traces of the storm gone, and he couldn't imagine saying good-bye in just a few hours.

They walked toward Katy's car, but before he opened her door, he stopped and tenderly took hold of her hands. "Pray with me, Katy."

She smiled and closed her eyes.

Dayne took a moment before he began. When he did, his voice was thick with emotion. "I just want to thank You, Lord. This place, the view, the lake. It's perfect and already it feels like home." He tightened the hold he had on her hands. "Please, God, let the time go quickly. You know how I feel, how all I want to do is leave everything behind and marry Katy tomorrow. Help me be patient, and help us stay strong—" there was a smile in his voice—"every time we wander into shallow water. In Christ's name, amen."

"Amen."

As they climbed into their separate cars, Dayne was overwhelmed by God's mercy, His goodness. He was engaged to a woman who knew him—the real him. A woman who loved him more than life, one he honored and respected. And over the next several months she would create a home out of an old pile of rotting wood, a place where they could build a future together, where one day they would raise a family. All of that and the possibility of starring in a movie with her someday down the road. The future was better than any movie he'd ever made.

A wave of sorrow hit him, because in a few hours he'd be gone again. But not for long. One day soon these short trips would be a thing of the past. Now all they had to do was count down the days until then.

CHAPTER SEVEN

BAILEY FLANIGAN could hardly believe they'd been invited.

Dayne Matthews was in town, and he and Katy were having dinner with his birth family—the Baxters. But Katy had asked the Flanigans to come too, and it was all Bailey could do to keep from calling everyone she knew and telling them. She was having dinner with Dayne Matthews!

Her three adopted brothers were in Indianapolis at a soccer tournament, and Connor was spending the week camping with the Shaffers. So it was just her youngest brother, Ricky; their parents; and Bailey driving to the Baxter house.

In the backseat of her parents' SUV, Bailey was texting Tim Reed, her friend from CKT. *I'm having dinner with Dayne Matthews,* she wrote.

His answer was quick. *No way!*

I am . . . well, not just me. :) She tapped out her response. *My family and the Baxters. Oh, and Katy.*

After half a minute her phone beeped three times. She flipped it open and read his message. *I wish I were there.*

She smiled and began tapping the keys. *Don't worry. . . . I'll get you an autograph.* She sent the message.

Tim had been with her last year when Dayne was in town filming *Dream On.* The two of them had sneaked Dayne a message from Katy, and he'd treated them like equals. He'd even told Tim that he was doing a good job acting in the play.

Three more beeps. She opened her phone and peered at the screen. *Not because of Dayne . . . because of you.*

Bailey sucked in a quick breath. "Tim, my friend," she whispered, "what's all this?"

"What?" Her mother looked over her shoulder.

"Oh, nothing." Bailey smiled. "Just talking to myself."

Her dad caught her eye in the rearview mirror. "Who're you texting?"

"Tim Reed." She made a funny face. "He wishes he was going to dinner with us. That's all."

Her mom turned her attention to her father. "Did you bring the salad?"

"Of course." Her dad reached over and patted her mom on the knee. "Don't be nervous. Dayne's a regular guy, Jenny. You said so yourself."

"I know." She smoothed a wrinkle in the sleeve of her blouse. "It's one thing to have a few words with him once in a while when he comes looking for Katy. But dinner? Just shake me if I don't act like myself."

"He's moving here, right?" Ricky hadn't said much since they left home, but now he sat a little straighter. He was eight, and his blond hair was bleached almost white from a summer of swimming and boating on the lake.

"He is, buddy." Their dad gave him a quick smile.

Ricky tossed his hands in the air. "So what's the big deal?"

Bailey stared at her brother. He clearly didn't understand. "That's okay. You can play with Cole, Mrs. Blake's little boy."

"I will. I met him before." Ricky settled back in his seat. "He says his papa has a fishpond."

"There you go." Bailey's phone beeped again. She opened it and saw another message from Tim. *Did you leave me?*

She tapped out her response. Predictive text was so much faster than the ABC method. *No . . . but we're almost there . . . ttyl.* She hit Send and closed her phone once more. Not that she'd really talk to him later, but she might text him. Lately they'd been talking through text almost every day—this after six months of hardly hearing from him.

Bailey was sixteen, about to start her junior year at Clear Creek High School, but if she lived a hundred years she didn't think she'd figure out Tim Reed. He was a year older than she, and since January he'd been in a serious relationship with a girl from his church. Now, though, he was single and acting like he had feelings for her. Which wasn't possible. Not when everyone in CKT knew he still had feelings for his old girlfriend.

Bailey sighed and stared out the window. Besides, even if Tim was over the girl from church, the timing was all wrong. Bailey was seeing Tanner Williams, the quarterback at Clear Creek, the guy she'd known since fourth grade.

Things had changed around Christmastime. He'd called her one night and bared his heart the way he'd never done before.

She could still hear his voice. "I can't do this anymore, Bailey."

"What?" She was washing her face, and she had him on speaker-phone.

"I can't . . . I can't be your friend. It's too hard."

Bailey had rubbed the cleanser into her cheeks and stared at the phone. "Tanner, what in the world do you mean?"

He groaned. "Take me off speakerphone. Please."

"Fine." She clicked a button and held the phone to her ear, leaving just enough room so that the white cream on her cheeks didn't touch the receiver. "Why can't you be my friend?"

What he said next nearly knocked her off her feet. "Because

I'm in love with you." He made an exasperated sound. "Am I that hard to read?"

"Um . . . let's just say you'd be good at poker." She'd tried to laugh, but her heart was beating too hard. She reached for the washcloth that hung over her shower door, but as she did, she knocked over her facial toner. "Yikes." She grabbed a towel, sopped up the toner, and in the process dropped the phone into the sink. "Ugh!" She kept her voice too low for him to hear. "I'm a wreck." She stood the bottle right side up again. Then she grabbed the phone from the sink. "Tanner? You there?"

"You're not making this easy for me."

Suddenly she realized exactly what he was saying. "You're serious, aren't you?"

"Yes." He mumbled something. "Bailey, I want you to be my girlfriend. That's all I've ever wanted."

She hadn't thought she was ready to have a serious boyfriend, and her mom agreed. "Better to be friends for now, Bailey," her mom always told her. So that's what she told Tanner. But he had been adamant. He couldn't be her friend, not anymore. Not when every time they passed in the hall or hung out with the same group of friends all he could think about was her.

His revelation had caught her off guard, and by the end of that week she agreed to be his girlfriend. They could say they were going out, but he had to promise that things wouldn't get too serious. "No matter what happens in the future, I want to be your friend, Tanner. That matters more than anything."

They'd been an item since then. Not like her friends who were getting so serious with their boyfriends. So far Tanner hadn't even kissed her, and since they'd had their driver's licenses for less than a year, neither of them was allowed to have other teens in the car.

But she sensed Tanner getting anxious. The last time they hung out at her house, he took her up on the back balcony once it was dark. They held hands and talked about his football camp. Before he hugged her good night, he asked if he could kiss her.

"I'm not ready," she told him. "Not yet."

The truth? She didn't want to disappoint her parents, and even more, she was afraid. Afraid she'd make a mockery of what she stood for. Her faith and her decision to wait until she was married. But she was also afraid of her feelings. Once she kissed Tanner, everything would change. Maybe she would feel obligated to him, or maybe she'd fall so hard for him there'd be no turning back. Already their phone calls weren't as fun as before. He spent ten minutes every time asking her who she'd talked to, who'd been texting her. That sort of thing.

Whatever kissing him might do to their relationship, she wasn't ready to find out.

Bailey glanced out the window just as her dad pulled into the driveway of the Baxter house. She hadn't been here before, but the house looked warm and inviting, right in the middle of an enormous grassy yard. They parked and went inside.

Dayne gave her a big smile when he saw her. "How's my favorite CKT dancer?"

She opened her mouth, but it took a few seconds before she found her voice. "Good, thanks."

"Katy tells me you're going to drama camp in August."

"Yes, sir." She felt herself settle down. "Maybe you can come to the show."

"I'll be there." He shared a private look with Katy. "I already promised."

Bailey wanted to keep the conversation going. How many kids at school could say they'd actually talked to Dayne Matthews? "When you move here, maybe you could give me and Connor tips. You know, for acting and stuff."

Katy nudged Dayne. "Tim Reed's still talking about the compliment you gave him when you were here on location."

"Definitely." Bailey raised a single eyebrow at Dayne. "He used to be humble, but now . . ."

The three of them laughed. Someone called Dayne into the

kitchen. Bailey watched him go, and only then did she exhale. Katy was right. Around them, Dayne was like any other guy. Except he was the country's most famous movie star. She stifled a giggle as she took the seat across from him at the table. No matter how down-to-earth he was, her friends would never believe this.

Over dinner, she studied the interactions between the Baxters and Katy and Dayne. John Baxter seemed proud of his oldest son, anxious to help him find a place in the family. Katy had told them that, and from the way John asked about Dayne's latest film it was clear she was right. Ashley Blake was the same way. She sat on the other side of Dayne and hung on every word he said.

But most of all Bailey got caught up in watching Katy and Dayne. They weren't into all the touchy-feely stuff. At least not here. They held hands before dinner but nothing more. No close hugs or kissing. Bailey liked that. It was obnoxious when two people acted that way in public. Like her mom always said, "If you're acting that way in front of people, we don't have to wonder what you're doing behind closed doors."

What was beautiful about watching Katy and Dayne was the way they looked at each other. When Katy's eyes met his, the rest of the world seemed to fall away. And when Dayne looked at her, his expression held something Bailey had never seen on the big screen. She sighed to herself as she studied them.

After dinner Ricky went upstairs to watch *Finding Nemo* with Cole. The rest of the group moved into the living room, where they talked about the wedding. And that made everything about the night even more romantic.

"So, you've found someone who can help keep it a secret?" John Baxter looked happy at the thought.

"I think so." Dayne put his arm over the back of Katy's chair. "We'll see."

"In other words," Katy said, "we won't let a photographer or a helicopter ruin the day. That's for sure."

The sound of voices around Bailey faded. How lucky Katy

was—being engaged to Dayne, planning a wedding, and knowing everything about her future. All her life Bailey's parents had reminded her of the Bible verse Jeremiah 29:11: "'For I know the plans I have for you,' declares the Lord, 'plans to prosper you and not to harm you, plans to give you hope and a future.'"

God had good plans for her; she believed that. But it seemed like forever until she'd actually know what those plans were. One far-off day would she be having this same conversation—talking about wedding plans and honeymoons—with Tanner by her side? Or would it be Tim Reed? Or maybe even Cody Coleman, the guy from down the street? His mom had been arrested a few weeks ago on a drug charge, and now she was in jail, so Bailey's parents had agreed that later this week Cody could move into the downstairs guest room. At least for his senior year.

"He can come on one condition," her parents had told her the night before.

Bailey knew where the conversation was headed. "Nothing but friendship between the two of us."

"Right." Her mom's voice had been kind and understanding, but her eyes looked worried. "I know how you feel about that boy. Never mind Tanner or Tim Reed. Cody's always caught your eye, honey."

"That's just it." She gave them a sad smile. "I think he knows that we're . . . you know, different. Like from different planets in terms of our backgrounds and stuff."

The lines on her dad's forehead relaxed a little. "Exactly. Cody's a nice kid, and we want to help him. But that's as far as it goes."

Bailey smiled to herself now. She'd told her parents the truth. Cody might still take her breath away, but she wasn't interested in him. They were way too different. So maybe it would be someone completely new, someone she hadn't met yet. Maybe she'd go to CKT's summer camp in August and there'd be a new guy. Someone tall and strong, with a good sense of humor and a voice that would drop her to her knees. Someone like Dayne Matthews.

But as the evening wound down, as they said good-bye and piled into their SUV for the ride home, a shadow fell over Bailey's heart. None of the guys she knew were anything like Dayne. They were fickle and confusing and sometimes a little too possessive.

She stared at the starry sky over Bloomington. This wasn't the time to feel down about love. Even if nothing felt quite right about the guys in her life. Because one day . . . one day they would grow up. That's what her dad said. And then she'd find the hope and future that God had planned for her. Someday she would even find forever.

Just like Katy Hart.

ﰤ

The house was empty, and John Baxter lay in bed, too much on his mind to sleep. He had enjoyed every minute of the dinner with Katy and Dayne, but that didn't ease the tension brewing all evening just beneath the surface.

Ashley and Landon and the boys had arrived an hour early—so Cole could look for frogs near the pond, Ashley said. But they caught John off guard because Elaine was still at the house. She had helped him bake an apple crisp for the evening, and she was still cleaning up the kitchen when Ashley walked in.

He felt the awkwardness of the moment again. Ashley had stopped cold, her eyes drilling holes into Elaine's back.

His friend must've heard the door open, because she said, "John, when did you say the others would be—?"

"Now." Ashley moved slowly toward the table and set her things down. She found a stale smile. "We're here now." She put the baby carrier on the table and looked in on a sleeping Devin.

"Hi, Ashley." Elaine smiled. "I helped your dad fix dessert."

"I didn't . . . didn't know you were coming for dinner."

"I'm not." Her smile faded. "I'm almost finished here."

Landon came up beside Ashley, kissed her cheek, and gave her a look. John knew what the look meant. It was a warning, a plea. John wanted to add his vote. The moment was strange enough without Ashley's attitude.

John almost left the kitchen with Landon and Cole, but he couldn't do that to Elaine. Instead he crossed the room and took the spot next to her. He grabbed a dish towel. "I'll dry."

Finally, after what felt like half an hour, Ashley took Devin from his carrier and went into the next room.

When they were alone, John leaned his forehead on Elaine's shoulder. "I'm sorry." He lifted his head and saw the pain in her eyes. A pain she was trying to hide. "Ashley hasn't acted like that since she came home from France."

"It's okay." Elaine still had soapsuds halfway to her elbows. She looked down at the sink and ran the scrubber around the inside of the mixing bowl. "She loves her mother; that's all. And I'm not her."

"That doesn't excuse her for being rude." Defeat rang in his tone. He and Elaine were spending more time together. Taking walks and fixing an occasional meal at his house or hers. "I'm allowed to have friends."

What happened next was the reason he was still lying awake.

At his mention of their being friends, Elaine slowly found his eyes again. Sadness shone in her expression. "Friends, John?"

"Of course." His answer was quick. "You're my friend. Ashley and every one of my kids will have to figure that out."

She nodded, and after a moment she turned her attention back to the sink. "You're right. And she will. She'll figure it out."

A few minutes later they'd finished the dishes and Elaine had left. But John couldn't shake the feeling in his heart. Not then or for the rest of the evening. Elaine's entire attitude had changed when he called her his friend. At first he'd been sure about what she meant. *Friends, John?* As if she wanted to make sure he saw her that way—as a friend and not merely an acquaintance.

But even before she left, he hadn't been so sure. And now the meaning of her words seemed even clearer. *"Friends, John?"* As if to say, "Is that all?" After a year of talking about their families and finding joy in their hours together, was that all he saw her as? A friend?

Even that wasn't so surprising. Of course she would wonder. She'd been widowed for many more years than he had. But the hardest part was this: the conversation at the sink had made him wonder too. He was always quick to call her his friend, but was the reason so he wouldn't let his heart wander beyond the line of friendship?

Or was it too late for that?

John closed his eyes, and the quiet words came from the broken pieces of his heart. "Elizabeth . . . where are you?" He stretched his hand across the empty place in his bed. "How can you be gone?"

His feelings for Elaine, the tension he felt from Ashley the rest of the night—he never asked for any of it. This wasn't how these years were supposed to unfold. Elizabeth was supposed to be sitting next to him at the table, where tonight she would've held his hand and shared an occasional look that only the two of them could understand. Her eyes would've sparkled as she watched her family, amazed that finally . . . finally their oldest son had found his way home.

She was supposed to be here to marvel over Devin's birth, Cole's fascination with tadpoles, Jessie's bravery on the kneeboard this summer, and Hayley's miraculous progress since her near drowning. He spread his fingers over the sheet. Elizabeth was supposed to be here. Beside him.

As he fell asleep, he couldn't worry about Ashley or the doubts on her face whenever she looked at him tonight. He couldn't worry about Elaine or the meaning of her statement at the kitchen sink or where his actions were taking him in his friendship with her. His heart was completely and totally filled with the love of his life, the one he still missed with every breath.

His precious Elizabeth.

CHAPTER EIGHT

LUKE BAXTER wasn't sure which was higher—the heat or the humidity. But it didn't matter. Whatever the combination, he and his wife, Reagan, had picked a lousy afternoon for a stroll through Central Park with their kids. They had a double stroller these days—a place for Malin, less than a year old, and a spot at the back for three-year-old Tommy, who usually tired of walking after ten minutes or so.

It was four o'clock on the last Saturday in July, and Tommy had fallen asleep half an hour ago. They'd taken their usual route, south through the park toward the pond and the zoo, past the horse-drawn carriages and the sketch artists and hot dog vendors and back again. They were on the return leg of the walk, their pace slower than usual. The walkway was crowded with tourists, creating a frustrating obstacle course for the occasional jogger or speed walker who dared attempt the park on a summer weekend.

Five minutes had passed since either Luke or Reagan had said anything to each other. Luke had the stroller, pushing it forward the same way he wanted to push everything about their life forward. The results of his bar exam, his first official position as an attorney in his law firm, a place for him and Reagan and the kids outside her mother's uptown Manhattan apartment. All of it.

He glanced at his wife, but she didn't notice. Reagan looked tired, her blonde hair pulled back in a tight ponytail, dark circles under her eyes. Kids did that to you. Luke was tired too.

Reagan grabbed her water bottle from a holder near the handle of the stroller and took a long drink. She broke the silence first. "You sure nothing's wrong?"

Luke narrowed his eyes and kept walking. "Yep." He stretched his neck, first to the right, then the left. Why did she have to ask that? Every time they were together lately Reagan asked the same thing. He picked up his pace. Maybe it wasn't the heat and humidity. Maybe the dense, suffocating cloud was only the tension between them. What felt like tension, anyway. It reminded him that he wanted to be closer to Bloomington. At least he had wanted that before he found out Dayne was moving there.

He looked through the trees and caught a glimpse of a residential tower. One of dozens that lined the park, much like the one where he and Reagan and the kids still shared an apartment with Reagan's mother. Maybe that was the problem. Living with her mother. She was a soft-spoken woman, and she meant well. But what sort of husband was he, unable to provide a home for his wife and kids after more than two years of marriage?

Reagan's mother had hinted about it the other day. "How did the bar exam go, Luke?" She was setting the table, and she raised her eyebrows just enough. That subtle raise that suggested weariness and doubt at the same time.

"It went well." He felt Reagan looking at him from across the room. Now that he'd finished law school and taken the test, both women seemed to hold their collective breath, as if his entire worth would be proved by the passing or failing of this single test. "I think I passed it. I'll know in November."

She smiled, but it didn't reach her eyes.

The conversation faded from his mind. He massaged the muscles at the base of his neck. So much tension. Wasn't he supposed to feel better now that the bar was behind him? Malin stirred and her pacifier fell from the stroller. He stopped, and Reagan pulled up beside him. Luke picked up the pacifier, checked it, and dusted it off on his shorts. Then he gave it back to his daughter. With two kids consuming all their free time, the days of washing off a dirty pacifier were long over.

Luke remembered his conversation with Ashley Thursday night. He'd been sitting in the living room of the Manhattan apartment. "Thanks for getting back to me. I didn't think you'd find the time."

Ashley had hesitated, and when she spoke confusion rang in every word. "Is something wrong, Luke? Something I don't know about?" She let loose a single, sad-sounding laugh. "It seems like every time we talk lately you're mad. Angry at Dad or angry at the time you spent studying for the bar. Even grouchy at me."

"I'm fine." He didn't want to talk about his anger. He wanted to talk about Dayne Matthews. The wonder guy. Oldest Baxter sibling. Firstborn son. His brother. And how it was that overnight Luke had been relegated to a name on a list. Brooke, Kari, Ashley, Erin, and Luke. The other Baxter siblings. The not-so-famous kids of John and Elizabeth.

Ashley had sounded excited about her meeting with Katy Hart and Dayne. "The house is going to be unbelievable—nicest place on the lake for sure."

"Yeah. Great. I'm sure he won't have trouble affording it."

She didn't hide her shock. "Luke Baxter! What's gotten into you?"

He had tried to explain it to her. Dayne hadn't called since the trial, hadn't even formally acknowledged that they were brothers, that the news was true. Rather, all communication from him came through his dad or Ashley. Dayne was busy filming, and Luke was busy cramming for the bar exam. Maybe that was the problem.

The two of them hadn't connected. Or maybe the turmoil inside Luke had nothing to do with Dayne.

Out along Fifth Avenue a car passed, blaring heavy rap. The bass notes rumbled through his body, reminding him that at least some areas of his heart were empty.

Reagan tried again. "Everything still on for Thanksgiving?"

He shrugged. "If I can get the time off."

"You work at a law firm." Reagan sounded impatient. "There won't be a lawyer in New York City working over Thanksgiving weekend. Of course you can get the time."

"Maybe."

She stopped, exhaled hard, and faced him. "We're married, right?"

Luke planted his feet a yard from her. If she wanted to fight it out here in Central Park, fine. That's where they'd fight it out. "Yeah, so?"

"So that means I depend on you." She raised her voice, not enough to be yelling but louder than before. A few people stared at them as they passed. She pointed at the stroller. "Tommy and Malin depend on you." She took a step closer. "And all you've given us in the past few weeks are one- or two-word answers." She seemed to notice where they were and the scene she was making. She lowered her voice to a hiss. "Why won't you let me inside, Luke?" She spread her fingers over her heart. "I love you, remember?"

Luke shoved his hands in the pockets of his shorts and stared at the ground. "Let's sit down."

Reagan waited a beat, probably gathering her emotions. "Fine."

He pushed the stroller off the walkway to an empty bench a few feet away. Luke checked, but Tommy and Malin were sleeping. He parked the stroller and sat down. Reagan took the spot beside him. For a long time he only looked at her, studied her face, her weary eyes. She'd never looked that way before—back when they lived in Bloomington and life looked like it would roll out like a beautiful tapestry. "It's hard, isn't it?"

"Yes." She stared at her hands. "Harder than I thought."

Luke lifted his eyes to the trees and squinted, trying to see back to those long-ago days. Back before Reagan's father was killed in the World Trade Center collapse. Before Reagan got pregnant and moved to New York City. Before his life became consumed with studying minute facets of the law and taking turns staying up all night with a colicky Malin. Back before diapers and bottles and burp rags and feeding schedules.

Before Dayne Matthews.

He turned to Reagan. "My parents always made it look so easy. Love and laughter, fun times and family dinners, one season after the next. Year after year after year."

"Hmm." She kept her distance. "Mine too. And they didn't have their housing handed to them."

Anger rose to the choppy surface of his soul. "See? There it is." He waved his hand, dismissing further talk. "Forget it, Reagan." He started to stand up. "You're always undermining me. Making me feel like a freeloader."

"Wait." Instantly her expression changed to one of remorse. She applied a gentle bit of pressure on his knee. "Stay, Luke. I'm sorry. I don't mean it that way."

He gritted his teeth and settled back down. "It doesn't matter how you mean it. You bring it up all the time. You're tired of living with your mom, you're ready to branch out, and you're anxious for me to get a real job."

"I didn't say that."

"You didn't have to." He leaned hard against the wooden bench. "It's implied every time we talk." Defeat replaced the anger. "I know you. I can hear it in your tone."

Ten or so kids in red T-shirts on bicycles were approaching, laughing and chanting something unintelligible about soccer.

Reagan waited until they passed. "I know you too, Luke. This isn't only about me or your job. It's about Dayne Matthews." She hesitated. "Right?"

He wanted to shout at her, wanted to tell her no, this wasn't about Dayne. It was about them and how they'd managed to slip into a rut in just two and a half years of marriage. He opened his mouth to say so, but the words wouldn't come. Slowly he slumped forward and rested his forearms on his knees. He stared at the ground and exhaled long and hard. "Maybe it is."

Around them the sound of conversations and people walking and traffic on the boulevard faded.

"Luke—" Reagan's tone softened—"talk to me."

"It's wrong; that's all." He lifted his chin just enough so she could hear him. "All my life I'm the only son, and then in a single phone call everything changes."

"Everything?"

"Yes." He met her eyes. "Everyone's talking about Dayne, and now . . ." Emotions welled up in his throat, and he struggled to talk. He looked at the space between his feet and coughed. When he had more control he finished his thought. "Now Dayne's moving to Bloomington and I can picture it." He sat up, gripped the edge of the bench, and turned toward Reagan. "Dayne and my dad getting close, making up for lost time while I'm busy making a life for us here in New York."

She covered his hand with hers.

"This—" he motioned toward the busy walkway and the towering residential buildings and even toward her—"this wasn't how I pictured life, Reagan." He spoke through a clenched jaw, struggling to keep his feelings in check. "I was going to get some city experience and then find a wife and settle down in Bloomington. After that I was going to have kids." His eyes filled as he looked at her. "And my mom was going to be there to love my kids and be the best grandma ever."

The sudden hurt in her face was so strong it took his breath. "Is that what you think? That this isn't how you pictured your life?" She stood and put her hands on her hips. "Well, guess what? This wasn't how I pictured mine either." She did an exaggerated laugh and spun so that her back was to him. Then just as fast she turned and stared at him. "I was an athlete once upon a time, remember? I was supposed to play sports through college and earn a degree. I wanted to work in marketing or publicity or broadcast journalism." She wasn't loud, but her tone shouted at him. "After that I was supposed to get married to a guy who had his life figured out." She paused and gave him a pointed look. "Then somewhere down the road we'd have a family, and I could stay home."

He hung his head. She'd made her point. He earned so little as a legal clerk that she was forced to work part-time as a secretary so they'd have enough money to pay their share of the utilities and groceries. Her mother was still covering rent or they never could've afforded to live in Manhattan. They needed to live in Manhattan because that's where Luke's firm was located. And it was a good firm. It had paid Luke's way through law school and was a member of Meritas—the most respected legal network in the world.

Reagan wasn't finished with him. "Go on and hang your head. But don't you dare sing me your sad song about how life was supposed to turn out." She leaned a little closer. "You're getting your dream. Big-shot lawyer and all." She'd never sounded so angry. "But what about me, huh? Do you ever step outside your pity party long enough to ask that question?" She jerked back and took hold of the stroller. "I'll see you at home." She set off down the path without looking back.

Luke thought about chasing her down, but he didn't have the energy. Besides, it was too hot and muggy. He closed his eyes and leaned back. Everything was wrong. They'd made one mistake; they'd given in to temptation on September 10, 2001. The day before the terrorist attacks. And now they were paying for it with everything they had. He'd lost and she'd lost, and even now there was no shining light at the end of the tunnel. He had to wait four months to hear about the bar, and then if he passed, it would still take another month before he had a significant paycheck from the firm. He was easily a year away from having the sort of steady income that would allow them to branch out on their own. A year of seeing Reagan's mother raise her eyebrows and wonder when her son-in-law was going to figure out how to support her daughter and grandchildren.

Meanwhile, Dayne Matthews drew what, ten million a film? Fifteen maybe? Three films a year. The figures were mind-boggling. No wonder Dad was proud of him, anxious to make a connection with him. Not that Dad would've been impressed by income, but Dayne was beyond successful. He'd already made such a presence in their family that the girls had practically forgotten Luke existed. Even Ashley, the sister he'd always been closest to. Well, almost always. There were those awkward years after she returned from Paris pregnant with Cole. But since the terrorist attacks, they'd been closer than ever.

Until Dayne.

Luke stood and ambled along the path, slower now. What was the hurry? Reagan would be at home with the kids, warming up a bottle for Malin and fixing dinner for the rest of them. Her disgust with him would linger long after a talk like this one, clouding the air in the apartment and suffocating him, reminding him that he and Reagan might never have the lives they had separately dreamed about.

He was almost to the part of the walkway where he would veer off to find the crosswalk, five minutes from home, when he spotted the new receptionist from the firm. She was jogging in his direction. He watched her and felt the attraction. She was tall with dark hair, twenty-one or twenty-two at the most. Hannah, right? Wasn't that her name? She wore pink nylon running shorts and a T-shirt. He slowed his steps even more.

All the guys in the office were talking about her, how she was unattainable, a rare beauty even in a city like New York. Luke swallowed hard and glanced at the shrub ahead on the right, the one that signaled his path home. Then just as quickly he looked at Hannah again.

She didn't notice him until she was a few yards from him. Then her eyes lit up like Times Square, and she bounced to a stop. "Hey . . ."

"Hey." Luke forced himself to keep his gaze at eye level. "You're one of the brave ones, huh? Jogging with the tourists on a weekend."

Her forehead was damp from running. She wiped the back of her hand across it and laughed. "I guess so." She checked her watch. "I've got worship practice tonight at church, and I'm busy tomorrow—singing at both services." She gave him a shy smile. "It's hard to get my workouts in now that I'm at the firm. I never have any free time."

He held out his hand, almost as an afterthought. "I'm Luke. I'm not sure we've met officially."

She smiled. "I know who you are." She took his hand but didn't linger any longer than was appropriate. "I'm Hannah. Nice to meet you officially."

Without thinking, he took a step back. He'd caught her eye more than once since she started working, and always they exchanged a smile. If he slid his chair to the far side of his desk and leaned to the left, he could see her at her workstation. Once when his door was open, he overheard Hannah's coworker saying that Luke Baxter was the one who looked like Dayne Matthews. Hannah's cheeks had been red for ten minutes after that. But something in her eyes had always told him that she wasn't looking for a backstreet affair or a friend to flirt with. Now he knew why. She was one of the good girls. The kind of genuine girl he might've asked out on a date if his entire life wasn't already decided for him. "Well, hey . . ." He took another step back. "I'll let you get back to your run."

"Luke . . ."

He stopped.

"Are you married?" Her eyes were enormous, transparent. The sort of eyes a guy could get lost in.

"I am." He sensed a discomfort he wasn't familiar with. Somehow knowing that his intentions toward Hannah hadn't been right from the beginning.

Something changed in her eyes—the raising of a wall maybe. "I wasn't sure." No visible regret, no obvious curiosity over whether Luke's marriage was a happy one. No mention of his resemblance to Dayne Matthews, movie star. Just a closed door. Period. She wiped her forehead again and lifted her lips in a sensible smile. "See you at the office." With that she jogged away.

Luke realized something. He'd been holding his breath. Barely taking in enough oxygen so he wouldn't faint right there in front of her. He exhaled and headed for the path that would take him home. With each step his heart thudded hard against his chest, chiding him, warning him, shouting at him. Not because he'd done anything wrong or given Hannah even the slightest hint of impropriety. He hadn't winked at her or let on about the troubles he was wrestling with, and he hadn't asked her anything personal. He made no insinuation whatsoever toward an affair.

No, his heart was pounding for another reason. Because for a few minutes on a blazing-hot Saturday afternoon he had done the one thing he never imagined doing.

He'd considered it.

CHAPTER NINE

JENNY FLANIGAN was scraping a spatula through a pan of scrambled eggs when Bailey came running down the stairs. It was the end of August already, and they were half an hour from leaving for CKT teen camp, the first one Bailey and Connor could attend together.

"I have nothing yellow!" Bailey made an exasperated sound. She tore through the kitchen toward the downstairs laundry room. "I'm on the yellow team, and I don't have a single yellow T-shirt."

"Bailey, wait!" Connor came running down the stairs. "I found the box of costumes. There's tons of yellow in there."

"Really?" She spun around and jogged back through the kitchen and up the stairs behind him.

Katy rounded the corner at the same time. "I can't believe it." She grinned at Jenny. "I'm actually packed before Bailey."

"Yeah, but your color's blue." Jenny giggled. "Practically everything you own is blue."

"Good point." Katy laughed. She pulled a loaf of bread from the fridge. "I'll make the toast."

"Thanks."

Like always, once they checked in at teen camp the kids would meet with their teams. Then throughout the week they would share games and Bible teaching and grueling rehearsals. At the end of the week they'd perform a shortened version of a Broadway musical. This year the show was *The Wiz*. Jenny had already talked to Bailey and Connor about the casting, same as she did before every CKT show. Just because Katy lived with them didn't mean they'd have a better shot at a lead part. And placement in the ensemble was often more fun than a starring role. Neither of her oldest kids seemed too worried about the casting.

Jenny flipped a section of eggs and diced it with the edge of the spatula, then turned off the heat. Her kitchen sink butted up against an enormous window that overlooked the backyard. She peered out and smiled. Jim and the four younger boys were out back working on the old gazebo, a worn-out structure that Jim had intended to restore ever since they moved in. Finally, yesterday Jim bought the supplies he'd need—paint, roofing shingles, a few spindles, and a box of nails. The boys started work early since the day threatened to be one of the hottest of the summer.

Jenny angled her head, studying her husband as he supervised their sons. Each one had a piece of sandpaper and was stationed at a section of the railing that made up the lower part of the gazebo.

You're so good at keeping Jim busy, Lord. Thank You.

Just last night Jim had been restless again, sorting through the messages from half a dozen pro football teams looking to hire him. This time of year the routine was always the same. NFL teams in need of a new coach would sift through the list of retired or out-of-work coaches and see who was interested.

Every year the offers were more tempting.

"It'd be good for the boys, seeing pro football up close like that," Jim had told her. "Every one of them is interested in football."

"Not Connor."

Jim had been quiet for a moment. "No. Not Connor."

"Honey—" she entered these waters carefully—"Bailey and Connor would be lost without CKT, and we both know there are only a handful of states that offer the program."

"I know."

"Connor has five more years. Then we can talk about it, all right?"

He narrowed his eyes. "It's just, the other boys would love it."

"They love what you do now." She'd kept her tone gentle. "Have you seen them on your sidelines, Jim? Clear Creek High's the big time, and you're their biggest hero."

He smiled. "It's not that. . . ."

"I know." She'd kissed him on the cheek. "You'll be back in the NFL someday. And we'll say good-bye to everything here in Bloomington and move ahead with full hearts." She kissed him again. "Just not yet, okay?"

The excitement in his eyes had dimmed a little. "Okay."

But when she woke up, Jenny had the sense that it was harder for Jim to say no to the pro teams this time. That's why the gazebo project was a good one. She gave Jim a last look. At the same time, she heard someone enter the kitchen and turned around.

Cody Coleman waved at her and Katy. "How are you ladies this fine morning?"

"Running ragged." Katy had buttered twelve pieces of toast. She didn't look up, and her next comment was directed at Jenny. "The boys haven't eaten yet, right?"

"Right." Jenny kept herself from smiling. Katy was doing a good job discouraging Cody's recent advances. She had told Jenny privately that Cody's flirting sometimes got on her nerves. Jenny had agreed to have Jim talk to the young man about his behavior. "So—" Jenny wiped her hands on a kitchen towel—"how're the wedding plans coming?"

Cody clucked his tongue against the roof of his mouth. "Here we go again." He planted himself a few feet from Katy. "How can you marry Dayne Matthews—" he thumped his chest—"when you could have me?"

Katy took her plate and sat several seats from Cody. "It's hard to imagine."

Cody shrugged and snagged a plate. "Have it your way. I'll be here waiting when things don't work out."

Bailey darted down the stairs again, Connor close behind her. They had sleeping bags slung over their shoulders and were heaving duffel bags along in front of them. "The costume box worked!" She dumped her things at the foot of the stairs and hurried into the kitchen. "Connor's brilliant."

"Yeah, only now she'll have better stuff for the color-wars contest than me." He made a face. "Me and my big mouth."

Bailey set her phone on the counter and hurried to grab a plate and some eggs. "We can't be last; I'll get the worst bunk."

Cody set his fork down. "You two make me dizzy." He grinned at Katy. "I thought camp was supposed to be fun."

Jim walked through the back door, the four younger boys in tow, just in time to hear Cody's comment. "Fun? Are you kidding?" He chuckled. "Two-a-days start next week, Coleman. Let's see what you think about fun after that."

Cody exhaled hard. He looked at Connor. "About that big mouth of yours? I can relate."

Jenny leaned against the kitchen sink and studied her family. The boys were diving into the eggs, heaping their plates, and Bailey and Connor were deep in conversation about the games most often played at CKT's teen camp. Jenny smiled. Her home was overflowing with conversation and kids and more love than she could've imagined once upon a time.

She set her dish towel down and walked around the counter to the spot between her two oldest kids. "Toothbrushes?"

"Check," Bailey and Connor answered in unison.

"Pajamas?"

"Check." The tone in their voices told her they were used to the last-minute list of necessary items for a trip.

"Bibles?"

"Definitely." Connor raised his finger and smiled at her. "I'm winning the sword drill, hands down."

"He has no idea." Bailey turned and made a face in Katy's direction. "Newbies never win the sword drill."

"Sword drill?" Cody swallowed a mouthful of eggs. He raised his eyebrows, curious. "Someone wanna clue me in here? I thought it was a drama camp."

Jim laughed. He took his plate and sat next to his star football player. "Christian groups have these contests. See who can find a Bible verse first. As long as I can remember they've called it a sword drill."

"Oh." Cody took a bite of toast.

"Let's just say it's a good thing Dad doesn't have sword drills for the football team." Bailey lifted her chin and shot a haughty look at Cody. "Otherwise you'd be running lines from morning to night."

"Bailey." Jenny kept her tone lighthearted, same as the mood in the kitchen. But she understood. There was a little more to Bailey's statement than simple teasing. Ever since Cody had been paying attention to Katy, Bailey had been put out. The digs she sent Cody's way were nearly constant. Jenny waited until she had Bailey's attention and used her eyes to convey the deeper seriousness of her warning. "Be nice."

"Yeah, be nice." Cody leaned around Jim and stuck his tongue out at Bailey. "Some of us didn't spend our summers at church camp, okay?"

Bailey glared at Cody and returned the gesture.

Before Jenny could continue the checklist, Bailey's phone sprang to life, and a song began to blare from the tinny speaker. Something about holding on to every moment. Bailey snatched her phone and hurried out of the kitchen into the dining room to answer it.

Jenny wanted to follow her, to listen to her end of the conversation, but she resisted. Lately Bryan Smythe had been calling,

showering Bailey with flowery compliments and brazen procla-
mations. Last night after his call, Jenny had found Bailey lying
on her bed. Jim was in the living room with the boys, talking to
them about fall sports and whether they wanted to play soccer or
football.

"I'm so confused." Bailey sat up. Her shoulders sagged forward.
"I'm dating Tanner, and I still like him. I've liked him since fourth
grade. But every time we talk, I wait for him to ask me about
dance or drama—something that's interesting to *me*."

"Hmm." Jenny didn't want to steer her daughter in any one
direction. But she needed to help her see the whole picture.
"Tanner's never seen you dance, honey. He's never been to one of
your shows."

"Exactly." She exhaled hard.

"But . . . you've never invited him to a performance either."
Jenny sat cross-legged on the bed and leaned her elbow on her
knee. "Right?"

"Of course not." Bailey had looked horrified. "I'd be so embar-
rassed having Tanner in the audience. He's used to seeing me in a
cheerleader's uniform, not in a costume acting onstage."

"Okay, so all I'm saying is you can't judge him for not asking
about dance and drama. Not when you haven't allowed him a
window into that part of your life."

She ran her fingers along the bedspread between them. "True."

"So which part's confusing?"

Bailey lifted her chin. "The Bryan part."

"Bryan Smythe from CKT?"

"Yes." Her voice had taken on a dreamy quality. "He's tall and
dark and broad shouldered. And no one can sing like Bryan.
No one."

"He called you again, didn't he?"

"Yes." She fiddled with the promise ring on her left hand, the
ring Jenny and Jim had given her on her thirteenth birthday as a
symbol of her determination to stay pure. "Tim Reed's flitting

around talking to every girl he comes across, but Bryan . . . Bryan's crazy about me, Mom."

Jenny reminded herself not to react too strongly. She enjoyed these talks with Bailey, and she couldn't jump to conclusions. But to Jenny something about Bryan Smythe didn't feel genuine. "What did he say?"

"Well, he asked me if I was still with Tanner, and I said I was. Then he told me that one day—even if he had to wait a long time—I would see the light."

"See the light?"

"You know, like dump Tanner and go out with him. He said he'd be right there waiting for me, because one day—" her eyes got big—"he's going to marry me, and then I'd belong to him forever." She leaned in, her voice full of excitement. "Isn't that amazing?"

Jenny winced. She wanted to tell her daughter the entire conversation was ridiculous. Bailey and the guys she knew were too young to talk about anything so important. But if it felt real to Bailey, Jenny knew better. She had to take the discussion seriously. "Dump Tanner? I don't know. Something about it sounds awfully callous, honey."

"I know." She straightened, more serious again. "Those were his words. I'm just saying, at least he's pursuing me. My talks with Tanner are so . . . I don't know . . . so simple. 'How's baseball?'; 'Good.' 'How's your family?'; 'Fine.'" She groaned. "Where's his passion? It's like he's barely alive sometimes."

Jenny's memory of last night's conversation faded as Bailey returned to the kitchen. Her eyes shone brighter than before, and there was a spring in her step. She looked at Katy. "Bryan's going to teen camp too. I guess he signed up at the last minute."

"Good." Katy stood and rinsed her plate in the sink. "The more guys, the better the show." She looked over her shoulder at Bailey and Connor. "I think it'll be a strong cast."

"Great," Connor mumbled. "Tim and Bryan in the same show? There goes my chance at a lead."

Katy pretended not to hear him, but Jenny stepped in. "That's the wrong attitude, buddy."

Connor rebounded quickly. "I know. Sorry." He cleared his plate, rinsed it, and stuck it in the dishwasher. His tone improved almost instantly. "You're right. Anyone can win a part on any given day."

"Exactly!" Katy grabbed her suitcase and sleeping bag. "The kids and I will load the Suburban."

"Five minutes and I'll be out there." Jenny watched them grab the gear and head out to the garage.

Cody finished at the same time and headed for his room downstairs. "Workouts at ten today, right, Coach?" he called over his shoulder.

"Ten and two for you, Coleman. After last year, your two-a-days can start this week."

"Ugh." He disappeared down the hallway toward his room.

Jenny came up behind Jim and put her arms around his shoulders. "You doing okay?"

He swiveled his barstool to face her. "About the coaching stuff?"

"Yeah." Jenny eyed the boys. They were busy at the far end of the bar, comparing notes on who'd eaten the most toast. She turned her attention back to her husband. "If it's really on your mind, we can talk about it."

"No. You're right. The older kids need the stability. I won't even think about it until next summer, okay?"

Jenny was overcome with a combination of relief and anxiety, and she tried not to let either show. Only one more year in Bloomington? She loved this city, her involvement with CKT, and her relationship with the other parents. She loved the rolling hills and open farmlands and the proximity to Indiana University, where they could see theater and sporting events, and she loved their recent connection with the Baxter family.

One more year? What if that's all they had? Bloomington was the perfect place to raise a family, and the thought of ever leaving put knots in Jenny's stomach. But for Jim she would've moved to the moon and somehow figured out a way to enjoy it. After all, he had pulled out of the NFL for her. She could pull out of Bloomington if it meant seeing him do the job he loved.

She kissed him and searched his eyes. "You're sure? You love coaching. I know that."

"I *am* coaching." He brushed his knuckles against her cheek. "Clear Creek High needs me."

She rubbed the tip of her nose against his. "I love you, Jim Flanigan."

"I love you too."

"Yuck." Ricky, their youngest, wrinkled his nose and set down his piece of toast. "I'm never getting married. All that yucky kissing."

"I'm getting married." Shawn raised his fork in the air. "The sooner the better. That way I can love her longer."

His brothers turned on him.

"Sick."

"Gross."

Shawn pierced the air with his fork again. "Of course, by then I'll run as fast as a cheetah. If she wants to kiss me, she'll have to catch me first."

Jenny's heart melted. Shawn, the oldest of their kids adopted from Haiti, was always the tenderhearted child. Tenderhearted and obsessed with animal facts. She could hardly wait to see what God did with that combination in the years to come.

"All right, guys." Jim maneuvered his way around Jenny. "Let's finish eating. The gazebo's calling us!"

Jenny gently took hold of his arm. "I'm leaving. The camp's on the other side of Lake Monroe—at the retreat center. I'll be back in a couple hours."

"Be safe. Tell the kids I love 'em."

At that instant, Bailey and Connor appeared and piled on top of their dad.

"We couldn't leave without saying good-bye." Bailey planted a kiss on her father's cheek. "Pray for us, okay?"

"I will." Jim chuckled and hugged Connor. "Keep an eye on your sister."

"I will."

Jenny waved at Jim and the boys and then put her arms around the shoulders of Bailey and Connor. "Let's go. You'll wind up sleeping on the floor if we don't hurry."

"True." Bailey hurried her pace. "I call front."

"Katy's got the front," Connor pointed out.

And with that they made their way to the Suburban in the garage, the adventure of teen camp just an hour away. And as the bantering continued, as Katy chatted with Jenny about Dayne Matthews and his struggles with his current film, as Bailey talked to Connor about Bryan Smythe and Connor guessed about whether Sydney or Chelsea would be on the blue team, Jenny couldn't help but be grateful for one very wonderful thing.

No matter what the future held, they still had one more year in Bloomington.

Katy was glad for the distraction.

CKT teen camp was one of the most anticipated events of the summer, and this year's group figured to be the best ever. She would roll up her sleeves and dive in, working alongside the other counselors to make sure they somehow had enough time for all the activities scheduled. Katy was heading up the blue team, and her close friend Rhonda was in charge of yellow.

Beyond that, they had a new guy joining them—Aaron Woods, a twenty-four-year-old youth pastor from a church on the north side of Bloomington. He'd called in February asking how he could help, and Katy had checked his references. He had played football at Oregon State University and had an impeccable résumé.

He'd been a speaker at several youth church camps. Katy had him slated for games and the evening talk.

Even so, she'd be busy from early morning until late night. Which meant she'd have less time to worry about Dayne and the final scenes he was working on with Randi Wells this week. The movie was finished, and the early buzz predicted it would be a huge hit. Maybe Dayne's biggest. But the director wanted them to retake a few of the love scenes. More kissing, more togetherness. More of everything he thought they'd done so well. Dayne planned to argue that what they had was already perfect. Decisions on the various shots would be made later today.

Katy's conversation with Jenny dropped off, and Jenny turned the radio up. The song wasn't on the Christian station, but it was a popular one by Switchfoot: "Dare You to Move."

Katy stared out the window and lifted her eyes to the clear blue sky over Bloomington. Anxiety nipped at her heart. More passionate love scenes between Dayne and Randi? The thought formed a picture in her mind, one she couldn't dismiss. If only it were Thanksgiving already. He would be ready to move to Bloomington, and she would be wrapping up *Cinderella*. November was just three months away, but it felt like an eternity.

The song says it, Lord. Like the enemy is daring me to move, to try and keep on going when the man I love could very well spend the week in the arms of another woman. She kept her prayer silent, between her and God. *I don't want to worry, and I don't want to be jealous. I know Dayne's heart belongs to me. But please . . . let him have influence over the director. He's trying to do the right thing, Father. Go before him this morning.*

She heard no immediate answer, but she felt a sense of knowing deep within her. God would take care of the situation with Dayne. She felt herself relax. The Lord would go before her fiancé, and all week long God would go before her, too. They had work to finish before they could move forward with their wedding plans. And God would help them get things done in a way that brought glory to His name. Dayne's meeting with the director, her work with the teens—God would be there through all of it, one step at a time. He had brought them this far.

Certainly He would see them through Thanksgiving.

CHAPTER TEN

DAYNE MATTHEWS stood outside the director's door five minutes before their scheduled meeting. The rest of the cast didn't know about the talk they'd planned for today. But Dayne had no choice. All last week he'd dreaded the retakes scheduled for this morning. Ross wanted more passion, but why? When they'd shot the scenes the first time, he'd been thrilled with what they'd caught on film.

There had even been rumors on the set last week that the director was going to up the ante, offer them a hefty bonus if they'd agree to partial nudity or a steamy shower scene. Dayne wasn't doing either, no matter what was offered. And if Ross demanded the scenes, he'd simply walk off the set. His agent could work out the details.

He knocked on the director's door, and a voice inside said, "Come in."

Dayne entered and shut the door behind him. He crossed his arms and drew a long breath. "We need to talk."

"Fine." Ross seemed relaxed. He gestured for Dayne to sit down. "I want your input, Matthews. You know that."

Dayne took the seat opposite the director and gripped the chair's arms. "It's about the retakes. Why more passion? I don't get it."

Ross stood and walked around his desk. He flashed one of his laid-back grins. "You look uptight, Matthews. Something wrong at home?"

"Nothing's wrong." Dayne knew better than to rush ahead. His request had to be rational, not based on emotions. He crossed one leg over the other knee. "Remember when we shot the love scenes? You thought they were amazing. So why change them?"

Ross leaned against the edge of his desk. "More is better. It's the industry trend. You should know that. More steam, more passion. We reshoot, throw in a few shower and bed scenes, the tabloids get wind of it, and all of a sudden half of America can't wait to see what edgy level of acting you and Randi are bringing to the picture."

It was the answer Dayne expected. He nodded, thoughtful. "What about the other industry trend? The cleaner the film, the more money it makes."

Ross tilted his head. "True." He allowed an easy laugh. "But with you and Randi, we make money either way."

"Okay, here's the thing." Dayne planted both feet on the floor. "I have a problem with making the scenes hotter. We do that and we change the whole genre." He waved his hand in the air, trying not to let his frustration show. "It goes from being a date movie to being an edgy project. And when that happens, we make less money. It's that simple." He worked to keep his composure. "At this point in my career I can't afford to go backward."

"Is that right?"

"Yes." Dayne felt a twinge of guilt. He could get his way with this argument, but it wasn't the entire truth. His faith, his dedication to Katy—those were the real reasons he was uncomfortable with heating up the love scenes. But if he said so, Ross would never take him seriously again. Hollywood didn't look fondly on a principal actor or actress making requests for morality's sake. All acting was considered art, regardless of the lines it crossed.

Ross looked at him for a long time. "You may have a point."

"I do." Again he felt like he wasn't saying enough. *God . . . they'll think I'm weird.*

"No one lights a lamp and hides it in a jar." The verse sliced through his conscience. He'd read it at home last night after talking to Katy. He'd been sitting on his balcony, overlooking the Pacific Ocean, when he found the Scripture. As he reread it, he could almost hear God Himself saying the words. Standing right in front of him and making the point.

The commentary on that verse in his study Bible was even more hard-hitting. Below it in a small shaded box was a paragraph titled "Never Enough Time." It detailed a young man who had understood God's mandate to be an example, to let the light within him shine for those around him. But the man kept quiet about the Lord day after day. "Someday, God," he'd say at night when he prayed. "Someday." But one day the guy was on his way home from work when an 18-wheeler beside him lost control. In a flash, the man's life ended and the light he had always intended to shine was put out.

Dayne had shivered when he read the story. Everything about his life was finally going right. He was engaged to the woman of his dreams, he had plans to leave Hollywood, he'd found his birth family, and they had welcomed him into their lives. Even the tabloids didn't bother him as much. The idea of having it all end in an instant was sickening.

Then and there he had promised God that he wouldn't wait, that he would shine the light of Christ's truth and grace whenever he had the chance. Dayne understood the score. He'd been given a tremendous light when he accepted Christ as his Savior. But what had he done about it since then? Sure, the light had guided him to make the right decisions about Katy and his connection with the Baxters. But what about his role as a movie star? Had he mentioned God in any interviews or shared more than a passing acknowledgment about faith with his costars?

And now here he was, hiding the light again. He swallowed hard. "The movie's good the way it is. It'll be huge; everyone knows that."

The director gave him a wary look. "This isn't about that Indiana woman, is it?"

Before he could stop it, the easy answer tumbled across his lips. "It's acting. I'll make the film work, whatever it takes." He tightened his grip on the chair arms. "This time I think cleaner, sweeter, works better. It'll sell better."

The director straightened and made his way slowly around the desk and back to his seat. "I see your point." He jotted something down on a notepad. When he looked up, his expression said his decision had been made. "We'll leave it as it is. No more passion, nothing steamy. But let's retake the entire street scene, the one at the middle of the film. I want you and Randi closer to each other. Get the audience anxious for your first kiss a few scenes later."

"Fine." Dayne stood. "That'll work."

"I know." Ross wrote something else on his pad. He grinned at Dayne. "Everything you do works. That's why this film is going to be huge."

Dayne thanked Ross, but when he was out in the hall, when the door was shut behind him, he leaned hard against the wall and closed his eyes. He'd had the perfect chance to be a light, to tell the man the truth. That God couldn't possibly bless a film that was passionate and steamy merely to feed the prurient interests of a select percentage of their audience. It would fail because it was wrong.

Instead Dayne had taken the low road, the easy way out. The fact that he'd won brought little comfort in light of the opportunity he'd missed.

He opened his eyes in time to see Randi Wells enter the hallway. She smiled when she saw him. "Hey, gorgeous."

"Hey." He straightened and faced her. "Talked with Ross."

"About?" She reached him, leaned up, and kissed his cheek. The sort of greeting that was common in Hollywood.

"The retakes. He agrees with me." Dayne slipped his hands in his pockets. "The film has enough passion already."

"Oh." Disappointment cast shadows on her expression. She touched his chin and let her finger drag softly down his chest. "I was looking forward to the changes."

Here it was, another chance. But the more familiar words were out of his mouth first. "We want a hit, right? Wasn't that the goal?" He smiled at her the way a brother would smile at his petulant younger sister.

"Of course." She lowered her chin, giving him her famous pout. "The steamier the better, right?"

Dayne pursed his lips. "Not anymore, Randi. Clean's in. Besides—" he crooked his finger and touched it gently to her cheek—"better to have the audience aching for the first kiss than covering the eyes of the kids when things get too hot."

Randi thought about that for a minute. Suddenly she dropped the silly, flirty behavior and took on the seriousness that made her an actress in demand. "True. As it is, everyone who sees it will be practically desperate."

He nodded to the director's door. "That's what I told Ross."

"Hmm." She thought for a few more seconds. "Yeah, good call, Dayne. I like it. So what'll we work on today?"

Dayne told her, and all the while she maintained her professional demeanor. But before she left she elbowed him. "Too bad about the change. Really. I was looking forward to today."

He didn't have to ask what she meant. The look in her eyes told him enough. He smiled at her, keeping the air between them light. "I'll have to make it up to you."

"Oh yeah?" She touched his arm. "Meaning what?"

He took her hand and slowly moved it back to her side. "Meaning lunch Friday. My treat. Before I fly out."

Something in her expression changed. "To Indiana again?"

"Yes." He studied her. "How're things with your husband?"

She held his gaze, but her lip quivered just a little. "Not good."

"I'm sorry."

"That's okay." She sniffed and started walking. He fell in beside her. "We lasted longer than most, I guess." She kept her pace slow, and she looked at him, the kind of look that said whatever she was about to tell him, she was no longer teasing. "What about you and Miss Indiana? Think you'll make it longer than three or four years?"

He didn't hesitate. "I know so."

She stopped. "You sound so sure."

"I am." Here was another chance to be a light. He held his breath and plunged ahead. "We both have our faith, Randi. Something Hollywood's forgotten about." The words felt beyond right as he spoke them. Like the light inside him was screaming to get out. "We've made a promise to put God first."

She looked doubtful. "And you think it'll be enough to keep you together?"

"Yes." He imagined Katy sitting beside him on the lawn outside their home, the fixer-upper on Lake Monroe. He smiled. "Forever."

"Well—" Randi started walking again, her gaze straight ahead— "if you won't spend the day filming steamy love scenes with me, then the least you can do is take me to lunch on Friday." She glanced at him. The sadness in her expression was still strong. "Maybe we can talk about forever over a couple of turkey sandwiches."

Dayne laughed. "Deal."

❧

The camp was only five hours old, and already Bailey's head was spinning. She'd won the lead role of Dorothy, and Connor was one of four kids who would wear yellow T-shirts and act as a moving yellow brick road. But that wasn't what made her mind dizzy.

Tim Reed had the part of the Tin Man, and Bryan Smythe was the Scarecrow. That meant every scene would involve the three of them. Only how was she supposed to handle that? Tim had been around for a long time, a friend more than anything. If she was honest with herself, she'd had a crush on him since their first CKT show. But Bryan . . . everything about him was smooth and deliberate.

She'd have to call her mother. Talking to her mom always helped her sort through tough situations. She remembered how the morning had gone. Katy had asked them to take their places. "Tin Man on one side of Dorothy. Scarecrow on the other. Link arms. You're both supposed to think the world of Dorothy. Ready . . . places."

Tim had taken one of her arms, but Bryan made sure he caught her eyes as he came up beside her, closer than necessary. "Who said acting was work?" Katy was giving directions to the four kids representing the brick road, so Bryan leaned in and continued. "I could get used to this spot, Bailey. I mean it."

"What?" Tim looked at them. His expression said he hadn't picked up on Bryan's comments.

"Nothing." Bryan winked at her. "Some things aren't supposed to be shared."

They were on a break now, and Bailey needed more than fresh air and water. She needed perspective. The moment she sat down on top of the picnic table outside her dorm, her phone rang. She set her feet on the bench and looked around. Cell phones were against the rules except on breaks and for a brief period at night. She glanced at the caller ID window. It was Tanner Williams. She flipped her phone open. "Hello?"

"Hey . . . I didn't get to say good-bye."

Her heart melted. Tanner cared more than she had given him credit for lately. "That's okay. It was a busy morning."

"I should've come by last night. I was working with my dad, throwing the ball, getting my accuracy down. That sort of thing."

"Oh." Did he even know what camp she was at? "I guess you'll be ready to lead the team when school starts."

"Hopefully." His voice was tender. "We have a team meeting tonight, but I had to call. You're at church camp, right?"

She bit her lip. Hadn't she told him that the end of August and first part of September were for CKT? She checked the time on her phone. Two minutes till break was over. She held the phone back to her ear. "Yeah, church camp. It finishes on Saturday."

"And next week I have two-a-days."

At that moment, across the field, Bryan Smythe noticed her. He locked eyes with her and closed the gap between them.

Tanner cleared his throat. "So, can we go out Saturday night or something?"

Bryan reached her and covered her knees with his hands. "Break's almost over," he whispered near her ear. "Who's on the phone?"

Bailey waved him off. "Saturday night? Uh, maybe . . . I'm not sure what's happening after . . ."

"Saturday night?" Bryan's voice was a gentle caress, one that sent shivers down her spine.

She pushed him away and tried not to giggle.

"You still there?" Tanner didn't sound frustrated, just confused. He didn't know that she was at a drama camp or that Bryan Smythe even existed, so he had no reason to sound concerned.

"Yeah, sorry."

Bryan grinned and took the spot next to her. He slipped his arm around her shoulders and whispered into her ear once more. "Tell lover boy I said hi."

Tanner was waiting for an answer, so Bailey said, "Saturday night could work. I don't finish up here until late. How 'bout I call you Thursday or Friday?"

"Okay." Suspicion crept into Tanner's tone. "Everything's good, right? Between us?"

Bailey shaded her eyes and looked out across the field. She spotted Tim Reed surrounded by a group of girls. She tried to focus. "Yes, Tanner. Everything's fine."

Bryan leaned to the side and studied her appreciatively. "Very fine, I'd say."

She covered the receiver and gave him another playful push. "Stop," she mouthed. "I'm serious."

"Okay, then." Tanner sounded bewildered. As if something really might be wrong but he couldn't quite put his finger on it. "Call me later, I guess. I was thinking of you; that's all."

"Me too." She closed her eyes because it was the only way to keep Bryan and Tim from crowding her thoughts. "I'll talk to you soon."

As soon as she hung up, she pushed Bryan harder than before. "That wasn't nice." There was laughter in her tone. "What if he would've heard you?"

"I almost asked if I could talk to him." Bryan reached for her phone. "In fact, maybe I'll call him back, because Saturday's my night. We wrap up the play and you and I go out for pizza."

She hid her phone behind her back and shook her head. "I have a boyfriend, Bryan. What part of that can't you understand?"

He moved closer inch by inch. "The part that knows I'm crazy about you, Bailey. Obsessed even." He came so close that she could feel his breath on her face. "I'm sorry if that makes you uncomfortable."

She stood up and created distance between them. "It does." She tossed her hair and took a step back. But even as she did, she could feel her eyes dancing. "Good work today, by the way. I love your solo."

"Thanks. And no one could play Dorothy but you. Your dancing is amazing." He put his hands behind him and leaned back, appearing comfortable with himself. "About the Saturday night thing—have it your way. Whenever you're ready, I'll be here."

She gave him a final smile and turned and walked toward the auditorium. Behind her, she could hear two girls approach Bryan, their voices high-pitched and flirty. She looked over her shoulder, but he wasn't paying them any attention. He'd started walking back, the girls on either side of him. But his eyes were still on her. He waved in her direction.

She ignored the gesture and grinned to herself. Everyone said Bryan Smythe was a player, that he could pick up any girl anywhere in record time. But he didn't seem like a player to her. More like a sensitive, talented guy who would've walked across burning coals for her.

Near the auditorium door, Tim Reed caught up with her. His group of admirers had apparently gone inside. "Hey, I wanna talk to you." His expression was serious.

"About what?" Bailey checked the time on her phone. "Break's over."

"I know." He glanced at Bryan and the girls making their way across the field toward the auditorium. His eyes found hers again. "It's important."

Bailey sighed. Tim had always been this way. Interested in making his opinion known but never interested enough to pursue her. "Fine." She crossed her arms. "What?"

"Come here." He took her wrist and led her around the corner of the building. When they were alone, he said, "Bryan Smythe's making a fool of you. Can't you see that?"

She rolled her eyes. "He is not. We're friends, nothing more."

Tim let out an exaggerated laugh. "That's not what he's telling the guys. He says he promises that in less than a month you'll be broken up with Tanner."

Bailey made a face. "He didn't say that. He knows I'm not breaking up with Tanner."

"Yeah." Tim exhaled hard. "Not yet. But he's turning the charm on so thick you can't see straight. It's obvious, Bailey." He lowered his voice and looked at her, to the deep places reserved for those closest to her. "Be careful; that's all I'm saying. The guy's a player."

"I can see that." Her answer was quick. "Anyway, you should

talk. She looked back at a group of kids walking across the lawn. "You have more followers than Bryan."

Frustration filled Tim's expression. "Never mind. I'm just trying to warn you. The guy's no good." He put his hand on her shoulder. "You deserve better. That's all."

"Okay." She studied him for a few seconds, then gave him a quick hug. Her mom was right. She was too young for all this. The drama was better kept to the stage. "I'll try to remember that."

They hurried around the corner again and into the auditorium.

But by the time they were halfway through the first scene, Bailey had forgotten Tim's advice entirely. Bryan had been kind and thoughtful onstage, using his talent to showcase hers and whispering compliments or flirty one-liners every time he had a chance.

When they broke for dinner, Katy pulled Bailey aside and gave her a stern look. "This camp's production is something I take very seriously." Her voice wasn't angry, but there was no denying she meant business.

Bailey's mouth hung open. "Did I do something wrong?"

"Just be careful. I don't like all the attention Bryan Smythe's giving you." She allowed a tight smile. "This is a big part for you, all right?"

"All right." Her cheeks were suddenly hot. "I'm sorry if I didn't seem serious."

"You did. Just don't let Bryan distract you."

Bailey's mouth was dry by the time Katy walked away. And as she headed for the dining hall, she looked through a break in the trees to the sky overhead. *God, help me focus this week. And help me know if Tim's right about Bryan.* Tim's and Tanner's faces came to mind. At least Cody wasn't in the picture anymore. The guy was such a jerk, throwing himself at Katy when he knew Katy was engaged to Dayne. She kept her eyes on the sky and sighed. *Help me, Lord. Unravel this confusion. Please.*

Bailey had been looking forward to teen camp all summer, and now she had the leading role and Katy was worried she wasn't taking it seriously. Which meant she would have to find a way to ignore the distractions in her life—Tim and Bryan and Tanner.

That way what she did onstage really would be drama enough.

CHAPTER ELEVEN

WORK ON THE FILM took up so much time Friday that there wasn't time for lunch with Randi. Dayne met her around two o'clock. "Lunch is out obviously. No time today. Sorry."

"Dayne!" She put her hands on her hips and frowned. "That's not fair. I looked forward to lunch all week. I want to talk about my husband and your Miss Indiana and how come it's all going so good for you. Give me an hour for breakfast tomorrow, Dayne." She used her whiny voice, her head tilted. "You always have the best advice."

He hesitated. He had promised Katy he'd be there for the teen camp finale, the presentation of *The Wiz*. He had plans to meet his private jet at ten tomorrow morning so he could be in Bloomington by five o'clock. That would give him enough time to get to the seven o'clock show. He and Katy could have dinner together, and he would spend the night at John's house and have most of Sunday with Katy before flying back home Sunday evening.

Breakfast Saturday morning would be pushing it. Besides, if the paparazzi discovered Dayne and Randi were sharing a meal, it would make the magazines for sure. Not that the stories would amount to anything. It wouldn't be long before they figured out he was engaged, and then—for a while anyway—they would stop linking him with other women.

Dayne had already promised Randi, so he finally agreed and gave her a lopsided smile. "Bella's on PCH at eight."

Randi's face lit up. "Really?" She hugged him impulsively. "I can't believe it. Dayne Matthews taking time out of his busy life for me."

"I'll only have an hour. I've got a private flight to Bloomington set for ten."

"Again?" Randi sighed. "You're ridiculous. Does that woman even know what she's got?"

"Yeah." He patted Randi's arm as he turned back to his trailer. "And I do too."

*

It was Saturday morning, a few minutes before eight, and Dayne had three paparazzi cars on his tail. "Great," he muttered under his breath. He had tried the usual tricks, turning into a couple gas stations along the way and taking side streets. But nothing worked. They were on high alert today—probably bored. All of Hollywood's A-listers were minding their manners and staying out of the limelight. The tabs were rabid for a story—any story.

And this morning, the story was Dayne.

Halfway to the diner he gave up and fell in line with the rest of the traffic on Pacific Coast Highway. His packed bag was in the back of his Escalade, ready for his quick exit on the private jet. No question he wanted to lose the photographers by then. If they figured out he was using private air travel, they'd find out where he was going. And that would ruin the privacy he wanted between now and the wedding.

He parked in the diner's lot, climbed out, and shut the door.

Behind him he heard the squeal of tires as the three cars raced into the parking lot. Dayne didn't turn around. Instead he spotted Randi sitting on the restaurant's patio overlooking the ocean. She wore a wide-brimmed hat and oversize white sunglasses.

He lowered his head and made his way through the restaurant out onto the patio. He took the spot opposite Randi and let out a frustrated breath. "The scavengers followed me." He planted his elbows on the table and stared at the menu in front of him. "Not a minute's peace." He looked back at the door. "Maybe we should eat inside."

"No." She smiled. "They'll think we're hiding something."

"True." His frustration ate at him.

"Hey—" she touched his arm—"don't worry about it. They think we're fighting, remember?" She looked over her shoulder at the cameramen.

They were out of their cars, resting on their back bumpers or sitting on their trunks, camera bags open, already aiming lenses in their direction.

She looked back at Dayne. "What are they going to say? 'Dayne and Randi Back on Good Terms'? That could only help the film, right?"

"I guess." He glanced at his watch. Ten o'clock couldn't come fast enough. The weather forecast was clear, which meant it should be a smooth flight. Just a few hours and he'd be in Bloomington with Katy.

They'd talked last night, and she was so excited she could hardly stand it. "You're going to love the show," she'd told him. "Bailey finally got serious. She's amazing. Wait till you see it."

Dayne gritted his teeth and lifted his eyes to Randi. "Don't they ever get tired of chasing people, capturing their every move for the tabloids?"

"Doesn't look like it." Randi took a sip of her water and maintained her smile. Anyone whose face was in the magazines on a weekly basis knew better than to frown when a camera was pointed at her. Randi was a professional. If she had anything to say about it, she wouldn't let them catch her coughing or sneezing or frowning. She rested her forearms on the linen-covered table. "We'll keep our hands to ourselves, and everyone will win."

Dayne felt himself start to relax. She was right. The press thought he and Randi were fighting. Why not share a public breakfast on the beach, let the cameras catch them laughing and talking like old friends? Pictures like that *would* be good for the film.

The conversation shifted as they ordered and waited for their food. Dayne looked for an opening, a chance to bring God into the conversation. Randi was talking about her husband and how the two of them had planned to have a monogamous relationship, but that had changed after the kids came.

"I had a feeling six months ago that there was trouble." She lowered her chin and poked at her omelet. Egg whites and spinach, no cheese. The sort of breakfast that kept Randi in her size-two jeans. "He told me he was considering an affair."

Dayne felt sick to his stomach. "He *told* you that?"

"Mmm-hmm." Randi lifted her glass and took hold of the straw with her lips. After taking a sip, she swirled the ice in small circles. "He said sometimes an affair brings new life to an old marriage."

"Old . . ." Dayne turned his head for a moment and gave a sad laugh. As he did, he noticed the commotion in the parking lot. The three paparazzi cars had easily become a dozen. Every photographer had a camera trained on the two of them. Even with the backdrop of crashing surf and seagulls, he could hear the constant clicking. He tried to put it out of his mind as he turned back to Randi. "Old? You've been married four years."

"I know." She sounded defeated.

"Do you know how many guys would love to be in his spot? Guys who would love you the rest of your life?"

Randi leveled her gaze at him, and through her lightly tinted sunglasses he could see the depth in her eyes. "Not you, though, right? You're off the market."

"I am." He refused to let the conversation turn toward the two of them. "But your husband's wrong. Having an affair isn't the answer."

She lifted her shoulders and let them fall. "What is?"

Here was his chance to be a light, like he'd read about in the Bible earlier that week. He took a swig of his coffee and set his cup down. "The answer is God, Randi. Placing your faith in Him." His tone was serious. He was tired of dancing around the truth. If Randi didn't understand, so be it. At least he would've done what he was supposed to do. "Forever's what God's all about."

"Hmm." She looked like she might reach across the table and take hold of his fingers. But then she glanced at the parking lot and stopped herself. She lowered her hands to her lap and smiled at him. "I had a feeling you were going to say that." She paused, studying him. "You're a strange one, Dayne, but here's what's funny: I think you really mean it. About God."

He felt a surge of joy. She was listening, really listening. He kept his composure. "I do. Even here in Hollywood you can find that faith. I'll help you."

She nodded. "I might just take you up on that."

They ate the rest of their breakfast, both of them doing their best to take small bites and maintain their smiles, acting as if they couldn't see the cameras following every move they made.

"We should've had breakfast at your place," she said.

"Yeah, that would look good. Randi Wells, struggling in her marriage, spends the morning at Dayne's beach house. The press would have a field day."

"Sometimes I think we care too much what the press thinks."

"I do too. I read the other day how some top model stopped and gave a bunch of photographers a box of Popsicles. Every rag in town ran the story."

"Exactly."

"So maybe that's the answer." Dayne settled back in his seat and checked the time. "Hey, I have to run."

"I'll follow you out toward the airport. That way I can take a sharp turn before you get there. I'm the one with the rocky marriage. If they have a choice, they'll follow me."

"You might be right. They'll think I'm headed home." He stood and left a couple twenties for the bill. If the photographers hadn't been watching, he would've hugged her. The conversation had gone better than he hoped. Randi cared. And someday maybe she'd give her life to God.

They walked out of the restaurant to their vehicles, and Dayne waved at the throng of photographers. "Nice morning, huh?"

"Does this mean you and Randi are friends again?" one of them shouted over his camera.

"What about your husband, Randi? Does he know you had breakfast with Dayne Matthews?"

Randi laughed and shrugged in Dayne's direction. Then for the sake of the photographers, in a loud voice she said, "So you're going home?"

"Yeah. I need an hour in my home gym. You?" He loved this, the chance they had to trick the tabloids.

"I have that meeting." She pretended to look upset as if she'd let something slip that never should've slipped with paparazzi listening.

The photographers jumped on the moment.

"What meeting?"

"Are you seeing someone else already?"

"Is it the film's director?"

"Does your husband know?"

Randi held up her hand and gave a look of mock frustration. Then she turned to Dayne. "Thanks for breakfast."

"Bye." He kept himself from laughing. No wonder she'd won an Oscar. Her acting was beyond believable. He slipped into his SUV and only then did he allow himself a slight smile. Randi understood how badly he wanted to keep his trips to Bloomington a secret. And she'd been a friend to him, giving the press a reason to think she was up to no good.

He started his engine and reached the driveway just before her. His cell phone rang before he could make his left turn back onto Pacific Coast Highway. "Hello?"

"How was that?"

"Every one of them bought it." He chuckled. "You're good, Randi. If I didn't know better, I'd follow you myself. Just to see what was going on."

"Yeah, yeah. Whatever." She laughed. "Let's give 'em a run for their money. And, Dayne . . ."

"Yes?" He checked the traffic and pulled out.

"Thanks for being my friend."

"Thanks for being mine. I think I have a shot at getting to the airport without leading a parade."

"Well, you better focus on the road. We've got lots of company for now."

They ended their call. Randi stayed behind Dayne, and by the time they hit their cruising speed, twelve paparazzi cars were clustered behind them. There was no point trying to lose them yet. His Escalade had tinted windows, but they knew it belonged to him, same as they knew the red BMW convertible belonged to Randi. But if Randi's ploy worked, sometime before the stretch of homes on Malibu Beach, she'd turn and the paparazzi would follow.

Dayne checked his rearview mirror again. One of these days the photographers were going to cause a wreck, and then what? Would the craziness finally come to an end, or would it only make them more anxious, rabidly excited about being first at the scene?

Randi took the lead, grinning in Dayne's direction as she passed him.

Eleven paparazzi cars sped by him and tried to squeeze in on either side of Randi. Dayne understood what they were doing. Randi was blonde and pretty, and with her BMW top down and her designer sunglasses, a shot of her driving along PCH was bound to bring good money.

Still, the move was dangerous, and he watched her react to the nearness of them. At first she jerked her car to the right and then to the left. He could see her grab the wheel with both hands, trying to maintain control.

Alarm coursed through Dayne's body. *If she swerves . . . help her, God. Please!*

He sped up, trying to intimidate them, but still they hounded her. And now another photographer zipped around him and into the lane of oncoming traffic. Only a sports car was coming straight for the guy. The photographer snuck back into traffic at the last second but not before the sports car swerved hard to his right.

At the same time, a delivery truck in that lane swerved out of the way, lost control, and shot across both lanes and straight for . . .

Dayne had no time to analyze the situation, no time to imagine the ramifications of the scene playing out in slow motion before his eyes. No time to brake or turn the wheel. The truck flew at him like a runaway train, and in an instant he realized that this was how it happened. Every day in every city in the country someone stumbled into a moment like this, and that was all there was. Living life one minute and carried off in a body bag the next.

A hundred questions screamed at him. What about the wedding? What about the plans he had for later today and tomorrow and Thanksgiving? He hadn't had time to talk to Ross about Jesus, no perfect time to talk to Luke and Erin, the brother and sister he'd been meaning to call since the revelation that he was related to them. No time to call Katy and tell her good-bye.

He slammed on his brakes, but the steering wheel locked and there was nowhere for him to go. In the final split second before the truck slammed into the driver's side of his Escalade, he had just enough time to grieve everything he was about to lose. His place in the Baxter family, his years in the house on the lake, his life with Katy. But only her face filled his heart and mind and soul as the truck slammed into his SUV, as glass exploded and the sound of screaming, twisting metal filled his ears.

Something sharp and burning tore through his body, his head, as everything was going black, and his final thought was the saddest of all. The face in his mind was one he might never see again this side of heaven.

The face of his forever love, Katy Hart.

CHAPTER TWELVE

RANDI WELLS watched the whole thing happen in her rear-view mirror. One minute she was being squeezed by the paparazzi, fighting to keep control in her own lane, and the next there was a series of swerves and screeching tires and suddenly a truck was flying across traffic and smashing into the door of Dayne's Escalade.

Randi slammed on her brakes and jerked the gear into park. She was out of the car before the traffic around her had come to a complete stop. "Dayne!" she shouted, her body numb from the shock. "No . . . not Dayne!"

Around her, the paparazzi were stepping out onto the pavement. As she hurried around a few of their cars, she heard the click of cameras. Her entire body shook, and she turned on them, screaming like a madwoman. "Are you kidding me? You caused this, you vultures." She raised her fist and brought it down hard on the hood of the car that had pressed in on her left side. "Stop!" She hit the hood again and again; then she faced the photographer who had caused the accident.

"This isn't my fault," he sneered.

"It is too." She reeled back and pushed the guy to the ground. Then, only dimly aware of the other paparazzi still snapping pictures, she grabbed his camera and threw it, smashing it into a dozen broken parts. "There. You'll go to jail for this, mister. Look what you did to my—" She gasped. "Dayne! Someone call 911!" She turned and saw the truck driver trying to get free of his vehicle. But what about Dayne?

"Dayne . . . hold on!" She couldn't breathe, couldn't feel her feet. But somehow she made it to the side of his Escalade. Dayne was unconscious, pinned against the driver's seat, and bleeding from his mouth and ear. Randi clawed at the broken pieces of glass, desperate for an opening. She reached in and touched the tips of her fingers to his shoulder. "Talk to me, Dayne. Come on. Say something."

In the distance she heard a siren. *Come on. Get here. Get him out.*

Randi was shaking harder now, so hard she couldn't talk. Dayne was okay, right? Just knocked out? She tried again to reach him, to touch his face and tell him everything was going to be fine. But the twisted metal wouldn't let her any closer. She searched the other side of the SUV. Yes, maybe that was the way in. The other side.

She ran around the back of his smashed vehicle to the passenger door, half expecting it to be locked or too badly damaged to open. *Please let me inside!* She lifted the handle and pulled with all her might. To her shock, it opened. She squeezed her eyes shut. *Please talk to me, Dayne.* Randi opened her eyes again and lifted herself onto the passenger seat. Shattered glass was everywhere, and the engine was still running. She turned off the ignition and put her hand on Dayne's leg. "Dayne, wake up. Talk to me."

He was breathing. Not much and not very hard, but his chest was moving. Randi felt a wave of relief and realized that until that moment she hadn't been sure if he was even still alive. She tried to listen to his lungs above the pounding of her own heart. There was a rattling sound in his chest, and his head was hurt too. Badly.

And the bleeding near his mouth meant internal injuries, right? Wasn't that what she'd learned on some film set five years ago?

What about the air bags? She peered around Dayne, but the SUV door was too damaged to see more than a small bit of plastic. She realized the impact was so sure and so fast that the air bag had deployed, but then it had been crushed by the twisting metal around it.

Even so, the initial deployment had probably saved Dayne's life.

Only then, as she surveyed the rest of his body, did Randi notice his leg. A long piece of metal, probably from the mangled driver's door, had pierced all the way through his upper thigh. Her eyes widened, and she felt overpowering nausea well within her. Around the place where the metal had entered him, Dayne's leg was spurting blood, though she guessed the piece might also be stanching some of the blood loss.

She spotted Dayne's cell phone on the floor of the passenger side and picked it up. He had a flight to catch, right? Who would notify the woman in Indiana that Dayne had been in a terrible car accident? She slipped Dayne's phone into her shorts pocket just as the paramedics rushed up to the SUV.

"We've got it, miss," one of the paramedics said.

"No. I have to stay with him." She turned and shook her head, begging the paramedic with her eyes.

"You're . . . . you're Randi Wells." The man hesitated. "Ma'am, I need you to step aside so we can work on him."

A pair of workers had started using machinery to separate the two vehicles. One of them exchanged a look with the paramedic near Randi. "Is this guy who I think he is?"

"It's Dayne Matthews." Randi inched her way out of the Escalade. She was shaking so much that her words were nearly unintelligible. "Get him out! He needs a hospital!" Her screaming had dimmed to a faint cry. She finally did as the paramedic asked and stood a few feet away. "Please hurry."

The paramedics worked as fast as they could, and their

conversation was hard to understand. Randi's head was spinning. When an officer asked if he could move her car into a nearby parking lot, she nodded absently. Her car? Did she drive here? Wasn't she with Dayne?

When the man returned and handed her the keys, she said, "I . . . I have to stay with Dayne."

"That's fine." The officer put his arm around her shoulders. "You can come with me. We'll follow right behind the ambulance."

At that moment, she had a sudden burst of sanity. She stared at the chaotic scene around her and pointed to the photographer she'd pushed a few minutes earlier. "Him." She pointed at another photographer and another. "They did this . . . they were ch-ch-chasing us."

The officer seemed to understand for the first time. "The paparazzi? They caused this?"

Randi hugged herself. Her teeth were chattering. "Y-y-yes." She whirled around, back to the place where paramedics almost had Dayne freed from the wreckage. "He's okay, right? He'll be okay?"

"Hold on." The officer held a radio to his mouth and said something about arresting anyone on the scene with a camera. Then he put his arm around her again and led her to the passenger seat of his squad car. "Stay here."

She started to sit, but then she jumped back to her feet. "What about Dayne? . . . He's okay, r-r-right?"

"They're taking him to UCLA Medical Center. He'll be in good hands there."

There was a commotion near the wreckage as four men lifted Dayne onto a stretcher and into the waiting ambulance.

Randi slid into the squad car and buckled her seat belt. Yes, Dayne would be okay, because now he was in an ambulance. And that meant he was on his way to the hospital, where they'd fix him up good as new.

The officer got in beside her and drove skillfully through the stopped and slowing traffic. When he was behind the ambulance, he turned on his siren.

"Dayne . . . he has a plane to catch. He'll be late."

The officer didn't say anything, and Randi silently screamed at herself. Of course he would be late. It would take most of the day to stitch up his leg and make sure his head was okay.

She berated herself. What was she thinking? Dayne wouldn't be out of the hospital later today. He might not even live that long. He had been pinned to his SUV, his leg nearly severed, with very serious head wounds.

The officer was speeding south on Pacific Coast Highway, staying right behind the ambulance just like he'd promised. "The paparazzi will be charged for sure."

Randi wanted to say *good*. Good that they'd be charged. Only nothing was good at all, because charging them with a crime wouldn't undo the damage, wouldn't give Dayne a clear shot toward the airport and his waiting plane and the woman he loved in Indiana. She felt tears in her eyes, the first since the accident.

Finally they reached Wilshire Boulevard, turned left, and drove a few more blocks. Randi stared at the hospital. If anyone could help Dayne, the doctors at the UCLA Medical Center could. When they pulled into the driveway marked for emergencies, only eight minutes had gone by, and Randi silently celebrated. They'd made excellent time! Maybe they could still save him.

She jumped out of the car and ran behind the stretcher. She felt faint and dizzy. But sheer willpower kept her on her feet. The paramedics hadn't removed the piece of metal piercing Dayne's leg. It stuck out on either side of the gurney in a macabre way. She hurried after the stretcher, silently screaming, *Dayne . . . wake up! You have to be okay! Please be okay!*

When they were inside the emergency room, a nurse ushered her into a private room. "Ms. Wells, you can wait here. Mr. Matthews will be in surgery." The woman patted her shoulder. "We'll let you know as soon as we hear anything."

Strange how wherever they went—even here in a hospital room, the great equalizer—people knew who they were. Randi Wells and Dayne Matthews. But that's where celebrity treatment stopped. Death and destruction were no respecters of persons. Disaster could lay claim to a movie star as quickly and certainly as it laid claim to anyone else.

Before the nurse shut the door, Randi blurted out the only question that mattered: "Is . . . is he going to live?"

The nurse hesitated, and in that instant Randi knew just how bad things were, because if Dayne were only mildly injured, her answer would've been immediate. Instead the nurse paused just long enough so her words didn't come as a surprise. "He's fighting for his life." She looked pale, as if she herself was taking the news hard. And she probably was. The whole country felt as if they knew Dayne, after all. "Is there someone you can call? next of kin? They should have the chance to be here in case . . ." She didn't finish her sentence. "If there's someone we can call, please let us know."

Randi felt her shorts pocket. Dayne's cell phone; it was still there. "No." She pulled the phone out and ran her thumb over the top. "I'll take care of it."

"We're fielding calls from the media, Ms. Wells. We won't tell them a word about the accident until you and the doctors decide."

"Thank you." Her voice was robotic sounding, numb and lifeless. She felt sick again, and she almost asked for a bathroom. But before she could, the woman was gone and Randi was alone in the small room. Just her and God, if the God Dayne believed in really existed. She sat down, leaned over her legs, and dug her elbows into her knees. This couldn't be happening. *God, if You're there . . . let him live. Please.*

Randi opened the phone and saw that her hands were shaking again. She scrolled through Dayne's numbers, surprised at how few there were. But then, Randi hadn't heard about Dayne hitting the party scene since meeting the woman in Indiana. So she would be her first call.

Randi concentrated, tried to block out the images of a broken, battered Dayne Matthews and focus instead on the conversations they'd had about his love life. Katy, right? Wasn't that her name?

Randi ran down the list until she hit the *K*s, and there it was: *Katy Hart*. Yes, that was it. The director had talked about her at one of their meetings. She was a talented actress, apparently. Someone who had chosen to walk away from the part in Dayne's movie with Kelly Parker. Randi hit the OK button and then just as quickly hit Send.

The phone connected, but after four rings it went to Katy's voice mail.

After the beep, Randi forced herself to speak. "This message is for Katy Hart. This is Randi Wells. I'm an actress on the picture Dayne's working on." She paused. "There's been an accident. Please call me immediately so I can give you the details." She left her cell number and clicked the End button.

Who else? She stood and paced from one side of the room to the other. Any family or relatives? Dayne's parents had died when he was young, so who else could there be? She scrolled through the names, looking for a sign. As well as she thought she'd known Dayne, she really didn't know him at all. Didn't know who cared for him or who would want a call in a terrible situation like this one. She worked her way down the list, and partway through it she saw something that stopped her cold.

Under the *D*s was the name *Dad*. She checked the number, and the area code was the same as Katy Hart's in Indiana. In the notes section for the listing was something else. The name *John Baxter*, which meant the man probably wasn't Katy Hart's father. Randi stared at it for a moment before making the decision to call the man. This must be something Dayne was hiding. There could be no other explanation.

Because the world thought Dayne parentless.

CHAPTER THIRTEEN

KATY HAD NO CHOICE but to be understanding.

Dayne had promised he'd attend the show, but his schedule didn't allow him the freedom to always make his own choices. It was that simple. Showtime was in fifteen minutes, and only Bailey and Connor knew that Dayne was supposed to be here. Bailey came running up to her while she was giving final instructions to a crew of kids near the wings backstage.

Katy dismissed the other teens. As Bailey approached Katy caught her breath, almost as if she were seeing the girl in a different light for the first time. Every morning they shared breakfast and every evening they told each other good night, but somehow Katy had missed the obvious. Bailey was growing up. She had never looked more adorable, her hair in pigtails and big, colorful, eighties-style jewelry finishing off her look. The kids had been told to bring black clothes for the show and accessories to dress up their outfits. Over her black tights and long-sleeve black T-shirt, Bailey wore a short, bright pink skirt and a pink, form-fitting jacket. The picture of *The Wiz*'s offbeat version of Dorothy.

Bailey leaned in close. "I looked through a crack in the curtains. I don't see him."

"He's not here." Katy peeked around the curtain and searched the audience the way she'd done a dozen times in the last few minutes. Rhonda was standing near the back next to Aaron, the guest speaker and activities director. He'd turned out to be a great guy, and he seemed to hit it off with Rhonda. Katy wouldn't be surprised if he asked Rhonda out once they got back to real life on the other side of the lake.

But Dayne was nowhere.

Bailey frowned. "I thought for sure he'd come."

"Me too. He was probably sucked into a meeting. Directors can do that."

"Yeah." Bailey grinned at Katy. "Tell me about it."

"You doing okay with Tim and Bryan?"

"Fine." She giggled. "I invited Tanner to the show. That oughta keep them both quiet."

"I'd say."

Bailey looked at the stage. "My mom says I have to give him a chance to like theater. Maybe then we'll have more to talk about."

"Good advice. Besides, Tim and Bryan both have pretty big egos. If your boyfriend's here tonight, they might still have a chance to fit through the doorway at the end of the show."

"Right." Bailey held her hands out. "Pray with me?"

"Sure." They bowed their heads together. Katy asked God for His protection and provision throughout the night, that Bailey and the others would remember their lines, and that the entire show would be glorifying to Him.

When Bailey ran off to join the others, Katy worked out a few more kinks in costumes and blocking assignments; then she took her place in the front row. Rhonda and Aaron sat on her right side; Bethany Allen, CKT's coordinator, on her left. Up until the moment the lights went down, Katy searched. Time and again she looked over her shoulder and scanned the auditorium.

But there was no Dayne.

She hid her disappointment. Even Rhonda didn't know she'd been expecting him. It was time to dismiss all other thoughts so she could focus on the matter at hand. Her finest teen-camp production so far.

The lights faded to dark, and a single spotlight appeared onstage.

"Dorothy?" The teen playing Aunt Em craned her neck as she looked out over the audience. "Dorothy, it's time to come in. I've got supper on the table and a storm's coming."

Bailey came running down the side aisle and up onto the stage. "Here I am, Aunt Em."

The lines, the acting, the timing—all of it was perfect. Again Katy felt the ache of disappointment. Dayne had really wanted to see Bailey and Connor in a show together. And more than that, she had been looking forward to after the show, to finding a quiet place where she could lay her head on his chest and let him wrap his arms around her.

The show moved along without a hitch. Bryan was perfect as the Scarecrow, standing on the inside edges of his feet and letting his arms dangle, regardless of the scene. Same with Tim, who managed to use robotic movements whenever he needed a little oil. Even the Cowardly Lion was good—played by a wiry teen who had no trouble acting timid. His song drew more laughs than all the others combined.

When it was over, Katy looked once more. She saw Tanner Williams sitting with Jenny and Jim Flanigan. But Dayne wasn't here. Whatever had happened, he wasn't in Bloomington. Because if he were, nothing could've kept him from being here tonight. The cast took their bows, then stayed onstage to sing three praise songs.

This was what she really wanted Dayne to see.

No matter how victorious the show, the kids never forgot this part. They linked hands—Bailey and Connor and Bryan and Tim, the Schneider girls and the Shaffer kids. The Rogers and Farleys and Pick boys. Parts no longer mattered, but only the one voice they lifted to heaven. "I love You, Lord . . . and I lift my voice. . . ."

Katy felt tears in her eyes. *Thank You, God, for these kids. And for reminding me every time they take the stage why I'm here.* Nights like this she almost felt like Dorothy. There really was no place like home. *And, Lord, thanks for showing me again. There's no other place I'd rather call home. Just hurry the time so Dayne can be here with me. All the time.*

Finally the houselights lifted, and the kids raced down the stage stairs and off to their respective parents. Around the auditorium, parents were handing kids flowers and giving hugs and snapping pictures. It was a familiar scene, and usually Katy would make the rounds, posing for pictures with the kids who called out to her.

She was walking up the aisle toward the back of the theater when she spotted a man who looked like John Baxter near the door. He was talking to Bethany, and his face looked tightly drawn, serious. *Strange*, she thought. She continued toward them. She hadn't seen the Baxters in attendance. Ashley had hoped to make it with Landon and the boys, and even Kari had talked about bringing her husband and their two children. But until now Katy hadn't seen any of them.

As she came closer, she saw she was right. The man was John Baxter. He turned and their eyes met. That's when Katy saw that his eyes were red and swollen. His lips parted but he said nothing, only shook his head.

Bethany pulled away, touching Katy on the elbow briefly before she walked off.

"John?" Katy closed the distance between them. "Is something wrong?"

"Yes, Katy."

Katy gripped his forearm. That wasn't the right answer. Her question had been rhetorical. If someone looked upset, you asked if something was wrong. Most of the time the sad-looking person would shake his head and decline to get into details. "Everything's fine," he would say. Or "Don't worry. It's no big deal." Never was a person supposed to answer the way John Baxter just had.

Katy searched his face, his eyes. Was it Ashley? Had something happened to her friend on the way to the show? "Talk to me. What happened?"

"There's been an accident. Dayne's SUV was hit by a truck this morning." John sniffed, and his lower lip trembled. "He's in the hospital in intensive care. They . . . they don't know if he'll make it."

Katy's head began to spin and her mind raced. What was he talking about? Dayne wasn't in an accident. She'd talked to him just last night, and everything was all set. He would board a plane at ten this morning and meet her at the auditorium in time for the show. She looked slowly over her shoulder at the rows of seats. Only he had never showed up, so maybe . . .

She turned back to John and shook her head. "Not Dayne." Her voice was a painful whisper, each word taking every bit of her strength. Her knees shook, and she had to blink hard to keep from passing out. *Not Dayne, God. Not him.*

John took her in his arms and held her. Then he led her outside and around the corner. The summer air did nothing to stop the chill that suddenly ran through her. "I'm leaving first thing in the morning. Ashley's coming too. I thought you'd want to join us."

No, she didn't want to join them. She wanted to walk back into the auditorium and see Dayne Matthews signing autographs for the CKT kids. She wanted to see Bailey and Connor run up to him and beg him for his opinion of their show. She didn't want to fly to Los Angeles and find him in a hospital room. She held on to John with both hands and squeezed her eyes shut. She had to focus, had to make herself think.

Katy blinked and looked at him again. "What happened?"

Disgust and anger mixed in John's expression, and he clenched his jaw. "Paparazzi. Dayne and Randi Wells were leaving breakfast in separate cars, and a dozen photographers chased them. One of them veered into oncoming traffic and started a chain reaction. An oncoming delivery truck lost control and shot straight into Dayne's door."

Katy gasped and brought her hand to her mouth. "Is Randi with him?" Someone had to be. He couldn't be lying there in a hospital room fighting for his life without anyone nearby.

"She's there. They won't let her in yet." John glanced at the ground, clearly fighting tears. When he found her eyes, he looked like whatever he had to say next was maybe the hardest part of all. "He has a brain injury, Katy. Also, he may lose his left leg. Internal bleeding, organ damage. The accident was horrific." He pulled her close again. "We have to pray for a miracle."

Brain injury? Katy pictured the handicapped brother of one of the CKT kids. The child had been riding his bicycle without a helmet when he was hit by a car. The accident took everything but his life. It left him in a near-vegetative state, unable to walk or talk or think beyond an infant level. Katy shuddered. "Yes. We have to pray."

"Should I book you a flight?"

"For tomorrow?" Suddenly the urgency filled her heart and mind and raced through her veins. "What if . . . what if that's too late?" She took a few backward steps. "We need to go now. The next flight, John. Don't you think?"

"I've checked." John caught up with her and put his arms around her. "Don't panic. Dayne needs you to be calm, to pray. Come on." He gently led her toward the parking lot. "I'll take you home so you can get some sleep. I'll pick you up at four in the morning. The flight leaves at seven." He explained that Bethany and Rhonda had come in one car, and later Rhonda would collect Katy's things and drive Katy's car back. Bethany would follow her to the Flanigan house.

"Yes." Katy was numb. "Take me home, please." Nothing made sense, and all she wanted to do was find a way to Dayne. Even if she had to walk all night. She buried her head in John's shoulder as they walked.

On the way home, she said nothing because everything felt like a horrible nightmare, so surreal she couldn't believe it was happening. She hadn't seen Dayne for a month, so today was going to be about more than the show. By now they should've been almost finished with the aftermath from the camp, and they would've found a quiet spot on Lake Monroe where they could talk and hold hands and dream about their future.

Only now nothing was certain, not even Dayne's next breath.

When they reached the Flanigans', Katy thought of another question. "When will we know more?"

John understood. The dark shadows on his face, the tears that pooled in his eyes, told her the answer before he spoke. "His injuries are very serious. We have to beg God for His help, for every minute he survives."

"Dear God . . ." She couldn't finish, couldn't find the words. It was already too late. Dayne was so badly hurt that she didn't know where to begin.

John took her hands in his and finished the prayer. "I've seen You work miracles, Lord. I've seen You allow life in little Hayley, and I've seen you take the woman I love home to heaven." For a moment his emotions seemed to prevent him from speaking. After several seconds he coughed and continued. "Lord, Dayne is only beginning to live. He has found You and us and Katy . . . all in the same season of life. Please—" his tone grew desperate— "please, God, heal his wounds, his brain, and his leg. Breathe life into Dayne so we see a dramatic change in the morning. In Jesus' name, amen."

Katy couldn't speak. She thanked John with her eyes; then she leaned over and hugged him. She wasn't sure how she stepped out of the car and made it to the front door. Jenny and Jim met her there. Their ashen faces told her they already knew. They must've left the play immediately so they could be here for her.

"Katy . . . oh, honey." Jenny wrapped her arms around her and held her close. "I'm sorry. The story's all over the TV."

TV? Katy sagged against Jenny. How could they? The same paparazzi who had caused the accident were now providing the networks with pictures and video? Couldn't they give Dayne privacy even in this? Anger built inside her, and it gave her strength. She searched Jenny's face. Jim stood on Katy's other side, his hand on her shoulder. Katy tried to focus. "What . . . what are they saying?"

"It's bad." Jenny looked hesitant. "He's in intensive care."

"I know. John Baxter got a call from Randi Wells." Katy felt faint again. She walked slowly down a short hallway toward the kitchen and great room. The television was on, and she wanted to see it for herself. Maybe the information they'd heard was wrong. Maybe the news would say Dayne hadn't been injured but only stuck in traffic after a fender bender. Something like that.

She rubbed her temples as she took a seat directly in front of the Flanigans' big-screen TV. Jenny and Jim took the spots on either side of her. They didn't have to wait long. A woman anchor appeared on the screen beneath a banner that read, "Dayne Matthews in Critical Condition."

Katy held her breath. *No, God . . . no, please.*

Using the tone reserved for grave matters, the anchor drew a slow breath and began. "Actor Dayne Matthews is fighting for his life in a Santa Monica hospital tonight, victim of a paparazzi chase gone awry." She gave the details of the crash, the same ones John had explained to Katy earlier. "Tonight doctors are trying to prevent amputation of Matthews' left leg."

The station cut to a clip of a doctor speaking before a throng of reporters and photographers. "Dayne Matthews' condition is extremely critical." He made a straight line of his lips and hesitated. "We're doing what we can, but several of his injuries are life threatening."

Back to the anchor. "Dayne Matthews' agent said he expects another press conference from doctors in the morning. The accident is sadly reminiscent of the one that took the life of Princess Diana." She paused. "In other news . . ."

Jim clicked the TV off, but Katy barely noticed. She could no longer lie to herself, convince herself for another breath, another moment, that maybe the facts were wrong or that it wasn't such a serious accident after all.

She collapsed in Jenny's arms, and finally her tears came. Floods of them, desperate for a way to release the sorrow building inside her, filling her heart. She would find a way to exist between now and four in the morning, and then she would pray with every passing second that by the time she reached Dayne's side, he would still be alive. Because the accident, the details of his injuries, his prognosis—none of the information she'd already heard had been wrong or exaggerated.

Katy had no idea how long she stayed in Jenny's arms, sobbing, aching for Dayne to walk in and tell her it was a horrible mistake. But it wasn't, so there was nothing left to say.

The TV news had said it all.

CHAPTER FOURTEEN

THE MIX OF EMOTIONS had become an angry, churning sea, and Ashley Baxter Blake was so far underwater she couldn't see her way to daylight. Landon had called the fire station and asked for a few days off so he could watch the boys and Ashley could join her dad and Katy in LA. Ashley was grateful. She couldn't imagine coming this far in the search for Dayne only to lose him.

It was four o'clock Sunday morning, chilly and still a long way from sunrise, when Ashley and her dad pulled into the Flanigans' circular drive.

Katy appeared and jogged to the car. She had just one small suitcase.

Ashley opened her door, stepped out, and met Katy's terrified eyes. "I'm so sorry, Katy."

"We have to get there."

"Yes." Ashley could barely stand up under the rush of sorrow. The two of them hugged, and Katy took the backseat.

As they pulled out, she leaned up and directed her question at Ashley and her father. "Have you heard anything?"

Ashley watched her dad's reaction. His face was a mask of thinly veiled fear. "I spoke to his doctor half an hour ago. So far they've been able to save his leg, but he's not out of the woods. Infection's a big threat."

"What about . . ." Katy was breathless. She sounded scared to death. "What about his head injury?"

"He's in a coma. They removed fluid late last night, but swelling in his brain could still be a problem."

Ashley leaned her head back and closed her eyes. Swelling in his brain? A coma? Infection that could result in Dayne's losing his leg? Every bit of dialogue was like something from a horrific nightmare. And all because the paparazzi wanted a photograph. The situation was maddening, and Ashley intended to do something about it. After all, Luke was practically a lawyer. Maybe they could file a lawsuit against the tabloids, ordering them to keep their distance from now on. Something had to be done. Otherwise even if Dayne survived, they'd only chase him into another dangerous situation.

She angled herself so she could see Katy better. Her friend was shivering, her arms crossed tightly in front of her. Ashley wished with everything in her that she could whisk them back in time and find some way to protect Dayne, some way to undo the damage. She reached back and put her hand on Katy's knee. "The paparazzi did this before, didn't they? When you were in LA for the trial?"

"Yes." Katy's teeth were chattering. "They ran us off the road."

Ashley knew the rest of the story. The incident had convinced Dayne that his lifestyle was too difficult for Katy, too dangerous. They had called off their relationship, and things didn't work out until Dayne surprised her with an engagement ring over the Fourth of July holiday and shared his plans to move to Indiana.

Her older brother was anxious to live in Bloomington, marry Katy, and become a part of the Baxter family. Dayne had told her so himself the last time he was in town. "All the insanity is about to calm down." He had smiled at the others around the table at the Baxter house. "I feel like my real life's just about to start."

His words haunted Ashley as they neared the airport in silence, and another concern began to take root, but it wasn't one she wanted to talk about near Katy. Katy had enough to worry about.

They arrived at the airport and boarded the plane as part of the last group of passengers. Ashley was seated by her father, and Katy was a few rows up. They'd been the only seats left on the plane when her dad booked the tickets.

When the plane reached its cruising altitude, Ashley turned to her father and voiced the concern that had stayed with her since the drive to the airport. "What about the media?"

Her father nodded, his eyes filled with a knowing. "I've thought about that."

"And?"

"What can we do?" Her dad didn't look fazed. "The doctor knows we're coming; he knows we're family."

"Immediate family?" Ashley was stunned.

"Yes. That's the only way we'll have access to Dayne."

Ashley could barely take it in. All along this had been the obstacle, the barrier between having an open relationship with Dayne and keeping every conversation and contact a secret. Ashley hadn't cared, but what about the others? Everything was happening so fast—the accident, the trip to Los Angeles. Certainly the media would wonder who they were and why they were allowed in Dayne's hospital room. "Have you talked to the others?"

"Yes. None of them had any issue with it."

Ashley held her breath. "Even Luke?"

"He didn't say much. I think he was in shock."

Ashley exhaled and kept her mouth shut. Her recent conversations with Luke told her that maybe his reaction was more than shock. Luke didn't want his name publicly linked with his older brother's. At least not yet. Anyway, the last thing they needed to worry about was the tension Luke had been feeling.

Her dad pinched the bridge of his nose, and Ashley realized he was fighting tears. "All that matters is Dayne. If the media turn on us, so be it." He swallowed, finding his composure. "If the paparazzi figure it out, maybe we can take the heat off him."

A sense of awe came over Ashley. Her father wasn't only interested in Dayne, anxious for a relationship with him. His feelings were much stronger than that. Her dad loved Dayne, and now—faced with losing him—he would throw himself at the mercy of the tabloids if it meant helping his son.

Ashley put her hand on her father's and gave it a gentle pat. "God'll take care of us, whatever happens."

"Yes. That's what I've always believed." He drew a long breath. "Dayne was the one who worried about our privacy." He slid his fingers around hers. "I have nothing to hide. Dayne's my son. He's always been my son."

Ashley felt her father's passion to the core of her soul. If anything happened to Dayne now, after her parents had spent their entire married life wondering about him, she wasn't sure her dad would recover. "We need a miracle."

With his free hand, he pulled his wallet from his pocket. Inside were photographs tucked safely in worn plastic sleeves. Her dad flipped them slowly, painstakingly, until he reached the most recent photograph of Brooke's daughter Hayley. He stared at the picture for several seconds and then tapped it gently. "God's given us a miracle before. I'm begging Him to do it again."

Ashley looked at the photo of her niece and remembered other times. Landon's unexplainable recovery from the burns his lungs received when he'd rescued a child from a fire. Her own clean bill of health. For that matter, the story of their lives had been marked at every turn with one or more miracles. Even her mother's death had its own glimpses of God's handiwork—she'd seen her dream come true by meeting Dayne before she died.

Ashley was quiet the rest of the flight, talking to God and asking every few minutes that He might breathe healing into Dayne.

When they landed, she saw something different in Katy, a fear that hadn't been there before, as if now that they were in Los Angeles everything about Dayne's accident, his condition, felt so much more real.

Ashley's father rented a car, and the tension built with every mile as they neared the hospital. At one point Ashley turned on the radio, and a few minutes later a news report updated an anxious city that Dayne Matthews was still fighting for his life. They would give more news when it became available. Ashley turned it off.

"They don't know everything." Katy sounded stiff and robotic. "Let's just get there."

Ashley noticed her father driving faster after that. She stared straight ahead as they maneuvered through LA traffic. Scenes kept flashing in her mind: the way she'd found her mother's letter in an envelope marked *Firstborn*, how she'd known her parents' secret before the others, and how that had led to her eventual discovery that her older brother was Dayne Matthews.

She was replaying that first conversation with him when her dad turned into the hospital parking lot. Filling an entire side lot were dozens of media cars and trucks and vans with news-station call signs splashed across the sides and satellites shooting high into the air. Ashley surveyed the front of the hospital. Members of the press were clustered on either side of a long walkway.

They wouldn't recognize her dad and her, but Katy Hart . . . certainly some of them would remember her. She had been part of one of the most sensational trials to hit the national media all year, and after that she'd been the focus of the tabloids for several weeks.

Her father parked, and the three of them headed toward the walkway. Without saying anything, Ashley and her dad each took one of Katy's arms to support her.

Ashley leaned her head in close to her friend's. "Keep your eyes down; maybe they won't figure out who you are."

Katy narrowed her eyes. "I've run from them ever since I met Dayne. Not this time." She clenched her jaw and lifted her chin.

They were ten yards from the first set of cameramen when a reporter shouted, "Katy Hart, everybody! It's Katy Hart."

The press moved in like sharks around a kill, and Ashley tightened her grip on Katy's arm. For a few seconds she had the urge to run. Was this what Dayne lived with every day? She felt sick to her stomach at the thought. Cameras were aimed at them, and the air was filled with the sound of clicking and shouting. Constant clicking and shouting.

"Katy, can you tell us how Dayne's doing?"

"What's his prognosis?"

"Do you have any comments for the photographers who were chasing Dayne and Randi Wells before the crash?"

Katy stopped and faced the reporter. Her eyes grew steely, and her lips parted.

Ashley wasn't sure if she should urge Katy through the throng or stand by while she had her say. Her father seemed to be struggling with the same dilemma. Even the reporters stopped yelling their questions.

But instead Katy turned back to the hospital doors and worked her way through the crowd, which parted just enough to let the threesome through.

"Vultures," Katy muttered once they were inside. But when they reached the elevators, she exhaled hard and hung her head. "Stop me if I say that again. This can't be about them, not when Dayne's—" Her voice caught, and she brought her hand to her mouth.

The elevator doors opened. Ashley put her arm around Katy as they stepped inside. "He's going to be okay. I believe that."

Next to them, Ashley's father said nothing, and Ashley wondered if he was thinking about her mom. The last time the family had gathered at a hospital, it had been to say good-bye. Ashley prayed that this time would be different.

They reached the intensive care unit and were immediately met by a uniformed officer. "Name of the patient you're seeing?"

Ashley was glad for the security. It was the only reason the entire floor wasn't crawling with photographers.

Her father took the lead. "Dayne Matthews."

"Your relation?"

Her dad didn't hesitate. "Family."

The police officer checked his clipboard. "Your name?"

"John Baxter." He pointed to Ashley. "My daughter Ashley and Dayne's fiancée, Katy Hart."

The officer looked at their IDs and made three check marks on the paper. "Thank you. Go on to the nurses' station."

Sitting in the hallway between the elevators and the nurses' station were two women. They had the appearance of people waiting for news about someone in intensive care. But Ashley had her doubts. As they passed, one of the women took out a cell phone and made a call. Clearly no cell calls were allowed on the floor. Ashley could've bet the woman was alerting someone that the two people with Katy Hart were Dayne Matthews' family.

Or maybe Ashley was only imagining things.

They reached the nurse, and she checked their names. Then her lips formed a sad smile. "We've been expecting you."

"Can we all go in?" Katy's voice trembled.

"That's fine. Room nine. But only for a short time."

Ashley looked at her dad. He nodded for her and Katy to go in first. Then he turned his attention back to the nurse. "I'm a doctor. Can I speak to the attending physician?"

"Absolutely."

Ashley forced herself to be strong. She led Katy across the hall into the room. The lights were dimmed, and half a dozen machines were stationed around the bed. The man in the bed looked almost nothing like the movie star everyone knew and loved. His head was bandaged, and his leg was wrapped to nearly twice its size. Swelling distorted his face, and bruises colored the area below his eyes.

Katy reached his side first. She put her hand on his shoulder, leaned over him. "Thank You, God," she whispered. "Thank You."

Ashley came up beside her.

Katy's cheeks were wet. She didn't take her eyes off Dayne. "This is all I've wanted. Ever since I heard about the accident."

"This . . . seeing him?"

"No." Katy closed her eyes. "Standing here beside him and hearing him breathe. Just knowing for sure that he's alive."

For the first time since Ashley got the news about her older brother, the mix of emotions having their way with her reduced to only one. A great and all-consuming sorrow. It wasn't fair. After all the years her parents had missed, all the birthdays and Christmases and milestones, for Dayne's life to be cut short in any way was wrong. She took hold of the bed rail and looked at his face. *Please, God, let him live. Please put him back together.*

And then she felt compelled to add one more thing. Because now that she was here, now that she could see how truly critical the situation was, another fear was slowly making itself known. So in her next breath, she asked God not only that Dayne would live and that the doctors could save his leg and his mind once he woke up. But something else.

That he'd remember them.

Two hours had passed since they arrived at the hospital, and John had been in to see Dayne twice. Now he and the neurosurgeon, Dr. Cynthia Deming, were talking in hushed voices a few doors from Dayne's room. The prognosis wasn't good.

"We're still watching for edema, obviously. We'll need three days before we're out of the woods on that."

"And responsiveness?" John felt sick even asking.

"Nothing. Not since medical help arrived on the scene. Probably not since the point of impact."

John felt his heart sink. This was the sort of news he dealt with every day, news he had shared with grieving family members in a hallway like this one more times than he could count. Head injuries were always riddled with uncertainty. Much depended on which lobe sustained damage and whether that damage wound up being permanent or not.

Comas were graded on two different scales, giving doctors a way to determine whether a patient was making progress. By those standards, Dayne's coma was easily the most severe type. That was to be expected. Typically, the first three days were the worst after a brain injury—especially a traumatic brain injury, or TBI. After the brain stopped swelling—if a victim survived that long—healing could take place. At that stage, tests could more accurately pinpoint the areas of damage and the coinciding consequences.

The neurosurgeon was an articulate young woman with a gentle manner and a keen understanding of TBIs. She was known throughout the medical community for her work at UCLA. John had researched her last night when he couldn't sleep. Dr. Deming was thirty-seven, married, and expecting her first child, though she barely showed. She was a risk taker, one article said, using her off time to skydive and scuba dive and hike trails everywhere from Oregon to Hawaii. She loved the outdoors and every living thing. But she was passionate about saving brain-injured patients. In the decade that she'd been practicing neurosurgery, she'd become a legend.

John wouldn't have wanted Dayne in any hands but hers.

"Obviously you understand what we're facing here, Dr. Baxter." Dr. Deming tucked Dayne's chart beneath her arm. "Your son's injury is very serious. The odds of his ever coming out of the coma are small."

"How small?" The moment felt unreal, as if someone else were asking the question.

"My best guess is 10 to 15 percent."

John closed his eyes and waited several heartbeats before he opened them. "And if he does?"

"It's hard to tell." The doctor brought her lips together and shook her head. "He could have loss of memory, loss of motor skills. Even complete loss of all cognitive bodily functions."

"That's the worst-case scenario." It wasn't a question. All doctors knew that every now and then a case defied the odds. With every breath, John was silently praying that Dayne's case would be one of those.

"Of course." Dr. Deming frowned. "I have to be honest. A complete recovery would be very unlikely. But I won't rest until we try everything possible to make that happen."

John nodded. *Please, God, a complete recovery. I just found him.*

"About the others . . ."

"I'll tell them." John thought about his earlier conversation with the vascular surgeon. There was still a possibility that Dayne would lose his leg. He fought the heaviness inside him. Ashley and Katy knew none of what he'd learned. He kept waiting, hoping for something good to tell them. But there was nothing.

John thanked the doctor and returned to Dayne's room. Ashley and Katy both turned to him, and he motioned them into the hallway. No matter how badly Dayne was injured, there was a chance he could understand what was being said around him. In that case, it was imperative that they keep negative conversations outside his room.

Ashley's face was a mask of concern. As they rounded the corner and moved a few doors down, she whispered, "Tell us what you know."

"I can't read the machines." Katy hugged herself. Her face was pale, the way it had been all morning. "I keep looking at them and willing them to show something, a sign that he's getting better."

John leaned against the wall. The two young women standing before him had no idea what they were up against, what they were all up against. *God, help us stay strong.*

I am with you, son. I will never leave you. . . .

The reassurance that only Christ could give filled John's heart and mind. He couldn't wait any longer. He started at the beginning. "Dayne's had a traumatic brain injury. It'll take as much as three days before the swelling in his brain will stop." John tried to keep things simple. "The more the swelling, the worse things get."

Katy's eyes were wide. She looked like she could barely draw a breath. "Is . . . is there swelling now?"

"Yes." John pressed his shoulder into the wall. *Hold me up, God.* He could still hardly believe they were even having this conversation. "Once the swelling stops, we'll have a better idea of how much damage he's suffered."

Ashley massaged her brow. "So we're assuming brain damage? Is it a fact at this point?"

"Everyone's different. I don't want to assume anything yet." He paused. "Dayne has one of the best doctors in the field."

"Good." Ashley put her hand on Katy's shoulder. "I told you. He's in great hands."

John started to tell them that the odds were dramatically against Dayne's waking up the same person he was before the accident. But he changed his mind. If they were asking God for a miracle, they needed to believe it was possible. At least for now when so much was uncertain. One way or another, God would show them soon enough. John decided to move on. "He has a fever from the infection in his leg. There's still a chance they might have to amputate."

Katy stared at a spot near her feet. She shifted and crossed her arms more tightly than before.

John watched her and wondered what she was thinking. He knew Katy but not that well. The good times rarely showed the character of a person, and maybe here, now, he would learn something about Katy Hart that he hadn't known before. The news hitting her on every side had to be overwhelming. Was she thinking that she could hardly stay around for a guy with a brain injury or that a one-legged Dayne might be more than she could handle?

Katy looked up then, almost as if she could read his mind. The look in her eyes was rock solid. "I want you to know something." She glanced from John to Ashley and back. "Whatever happens after this, I'm not leaving." She pointed toward Dayne's room. "I love him. I've never loved anyone the way I love him. No matter what, I'm not leaving." Tears choked her voice. "When he wakes up, I'll be right there. Beside him."

It was a breaking point, the final drop in a bucketful of gut-wrenching moments. Ashley hugged Katy, and after a few seconds John joined in. They stayed that way for a long time, lending each other strength, silently begging God for a miracle that seemed all but impossible.

The day wasn't over, and already John knew so much more than he'd known this morning in Bloomington. He knew that he cared for Dayne the same way he cared for any of his kids and that his family would rally around the young man as if they'd known him their whole lives. He'd received confirmation about that from everyone—everyone except Luke. And that was only because Luke was distracted. Beyond that, John now knew more about the battle they were facing to see Dayne restored to health. But most of all, he knew the impeccable character of the young woman who had pledged her life to his older son.

A woman named Katy Hart.

CHAPTER FIFTEEN

KATY SAT in the hospital room alone with Dayne, where she had been almost constantly since she arrived. It was Tuesday afternoon, three days after the accident, and still she'd received no reports about the swelling and whether it had slowed or stopped. No matter how optimistic Ashley was, Katy had heard the truth in John Baxter's words. For a person with a traumatic brain injury, the first three days were the most critical. Life hung in the balance.

They'd passed that first tenuous goal. Three days and Dayne was still alive. She held on to that one fact alone. Katy stared out the window. It was the first week of September; Labor Day had come and gone. A strong wind moved the trees below Dayne's hospital room, clearing out the fog and smog and making the sky bluer than usual. Ashley and John kept vigil with her most of the time, but they spent the nights at a hotel down the street.

At this moment, John was talking with Dayne's doctors, and Ashley was getting a sandwich in the cafeteria. Katy wasn't hungry. The news about the paparazzi was as bad as any of them had expected, though Katy had been spared by never leaving the intensive-care floor. Ashley and John had been careful to keep most of the details from her, but when she pressed them this morning they'd had to admit that everything they'd feared had indeed happened.

"They know who we are," Ashley had told her. "Their questions tell the story. They're asking if I'm Dayne's sister and if Dad's his father. They've got it figured out for sure."

Katy sighed. The first tabloid stories would hit in just six days, and after that the frenzied hunt for information on Dayne's biological family would—at least for some time—become all-consuming.

Even so, Ashley hadn't seemed concerned. "We knew about this risk when we contacted Dayne. If the world wants to stare at us through a magnifying glass, fine. Nothing will change back home. We'll still be the same Baxter family."

Katy hoped so. The pulse and rhythm of the machines soothed her nerves. She preferred this now—just the sound of the equipment helping Dayne survive, monitoring whatever progress he might be making. She'd stopped watching news reports last night after tuning in to a special about Dayne. The reporter reminded viewers of Dayne's relationships with several of his leading ladies, including Kelly Parker.

What the special didn't mention was the baby Dayne had fathered. The one Kelly aborted. Katy had turned the TV off then, and it had stayed off since. In one of their last conversations before the accident, Dayne had mentioned the baby, the way he did every few weeks. The child would've been almost three months old. He followed the dates, and the regret never quite went away.

In the first full day at the hospital, when sleep had been impossible and her mind raced to all sorts of extreme places, Katy had been comforted by the fact that if Dayne didn't survive, he would have the chance to see his baby in heaven. To hold him or her the way he never had the chance to on earth. Imagining that brought quiet rivers of tears, and for a few minutes it almost seemed like a good thing that God would release Dayne from the bonds of earth and allow him to meet his child.

Then her mind had veered in the other direction. The unborn baby was safe now, in that special place in heaven for all children who never had the chance to live. The baby didn't need Dayne. Not when Katy wanted to spend an entire lifetime with him. They were supposed to marry and have a houseful of children. But Dayne had to live first. He had to find his way back to daylight and to everything that had made him who he was.

The back of the chair felt hard against Katy's spine. She shifted and turned toward Dayne. The swelling in his face was almost entirely gone. Maybe the same was true for his brain. She let her eyes travel down the thick bedsheets to where his leg was still heavily bandaged.

She wouldn't leave him, no matter what. She'd told John Baxter that, and she'd meant every word. But in the darkest moments, when it was just Dayne and her alone in the hospital room, the future loomed like a black hole. A brain-damaged Dayne Matthews? Struggling day to day with only one leg?

She shuddered at the thought, but before she could ask God for strength, beg Him for a positive mind-set, there was a knock at the door. "Yes?"

The door opened and John and Ashley came in. Both of them were smiling, and Ashley had tears in her eyes.

John reached out and took Katy's hand. "I have good news."

Katy sucked in a quick breath. "Really?" For three days she hadn't heard those words in the same sentence. A rush of heat filled her veins, and she squeezed John's hand. "Tell me. Please."

John smiled, but his chin quivered and it was clear he was fighting to find his voice. Finally he cleared his throat and shook his head. "I didn't think we'd see this day."

Ashley took the place on the other side of her father. "The infection in his leg's turned a corner." Her voice cracked, and she put her fingers to her lips. "They won't have to amputate."

Time seemed to stop. "Thank You, God. . . . Thank You." Katy's whispered prayer came instantly, instinctively. Whatever lay ahead for the two of them, Dayne would have his legs. She looked at John. "You just found out?"

"Yes." He leaned over and hugged her shoulders. "There's more."

A dizzy sense of elation wrapped its arms around her. "More?"

"The tests they did this morning show the swelling has stopped and is already receding at a rapid rate."

"So . . ." She held her breath, waiting.

"He's going to make it, Katy. He's going to live."

"I told you." Ashley put her hand on Katy's shoulder. She was crying openly now. "God has plans for the two of you. For all of us."

Katy couldn't have stood if she wanted to. She breathed more thanks to God and then voiced the only question that remained. "His brain?"

John's smile faded some. "They're not sure. Tests show much less damage than they originally thought, but his coma is still at the most severe level." He took a step closer to his son and rested his hand on the bed rail. "It's imperative that he come out of the coma soon."

Katy understood. John didn't want to say that a lengthy coma could have serious ramifications for Dayne or that the longer the coma, the more serious his brain injury. They'd been told many times that Dayne might be able to hear them, so John was doing what he ought to do. He was presenting the facts in the most positive way possible.

Dayne needed to wake up. Period.

Even so, if the tests couldn't see the serious damage Dayne's doctor had feared, then there was reason to celebrate. Already God had worked the impossible.

Katy stood and hugged Ashley first, then John. "This is what we've been praying for."

"Yes." John took hold of one of her hands. "It's as much as we could've dared hope for at this point."

The look in John's eyes told Katy that they easily could've been talking about a funeral, and even if Dayne kept his leg and his life, he was not in the clear yet. Not until they understood the extent of his brain injury.

Katy tried to get a handle on everything she was feeling. "You and Ashley are leaving today, right?"

"In a few hours." Ashley directed Katy to sit back down. Then she pulled up a chair. "We need to talk." She sniffed. Her eyes were dry now, though her cheeks were still tearstained.

John took a few steps back and pointed to the door. "I want to meet with Dr. Deming again. I'll be out there if you need me."

When he was gone, Ashley's face filled with sincerity. "You're staying?"

"Yes." Katy looked at Dayne and her heart swelled. He was going to survive. More than that, he was going to recover. This was only the beginning. She turned back to her friend. "I won't leave until he's okay. However long that takes."

Ashley frowned. "You can't stay here, Katy. You look like a wreck." She surveyed the room. "You're spending the nights here, in the chair?"

"It reclines." She patted the arms. "The nurses bring me pillows and blankets."

"But that's not real sleep."

Katy nodded. She'd thought about this, even though it hurt. "If he doesn't . . . ." She stopped herself. "If we're here much longer, I'll start spending nights at a hotel."

Ashley looked torn. "I'd stay if I could. You know that."

"Of course." She sat up straighter. This was her job, her watch. No one could do it but her. "You have Landon and the kids. I can't believe you stayed this long."

"I wanted the whole family to be here. Erin. Kari and Brooke. Even Luke. So he'd know we're all pulling for him."

Katy hesitated. "About Luke . . . have you talked to him?"

"Only for a few minutes, the day after the accident." Ashley looked uncomfortable. "Pray about him, will you? I'm not sure what's wrong with him. He just took the bar exam, so he's been under a lot of pressure. But still . . ."

"You really think he might be struggling with having a brother?" Katy uttered the question before she remembered that Dayne might be listening.

"He's struggling." Ashley glanced toward the hospital bed and shot Katy a look. "We'll talk about it later. Just pray for him."

"I will."

Ashley's eyes were damp again. "I can't stay, but I'll do whatever you need back home. CKT stuff, the new house—anything."

"Talk to Bethany about CKT. I won't be there for fall tryouts—at least it doesn't look like it. Anything you can do to fill in would be huge. And the house . . ." Katy looked out the window. "I have no idea what to do next." She'd barely thought about it since the accident. They were in escrow, and already a home inspection had been done. Besides the obvious disrepair, the structure had only a small amount of wood rot and no termite infestation.

Sometime this week Katy was scheduled to meet with the contractor who would oversee the renovation process. They were supposed to talk about windows and walls and doors and appliances. In their initial conversation Katy had learned that the process could take a year and that quality subcontractors in the area were hard to book, especially for renovations. She'd called around, but everyone she talked to said the same thing. There was no way the house could be fixed up by Thanksgiving.

Katy explained all this to Ashley and then lifted her hands and let them fall on her lap. "It feels hopeless, honestly. I can't ask you to work with the contractor. The process will take hours at a time. Besides, there are a million little decisions only Dayne and I could make."

Ashley wouldn't let up. "Tell me. What's your vision? What sort of doors and windows? What's the feeling you're looking for?"

The question allowed Katy to dream for a moment. The break

from worrying and praying about Dayne was like someone had opened a window in the boxy hospital room. For the next half hour, Katy shared her vision with Ashley. The way she had hoped for exposed wood beams on the inside and rugged natural tile on the floor in the kitchen and dining room. She talked about alpaca rugs and walnut cabinets and granite counters in browns and blacks.

By the time John came back, both of them were giggling. "That's what I like to hear." He came closer. "What did I miss?"

Ashley smiled. "We just renovated Katy and Dayne's house in thirty minutes."

"The contractor says it'll take a year." Katy still felt weary. But the distraction was a good thing. "We figured out the entire job just like that."

The corners of Ashley's lips fell. "Really, Dad, don't you know someone who could get the work done sooner?"

John looked at Dayne, and for a while he said nothing. Katy could guess what he was thinking. If Dayne didn't come out of the coma soon, his recovery period would take months. Years even. There was certainly no rush getting the house fixed.

But if that's what he was thinking, he said nothing of the sort. Instead he gave a slow nod. "I know a few people. Elaine does too. She's had some work done on her house."

At the mention of Elaine, Katy shifted her gaze to Ashley in time to see her friend bristle. More than once Ashley had shared that she didn't want her father spending time with Elaine. According to Ashley, the woman was trying to move in on her dad, only a few years after her mother's death. Ashley let the moment pass, but Katy was pretty sure Ashley would say something to John later.

For now, Ashley only patted Katy's hand. "I'll make some calls. There has to be something we can do to get the place ready."

"I'm glad you're still going through with it." John walked to the edge of Dayne's bed. "I was afraid you might change your mind."

Change her mind? About their dream house on the lake? The

idea hurt too much to even think about. "No. I'll never change my mind about that."

They talked a few more minutes about contractors and work that needed doing and how impossible the task felt to Katy.

Then John checked the clock on the wall. "We have to get going." All the time he'd been here, he hadn't said more than a few words to Dayne. He'd been crucial in aiding communication between Dayne's doctors and Ashley and Katy, but he'd kept much of his feelings to himself.

Not now.

John put his hand on the top of Dayne's head and leaned over his son. "You're going to get through this. I've talked to the doctors and . . . I've prayed for a miracle." His voice filled with emotion. "It's going to happen; I can feel it. We just need you to get out of here and show everyone how amazing God is." He stroked Dayne's forehead. "I never got to hold you or watch you take your first steps . . . or help you ride a bike. So we have a lot to make up for, Son. Hurry and wake up, okay?" He blinked and two tears slid down his cheeks. "I love you, Dayne. I've loved you since you were born." He bent down and kissed Dayne's forehead. With a last nod toward Katy, he left the room.

It was Ashley's turn. She took her place near the edge of the bed and angled her head. "We haven't even had time to get to know each other." She took hold of Dayne's hand and lifted it a few inches off the bed. Katy tried not to notice how lifeless his fingers looked. Ashley had a cry in her voice when she continued. "Now listen, Dayne, you fight to get better, okay? God's working a miracle here. I believe it and Katy believes it. We all do. Now . . . now you have to believe it too."

Katy's eyes stung, and she blinked so her tears wouldn't cloud her vision.

"No matter what we've missed, you're our brother. We have a lot to catch up on, so we need you back in Bloomington." Ashley lowered herself over his bed a little more and brought his hand to her cheek. "We all love you, Dayne. We'll keep praying." She used her free hand to dab beneath her eyes. "I'm not saying good-bye, because . . . because we just said hello. Call me when you wake up, all right?"

She held his hand to her cheek a moment longer, then carefully lowered his arm back to his side. Katy was on her feet by the time Ashley turned to her. They hugged again, both of them too emotional to speak.

Finally, when Katy thought she could find enough air in her lungs, she whispered the only thing that had to be said. "Thank you. I couldn't have survived this without you."

Ashley met Katy's eyes. Her look said that there was still much ahead, much to survive. "I wish one of us could be here with you."

Katy shook her head. "I'll be okay. You go take care of your family."

"I will." Ashley gave her a final hug, and before she left the room she promised to call tonight.

Katy watched her friend go. When the sound of her footsteps and John's faded in the hallway, she turned back to Dayne. For an insane moment she wanted to crawl into bed beside him and take him in her arms. But nothing about such a move would've been appropriate.

Instead she slid her fingers between his. The sensation wasn't at all what she wanted it to be. His hand was cold and unresponsive, not what she was used to feeling when she and Dayne touched. She resisted the urge to pull away, and one heartbeat at a time her resolve grew.

"Were you listening, Dayne?" She searched his closed eyes, his still face. "I meant what I said. Somehow we're going to get the house fixed up, and you're going to get better." Her eyes filled again. A few tears fell onto Dayne's sheet, but she held the sobs back. "You're going to move to Bloomington, and we're going to get married in the spring."

Again she waited. *Please let there be a sign, a slight movement, anything. Let me know You're here, Lord, and that You're healing him.*

She stared at the place where their hands were connected. *Please . . . a twitch or a small bit of pressure.* She held her breath, looking at his hand for any sign. But there was nothing. Her eyes moved to his, and she studied him, willing him to move. He looked like a person so deep in sleep that nothing could wake him.

Then, as if God was directing her movements, Katy let her gaze settle on Dayne's chest. She watched the subtle rise and fall, rise and fall, and suddenly she was filled with God's peace. His presence. It had been only three days since the accident. Here, then, was sign enough. Not that Dayne was moving or twitching or coming out of the coma. Not that he could respond to anything she might say, even her deepest thoughts.

But that he was breathing at all.

CHAPTER SIXTEEN

LUKE TOOK the first open seat on the subway, settled back, and stared at the dirty rubber floor mat. Nothing about his life felt right, and here—on the fifteen-minute commute to their apartment—was the only time he could really think about it. The subway lurched into motion, and he grabbed hold of the silver pole on his left side.

Ashley had been home for more than a week, and she'd called twice. The problem was, he didn't feel like talking—not about Dayne, anyway. And Ashley hadn't called to talk to him about anything else since they found out that Dayne was their brother. Especially since the accident.

The familiar knots tightened in his gut. Guilt was certainly part of what he was dealing with. He'd heard about the crash on TV before he took the call from Ashley. Press had been at the scene of the accident, obviously. Of course the world would know before the actress Randi Wells decided to look through Dayne's cell phone and find their father's number. Luke had been sitting on the couch midday Saturday watching an NFL preseason special when the news bulletin had interrupted the program. He could still remember every word of what came next.

"We have received confirmation that earlier today actor Dayne Matthews was in a serious car accident. Though details are sketchy, reports are that Matthews is in critical condition and might not survive the night."

Luke kept his eyes on the floor of the subway. His first reaction should've been shock and grief. He should've jumped up and called his dad or Ashley or one of his other sisters. Instead, for the ugliest minute, he'd felt something closer to relief. If Dayne was out of the picture, so be it. The Baxter family could carry on, same as always. No threat of national attention, no figuring out his place in the family now that he wasn't the only Baxter son, none of the awkwardness that was bound to come from having a movie star at their Thanksgiving celebration or Christmas dinner.

It had taken a few minutes for Luke to catch himself, for him to realize that his attitude was not only ugly but selfish and petty and downright sinful. He'd called Reagan into the room and told her the news.

She reacted the way he should've. She gasped and sat down slowly on the sofa. "That's terrible!"

"I know," he finally said. Only then did he reach for the phone and leave messages for his father and Ashley. As it turned out, neither of them checked their messages and Randi Wells got word to them first. In the meantime, he'd talked to Brooke, Erin, and Kari. They were appropriately concerned, praying for their older brother constantly.

So what was wrong with Luke?

The subway rumbled through Lower Manhattan, up along Broadway toward Midtown. He and Reagan weren't getting along, and Hannah from work had stopped smiling at him. One time since seeing her in Central Park he had approached her and asked if she wanted anything from Starbucks. She declined and said, "Luke . . . I'm not interested. I have to be clear on that."

Which only made him feel like more of a loser. Because if his subconscious interest in the receptionist was that obvious, then he was betraying Reagan. Even if only in his thoughts.

He pulled a piece of gum from his pocket, unwrapped it, and popped it in his mouth. He and Reagan were still barely holding more than functional conversations—whatever it took to feed and dress and bathe the kids and the usual formalities that were expected of each other.

Reagan blamed the change on the bar exam, the stress of preparing for it, taking it, and now waiting for the results. But if he was honest with himself, there seemed to be a deeper connection with the situation regarding Dayne. The feeling overtaking him from the inside out was one of emptiness, uncertainty. As if he no longer felt comfortable in his own skin. The confident Luke Baxter he'd always been was now just another guy trying to figure out his life.

In some ways he felt the way he had after 9/11. He'd turned his back on God and his family and moved in with a coed who laughed at the idea of Christianity. But after Ashley helped him find his way back to Reagan and Tommy and even their parents, everything seemed right again. He had been there—the rock for his sisters—when their mother died, and often he and Reagan talked about moving back to Indiana.

The subway stopped. A swarm of people rushed to the exit while others, jostling briefcases and backpacks, found their way onto the car and took seats. It was crowded today, stuffy and stale smelling. A dozen people stood, holding on to the ceiling straps, their eyes tired and vacant.

Was that what Luke had become? Another New York commuter trying to get through another day? Where were the thrill and excitement that had marked his existence a few months ago? And where was the passion he had shared with Reagan? Were the kids wearing them out, leaving both of them with nothing left for each other? He worked his gum, but already the mint flavor was wearing off.

The answers had to be somewhere. Luke leaned back against the window and stared at the ceiling. *God . . . I've never felt like this, so out of sorts. Even after 9/11, I had a purpose and a passion. The wrong one, yes. But I didn't feel so lost.* The vibrating window hurt his head, so he leaned forward and planted his elbows on his thighs. He covered his face with his hands. *I feel disconnected. Help me find my way back, Father.* He opened his eyes and studied his shoes. *Life means nothing without family, and everywhere I look my connection with family is falling apart. I don't know. Just help me. I can't figure it out alone.*

He would've liked an answer, a response echoing somewhere in the distant recesses of his soul or a kind word from a stranger. Something to make him know God was listening. But there was nothing.

Luke sat up straight, and five minutes later the subway rattled to a stop at his station. He gathered his attaché case and checked that his cell phone was in his pocket. But as he walked up the stairs, he moved slower than usual. The hardest part of the day was just ahead.

The part where he had to face Reagan and the kids.

Reagan and her mother had been talking about Luke's attitude for several weeks. Her mother's opinion was clear. Luke's conflict was with himself. Now they sat at the dining room table waiting for Luke to return from the office. Reagan had Malin in the high chair beside her and Tommy in a booster seat on the other side.

Her mother sat across from them, her expression sympathetic. "He'll come around, honey. Luke's from a good family. Guys like him always figure it out eventually."

"But he's taking it out on us." Reagan was losing her patience with the situation. For the past few days she'd allowed herself to think the unimaginable. If Luke wanted out, fine. He could get his own apartment or go back to Bloomington. She and the kids didn't need to be around someone so defeated all the time.

Her mother's tone was gentle. "Men have a lot to figure out. He's young, and after taking the bar his career is kind of on hold." She paused. "Your father went through something like this."

Reagan put a spoonful of green peas on Malin's high-chair tray. "How'd you survive?"

"By loving him." She smiled, and her eyes held the distant sadness they would always hold when she thought about her lost love. "By praising him, finding ways to build him up." She refocused on Reagan. "Men need that. Even when you don't feel like doing it."

"But you've been down on Luke too. You thought he'd find us a place to live by now." She turned to Tommy and tore his slice of bread in half. "Take small bites, okay?"

"'Kay, Mommy."

Tommy's toothy grin melted her heart. Her little boy looked so much like Luke; the resemblance was always striking. It made her smile even now when she was so angry with her husband.

"I thought you'd have your own place, yes. But I didn't think he'd put so many hours into getting his law degree." Her tone was measured. "Actually, after you had Tommy, I sort of pictured Luke going into sales. I thought he'd give up on the dream of law school."

Malin pounded on her tray. "Mama . . . Mamamama."

Reagan handed her a sippy cup of milk. Her daughter took it with both hands and tipped it bottom side up.

"She's a good eater," Reagan's mother said. "Not like you. I had to work to get anything down you."

"She's a blessing, for sure." The adoption had gone through more quickly than they'd expected, and Malin's transition from China into their home had been going well for the most part. But something her mother had said surprised Reagan. "So you're saying you're proud of Luke?" She felt the puzzled look on her face. "I thought you were frustrated with him."

"How could I be? Everything he's worked for is to give you and the kids a good home." She sighed. "The early years of marriage are often hard. The key is to learn how to love. And for a woman, that means making her husband feel special, important."

Reagan was about to ask how she could do that if Luke wasn't even willing to be responsive when they spoke, but at that moment he walked through the door.

When he saw her and her mother at the table with the kids, a defeated look flashed on his face. "Sorry I'm late."

"No." Reagan stood and walked halfway across the room. "I thought I'd have the kids fed before you got home. That way I could get them down earlier. So we could talk."

"Oh." He gave a weary nod and waved at Reagan's mother as he headed for their bedroom. "I'll change clothes and be back out in a few minutes."

Reagan's mother's advice stayed with her. Maybe she was right. Luke might be feeling unneeded, useless. He wasn't making much of a living yet, and nothing would change until he passed the bar.

But Reagan had another suspicion. Maybe the trouble with Luke stemmed from the fact that Dayne Matthews had appeared in their lives. It was one thing when the guy was a client at the law firm, someone Luke could help out during a big, splashy Los Angeles criminal trial, the way he had last spring. But now that Dayne was his brother, the oldest Baxter sibling, Luke seemed almost jealous of him. Which was ridiculous, because no one could ever take Luke's place in the Baxter family. The group was way too close for that. Still, Reagan figured Dayne's role in the family might have something to do with the changes in her husband.

Reagan and Luke finally settled down on the sofa near the front window, the one overlooking the boulevard. The kids were in bed, and Reagan's mother was watching a movie in her bedroom. They were as alone as they'd ever be.

At first neither of them said anything. Reagan looked out at the rooftops of the buildings across the street. New York City had been hot and humid today, and the break in the weather that came in the fall still felt a long way off.

"So . . ." Luke folded his hands and leaned over his knees. "You wanted to talk?"

"Yes." Reagan pulled her knees up and hugged them to her chest. "I need to know what's wrong with us."

Luke sighed, and it sounded as if it came from deep within him, from a place he no longer allowed her access to. "I've been asking myself the same thing."

For a moment Reagan waited. What had her mother said? Compliment him, build him up. Fine, she would do that, but not until he told her what was wrong. "You go first."

"I don't know." He raked his fingers through his hair. "Nothing feels like it used to. Nothing feels right."

Anger breathed its hot breath on her, and she clenched her teeth. If she was going to get to the bottom of the situation, she needed to speak her mind. "You know when all this nonsense started?" She kept her voice low, but her tone was uncharacteristically sharp. "When you found out that Dayne Matthews was your brother."

"He's not my brother."

"He is your brother." Reagan was on her feet. She glared at her husband and exhaled hard. "See, I'm right! That's what this is all about. You're jealous because Dayne's part of the family now."

"Listen—" Luke's voice was louder than before—"just because my dad and Ashley are in contact with the guy doesn't mean he's part of the family. He's a Hollywood star, for heaven's sake." He jabbed his finger in the air. "He doesn't know the first thing about being a Baxter."

"Well, you know something, Luke?" Reagan felt herself losing control. "Lately neither do you." She spun around and stormed a few steps in the opposite direction. Then she whirled and pointed at him. "When I first met you, that's when you were a Baxter. You were devoted to God and kind to your family, and you treated me like a queen. That's the Luke I fell in love with."

He stood. "And you're saying I'm not that same guy anymore?"

"You were when we first got married. But not lately." She waved her hand. "One-word answers, stalled conversations, hardly any time with the kids." There was a cry in her voice. "I don't even recognize you anymore."

"So what are you saying?"

Everything her mother told her fell by the wayside. The way Luke was acting wasn't fair. "I'm saying grow up." She spat the words at him. "I'm the one who gave up my college dreams, and I'm the one working part-time and still taking care of the kids."

Reagan moved a step closer. The intensity in her voice ran through her veins. "Maybe we can stop sitting around trying to understand why poor Luke isn't feeling right, why nothing feels the same." She gestured toward the door. "You're the one out there working for your dream and coming home and treating me like a stranger." She felt like breaking down, but the anger inside her wouldn't let the tears come. Not yet.

For a few seconds it looked as if that last line might break Luke. Rather than the walls that had dulled his eyes recently, his look was transparent, full of pain. But instead of apologizing, he only returned to the sofa, sat down, and let his shoulders sink. "I'll move out if you want me to. Until we can figure something out."

"What?" she shouted. Just as quickly she lowered her voice. "Is that all I mean to you? Just some problem to figure out? Even if it means walking away?"

"I'm just saying maybe we need a break."

"No!" She backed up a few steps. "What we need is for you to remember who you are, Luke Baxter, before you come home one day and I've changed the locks."

That last statement brought the walls flying back up again. Luke looked at her, disgust written in the lines on his forehead. Then he stood and stalked out of the room.

At the same time, the phone rang. Reagan could feel tears building, but she refused them. She went to the phone and saw the name *John Baxter* in the caller ID window. She didn't want to talk to anyone right now, but she also didn't want her mother picking up the phone. If her mom and John talked, her mother might leak the fact that Reagan and Luke weren't getting along. News like that should come from her or Luke, not her mother.

She didn't hesitate another moment. She picked up the receiver, hit the Talk button, and held it to her ear. "Hello?"

"Reagan, dear, how are you?" Luke's father sounded serious— the way he'd sounded often since Dayne's car accident.

But the question released every ounce of emotion Reagan had been holding in. A lump formed in her throat, and she couldn't speak. She squeezed her eyes shut and dropped slowly to the nearest chair.

"Reagan?"

She pinched the bridge of her nose and forced herself to speak. "Yes. I . . . I'm sorry, John."

"Something's wrong?" The man's voice was thick with concern. "Is it one of the kids?"

"No." She couldn't do this to him. He'd heard this much, so she needed to explain herself. "It's Luke and me. We're . . . we're not doing very well."

John let out a breath, but it sounded like a sad groan. "I'm sorry. I didn't know."

The tears came in torrents, as if all the emotions she'd been feeling for the past month were trying to find release in that single moment. "He hasn't been himself, and now—" she covered her eyes with her free hand—"he's talking about a separation."

"Oh, Reagan." Luke's father had never sounded so distraught. "I had no idea."

"Maybe . . . maybe you could talk to him."

"I will. Definitely." His voice changed from shocked to weary. "I was calling to tell him there's no change with Dayne. He's still in a very deep coma."

"Oh." Reagan pressed her finger to her upper lip. "I'm sorry." She thought for a few seconds. Should she share how she was feeling? "I think Luke . . . he has a problem with the whole Dayne thing. I'm not sure I understand it."

John made a frustrated sound. "I think you're right. Listen, I promise I'll talk to Luke. In the meantime, I guess I can only ask you to have patience with him."

"I'm trying." Another wave of tears strangled her heart. "I'm not sure he wants to work things out."

"He does." John's tone was kind but adamant. "I know my son. He would never leave you or the kids. Whatever's going on must be eating him alive."

"Yes." She wiped at her eyes. "Should I tell him you're on the line?"

"No. I want to pray about this first. I'll let the two of you have your space tonight, and I'll talk to him when he gets home from work tomorrow."

They said good-bye. Reagan laid her head on the table, the receiver still in her hand.

The troubles in their marriage were Luke's fault, not hers. Her mother meant well, telling her she could improve things by building up her husband and making him feel important. But the fact was, the changes were the result of some difference in Luke—a difference in his attitude and tone of voice and desire to make her feel loved. They hadn't been intimate in nearly two weeks, which meant what? That he'd lost interest in her? Was she that undesirable?

No, the solution wasn't up to her. It was up to Luke and God and whatever conversation John might have with his younger son tomorrow night. If that didn't work, then maybe Luke was right. Maybe the only option facing them next was the one they had never dreamed possible.

A separation.

CHAPTER SEVENTEEN

IT WAS DUSK in Bloomington, and John hadn't been able to shake Reagan's terrible news. He was taking the walk around his property, the one he and Elizabeth had taken thousands of times before. Only this time—as was often the case lately—Elaine was at his side. He'd already caught her up on the latest news concerning Luke, and he was desperate for her insight.

Elaine glanced at John. "You agree with Reagan?" Their steps were slow, the fading sunset filling the air around them with a sort of quiet comfort. "That all this might be about Dayne?"

"It's possible. I haven't had a good conversation with Luke since he found out that Dayne's his brother."

They weren't far from the fishpond. When they reached it, Elaine crossed her arms. "Every time we're out here I can picture Cole, crouched down looking for frogs and fish." She looked over her shoulder at him. "The way I picture Cole, anyway. From his photographs."

John felt something strange stirring inside him. Did she mean something by the comment? Something deeper? He opened his mouth to ask her but changed his mind. The conversation tonight wasn't about the two of them. It was about Luke. He linked his arm through hers and led her up the walkway toward the house. They sat in the porch swing, and Elaine was quieter than usual.

"More than anything, I think Luke's struggling with himself. Who he is and who he's becoming." John narrowed his eyes and looked out over the grassy fields that spread across the landscape. "I remember feeling that way halfway through med school. You're trying to support a family, and you wake up one day and wonder if all the work's ever going to pay off."

"He's your son, John." Elaine lifted her gaze to the darkening sky. "He'll figure it out. Tell him how you and Elizabeth worked through things." She smiled at him, but there was a distance in her eyes. "That should help."

"I will." He set the swing gently in motion. "Dayne's still in the coma. I guess I told you that."

"Yes. Katy's staying with him?"

"She is. Now she's spending the nights at the hotel across the street. But she won't leave. Not for anything."

"Do you think he has a chance to pull out of it?"

John hated thinking about the situation. "Every day the odds of his recovery get smaller."

"But the God we serve isn't interested in odds." She looked at the sky again. "I've learned that much."

"So true." They rocked for a while before he spoke again. "Odds were the tabloids would smear our names across a dozen covers last week. But that didn't happen."

"Perfect example."

A bat dipped low in front of them and flapped off into the shadows. The first mention of Dayne's accident had hit the tabloids the Monday after they returned from Los Angeles. The news that he was in critical condition made the covers of every magazine that week. Details of the accident and the arrival of Katy Hart at the hospital along with her constant bedside vigil were the focus of every story.

But there was only a small boxed sidebar inside three of the rags that mentioned Dayne's biological family. "Mystery Family Members Accompany Katy Hart," one of the headlines read. The story said only that records showed Dayne Matthews was adopted, and sources confirmed that he'd located his birth family in recent months. The article questioned whether the two people who entered the hospital with Katy Hart might in fact be members of his biological family. End of story.

Even Katy had come out of the paparazzi frenzy fairly unscathed. The articles played on the sympathy of readers, painting a picture of the sweet, innocent Katy Hart, previously known as Dayne Matthews' mystery woman, now grieving beside him as he fought for his life. Sources were quoted saying that Dayne had never loved anyone the way he loved Katy, and if there was any power in love, having her by his side would help him pull through.

Indeed.

John gave the swing a soft push. "There'll probably be more about us in the weeks to come."

"I'm sure." Elaine's words were shorter than usual. Clipped. "You'll survive, though. You always do, you Baxters."

A whip-poor-will cried as it swooped low over the far field. John caught Elaine's expression in what remained of the daylight. It was definitely strained. "Something wrong?"

She didn't answer at first, only raised her chin an inch and kept a strong front. But the way she pinched her lips together told the story. Something *was* wrong, and John realized it was the first time since they'd struck up a friendship that she'd kept him guessing. Always before, if she was struggling with one of her kids or troubled by a sick grandchild, she would say so early in the conversation. This was different.

After half a minute, she exhaled in a way that made her sound beyond tired. "You ever wonder, John . . . how come we talk about everything else?"

His mind raced. First the comment about Cole, then the remark about the Baxters always surviving, and now this. "Everything else?"

"Your kids, my kids, your grandkids, mine. We talk about faith and fish and frogs." Slowly she looked at him. "But we never, ever talk about us."

The word hit John like a two-by-four. All this time, all the morning walks around the farmers' market and the strolls around his property and down by the stream behind his house. The hours they'd spent sitting in the porch swing and building their friendship, and through all of it he'd wanted nothing more than to avoid that one word.

Us.

Because as far as John was concerned, the word *us* could only represent two people: him and Elizabeth.

He grabbed the swing chain and squeezed it with all his strength. "You and I . . . we're friends, Elaine." He tried to hide the hurt in his heart, tried not to let her hear it in his voice. In that moment he ached for his lost wife more than he had in days, months. The smell of jasmine hung in the breeze. He turned to Elaine, searching her face. "I never meant to make you think it was more."

Tears glistened in her eyes, but she gave a quick nod and forced a smile. "I know." She stood and with both her hands took hold of his free one. Almost the way she might greet a stranger, she gave his hand a squeeze. "I need to go."

"Elaine . . . why? What's changed?"

A single tear fell onto her cheek. "Nothing." Her smile faded. "That's just it." Without saying good-bye, she turned and walked to her car, her back straight. She never once looked over her shoulder at John. She stopped at her car door, but even then she hesitated only a few seconds. Then she climbed in, started the engine, and drove away.

When he could no longer see her car making its way down

the country road that led away from his house, John sucked in a long breath and released his hold on the swing chain. *God, I don't understand.*

"I know the plans I have for you . . . plans to prosper you and not to harm you."

The verse nearly knocked the wind from him. It was the one he and Elizabeth had used so many times in talking to their children. When Kari was heartbroken over Ryan Taylor's football injury, when it looked like Brooke wouldn't get into med school. Erin's struggle with having children, Ashley's health scare, and Luke's frustration with God after 9/11. Always they'd told their children the same thing. Jeremiah 29:11—God has plans for each person. Good plans. The key was to walk with Him, step by step, so the Lord could reveal those plans to each of them.

Only now God had brought the verse to mind for John as he watched Elaine's car drive out of sight. Was Elaine part of the plans God had for him in this, the autumn of his life? Elizabeth had been gone over two years, and Elaine had been a widow for more than ten. Was it time he adjusted his definition of the word *us* to include Elaine? The thought made him ache, because deep down he knew that his friendship with Elaine was headed somewhere. And because he never intended to hurt her. Never.

But most of all because he still missed his dear Elizabeth.

He struggled to his feet, the weight of his sorrow like a chain around his neck and shoulders. Inside, he went to the one place where he could still see her, still feel her with him. Her rocker next to his recliner in the living room. Countless nights they would sit here together, side by side, talking about their kids, studying the pictures of them on the mantel.

He made it over to her chair, and with all that remained of his strength, he did what he did only once in a rare while. When the pain of losing Elizabeth threatened to stop his next breath. He took hold of the back of the rocker, the place where she would lay her head when her eyes were tired and the night grew late. He held it as if he were holding her, clung to it as though he might somehow bring her back to him even for a few minutes.

"Elizabeth." Her name was as right and real, as familiar as his own heartbeat. He tightened his jaw and barely squeezed out the next words. "God . . . I miss her so."

Standing there, gripping her chair that way, he could almost hear her voice, smell the subtle sweetness of her perfume. Gentle, loving, honest Elizabeth. How could she be gone, and how could another woman be wondering about her future with him? He hadn't realized it until now, but tears were hot against his cheeks. He held on tighter, willing a little of Elizabeth's strength to find its way into his heart.

Dayne was still in critical condition, Luke's marriage was in trouble, and Ashley was feeling the strain of balancing her life at home with her increased duties at CKT and her desire to get the lakeside house fixed up for Katy Hart. "Elizabeth, if you were here . . ."

"Do not be afraid or discouraged. . . . For the battle is not yours, but God's."

Yes, God, I hear Your voice. The Scripture was from 2 Chronicles 20, where he and Elizabeth had always gone when times got tough. The battle belonged to the Lord. In the hardest times, the only way through was to remember that much. Part of the text reminded God's people to take up their positions and stand firm and see the deliverance the Lord would bring.

I need that now, Lord. In so many areas.

At that moment, more than anything, John needed strength to stand, to once more let his dear Elizabeth go, the way he'd had to let her go a thousand times since her death. *She's Yours, God. I know that. Help me walk this journey without her.*

I am with you, son.

Slowly, painfully, John released his hold on Elizabeth's chair.

Then, with a peace and strength that were not his own, he trudged upstairs to their room and into the closet, where her box of letters still sat on the upper shelf. Times like this, he could always take the box down and find something that would bring him comfort, a piece of Elizabeth's heart that she could share with him even from as far away as heaven.

He sifted through the envelopes, and partway through the pile he felt one that was heavier than the others. Over the last two years John had discovered that once in a while Elizabeth had written a letter and made copies of it—one for each of the kids. It was why he knew he had to sort through all the letters one day. Because within them was a wealth of memories and wisdom that Elizabeth meant for her children. He was doing them a disservice not to make her words available to them.

He lifted the heavier envelope from the others and looked at it. Scrawled across the front in her own delicate handwriting were the words that graced the fronts of many of the letters: *My dearest John.*

The words soothed his heart and reminded him of all they'd shared. The idea that he might find that kind of love twice in a lifetime was absurd, and he needed to acknowledge that fact. He couldn't duplicate with Elaine what he and Elizabeth had shared. Not even if it meant losing Elaine's friendship.

He slid his finger carefully under the flap of the envelope, and sure enough, inside were several sheets of paper. He spread them on the bed. The top page was a letter to him. He lifted the paper to his face and breathed in long and slow. It wasn't his imagination. He could still smell her perfume on the pages, even after two years. Elizabeth had always kept her stationery in her perfume drawer—something her mother had taught her. And so the pages—though old—carried the smell that would always be hers alone.

He found the top of the page, the place with the date from ten years ago, and began to read.

> My dearest John,
>   Today I was volunteering with Elaine . . .

John's heart skipped a beat. He almost dropped the page. Of all the letters in the box, he had picked one in which Elizabeth mentioned Elaine? He stared at his friend's name and felt a chill pass over him. *God, is this a sign somehow? Am I supposed to remember that Elaine was Elizabeth's friend first, so she should never be more than a friend to me?*

He wasn't sure, and maybe it didn't matter. God wouldn't be giving him a message about Elaine now. He dismissed the entire idea. Instead he continued reading.

> Today I was volunteering with Elaine when one of the other women asked me a question. She said, "How do you do it, you and John? The way you look at each other, the love in your eyes— it's the sort of thing usually reserved for newlyweds." I smiled at her, and a thought occurred to me.
>   John, we really do have the most amazing marriage. So many times I find myself sharing our secrets with my friends. How I respect you with every breath I take and how you cherish me like I was the greatest gift God's ever given you.

A smile tugged on John's lips as he reread that last line. It was true. He and Elizabeth *had* been an example to so many people— and not because they never disagreed, but because somewhere along the way they'd learned the secrets to enjoying marriage, to loving each other actively and constantly. And in the process, they both won, every day that God had given them.

Sweet Elizabeth, taking the time to write this letter. The first thing he'd do when he saw her in heaven was thank her for leaving this piece of herself, these letters. The thoughts and glimpses of her heart.

He found his place once more.

> I decided that the things we've learned about marriage boiled down to ten points, and if we got those right, everything else

> would fall beautifully into place. I've shared this time and time
> again, but here I want to write those points down for our chil-
> dren. Because one day they'll most likely get married, and they'll
> find out, like we did, that marriage takes work. And it's not until
> you understand how to be happy together that the good times
> can really begin.

John let himself drift back. Elizabeth was right. The early years
had been rough for them too. The same way they were now for
Luke and Reagan. John had been in med school, and they were
struggling financially. On top of that, they were missing their firstborn son and on edge because they didn't feel the freedom to talk
about him. It wasn't until they had met with the associate pastor
at their church and brought their feelings into the open that they
could finally let go of those feelings and start learning to love.

Another chill passed over him. So here was the real message
from God, the real reason he'd found this letter first. The letter
held Elizabeth's advice about marriage. The exact bit of wisdom
Luke needed now more than ever. Since Elizabeth wasn't alive to
tell Luke herself, God had directed John to this letter.

John felt the presence of the Holy Spirit in the room with him.
You are so good to me, God. Thank You. This is just what I needed.

His hands shook a little as he continued reading.

> Anyway, I thought it was important, so I wrote down everything
> we've learned over the years. The secret to our love, I guess. I've
> made copies, one for each of the kids. I'll give it to them when they
> get married. I love you, John. Thanks for making it so easy.
>   Your Elizabeth

Her voice hung in the hallways of his heart, and the ache hit
him again. The one that served as a constant reminder that she
was gone. She must've forgotten about the letters, too busy with
wedding plans for each of the girls and too caught by surprise for
Luke's wedding. Still, God in all His goodness had brought her
words to the surface just when they were most needed.

John looked at the pages on the bed and wondered. He sorted through them. Sure enough, there weren't five copies; there were six. Because always and ever Elizabeth had included Dayne. He had been in her heart from the moment she first held him until her dying day. Her firstborn. She wouldn't have spelled it out, wouldn't have jeopardized the sanctity of their family. Especially as far back as ten years ago. If anyone else had stumbled onto the envelope prior to learning about Dayne, they would've assumed only that she'd made one too many copies.

But that wasn't the case. He knew her better.

Six children. Six copies. Period.

It was one of the ways she could keep Dayne's memory alive in her heart, including him when she thought about the future of her children.

Tenderly, John folded the pages and put them back into the envelope. He would give the letters to the girls later.

But he would mail Luke's copy tomorrow. His mother's advice couldn't be timelier. John remembered the hurt in Reagan's voice, the way she'd broken down during their conversation earlier tonight. Yes, he would send the letter right away.

There was no time to lose.

First thing the next morning, John was on the way to the post office when he spotted someone parked on the road at the end of his driveway. *Strange*, he thought. People looking for him would've come up the driveway and knocked on the door. Same as if the person was looking for one of John's neighbors. Maybe the driver was lost.

He headed down his driveway, and as he reached the parked car, a man jumped out and quickly held a black piece of equipment up to his face. For a split second John thought it was a rifle and the man was a lunatic trying to kill him. But as he made his turn, he realized that the piece of equipment wasn't a gun.

It was a camera.

CHAPTER EIGHTEEN

THE CHURCH SERVICE Sunday moved both Ashley and Landon.

Pastor Mark Atteberry had preached on service and how God's people were created to serve. "The 'one anothering' that goes on throughout the Bible is proof enough. Every day you should wake up and ask God what He wants you to do that day, how you can serve someone else. Whatever your troubles, serving others is one of the greatest cures."

When they'd collected Cole from his Sunday school classroom and Devin from the nursery, Ashley linked her arm through Landon's. "That sermon made me think of you."

"Oh yeah?" He had Devin's baby carrier hooked on his other arm. Cole danced merrily in front of them as they walked.

"Yeah." She nuzzled against his shoulder, then released his arm. "That's all you ever do. Serve people. Ever since I've known you."

"Well . . . I'm not sure about that." He grinned at her. "There was that one time at the last Fourth of July picnic when I tried my hardest to beat your dad in a fishing contest."

"You still ended up serving, Daddy." Cole turned around and flashed a smile at him. "Sort of."

"Is that right?" Landon rubbed the top of Cole's head. "How so?"

"Because Papa won, and you had to go in the lake with all your clothes on." Cole was reduced to giggles at the memory. "Maybe you didn't mean it to happen, but that was fun for the rest of us."

Ashley laughed too.

Landon set Devin's baby carrier down and did a reenactment of himself splashing around the shallow lake water in his clothes. "How's that?" He picked up the carrier again.

"Funny!" Cole laughed harder than before. "So funny."

"Yep, that's me." Landon found his place next to Ashley again. "Anything to keep the rest of you happy."

Cole's giggles faded as he skipped toward their Durango.

"I'm serious, though." Ashley looked up at Landon. "Pastor Mark spent the hour talking about service, and all I could think about was you. Out there fighting fires and saving lives, running off to New York City to find Jalen." Her voice fell a notch. "Chasing after me, even when I was a complete brat."

Landon smiled. "Is that what you were?"

"Sometimes." She gave him a wary look.

"Sometimes?" He stopped and faced her. His eyes danced.

"Okay, a lot of times." She loved the way they could stop on a dime and find that place of butterflies and magic, that crazy-in-love feeling that put them in their own world, even in the middle of the church parking lot.

"Yeah." He touched her face and worked his fingers into her hair. "A lot of times."

"But there you were . . . hanging around again and again for me."

"For you?" He chuckled. "That was for Cole, you mean."

"Guys!" Cole was hopping up and down near the SUV. "Hurry with all that mushy stuff. I have to go to the bathroom."

Ashley and Landon laughed.

"We're coming." Then Ashley eased her hand along her husband's neck and cradled the back of his head. She drew him closer and kissed him. "Okay, for Cole." There were no churchgoers nearby, so she kissed him again. "But see, you were thinking of everyone but yourself."

He brushed his face against hers. "You mean like when you framed a roomful of old photographs so a sweet old lady could live with the memories of her husband, or when you bought a saddle on eBay so an old man could remember the days of his youth?" He smiled. "Like when you dropped everything to go to California with your dad so you could make sure your injured brother would feel cared for? And when you keep stepping in and helping with CKT without any pay just because you like watching kids enjoy theater?" He took a step back, and the teasing in his eyes changed to something much deeper. "I think you know a thing or two about serving."

Ashley was touched more than Landon could ever know. That he had a servant's heart was obvious. But her? The selfish middle daughter who left Bloomington for Paris and had a shameful affair with a Parisian artist? The one who came home pregnant and alone and often allowed her mother to raise her son so she could pursue her painting dreams? Even now she didn't think of herself as particularly helpful or generous.

But Landon did.

She thought about Dayne as they drove home, packed a picnic, and headed for Lake Monroe. If anyone needed service it was Dayne and Katy. He was still in a coma with no sign of coming out of it. And Katy still needed help getting their house together. Because one day Dayne would wake up and he would talk and think like the Dayne he'd been before the accident, and come Thanksgiving he would need a house to live in. Ashley had an idea that could make all the repairs come together by then. Her dad was going to meet them at the lake, and Kari and Brooke and their families too. Temperatures were in the eighties—summer's last glorious ride before fall would take the reins. Before the afternoon ended, Ashley wanted to tell them what she'd been thinking.

They reached the familiar picnic spot first, and when they were settled at a table halfway between the parking lot and the water, Landon set up a canopy to keep the sun off them.

Devin was awake and cooing. He was jabbering in a precious language all his own, and he laughed whenever Cole was around.

"Can I catch him a snake, Mommy?" Cole peered in at his brother and patted his forehead.

"Babies don't like snakes."

"He might." Landon shared a conspiring look with Cole. "Go ahead. Just stay there in the grass where we can see you, okay, buddy?"

"Okay!" He looked back at Devin. "Wait'll you see the snakes they got out here. The big ones are four feet long!"

Ashley let out an exasperated groan. "All snakes must go to Daddy before they go to Devin. That's Mommy's rule."

Landon nodded, but he grinned at Cole. "Bring 'em here first, all right?"

"I will!" With that, Cole was off for the patch of grass a few yards away.

"He's pretty good at catching snakes, you know." Landon sat down on the edge of the table and put his finger out near Devin. The baby grabbed hold of it and smiled.

"He loves you."

"Yeah, well, I love him back." Landon leaned in and kissed the baby's head. He glanced at Ashley over his shoulder. "Don't worry about the snakes. They're harmless. Garter snakes, nothing more."

Ashley made a face. "I just wish he'd stick to frogs."

Landon laughed. He got up and took a few steps in Cole's direction. "Maybe I better go help."

"See . . . there you go. Always serving."

He waved at her, brushing off her comment, and jogged toward Cole.

Over the next half hour, the others arrived. Maddie and Hayley and Jessie joined the hunt for a snake. Then Kari's husband, Ryan, joined in.

They asked Peter to help, but he declined. "I saw enough frogs and snakes in biology courses. I'll sit here with the women."

"And me." Ashley's father was making his way toward them. "I'll sit with the women too. My snake-catching days are over. The old knees can't take all that crawling around."

Everyone laughed, and Brooke shrugged. "I thought we came to the lake so the kids could cool off in the water."

"Oh no. That would be too logical." Kari held on to little Ryan's hand. He wanted to play with the big kids, but he still needed constant attention. Otherwise he'd eat a rock or wander up to the parking lot. Whenever the family was together lately, Kari spent most of her time chasing after her son.

Ashley grinned at the picture her sister and nephew made together. Soon enough, that would be her with Devin. Already she couldn't believe how fast he'd grown. Just yesterday she'd found a picture of him at four weeks old. She put it in a box of images to include in a painting someday . . . when the demands of CKT and raising a baby and helping Katy Hart with the lakeside house all let up.

Which reminded her . . . maybe now was a good time to tell her family the plan she'd been cooking up, the way they could serve the older Baxter son. She was about to make an announcement when Cole stood straight up and raised both hands in the air. Stretched between them was the largest garter snake Ashley had ever seen.

"It's the biggest one ever!" Cole jumped around, settling down only because he seemed to become suddenly worried that the snake might not enjoy the commotion. He hovered over it, and in seconds he was surrounded by his cousins.

"Cole, that's so cool!" Jessie's face was shining with admiration. "Can I touch it?"

Hayley and Maddie weren't so sure. They kept their distance and only ventured near when Landon and Ryan assured them the snake wouldn't bite.

"Please, Daddy, can I show Devin?" Cole asked.

Ashley caught Landon's eye and shook her head. "Please," she mouthed.

"How about just from a distance?" He shot her a sheepish smile. Then he led the group of snake hunters over to the group of non-hunters. Ashley had already fed Devin, and he was still awake. Landon stopped and held up his hand. "No closer than this, Cole."

His cousins formed a half circle around him and everyone watched.

Cole held up the snake. "Look, Devin. I caught you a snake." His voice brimmed with excitement. "But you have to grow up before you can play with it."

Devin couldn't possibly have known what was happening, but Cole's voice made him look in that direction, and he almost seemed to see the snake in his brother's hands. Either way, just at that moment he let out a sudden loud squeal followed by a hearty laugh.

"See!" Cole looked at Landon and Ashley. "I knew he'd love it."

Everyone laughed, and Landon led Cole back to the grass so he could release the snake. "You can catch it again when Devin's bigger," Landon was saying as they walked away.

Finally, when the incident with the snake had passed, the group washed their hands and gathered in a circle of folding chairs for their late lunch.

Ashley surveyed the group. There would never be a better chance to tell them about her plan. "I loved the sermon today. How we all need to serve because, you know, it's God's plan for us."

Her father nodded. "The message was strong." He looked sadder than usual. Probably because of Dayne.

Ashley didn't point this out. "Anyway, I had an idea, something I want to suggest." She hesitated. All eyes were on her. "It's something we can all do together to serve Dayne and Katy."

"What's your idea?" Kari was first to respond. She had admitted since the accident that she felt terrible not helping Dayne somehow.

Ashley paused, gathering her thoughts. "I've talked with three contractors since I've been back from LA. The one Katy planned to work with and two others. All three say there's no way they can get the work on that lake house finished until next summer. Which is way too late."

"Have we heard anything new about Dayne's condition?" Peter was helping Hayley with her potato salad. The child was making weekly advances in her recovery from the near drowning, but she still needed assistance.

The question didn't surprise Ashley. Peter was a doctor and analytical. The point he was making was obvious. If Dayne was still in a coma, if the extent of his brain injury wasn't even known yet, then why rush to fix up an old house? Ashley prayed for the right words. She looked at her brother-in-law, willing him to understand. She needed everyone's enthusiasm for her idea to work. "No, Dayne's still in the coma."

"But we're praying for a miracle." Her father nodded at the faces around him. "We're all praying for a miracle."

"Exactly." Ashley kept the conversation moving. "The Bible says that anyone who asks God and then doubts is like a wave tossed around on the ocean. It says that in James."

"So . . . you're saying we have to believe that Dayne will wake up." Peter looked respectful but skeptical. "And we should move forward in that same belief."

"Yes." Ashley felt him catching her enthusiasm.

Peter nodded. "Okay, so what's your idea?"

"If the subcontractors in Bloomington are too busy to work a renovation into their schedules before winter, then maybe it's up to us."

"Us?" Ryan put his arm around Kari and leaned in closer. "You want us to call and bug the guys so they'll make it a priority?"

"No." Ashley smiled. She loved Ryan. He and Kari were perfect together. Ashley looked around the circle. "You've all seen that TV show *Extreme Makeover: Home Edition*, right?"

Next to her, she felt Landon sit a little straighter. "They bring in a crew and a bunch of supplies and fix up a house in just one week."

"Right!" Ashley could barely contain her excitement. "Now, among us we have some knowledge of building houses, don't we?" She looked at Ryan. "You used to do framing between school years in college, right?"

"I framed and did the roofing. Hours and hours of it."

Ashley clapped. "See, that's what I'm talking about." She glanced at Kari. "You have an eye for design. You could pick out the windows and molding and doors."

"And I could help hang them." Peter laughed. "I haven't worked in construction since high school, but that's something you don't forget."

"I could paint." Brooke put her hands on her knees. Her eyes sparkled at the thought. "After the tornado last spring I repainted the entire back porch, inside and out."

"I told her not to give up her day job." Peter kissed Brooke on the cheek. "She's too brilliant a doctor for that." He winked at Ashley. "But she can hold her own with a can of paint and a brush. That's for sure."

Ashley wondered if anyone else picked up on the underlying message. In their early years of marriage, Peter had always doubted Brooke's ability as a doctor. Especially when Maddie had suffered from unexplainable high fevers. But after Hayley's accident, he had a complete change of heart. Now his respect for Brooke's talent as a doctor was unmatched.

"What about Luke and Erin?" Kari directed the question to their dad. "Is there a way we could involve them?"

"About Luke . . ." The sorrow in their father's face was not something he could hide. "He and Reagan are having some trouble."

"What?" Kari and Brooke both responded at the same time. Kari's face lost some of its color. "How come we haven't heard about this?"

"I just found out." Their father rubbed his forehead. He looked like he'd aged five years in the last few months. "I think everything will be okay. I found something your mother wrote about—" he swallowed, clearly overcome by a sudden wave of emotion— "something she wrote about marriage. About the secrets to having a strong marriage. She made a copy for each of you. Even for Dayne. I'll make sure you get them later." He paused, as if he were trying to remember his point. "Anyway, I've sent a copy to Luke. I'm praying it'll help."

Ashley tried to take in everything her father was saying. Luke's marriage was in trouble? Was that why Luke had been so standoffish every time they'd talked lately? All this time she'd thought it had to do with his jealousy toward Dayne, but maybe there was something else going on. And then the bit about their mother? She'd written them a letter about marriage? As happy as she and Landon were, she was suddenly desperate to read what her mother had written, the wisdom that she thought was necessary for a marriage to flourish.

But they were getting sidetracked, so Ashley continued. "I don't think we can count on Erin or Luke, to be honest. Erin has four little girls running around. If she came, someone would have to watch them. And Luke isn't planning to be here until the Saturday before Thanksgiving."

Her father folded his hands. His knuckles were white, a likely sign that he was more troubled about Luke than he let on.

"Okay, so who else can we think of?"

Ryan held up his finger. "A few of the coaches worked together this past summer and built a deck on one of their homes."

"Do you think you could get them to help us out?"

"Yes." Ryan stroked his chin. A grin tugged at the corners of his lips. "For free tickets to a Colts game, I think I can talk them into just about anything."

A ripple of laughter eased the tension from the group. After that, conversations broke out all around Ashley. Ryan told Landon that he could probably get the football team involved, at least in the beginning when a couple workdays would be needed to clear out the debris. Brooke and Peter and Kari started talking about windows and interior paint.

They'd have to find someone to help with tiling and countertops and appliances, but as the excitement and enthusiasm built, anything seemed possible.

Before cleaning up the picnic, they prayed for Luke, that he and Reagan would work things out and that the letter from their mother might open his eyes to all that was at stake in his marriage.

By the time they headed for their cars, the entire group was buzzing about the work project. Even the kids were excited.

"I always wanted to do an extreme home makeover, Daddy." Cole held Landon's hand. "I'll hammer the nails, okay?"

Ashley imagined the way it would all come together. Dayne would wake up, and gradually he'd make a complete recovery. Then on Thanksgiving morning, they'd find a reason to ask him and Katy out to the lake house. And everyone who had worked on the project would stand around and cheer in the yard of a house that was completely made over.

Her heart swelled as she pictured Dayne's reaction. He would never again have to wonder if the Baxters wanted to include him as part of their family. He would know he belonged. The house would forever be proof.

The group kept walking. "I'll cut the wood." Maddie tugged on Peter's sleeve. "Right, Daddy? Girls can cut wood, right?"

They all laughed, dreaming out loud about the possibilities. Ashley was just about to suggest they hold another meeting in a week to bring in as many ideas as possible when her dad made a sudden stop.

"Everyone . . . get to your cars right away!" His voice was loud and stern. "Now. We can talk later."

It took a moment for everyone to react, but almost at the same time Ashley's sisters and their husbands seemed to see the cause of her dad's alarm. They sheltered the children and hurried toward their vehicles. Bags were tossed into the backs of their cars, and doors were locked.

Ashley secured Devin's infant carrier into the backseat and then slid in and shut her door. By then Cole had buckled himself in and Landon had started the engine.

Her dad was the only one not rushing. Instead he planted himself behind his car and stared across the parking lot.

Ashley followed his gaze, and she saw what he was looking at. Parked across the lot were two cars, and leaning out the windows were two men, aiming something straight at them. She'd spent enough time in LA to understand what was happening. The men were paparazzi, and the items in their hands were high-powered cameras. Whatever the tabloids were working on, the story was heating up.

The Baxters had been discovered.

CHAPTER NINETEEN

BAILEY KEPT UP on the situation with Dayne and Katy through her mother. Katy called almost every night, and afterwards Bailey would find her mom and get the latest. It was Wednesday evening, and Katy hadn't called yet. But yesterday's news was the same as every day for the past three weeks. Dayne was still in a coma. Everyone needed to keep praying. All of CKT was asking God to give Katy and Dayne a miracle.

In some ways the ordeal reminded Bailey of how things had been after the other car accident, the one that killed Sarah Jo Stryker and Ben Hanover, the little brother of one of the CKT kids. That time a drunk driver had done the damage, and Bailey had spent weeks afterwards being so furious she could hardly concentrate in school. In the end, a bunch of them had gone to the jail and met with the guy. He was young, still a teenager. All the CKT kids who went made a line, and one at a time they approached him and told him they forgave him.

Nothing had ever made Bailey feel so good. And even though the anger had returned dozens of times since then, always she would remember the drunk driver's face and how he'd wept because he didn't deserve to be forgiven.

"That," her mother had told them when they reached the car that afternoon, "is the way all of us should feel when we come to Christ. He steps into our lives and offers us forgiveness we don't deserve. And all we can do is open our hearts and weep over His amazing grace."

Her mom's words had stayed with her, but now the anger was back in a different way. Anger toward the paparazzi. All Dayne wanted to do was get to the airport. He was supposed to make it to the retreat-center auditorium in time to see *The Wiz*, but instead he never even made it on the plane. All because a dozen photographers were chasing him down some highway.

The situation was wrong, and the only way Bailey could keep it from eating at her day and night was by taking action. She'd created a MySpace page where she and the kids from CKT could post prayers and messages for Dayne and Katy. That way when he woke up—and he would wake up; she had to believe that—he and Katy could see the page and know how much people cared about them.

Computers at the Flanigan house were kept in the open in an alcove off the main walkway through the kitchen. There were three computers in that space, and Bailey sat down at the middle one. The boys were already in bed, even Connor. Auditions for CKT's *Cinderella* were in two days, and he wanted to make sure he wasn't run-down. She moved the mouse and brought the computer to life. At the same time she heard the front door open. She looked at the time on the screen. Just before nine o'clock.

"Cody, is that you?" Her mother was in the kitchen slicing vegetables for her homemade soup.

"Yep," he called from the entrance. "Right on time."

Bailey rolled her eyes. She typed in the address for MySpace and waited. Cody was always coming home right before curfew. He had a car, and when he lived at home with his mother—before she was sent to jail—he could come home at any hour, day or night. Now he agreed with Bailey's parents that structure was a good thing. But he never came home early.

She heard him walk down the hallway toward the kitchen. "Did I miss dinner?"

The page popped up before Bailey looked over her shoulder. "A long time ago."

"Hey—" Cody grinned at her—"I didn't see you there." He took the seat next to her. "Whatcha doing?"

"Checking MySpace."

"You're still into that?" He stretched out his legs and came very close to brushing up against hers.

"No. It's not for me." She slid over, making sure there was ample space between them. Everything about Cody was wrong for her, but no matter what he did to bug her—flirting with Katy, coming home late, or hanging out with the senior girls from school—she couldn't stay mad at him. And she couldn't stop herself from being attracted to him. She was breathing, after all. "It's for Dayne. It's the prayer page I made for him and Katy. You have to know the password to get in."

"Oh." Cody's voice held a level of remorse. "Do you have your own page?"

"Not since a year ago. It's too crazy, too much gossip." She glanced at him. "I have enough in my life without finding it on MySpace."

He winced. "Why do I think there's a message in that for me?"

She lifted one shoulder and let it fall. "Think what you want." She turned her attention to the computer screen. The main photo was a picture of Katy and Dayne taken at the Baxter house during the dinner they'd all had there in July. Where the usual profile was, Bailey had posted this message:

As you know, Dayne Matthews was in a serious car accident. Katy Hart is staying with him in Los Angeles until he recovers. At this time, we're asking everyone to post prayers and messages for Dayne and Katy. He's in a coma, and when he comes out of it, we want both of them to know how much we love them and how much we're looking forward to having him move to Bloomington, where the paparazzi won't be chasing him everywhere he goes.

Beneath her message were the posts from other people. Bailey had sent an e-mail to every family who had ever participated in CKT, giving them the password and asking them to keep the board private. The last thing they needed was the media finding out about Dayne's plans to marry Katy and move to Bloomington.

"Scroll down." Cody leaned in. Whatever cologne he was wearing—Abercrombie or Hollister—it smelled wonderful. Bailey tried not to notice.

She did as he asked, and together they read the most recent messages. There was one from Tim Reed that referred to the few times Tim had met Dayne. *We're all pulling for you. Can't wait to see you make a full recovery.*

After that was a message from one of the Shaffers and a beautiful prayer by Stephen Pick. The next message was in a weird font. The type size was a mix of small and large letters. As soon as Bailey started to read it, she felt her heart slam into double time.

Dayne Matthews is nothing but a vegetable. All you people are wasting your time. Give up and get a life.

Bailey shrieked. She stood and smacked her hand against the computer screen.

"Hey—" her mother's tone carried a warning—"you didn't pay for that."

"I know." She dropped back to her seat. "I'm sorry." She made a fist and pounded it on the counter. "How can they say that? And how did someone who isn't part of CKT get the password?"

"What happened?" Her mom must've put down the cabbage she was cutting. Bailey could hear her footsteps coming up behind her.

Bailey pointed to the screen. "Read that." She wanted to scream, but her voice broke instead. "How can someone say such a thing?"

She didn't want to cry, not with Cody sitting next to her.

When her mom finished reading it, she hugged Bailey's shoulders from behind. "I'm sorry, honey. That's a lie and it's mean."

The phone rang, and her mom gave her shoulder a final pat. "Let me get that. It's probably Katy." Bailey heard her walk across the kitchen to the far windows, toward the phone.

So far Cody hadn't said anything. But now that they were alone he put his arm around Bailey's shoulders. "That's terrible. The idiot has the sensitivity of a pit bull."

Bailey wasn't sure what she was feeling, but having Cody's arm around her took the edge off her anger. He gave her a sideways hug and then released her. Even then he leaned in close. "Here. Slide over a little."

She did, and he moved into her spot. His hands hovered over the keyboard, and he pulled up a message form. In the box provided he typed: *Whoever said Dayne Matthews is a vegetable is a moron. Dayne is in a coma, and the doctors think he's going to pull out of it. You should be begging God for a miracle, not assuming the worst. Whoever you are, this is a private board. Stay off.* Cody hit the Enter button. The message showed up immediately.

The anger Bailey felt a moment earlier was gone. She wasn't even sure what to say. She blinked back tears so Cody wouldn't see her cry. "That . . . that was the nicest thing, Cody."

He stood and took hold of her hands. Then he pulled her to her feet and slipped his arms around her.

His hug was nothing more than what she'd seen him give her mother a time or two, but her head swam all the same. A part of her didn't ever want him to let go.

"It's okay to cry, Bailey. You don't have to always be so strong."

She pressed her head against his chest and held on. "I can't believe it happened again. Another car accident."

"I know." He ran his hand over her back. "That's why it's okay to be sad." In the background, they heard her mom wrapping up her phone call. Cody eased back and put his hands on her shoulders again. "Hey." He searched her eyes.

The space around the computers was dark, and the moment felt strangely forbidden. Bailey tried to exhale. "What?"

"Sometimes you treat me like the enemy. How come?"

"Because." She couldn't meet his gaze another second. She looked down. Something about the moment, about the way he'd come to her rescue a few minutes ago, made Bailey more honest than she'd ever been before. She found his eyes again. "I don't want to like you. That's why."

He gave her a goofy smile. "Me?" He angled his head, his eyes looking way past the surface of her heart. "What did I ever do to you, Miss Bailey Flanigan? You're the one with the boyfriend."

A nervous giggle escaped her before she could stop it. "You flirt with every girl in sight. Here . . . at school." She tried to find her polished persona, the one she could usually whip out whenever Cody was around. But it wasn't there. "You're here because my family loves you, but you're a player. I can never, ever fall for you." She gently took his hands from her shoulders and returned them to his sides. "I promised my parents."

Cody looked hurt. "Really?"

"Yeah. Nothing against you, but . . . well, you know. My dad isn't, like, in the dark about your reputation. He wants me to see you as a brother." She grinned at him. The air between them changed; the danger from a few heartbeats ago had passed. "Most of the time it's pretty easy to do that."

"Oh." The hurt was gone, or at least he was no longer letting it show. "All right, Sis, so here's my new goal."

Bailey couldn't stop her eyes from dancing. She could feel the way they shone all the way to her core. The guy's charm was beyond anything even he could've understood. "What?"

"By the time I leave for college, I want you to look me in the eyes and tell me you saw a change in me. Tell me that I'm not a player anymore."

"Really?" Bailey heard the teasing in her voice. "Pretty big order."

"Only say it if it's true." He reached out and touched the side of her face. The sort of thing Connor had done a time or two when he was giving her a compliment. The lightheartedness in his voice faded. "And it will be. I promise."

Her mother walked up just then. She hesitated, looking from Bailey to Cody and back again. "Did I miss something?"

"Yes." Bailey recovered quickly. She would tell her mom everything later—she always did. But she didn't want Cody to know that. "Cody was just telling me how he doesn't want to be a player anymore."

"Turning over a new leaf, huh?" Her mom gave Cody a doubtful smile. "That's what we're praying for. It's why you're here."

"I'll keep that in mind. Good night, Mrs. Flanigan." He chuckled and nodded toward Bailey's mother. But then he shifted his attention to her, and there was something deeper in his look. "Good night, Bailey."

"Good night." Her cheeks felt hot.

When Cody had walked down the hall to the downstairs guest room and they heard him close the door behind him, Bailey's mom gave her a questioning look. "What was that all about?"

"I don't know." Bailey dropped to her seat and pressed her palms against her hot cheeks. "He's so confusing."

Her mom didn't look concerned. There was a trust between them, one that was stronger than any of her friends had with their mothers. "Wanna tell me about it?"

Bailey exhaled, and she realized she'd been holding her breath. "I wish my cheeks would cool off."

"What did he say while I was on the phone?"

"Okay, so you know that horrible post, the one about Dayne?"

Her mom took the seat next to her and looked at the computer screen. "Yes."

"Well, as soon as the phone rang, Cody had me move and he took over on the computer. He left a message saying that whoever made that post was a moron." She made a dreamy-sounding sigh. "Wasn't that so nice of him, Mom?"

She put her hand on Bailey's knee. "Remember what we talked about before Cody moved in with us." She raised her eyebrows. "You promised, Bailey."

"I know." She tried to sound sensible. "When I think about his past and the girls he's flirting with and how he could fall back into drinking at any moment, I'm not interested. Of course I'm not interested." She felt her expression soften. "Except why does he have to smell so good?"

Her mom laughed quietly under her breath. "How's Tanner doing?"

"Good. He and I are talking more. Whenever Dad's not driving him into the ground at football practice." Bailey smiled and thought for a moment. "He's really more like a great friend than a boyfriend, you know? He doesn't ever pressure me."

"He respects you." Her mom slid a little closer so their knees were touching. "And Tim?"

"I don't know." Bailey had seen a change in her CKT friend. He was driving now, and he seemed to spend more time with his church friends than before. "He's not interested in me."

"What about Bryan Smythe?"

"I'm not sure. He says all the right things, but I never see him. Only at CKT stuff. He's a player too. Just like Cody."

"That's the nature of a teenage boy, Bailey." Her tone was kind, gentle. "Eventually they grow up. But between now and then it can be a lot of heartache. You're lucky you have a friend in Tanner Williams."

"Yeah." She blew at a piece of her bangs. She wore them to the side these days, and they needed cutting. "None of the other guys are worth liking. Not at this point."

"Well then, that means our prayers are being answered."

"Prayers?" Bailey loved these moments when no one else was around and she and her mom could share their hearts so easily.

"Yes." She reached out and framed Bailey's face with her hands. "Since you were born we've prayed for you. Your father and I. We prayed that God would make you into that one-in-a-million girl who wouldn't be dragged into something you'd regret. We prayed that love wouldn't really awaken in you until it was God's timing. These years are for you and God, so you'll become who He wants you to be."

Bailey smiled. She'd heard this before, but she never grew tired of knowing that her parents loved her enough to pray that way for her. She did a quick survey of her life. "If the guys I know are any indication, I'd definitely agree. God's answering your prayers big-time."

Her mother's smile fell, and she lowered her hands to her lap. "We need to pray about something else too."

Bailey's heart raced, thinking it must be about Katy. Every other time she had called, the news had been the same: No change. Keep praying. But this time her mother looked almost sick. Whatever the news was, it couldn't be good. "Was that Katy on the phone?"

"Yes. She talked to the doctor today."

"And . . . ?"

"The news was pretty clear-cut. If Dayne doesn't come out of the coma sometime in the next week to ten days, the possibility of his ever coming out goes down to only 5 percent."

"What?" Bailey shrieked the way she had when she read the awful message. Then she waved her apology, lowered her voice, and tried again. Already there were fresh tears in her eyes. "Only 5 percent? That's really what they told her?"

"If he comes out now, there's still a chance for recovery." Her mom sounded defeated. "But if we go another ten days at the most, the doctors want Katy to know the situation will be very, very serious."

Bailey gripped the edge of the counter and slid her chair in front of the keyboard. "That means I need to post a message telling everyone to pray extra hard these next ten days. Because Dayne has to wake up, Mom." Two tears splashed onto her cheeks. "He can't just lie there the rest of his life. Katy loves him too much for that."

"She does. You're right. We have to believe in miracles." Her mom pulled her into a hug.

Bailey cherished the feeling, safe in her mother's arms, believing Dayne would receive a miracle and knowing that even if they ran out of time, God could still pull him through somehow. Because that's what her mother believed. And at that moment, Bailey would rather be in her mom's arms than anyone else's.

Even Cody Coleman's.

Before Bailey went to bed, she and her mom bowed their heads and asked God to wake up Dayne Matthews—the sooner the better—and to bring about healing for Dayne and Katy and anyone else who was hurting tonight because of what had happened.

Luke went online before he left for work in the morning and searched for Hollywood gossip magazines. The rest of his family had apparently been photographed by paparazzi—in Bloomington, of all places. New issues hit the stands each Monday, so if they were doing a story on the Baxter family it would appear today.

He did a quick check through three of the magazines but found nothing except more stories on Dayne. How he was still fighting for his life, and—according to the ever-available "sources"—he might never recover fully even if he did come out of the coma.

The stories focused equally on Katy Hart and the bedside vigil she was keeping. Each was accompanied by photos of Katy rushing through the doors of the hospital or getting into a car or walking into a hotel. In several pictures she had her hand or her purse up, shielding her face. Every shot made her look weary and frightened. Desperate to be free from the paparazzi—same as Dayne must've been.

The articles also detailed the prognosis of Dayne's injuries. He would keep his leg, but doctors questioned whether he would ever walk normally again. Also, the stories cited statistics on brain injuries—how the vast majority leave at least some lingering damage, and how in a great percentage of the cases after waking from a coma, the victims are simply not the people they were before the injury.

Luke closed out the screen. He felt sick to his stomach. It wasn't that he had a problem with Dayne personally. The guy had been nice enough when they spent the week of the trial together. Not cocky or full of himself.

The problem wasn't with Dayne; it was with Luke's family. Okay, so Dayne was related to them. So what? How were they ever supposed to have another normal Baxter reunion with a movie star hanging around? And where did the arrival of Dayne leave Luke? The lesser of two sons? Was that all his entire life up until this point amounted to?

The seriousness of the situation was wearing on everyone he loved. Ashley and his other sisters could talk about nothing else—as if by keeping Dayne's name alive in conversation they could will him out of the coma.

Luke pushed his chair back from the computer. He hated thinking like this; it made him feel small and mean and far from God. But every time he prayed for Dayne, every time he tried to think about the situation the way his sisters and his father thought about it, his mind led him on the same angry rabbit trail.

The change in him was obvious to his father. He'd called twice since Luke's blowup with Reagan.

His dad's voice had been heavy from the moment Luke took the call. "I talked to Reagan."

The statement knocked Luke back against the wall. "About?"

"About the two of you. She told me."

Anger spoke first. "She's already told you her side of the story, so what's to—?"

"Luke." His father's voice was firm. "She told me you were thinking of separating. Nothing more."

"We're not really." He'd been too busy at work, too busy thinking about the situation with Dayne to consider that a separation might actually take place. "I mean . . . we haven't made plans or anything."

"Sometimes divorce is as easy as opening a door, Son. Open it just a crack, and the winds of discontent and frustration can blow it wide open."

Luke hadn't been sure what to say. His father had always talked with him this way, whatever the situation. Over the years a handful of his father's profound statements had stayed with him. They would stay with him until the day he died.

This was one of them.

Even so, Luke downplayed the need for help or counseling or even fatherly advice. He pressed the phone closer to his head and tried to keep his emotions at bay. "Thanks, Dad." He tilted his head back and closed his eyes. "We'll work it out. We will."

Before the call ended, his dad had told him he'd put a letter in the mail. One that his mother had written years ago. "It's the secret to a happy marriage. Something she wanted each of you kids to understand." His voice had been riddled with sadness. "The years must've made her forget about the letters because she didn't hand them out. But I found them in an envelope, and I knew it was God's timing. Exactly when you needed it. She made a copy for each of you."

Luke's back stiffened. He opened his eyes and looked at the floor. "How many copies?"

"Six." His father hadn't missed a beat. "Like I said. One for each of you."

The conversation faded, and Luke headed for the front door. Six indeed.

For a moment he stopped and looked down the hallway toward the room he and Reagan shared. She was sleeping after another long night with Malin. Still . . . how long had it been since he'd stopped in to kiss her cheek on the way to work? Her secretarial work was only three days a week from noon to three, and with Malin's refusal to get on a schedule, Reagan was usually asleep when he slipped out.

But for months after Malin came home he would at least go to Reagan's side and tell her good-bye, remind her that he loved her more than life. Except now it had been—what?—all summer probably since he'd done that. His hesitation didn't last long. Reagan was still mad at him, still discouraged with him for more reasons than he could count. The timing was wrong to start trying to turn things around now. He was already running late because of the time on the computer.

Luke left the apartment, took the elevator down, and headed for the double doors of the lobby. The sky was filled with storm clouds, and he remembered that rain was in the forecast most of the day. He had no time, but he couldn't afford to show up at one of the most prestigious law firms in Lower Manhattan looking like he'd been dragged through the gutters.

He checked out an umbrella at the guard desk and hurried out for the three-block walk to the nearest subway station. Not until he reached the sidewalk did he see the photographer. The guy was ducking behind a parked car a few feet from the building's covered entrance.

It took no time for Luke to figure out what was going on. The guy was paparazzi. Somehow someone had figured out that Luke

Baxter lived in the city. They'd probably already found out where he worked and that he'd been with Dayne in the sensational LA criminal trial. No wonder they looked so much alike. No wonder the press was sometimes guilty of confusing Luke, the legal assistant, with Dayne, the Hollywood heartthrob.

In the time it took Luke to blink, a small, wiry guy with an arsenal of cameras and equipment jumped up and blocked his path.

A sudden rage filled Luke, and he glared at the man. This was just the sort of thing he wanted to avoid, the type of encounter he and his family never should've had to deal with. And all of it was because of Dayne, because his father and his sisters wanted so badly to work him into their lives.

The seething thoughts flashed in his mind but not as quickly as the camera lens. By the time Luke realized how he must've looked and how many photos the guy had already taken, it was too late. "Leave me alone!" His words carried an implied warning. With the umbrella and briefcase tucked under his left arm, Luke blocked the camera's view with his right and made a sharp turn north toward the subway. He tried to blend in with a handful of walkers.

But the photographer was relentless. "Luke Baxter?" The man was behind him now, keeping up with him. "You are Luke Baxter, right?"

Luke's heart pounded. He wanted to turn around, grab the guy, and wrap him and his camera around the nearest light pole. If it weren't for the crowded streets . . . He worked the muscles in his jaw and kept walking.

"Talk to me, Luke." The photographer was jogging to keep up, and by the sound of his steps he was dodging people as he came. "Just a few words and I'll leave you alone."

Still Luke didn't respond. He hit the first intersection just as the light turned red. He had two more blocks and nowhere to turn.

The man maneuvered himself through the people gathering near the curb so that he was facing Luke, and even as Luke tried to turn away, the guy wouldn't let up. "One question, that's all!"

He sucked in the quickest breath. "When did you find out Dayne Matthews was your brother?"

That was it. Luke faced the guy and stopped just short of grabbing his camera off his neck. "Dayne Matthews is not my brother. Blood does not make him a Baxter." The words barely made sense through his clenched teeth. He took a step back, rage like hot lava consuming him, flooding his veins. He didn't shout; no need to make more of a scene than it already was. Instead he put his face an inch from the photographer's. "Listen, jerk. I work in a law office, and if you can't respect my privacy—our privacy—you'll find yourself at the wrong end of the worst lawsuit you've ever seen."

Instantly a peace came over the man. Luke watched it happen. His shoulders and the expression on his face relaxed in the same instant. The fight was over, knockout in the first round, the winner barely out of breath. He smiled. "Thanks." In his eyes, victory slow danced with pride. Before Luke could react, the man lifted his camera and clicked another few shots. Then he pointed at Luke in a mock-friendly way. "That'll do it."

The man swung his camera over his shoulder, turned, and pushed through the pedestrians, who were by now making their way across the street.

Luke stood there, unable to draw a breath. Signs up and down busy Manhattan streets advised people of the one New York City sidewalk rule: No Standing. But Luke couldn't help himself. He felt the crowd of people moving past him, and only when they'd crossed the street did he finally allow himself to breathe.

What had just happened? How could he have said that to a photographer? The story would be splashed all over the tabloids in a week. Sooner, if the guy could find a way to use it. He faced the intersection again, but the light was red once more. He leaned against the street sign, his head spinning. What exactly had he said, anyway? And how would the man spin the story around the photos?

The light turned green and Luke crossed, but his pace was slower now. Never mind getting to work on time. He wanted to turn around and threaten the guy again—use his quotes and he'd have a lawsuit on his plate by next week. But a sea of people separated them, and Luke had no idea where to find him. Paparazzi didn't hand out business cards.

Luke reached the subway station in a kind of automatic mode, because he wasn't seeing the people and streets around him. He was seeing his own words in a magazine spread. Grief pierced him as he pictured the pain on the faces of everyone his words would inevitably hurt. People who had done nothing wrong and who had suffered enough. His father and his sisters and Katy Hart.

And most of all, the guy who hadn't asked for any of this, the guy who had tried everything—even avoidance—to keep the press from ever knowing about the Baxter family. While Luke had thought of no one but himself all summer, the one he'd hurt the most now lay knocking on death's door.

The guy who would forever be something neither of them could deny.

Dayne Matthews, his brother.

CHAPTER TWENTY

KATY SETTLED into the chair by Dayne's bed and studied him. The swelling was long gone, but the almost-normal look he'd had the week after his accident was gone too. Now his muscles had atrophied, and his face was noticeably thinner than it had been. Grayer too. As if the life was draining from him one day at a time.

Don't think that way, she told herself. *He needs your support.* She leaned over and touched his forehead. "Dayne, I'm here. Back from lunch." Her throat tightened, the way it always did when she talked to him. "I'm going to read the Bible to you, okay? I know you can hear me." She searched his eyes, his face. No twitches, no reaction at all.

She sighed, giving the pain and tension a way of escape. "I'll start where I left off in chapter twelve of Hebrews." She kissed her fingertips and pressed them to his cheek. "Probably some of thirteen too."

Touching his brow, his cheek, made her feel as if he were still healthy, still the same Dayne she had spoken with the night before the accident. Like he really was only sleeping. It was harder touching his hands, trying to hold his fingers. He was cool and somewhat stiff and utterly unresponsive. There was no way to reach for his hand without giving in to the sorrow, the tears that were always waiting.

She opened her Bible to Hebrews and began to read. "'Therefore, strengthen your feeble arms and weak knees. "Make level paths for your feet," so that the lame may not be disabled, but rather healed.'" She looked at Dayne. *Please, God, let him not be disabled but rather healed. Like the Scripture says. Please.* She waited, as if maybe this might be the moment when Dayne would move his toes or try to blink.

But he remained motionless.

Against her understanding of faith, hope faded. Some days it was all she could do to keep even a flicker of hope burning in the darkness, and this was one of those days.

She found her place and continued. "'Make every effort to live in peace with all men and to be holy; without holiness no one will see the Lord. See to it that no one misses the grace of God and that no bitter root grows up to cause trouble and defile many.'"

No bitter root. The words were like a personal warning straight to her soul. Some days, when the paparazzi blocked her way into the hospital or into her hotel, bitterness defined her. How dare they do this to Dayne and still have the nerve to show their faces? She had no place in her heart or mind to even begin to understand them. And so she would have to guard against bitterness the way people in the Midwest guarded against tornadoes. Constantly. Diligently.

Before she could read on, there was a knock at the door. Dr. Deming entered the room and motioned for Katy to follow.

It was the first week of October, four weeks since Dayne's accident. During that time she and Dr. Deming had shared many conversations. The woman was kind and compassionate and determined to see Dayne through to recovery. For that reason, when the doctor summoned her from the room she refused to panic. Instead she clung to the possibility that this would be the time when she had good news. Tests had been done, and Dayne was coming out of the coma—even if Katy couldn't exactly tell yet. The doctor could tell her that now, couldn't she? It was possible. Katy took another look at Dayne, then stood and followed the doctor into the hallway.

Dr. Deming led the way to an office three doors down and pointed to a pair of chairs. The walls were filled with photographs of animals and children. When they were seated, the doctor set a folder on her lap and folded her arms. "Do you understand the time frame we're working with?"

"Time frame?" Katy's blood ran cold. They'd talked about a time frame last week. She'd passed on the news to Jenny Flanigan, but since then she'd tried to put the information out of her mind. A Bible verse flashed in her mind. *Do not worry about tomorrow, for tomorrow will worry about itself. Each day has enough trouble of its own.* That's what she'd read to Dayne a week ago. It was from the book of Matthew. She blinked and waited for an explanation.

Dr. Deming reached for the folder. "The prognosis and outcome for people with traumatic brain injuries are different for each person. It's the same with the staging of a coma." Her voice was gentle. "The problem, Katy, is that Dayne's coma hasn't progressed from the first day. In cases such as this, we wait as long as we can—hoping for change."

Katy knew what Dr. Deming was going to say next. With everything in her she fought to stay seated, to not bolt from the room and run to Dayne and never, ever leave his side again. She gripped the edges of the chair. "Yes."

"Unfortunately, if we don't see some sort of sign in the next few days, we'll have no choice but to transfer him to a long-term facility. We'll begin the process tomorrow."

Tomorrow? The sound of it shook her, threatened to drop her to her knees. *Long-term* meant indefinitely. Months and months, then years and years. A lifetime even. *Where are You, God? Why isn't Dayne waking up? What's happening to us?* She tried to think of something to say, but nothing would come. The tick of the clock on the opposite wall grew louder. *Tick . . . tick . . . tick . . .* mocking her, laughing at her. Time was running out. Any day now the doctors here would wash their hands of Dayne, and then what?

Dr. Deming was saying something about the transfer and how Dayne would receive around-the-clock care, and that as long as he was breathing there was hope. "Physical therapists will continue to work his arms and legs and turn him on a regular schedule to encourage circulation."

Turn him? Katy shuddered. Was this really happening? She was supposed to be back in Bloomington working with Rhonda and Bethany and Ashley on the final details for *Cinderella*. So what was this nightmare she was caught up in?

The doctor seemed to be waiting for some kind of response.

Katy swallowed. "So we need a miracle."

"Yes." Dr. Deming didn't look confident of the possibility. "I'm afraid so." She stood. "I will be working with Dayne's team of doctors on a placement. There's a very capable long-term facility not too far from here." She pulled a packet from the folder and handed it to Katy. "The first page gives details on that particular location. You can look through a few other choices in the local vicinity." Her expression was shadowed with futility. "We'll be discussing options later today. I believe we'll all agree that the facility closest to the medical center would make for the smoothest transition." She took a few steps toward the door. "That's all. I'll keep you posted about the logistics of the transfer."

When Dr. Deming was gone, Katy covered her face with her hands. She was alone in the room, so it was okay to cry. So often she denied herself the chance. When she was with Dayne, her first goal was to stay upbeat. If Dayne could hear her, she couldn't sit at his bedside weeping. Never. Tears in Dayne's presence were silent and hidden. When she took breaks for meals, she slipped into a functional existence, numb from the entire situation. And when she finally made it back to her hotel, she was too tired to cry.

But here, with the latest news crashing over her like a collapsing building, the ocean of tears inside her finally overflowed. Dr. Deming's news was devastating. Not because anything had changed but because she was giving up. And she had seemed like she would never, ever give up on Dayne. Katy's tears became sobs, and the helplessness surrounding her became anger. God could've prevented this. He could've caused the paparazzi to stick to their lanes of traffic, and He could've let Dayne be ten feet farther up the road or ten feet back. Anywhere but in the path of an oncoming truck.

God, I'm so mad. Dayne and I . . . we've been through so much, and now this? Was it wrong to believe that life might actually turn out right? The doctors are willing to give up on him, and now You are too. Is that it?

Bitterness shot out another root, another branch, and her heart had little room to breathe. She wiped her tears, stood, and walked to the office window. *I'm sorry, Lord. I don't want to be bitter.* She caught a series of quick breaths. *Anger doesn't feel right either.*

Across Wilshire Boulevard she spotted a building with a garden on top—like the hotel where she and Dayne had found peace that night during the first part of the trial.

"I miss him so much." The words came in anguished whispers. "We need a miracle, Father. I know I'm just one person and . . . and You hear so many cries. But we need Your help. Tonight. Please, tonight."

Katy held her breath, needing an answer as badly as she needed her next heartbeat. She focused all her senses on just one—listening. But the only sounds were the tick of the clock and the distant hum of traffic on the streets below. She began to shiver, and she realized why. Back at the beginning of this free fall, hope had been a roaring flame, warming her to her core. But now not even a flicker of hope could be seen, and the dimly glowing embers that lay at the deepest, darkest places of her being were not enough to make a difference.

She exhaled and hung her head. Dayne couldn't have her like this, weeping, falling apart. So maybe she should go somewhere different. Dayne's studio had provided her an around-the-clock car and driver. It was the least they could do, the director had told her. She could contact the driver and ask to take a drive to the mountains or into the desert. Somewhere the paparazzi could not follow her to, a place where she could finish crying and beg God again and again for a change in Dayne. Yes, that's what she would do. Find a change of scenery.

Before she could find the will to turn around, before she could make herself locate the driver's number, she heard footsteps near the door.

"Katy?" It was a woman's voice.

She wiped her eyes and turned toward the sound. Standing there, her eyes red and swollen, was Randi Wells.

From the beginning Randi had been on the list of approved visitors. Katy had added a few more names—Dayne's current director, his agent, and several people whom the two of them suggested. Even so, Katy had seen almost no visitors. His agent stopped in once a week, and the director had come by twice. They would stand by Dayne's bed, helpless, and after a few minutes they would mumble something about being sorry and leave.

Not until now had Katy seen Randi Wells.

Here, in the harsh glow of the fluorescent hospital lights, she didn't look like America's golden actress. She looked like any other person stricken by grief, trapped in the maze of pain and uncertainty. She took a step closer. "Can I talk to you?"

"Yes." Katy motioned to the chairs where she and Dr. Deming had sat a few minutes ago. When they were seated, facing each other, Katy saw an abyss of fear in the woman's eyes. Dayne had mentioned that Randi didn't care much for Christianity or faith or God for that matter. One of his goals during the filming had been to change her mind.

Katy's heart went out to the popular actress. The tragedy was all but impossible with faith. How must it feel without it? "You've been in to see Dayne?"

Randi folded her hands and stared at them for a moment. When she lifted her head, her chin trembled. "You have to understand something." Her expression tightened, and she allowed a few gut-wrenching sobs. "I couldn't bear to come before this. I kept waiting to hear it on the news: 'Dayne Matthews makes complete recovery.'" She steadied herself. "See . . . Dayne was my rock for the few months before his . . . before this."

Dayne was Randi's rock? Jealousy tried to take over, but Katy resisted it. Dayne hid nothing from her. Katy knew Randi's marriage was in trouble and that she sought Dayne often for advice. The fact that he also spent his days on-screen pretending to be in love with the woman rankled Katy, but she let the feeling pass. "I'm sorry."

"I know. You've lost so much more than I have. I keep thinking how selfish I am, missing his friendship and stumbling around in the dark without him. But never once . . . never one time coming here to tell you how sorry I am for you."

The hopelessness in Randi's voice was terrifying, and it gave Katy a chilling glimpse of life without salvation. No matter how dim, she must never let the fire of hope inside her die. Never. She put her hand on Randi's shoulder and begged God for the right words. "Have you prayed for him?" She was no longer intimidated by the woman. Never mind that Randi was known throughout the world. Here she was just one more lost soul, a person deeply in need of the lifeline only Jesus Christ could offer.

"I saw the Bible on the chair." Randi sniffed twice. "Is it yours?"

Katy brought her hand back to her lap and nodded. "I read it to him. The doctors think maybe he can hear us."

"Great." She let loose a single sob. "Then he would've heard me crying."

She wasn't sure if Randi wanted to talk about the Bible, but it didn't matter. Dayne would've wanted her to pray. "If he heard you cry, then he'll be feeling sad. But maybe now you and I can go back in there and pray for him."

"Pray for him?" A frown creased her otherwise-smooth forehead. "How can you, Katy? After all this time?" She leaned back in her seat, defeated. "Dayne read his Bible every night; I'm sure you know that. He prayed for me and the cast and you." She jerked her thumb toward the hallway. "Jesus was the guy's best friend, and look where it got him." She narrowed her eyes. "What proof do you have that God isn't just a nice fairy tale?"

Her words hit Katy slowly. Understanding dawned in her heart, and she looked deep into Randi's eyes. No matter what the accident had taken from Katy, from Dayne, it hadn't taken her faith. She felt God giving her strength, felt the answer coming to her crystal clear. "He's alive, isn't he? He kept his leg." Passion filled her tone. "The Lord's been here with Dayne, with me, every day since the accident. More than that, if God calls Dayne home, he'll go straight to heaven. Forever." A smile lifted the corners of her lips. "What more could he want?"

Randi studied Katy as if she were an otherworldly creature. "You're serious, aren't you?"

"I am." She stood and reached for Randi's hand. "Come on. Let's go back and ask God for a miracle. You could do that, couldn't you?"

Randi looked like she wanted to shake her head, run back down the hall to the elevator, and never venture to the hospital again. But gradually the doubt in her eyes lifted, and her eyes had the guileless look of a trusting child. "That's what Dayne would want, isn't it?"

"It is."

Then, without further conversation or analysis, they walked to

Dayne's room. Katy explained that Randi didn't need to speak; she could agree in her heart with everything Katy was saying and that would be the same thing. Then for the next several minutes they did just that, asking God—once more—for a miracle this very day.

When they finished, the fear in Randi's face was gone. "I think—" she looked at Dayne, and her eyes welled with tears— "when he wakes up, I'm going to ask him about the Bible." She tried to laugh, but it came out like a cry. She leaned over him and kissed the top of his head. Then she turned to Katy. "I might as well see what the fuss is all about."

Again Katy kept her jealousy at bay. "I think Dayne would like that."

Randi thanked Katy and was halfway to the door when she stopped and turned. "I almost forgot." She pulled a stack of magazines from her oversize bag. "These came out today. You might not want to see them—" she frowned—"but I thought you should."

Katy's heart fell. More tabloid news. She took the stack. "Thanks." She gave the actress a sad smile. "I guess you know all about this stuff."

"It doesn't make it any easier." She looked at Dayne once more. "He's the real deal." Her eyes found Katy's again. "You're very lucky, Katy Hart." Guilt flashed in her expression. "The truth is, I would've stolen him from you in a minute, but he wouldn't bite. Not at all. All he's ever been to me is a friend. He only has eyes for you." A sad smile played on her lips. "But I guess you already know that."

There it was. The admission that Randi did indeed have feelings for Katy's fiancé. But something else. The proof that Dayne had never shown any interest. Katy wanted to be mad, but she couldn't. Randi Wells was only being honest, letting Katy know that she had nothing to worry about.

Katy closed the distance between them and took Randi's hands. "I do know. But thanks for saying it." She hoped her sincerity shone through her eyes. "And maybe someday after Dayne wakes up, you and I can be friends too."

"Yes." Randi squeezed her fingers, then moved toward the door. "I'd like that."

When she was gone, Katy had the sudden certainty that one day not too far off Randi would give her life to Christ, and she would most definitely become a friend. Maybe even a close friend. But before she could carry the possibility too far, she remembered the magazines. She couldn't read them here.

But maybe there was a place she could go. . . .

She found her purse and the envelope tucked inside, the one Dayne's agent had given her. It held the keys to Dayne's Malibu house. "Use it," the man had told her. "Dayne's plants might need a little water, and you . . . well, the water might be good for you too."

The possibility had hung in her heart since then, but she didn't want a parade of paparazzi following her. She looked at her watch. It was only two in the afternoon. The paparazzi were used to her schedule by now. She stayed at Dayne's side until ten or eleven every night.

The idea began to feel like it might work. She called for the car and asked for a pickup on Wilshire Boulevard—not in front of the hospital like usual. She told Dayne good-bye and promised to be back later that evening. Then she hurried down the elevator and out a lesser-known back door. She peered one way and then the other, but she could see none of the familiar cars. From there she walked to Wilshire and met her ride.

An hour later every one of Dayne's dying plants had been watered, and Katy slipped out onto the sand with a blanket and the magazines. The beach behind the string of multimillion-dollar homes was nearly empty, the way it often was in the fall months. She walked a little ways, spread out the blanket, and sat down.

Only then did she look at the covers of the magazines. At first they looked like last week's. "Dayne Matthews Still in a Coma."

But beneath that was a headline that made her heart sink. "Dayne's Biological Brother Lashes Out." Katy stared at the words, trying to comprehend the ramifications. The Baxters had been found, for sure. But what was this about Luke?

She couldn't turn the pages fast enough. When she reached the spread on Dayne, there was a large photo of a very angry Luke Baxter. Beneath it the caption read, "Luke Baxter wants nothing to do with his famous brother." Making up the rest of the layout were photos of each of the Baxters, complete with their names and a few sentences about them. Only Luke's had a brief story beneath it.

Katy's mouth hung open. *Dear God . . . no.* She found the beginning of the story on Luke and began to read.

> *Celebrity Life* has learned the identity of Dayne Matthews' biological family. Dr. John Baxter and his wife, Elizabeth, who died two years ago, had their first child—Dayne—before they were married and gave him up for adoption. They went on to have five more children—Brooke, Kari, Ashley, Erin, and Luke. Most of the family lives in Bloomington, Indiana, and is known throughout the community for their strong Christian beliefs.

Katy struggled to catch her breath. She could only imagine the details that filled the page. She read on.

> At least one of the Baxters isn't excited about his famous sibling. This week Luke Baxter, a legal assistant in New York City, told a reporter for *Celebrity Life* that "Dayne Matthews is not my brother. Blood does not make him a Baxter." In addition, Luke Baxter threatened legal action if his or his family's privacy was breached in any way.

No, Luke. Katy groaned. *Why would you say that?* She looked out at the ocean. Dayne would be devastated when he woke up and had the chance to see the quote. All those years of ignoring his desire to seek out the Baxters, to approach them, and now this?

She held the magazine up and read the few lines beneath the other photos.

> Brooke was born after Dayne. She and her husband are doctors. Three years ago their youngest child was involved in a near drowning, and Brooke's husband was addicted to painkillers.

Anger surged through Katy. An injured child was something private, not a detail to toss around in a gossip magazine. How could they print that? She moved on.

> Kari is married to a former NFL star. It is her second marriage. Her first husband was violently murdered by a stalker.

Katy closed her eyes. She wanted to throw the magazines into the water and never look at them again. The Baxters were private people. This information should never have been made public. But that wouldn't change the facts, and it wouldn't stop millions of people from reading this same information. She found her place.

> Ashley is an artist who was the single mother of one boy until she married a Bloomington firefighter. She is healthy after an AIDS scare two years ago.

Nausea welled up inside Katy. *Ashley . . . I'm so sorry.* This was exactly what Dayne had feared. And now it had happened in the worst possible way. About Erin, the magazine only said:

> Erin is married and living in Texas with her husband and four daughters.

Katy threw the magazine onto the blanket. No dirty facts on Erin, but the press would keep looking. The story was too sensational to resist. She stood and walked toward the water, the wet sand slipping between her toes. She kept walking through the foamy surf and in farther until the water was knee-deep. She wanted to shout at God. *Where are You, Lord? Can't You see me?* She tilted her face to the sky. *Can't You hear? Everything's getting worse, and I can barely remember how to breathe. Father, I'm desperate for Your help. Please . . . are You even listening at all?*

She looked to the horizon, as far as she could see, but before she could utter another prayer, her cell phone on the blanket came to life. She was using the song "I Still Believe" by Jeremy Camp for her ringtone. By the time she ran through the water and up the sand, the song was at the part about feeling God's grace fall like rain.

Please, God . . . let it be good news. . . .

She flipped open her phone. "Hello?"

"Katy Hart?" The voice sounded familiar.

"Yes?" She bent over her knees and exhaled so she'd have room in her anxious lungs for the slightest bit of air. "This is Katy."

"This is Dr. Deming. We need you back at the hospital right away."

Katy dropped to her knees, but even in that instant she refused to believe that the news could be bad. Hope roared to a mighty flame. "Is he . . . ?"

"He's moving, Katy." She could almost see the doctor smile. "He's coming out of the coma. I must warn you, though; a full recovery is still a long shot. But we'll do everything possible to make it happen."

"Dear God, thank You." She uttered the words loud enough for the doctor to hear. "I'll be right there."

Katy grabbed her things, ran up the stairs to Dayne's house, and rushed out to the waiting car.

All the way back to the medical center she felt as if she were floating, soaring even. God had heard her! She whispered a constant string of thanks to Him, her Lord and Savior. She'd asked for a miracle tonight, and God in all His merciful power had delivered. Dayne was waking up!

If that wasn't proof that God was more than a fairy tale, nothing was.

CHAPTER TWENTY-ONE

DAYNE COULDN'T SEE CLEAR of the darkness, but something strange was happening. One small pinpoint at a time, light was streaming through. Light and something else. A voice that he would've known anywhere—the only voice that mattered.

The voice of Katy Hart.

"Dayne, can you hear me? I'm waiting for you, right here beside you." She sounded distant, as if she were talking underwater.

Yes, I can hear you! With every bit of his strength Dayne tried to speak, and then he tried to shout, but his mouth wouldn't work so his words had no way out. Another tiny spot of light burst through the darkness.

Where was he? And why was the darkness so thick? It hung like the densest fog, filling the air around him, consuming even his senses. Was he dreaming? Had someone drugged him? He was in Bloomington, wasn't he? Celebrating the Fourth of July and admiring the ring on Katy's hand.

So why couldn't he wake up?

Katy . . . I can hear you! Why can't I talk?

"There's no question he's coming out of the coma." This time the muffled voice belonged to another woman, someone unfamiliar.

But who was coming out of a coma? Not him. He wasn't hurt or sick; he'd done nothing that would cause him to be in a coma.

"When, Doctor? When will we know more?" Katy was still there beside him; he could sense her. Whom was she talking to? Whom did they know who was in a coma, and why was he in such a deep, dark sleep?

Maybe if he thought a little harder, forced himself to think about the past, he could wake himself up. He went back in time—way back. He had made a lot of mistakes—his confusion over Kabbalah, his relationship with Kelly Parker. The baby she aborted, the child Dayne would never know. Thinking of the baby made him sad. Beyond sad. He felt like weeping over the loss, but almost as quickly he had a certainty that the child was a boy and he was in heaven—safe in God's nursery. The knowing was so strong that Dayne was immediately overwhelmed with relief. His baby boy was safe.

More pinpoints of light pierced the thick black fog. The first time he saw Katy at the Bloomington Community Theater and again that first day in Los Angeles at the audition. The crazy woman on the beach, his trek back to Indiana, and all the ups and downs ever since.

"Dayne, can you hear me? Please open your eyes." Katy sounded a little clearer than before.

I'm here, Katy. Wake me up; shake me. I want to see you! He felt closer to the light, but still his words wouldn't come. If remembering was helping, then maybe he needed to remember recent things. He was at the Fourth of July party and then . . .

Fragments of memories flashed in his mind—Dayne and an actress working on a hillside somewhere. He concentrated. The actress was . . . Randi Wells. The flashbacks stopped there. Frustration hit hard and he tried again. *God, please . . . why can't I remember?*

"Dayne, I'm here." This time Katy sounded clearer still.

But there was no use answering her. Not until he could open his eyes. If only he could get a clear picture of what had happened. There was Randi Wells. Only they weren't filming a movie; they were at a restaurant. And there were paparazzi everywhere.

A stream of light joined the tiny dots. He could feel his eyelids moving, but he couldn't see more than shadows. Moving shadows close beside him. He tried to reach out and see if the closest shadow belonged to Katy, but he couldn't lift his hand. *Katy, I'm here....* Again no words came.

He thought back once more. The memory was coming into focus slowly, like looking through the lens of a cheap video camera. He and Randi having lunch . . . no, not lunch. They were having breakfast and a dozen photographers were capturing every move, every bite. Then they were finished and getting into their separate cars and heading down Pacific Coast Highway. The pictures were slow and hazy, but they were no longer broken into short bursts.

They were driving and he was following her. The paparazzi cars darted around Dayne to either side of Randi; then one of them lost control. He could feel himself moving, turning from side to side. The paparazzi car pulled back into his lane, but at the same instant a truck was headed right for . . .

His eyes flew open, but the truck was nowhere in sight. Instead there in front of him in lines that weren't quite clear was the only sight he wanted to see, the one who had pulled him from the darkest night.

He didn't blink, didn't dare. He couldn't risk losing her again, falling into the darkness once more and maybe never finding his way out. Had he been hit by a truck? Was that what happened? He felt sick at the thought. He could've died, but he was alive. God had helped him find his way to daylight, because she was here and he was here. Together. And in that moment, for the first time in what felt like ages, he found the strength to say the only word that mattered.

"Katy . . ."

☙

Katy's heart pounded out a strange rhythm against the wall of her chest. Dayne talked! He said her name! His voice was scratchy and weak, but it didn't matter. Her name was the first thing he'd said. "I'm here, Dayne. I love you."

He opened his mouth, but no words came.

"It's okay." Her eyes stung, and the sound that came from her was half laugh, half cry. "I can't believe you're awake." She lowered the bed rail and leaned over him, careful not to put pressure on his chest. Then she did what she'd wanted to do since she first saw him here. She eased her hands beneath him and held him. He smelled like stale antiseptic, disinfectant, and something medicinal. But he was warm and alive and moving—even ever so slightly.

When she had first arrived back at the hospital and raced to his room, she could barely see what Dr. Deming was talking about. But after a minute or so she saw Dayne's fingers twitch, then his toes. With every half hour that passed, his movements had come more often, been more pronounced. In the past hour he'd started to move his lips and turn his head an inch in either direction.

Dr. Deming checked in often, amazed. "He's coming out very quickly." She would grin and make a notation on Dayne's file. "When victims come out quickly, it can be a good sign. The more severely brain-injured victims are very slow to wake up."

And now . . . now Dayne had opened his eyes, and he'd seen her. Katy had spent enough time talking to Dr. Deming to know that blindness was a possibility. But he wasn't blind! And he was well enough to know her name, which meant two wonderful things.

First, he remembered her! All this time, every minute of every day for the past month, she'd lived with the fear that he might come out of the coma only to have lost his memory. Now that wasn't a concern. And second, he could speak clearly. He was groggy, but when he said her name, even through his slurred speech, she had no doubt what he was saying.

She pressed her face against his and whispered, "Everything's going to be okay, Dayne. You're back now. God gave you back to me."

"Wha . . ." The sound was thick, and it seemed to take all his effort.

"Shhh." She straightened and sat on the edge of his bed. "Don't make yourself tired. The words will come eventually."

He relaxed, and for the next three hours he made only an occasional attempt at talking. But the entire time he didn't take his eyes off Katy. He refused to sleep, as if by closing his eyes he might fall back into the coma. During that time she told him nothing about the accident, only that she loved him, she was praying for him, and he was going to be okay. For a while she read the Bible to him. More from Hebrews and part of James.

Later Dr. Deming came in to check on him.

Like the breaking of a dam, Dayne's ability to talk returned. "Tell me . . . what happened." His words were painfully slow. But there was nothing slow about his thinking.

Dr. Deming leaned over him. "You were in a car accident. You've been in a coma for thirty days." The doctor smiled at Katy. Only the two of them knew the significance of Dayne's coming out of the coma the evening of his thirtieth day. The day before he would've been considered a long-term case.

Dayne struggled to swallow. His eyes expressed his disbelief at the news. "A . . . month?"

"Yes."

"A . . . truck hit me."

"That's right." Dr. Deming shot a beaming look at Katy.

Katy understood, and silently she celebrated the unbelievable victory. If he could remember that detail, then his damage might be only minimal. He could still have motor-skills issues, but at least his brain was working. And that meant she had Dayne back, the Dayne she loved more than life.

Dayne looked at her. "I love you." His gaze shifted to the doctor. "I want to go home."

Concern flashed on Dr. Deming's face. "You've been asleep for a very long time, Dayne." She pressed her lips together. "I want to be honest. You'll need at least three months' rehabilitation before you'll be in any shape to go home. And that would be a best-case scenario."

Dayne narrowed his eyes and looked at the doctor for a long while. Then for the first time since he'd been awake, he lifted his hand. Not the sort of slight movements he'd been making before. This time he trembled as he lifted it all the way up, so his forearm was completely vertical. He turned his attention to her. "Katy . . ."

She took his hand. Gradually at first, then with an increasing intensity, he squeezed. "I'm here, Dayne. What do you need?"

A fine layer of sweat broke out on his forehead. Clearly he was working as hard as he'd ever worked before. She could almost feel Dr. Deming about to warn her not to push him. But the doctor stayed quiet. She probably felt the same way Katy did. After a month in a coma, if Dayne wanted to talk, no one should stop him.

He looked more alert than even five minutes earlier. But he was tiring out. "What day . . . is it?"

"October 2." She searched his face.

He looked like he was calculating, though that seemed impossible for someone who had been in a coma. "Three months . . . I can't go home . . ." He rested for a few seconds. His words were coming slower than before, but his thinking still seemed sharp. He found the doctor again and picked up where he left off. ". . . until January?"

"That would be the soonest." Dr. Deming gave Dayne an understanding smile. "Your progress at this point is beyond my explanation. But rehabilitation follows a predictable path. Three months, Dayne. It'll go quickly."

He shook his head. "We bought a house. I'm going home for . . . Thanksgiving."

A rush of emotion came over Katy. She replayed his words in her mind. If he wanted to go home for Thanksgiving, then home wasn't here in California. It was with her, in Bloomington. Her heart soared. *God . . . can this night get any better? This must be how Peter felt when he watched You walk across the waves.*

"Thanksgiving is in seven weeks. From a medical standpoint, it would be impossible to leave a rehabilitative setting by then."

Dayne looked like he might cry. For a minute he only worked his mouth, but no words came. He squeezed Katy's hand again. "Help me . . . please, Katy. Seven weeks. Help me get home for Thanksgiving."

She couldn't see for the tears in her eyes. "Yes, Dayne." She kissed his fingers. "I'll help you."

Dr. Deming appeared to want to say something to discourage Dayne from such unrealistic dreams, but she took a step back instead. "I'll leave you two alone. I need to schedule some morning tests for Dayne." She glanced at the file in her hands. "We'll wait until tomorrow afternoon to tell the press. That way you won't have to deal with a bunch of phone calls between now and then."

Katy thanked her. When she was gone, Katy brought her face close to Dayne's. "You're really back."

"Thank you." His strength was almost entirely gone. But he brushed his cheek against hers. "For helping me."

Katy could hardly believe they were having this conversation, that he was really alive and awake and talking to her. She looked to the deepest part of him, and when she spoke her voice rang with conviction. "God gave us a miracle tonight." She massaged her throat, loosening the emotion that was stuck there. "If we work together, maybe He'll give us another one."

He started to say something, but his eyes closed and after a minute his breathing changed. It was scary, watching him sleep. Maybe it always would be. But she only had to tell herself the truth. He wasn't in a coma any longer. He was resting. So that come tomorrow he could talk better and move better and start the long journey back to health.

She picked up the phone near Dayne's bed. Ever since she heard the news that he was coming out of the coma she'd wanted to call Ashley. But she wanted to make sure she had as much information as possible. And once Dayne was awake and talking, she couldn't tear herself away. Now she couldn't do anything until the Baxters heard the news.

Dayne had long-distance privileges from his room phone. That way she'd been able to keep in contact with Jenny Flanigan and Ashley and John without having to leave the hospital and use her cell phone. She started to dial Ashley's number, but then she stopped. Dayne was John's son. He deserved to know first. She pulled out the notepad from the top drawer in the nightstand and found his number.

He answered on the first ring. "Hello?"

"John, it's Katy." Her voice cracked. "I have . . . good news."

"Thank God." There was relief in his voice. "What's going on?"

She pressed her fingers to her lips and steadied herself. "He's awake, John. He came out of the coma and he talked to me, talked to the doctor too. He . . . he still wants to come home for Thanksgiving."

The other end of the phone was silent.

Katy could only imagine what he was thinking. John more than any of them knew how dire Dayne's condition had been. And now more than anyone he was probably stunned by the news. He had found his son only to come far too close to losing him. But Dayne was whole and alive and awake, which made them witnesses to a miracle. The sum of it must've been more than Dayne's father could take. Katy knew this not because of what he said, since he hadn't spoken a word yet, but by the muffled sound she heard coming through the phone line.

John Baxter was crying.

CHAPTER TWENTY-TWO

ASHLEY STARED at the magazines on her kitchen table with no idea what to do next. She'd read everything—every cover page, every index, and every splashy spread at the center of each tabloid.

Twice.

And still she was baffled. She understood how someone would've figured out that the Baxters were Dayne's biological family, and she'd expected something this week—since every one of them had been photographed in the past ten days. With enough money and motivation, it was not a shock that the paparazzi would find the juiciest details to smear beneath each of their pictures or that they would contrast those with the fact that the Baxters were—as one magazine put it—"supposedly Christians."

What shocked her was Luke.

The anger and hurt she felt toward him were so mixed she couldn't tell one from the other. How could he say that about Dayne? "Blood doesn't make him a Baxter"? Was that all he'd picked up along the journey of living with their mother and father, of seeing the way they always made family a priority over everything else?

It was long since dark, and Cole and Devin were asleep. Landon was working a swing shift, and he'd be home soon. She stood and paced across the kitchen to the telephone on the counter. When she'd first seen the story, first read the quote from Luke, she'd picked up the phone and started to dial before she stopped herself. Whatever was causing Luke to act and feel this way couldn't be dealt with in a barrage of furious words.

Instead she'd returned to the table, where she'd spent the last hour reading and praying and trying to make sense of the situation. She stared at the phone. She hadn't talked to any of the others yet. No doubt they were sorting through the stories, taking stock of how the notoriety would affect each of them.

Ashley had played out the story for each of her family members. Brooke and Peter would be fine. They were private people, and very few patients would ever connect the dots between them and the magazine story. Erin would be fine, of course, and Kari too. Their friends and neighbors might mention the connection, and the visibility might hurt for a while. But they'd get over it, as would their families.

Ashley and her father had already made their decision before they chose to travel to LA after Dayne's accident. They would shout from the Hollywood hills if they had to. Dayne was family, and family didn't shirk into the shadows just because a situation was difficult.

More than the embarrassment and hurt from what the tabloids had dug up was the inconvenience that would likely follow. People looking for a path to Dayne might try to find it through one of the Baxters. They would need to change their phone numbers to unlisted, and at family dinners and holidays they would have to be aware of paparazzi.

Yes, the hardship of being Dayne's biological family definitely had the potential to be more damaging than the dirt splattered over today's issues. Ashley was tired of looking at them. She collected them in a stack and put them on the seat of the chair beside her. Cole didn't need to see his mother's picture in a magazine. He was too young to understand any of it.

She crossed her arms and thought about Luke. How could he do it? He must've known the photographer would use every word he said. A thought hit her. What if he hadn't said it? He could've walked out the door and into the photographer's trap. The guy could've taken an angry picture of Luke and made the whole thing up. If so, right now Luke would be crushed by the stories in the tabloids.

Hurt took the upper hand over her anger, and she didn't want to wait until tomorrow. There was no better time to make the call.

She picked up the receiver and dialed his number. *Please let it be a mistake.* On the third ring, Reagan's mother answered. Ashley identified herself and apologized for calling so late.

"Not at all. We never have lights out before eleven." Reagan's mother sounded upbeat and friendly, the way Ashley remembered her from Luke and Reagan's wedding. But her tone sounded strange in light of today's news. She couldn't possibly have read the tabloids. Otherwise she never would've sounded so cheerful. In that case, maybe Luke hadn't seen the magazines either.

They spent a few minutes catching up; then Reagan's mom went to get Luke.

"Hello?" Luke sounded gruff, as if he'd been called away from something far more important than his sister.

"Hey." Ashley took the phone to the living room and curled up at the end of the sofa. *Curb my anger, God. . . . Give me kind words.* She stared across the room at a framed photograph of the Baxters—taken before any of them were married. "I figured you'd be expecting my call."

"I guess."

Ashley made a face. "I'm talking about the tabloids. You've seen them, haven't you?"

"The women at the office brought in bunches of them."

"Okay then." There was no easy way to broach the subject. She took a breath. "Those things they printed . . . did you say them?"

"I don't need this." He muttered the words so low they were barely audible.

"So you did say them?"

"Yes, okay?" The gruff voice was one that didn't fit him, didn't even sound like him. "I said it and I meant it."

"What?" She was on her feet. "Dayne's not your brother? Is that really how you feel?"

"He's not. Not the way you and Brooke and Kari and Erin see him." Luke let out a frustrated breath. "Mom and Dad gave him up, Ashley. He was raised in another family, so that makes him someone else's son."

"I see." Ashley felt her face getting hot. "So that's why the comment about 'blood doesn't make him a Baxter'?"

"Yes." Luke sounded defensive. "I didn't know until it was too late that they'd plaster it across the magazine. Anyway, no one sees my point."

"No." She walked closer to the Baxter family picture and studied the image of Luke. *What happened to you, little brother? How could you grow up a Baxter and miss the whole point of family?* She forced herself to stay calm. "Your point doesn't matter. Neither does mine or our sisters'. What matters is that Mom loved Dayne. Dad loves him still. Think about it. If you and Reagan gave a child up for adoption before you had Tommy, you'd spend the rest of your days wondering about him, looking for him, hoping his life was everything you ever dreamed it would be."

Luke was silent.

"You could tell each other not to talk about him, but that wouldn't make him any less real." She heard a catch in her voice. "Any less your son."

He remained quiet for a beat. Then he sighed. "I get that part." For the first time in months, there was compassion in his voice.

Compassion and pain. The real Luke, the one they all loved, was still there. Confused maybe, but deep inside he hadn't changed completely.

Ashley walked back to the kitchen. "Okay. If you get it, then why, Luke? . . . Why would you say that?"

"Because I liked the way our family *was*." The anger was back, though not as strong as before. "Back before I had to be chased down the street by a photographer shouting questions at me." He laughed, but there was no humor in it. "Back before I had to assure the women at the office that no, I couldn't get them a date with Dayne Matthews. Before I had to imagine every family gathering centered around a celebrity."

Luke's bitterness shocked Ashley. She leaned against the nearest wall. "That's how you see it? What happened to you, Luke? You and Reagan are in trouble, and now this? I mean, come on!" She didn't pause long enough for him to interrupt. "You spent a week with Dayne in LA, remember? And you told the rest of us Dayne was a nice guy, genuine." Ashley raked her fingers through her hair. Passion filled her tone. "You said he wasn't at all the way you'd picture a movie star. Remember that?"

"Look, what happens between Reagan and me is our business." His words were clipped. "I have to go. Malin's crying."

Ashley wondered. She strained to hear, but the line was quiet other than Luke. "Okay, but we have to talk this out." Her eyes caught another picture, a small framed snapshot of Dayne, Kari, Brooke, and her at the lake on the Fourth of July. "You can't change the facts. Dayne's our brother, and he'll be a part of our family whether you like it or not."

"Yeah." He sounded colder than before. "And maybe I won't be."

Luke said good-bye and hung up before Ashley could question him, before she could express her outrage at his attitude. How come everyone else in the family was okay with the curve they'd been thrown? All of them had reason to struggle with it, and at times all of them had. Mostly they'd struggled with their parents and how they could've kept such a colossal secret for so many, many years.

But how did any of them have a right to struggle with Dayne? None of this had been his fault. He had been adopted by missionaries and given a lonely childhood in an Indonesian boarding school, and before he graduated his parents had been killed in a small-plane crash. Yes, he'd gone on to take drama classes at UCLA and made a string of hit movies, but he had no control over what happened after that—being placed at the center of America's fascination with celebrities.

Ashley closed her eyes and turned her back on the small snapshot. She could understand Luke's having concerns about the change in their family if he hadn't met Dayne. But he'd spent a week with him. How could he lash out about having Dayne as a brother after knowing Dayne? She covered her face with her hands. *God . . . our lives are a ball of knots. I can't even begin to unravel it by myself.*

She heard a key in the front door and the sound of footsteps. Ashley peered through her fingers. She could smell smoke long before her husband reached her.

"Rough night?" Landon had dark smudges on his face and his uniform. He grinned, but his eyes were warm with sympathy. "I'd kiss you, but then you'd smell like me."

"You fought a fire?" There was no reason to sound surprised. Her husband was a firefighter. Still, she always felt a ripple of alarm when she knew he'd been face-to-face with a wall of flames. Especially since he'd nearly lost his life in a burning building twice before.

"We put it out." He set his helmet on the counter, grabbed a glass, and filled it with water. "No victims, no injuries. Just a blazing warehouse." He rubbed his eyes with the back of his hand. "It got a little crazy. Nothing serious."

Ashley lowered her chin. "Landon . . . you're telling me the whole story, right?"

"Yes." He angled his head, the way Cole did when he laid on the charm. "It was perfectly safe."

She pictured him walking through a building full of flames and falling beams. "Never mind. You're home. Thank God."

He winked at her. "I have." He guzzled the glass of water in four swallows and filled it again. "Unless you were playing hide-and-seek, I'd say your night might've been a little rougher than mine."

She laughed out loud. She must've been a sight, standing in the kitchen with her hands over her face when he walked in. The laughter felt good, but it didn't last. Her smile faded. "It was pretty bad. I talked to Luke."

"About the tabloids?" Landon had been home when Ashley came back with the stack of magazines. He hadn't had time to read them, but he saw the pictures and he knew the news wasn't great.

"Yes." She motioned toward the tabloids on the kitchen chair. "He said Dayne wasn't his brother." For the first time since she'd opened the first magazine, her eyes grew damp. "But he *is* our brother. And now the whole thing could split our family down the middle." She moved closer and slid her arms around his jacket. "I don't care about the smoke. I need you."

Landon cradled her close and rubbed her back. "Honey, nothing could split your family. Not time or distance or even death." He kissed the top of her head. "Definitely not this."

The smell only reminded her how blessed she was. Landon had survived another fire, and God had brought him safely home. One more time. "Thanks." She snuggled against him.

"For what?"

"For always knowing what to say." She took a step back. "Go shower. I'll make you a sandwich."

He reached for his helmet. "You know what I think?"

"What?"

"I think you ought to take the afternoon tomorrow and paint."

"Hmm." She smiled. Weeks had passed since she'd pulled out her brushes and sat in front of an easel and an empty canvas.

"Sounds wonderful." She wrinkled her nose. "But Kari and I are taking the babies to the park midmorning, and then I've got a CKT meeting after lunch." She felt most tired about what came next. "Then there's Katy and Dayne's house." Her shoulders sagged. "I'm not sure I even know where to begin."

Landon's eyes shone with love and understanding and strength. "Start where we always start, Ash." He pointed up. Then he smiled and headed into the hall and up the stairs toward their room.

Ashley watched him leave, amazed at the way he loved her, the way he always loved her. He was her rock in times like this, and here was why. *"Start where we always start, Ash. . . ."*

And, of course, that's exactly what she would do. It was what she had been doing. Only most of the time throughout the day praying hadn't felt like enough. But it was. It always would be. Peace stilled the rough waters in her soul, and she lifted her voice to God then and later with Landon after he showered and came back down.

They prayed that God would remove the bitterness and anger in Luke and replace it with compassion, and they prayed as they'd done each day that Dayne would wake up and that he'd have a full recovery. This time they prayed that Ashley wouldn't gain one brother only to lose another.

Three minutes after they finished praying, the phone rang. Landon jumped up and jogged to the kitchen. He answered it, and after a minute, he headed toward Ashley. He looked like he was trying to hide a smile. "It's for you. It's your dad."

"Thanks." Ashley stood and reached for the phone. Somehow everything would work out. God was always faithful, whether a person was in a season of blessing or a season of growing, whether in triumphs or trials. It was like her mother had always said: In the journey of life, it was a better ride if a person took the passenger seat and let God do the driving. Because along the way there were bound to be unexpected turns.

And some turns only God could maneuver.

She picked up the receiver. "Hello?"

"Ashley . . ." Her father sounded funny, like he'd been crying.

Ashley frowned. Why would he be upset? An idea hit her. This better not be about Elaine. Apparently her dad and his friend had gone through some kind of falling-out. She wondered once in a while if their trouble had anything to do with the way she had treated Elaine that night when Elaine was helping in the Baxter kitchen. The woman had no right to access their family. The trouble between her dad and Elaine was just as well. Her father had mentioned the other day that he hadn't talked to his friend in weeks. Ashley was glad. Her father needed time with his memories.

She pressed the phone to the side of her face. "Dad, is everything okay?" She glanced up. Landon was grinning bigger than he had at any time tonight.

"I . . . can't believe it." Her dad cleared his throat.

"What?" This wasn't about Elaine. It was something bigger. Much bigger.

It took a while for him to speak, but when he did the words came in a hurry. "It's Dayne. He's awake."

CHAPTER TWENTY-THREE

REAGAN SAT on the floor across from Tommy and Malin. They were building a tower with oversize plastic LEGO blocks, and it was all she could do to stay awake. But then, the exhaustion was becoming part of life.

"Tommy need a green one." Tommy was talking very well lately. With his light brown hair and big blue eyes, he looked more like Luke all the time.

Reagan reached across the carpet and found a green block. "Here you go."

Tommy concentrated on the masterpiece in front of him. He placed the block and clapped. "Big castle."

Neither of them spotted Malin until it was too late. She wasn't quite walking yet, but she could crawl faster than any baby Reagan had ever seen. She reached Tommy's building and tried to stand up against it. Reagan barely had time to catch her, but it was too late for the tower. It tumbled to the floor and broke in five sections.

Tommy screamed and then froze. He turned and shouted, "No, Mali, no! Bad!"

Malin didn't know what to make of her brother's anger, and combined with her near fall, her expression changed. She opened her mouth, and after a buildup that seemed to take a minute, she began to cry. The problem was, when Malin cried it was more like a scream. A temper tantrum even.

"Tommy, please . . ." Reagan stood and lifted Malin onto her hip. Her daughter's screams were so loud that she doubted Tommy could even hear her. "Your sister didn't mean to hurt your tower. Mommy can help you build it back."

Tommy started crying too. Then he glared at Malin, pointed his finger at her, and made a firing sound. "Tommy shoot her!"

"Wonderful," Reagan mumbled. She shifted Malin to her other hip and stooped down to Tommy's level. "We do not shoot people, Tommy. I've told you that."

She left Tommy sobbing in the middle of a pile of LEGOs, his gun finger still cocked and ready to fire. She carried Malin to the kitchen. A pacifier would lighten the mood, if only she could find it. Reagan looked beside the sink and between the canisters and in a basket near the fridge where she usually kept a spare. But there was no sign of it.

The phone rang, and she answered it on the run. "Hello?" she shouted above the crying and screaming.

"Hi." It was Luke. He paused. "What's happening?"

"Just another—" she bounced Malin back onto her hip— "happy afternoon."

"Oh. Well . . ." His voice was too faint to hear above the noise.

"What?" She moved a fruit bowl to the side. Where was the pacifier? "I can't hear you."

"Never mind." He was shouting now. "I'll see you tonight."

"Fine." She hung up without saying good-bye.

Malin's crying rose a notch. She held out her hand for her pacifier. "Poppy . . . poppy, Mama." Then she dropped her head back and shook her shoulders. The full-blown temper tantrum was right around the corner. Part of the reason was the pain in her ears. Yesterday she'd been diagnosed with another ear infection. Her third in the past six weeks. The doctor was talking about surgery and putting tubes in her ears.

Reagan had her hands full between Malin's ears and Tommy's recent fascination with guns. Yesterday Tommy had gotten a checkup at the same time. When the nurse was taking his blood pressure, he slowly looked up at her and scowled. In the corner bouncing a moaning Malin, Reagan knew what was about to happen. She could only hope she was wrong.

As the cuff tightened on Tommy's little arm, his scowl got deeper. He made a gun with his finger, aimed it at the nurse, and uttered a firing noise. Immediately the doctor—a guy—burst out laughing.

But the nurse made a face and sent Reagan a disapproving look. "That's not funny."

At least he hadn't finished off the job with the announcement he'd been making more often lately: "Tommy shoot her." Luke thought the whole thing was funny. In fact, Tommy was the only one who could make him laugh these days.

Reagan tried her best to convince their son that he should shoot only the errant dinosaur or tiger that had managed to get into the house, and once in a while she succeeded. Earlier that week he'd come running out of his room, carefully aimed his finger at nothing, and fired loudly. He proceeded to clear the apartment of approximately seventeen dinosaurs, six snakes, four bears, two tigers, and a swarm of bees.

But an hour later Tommy ran from her, and before she could catch him, he turned around and fired straight at her. Reagan's mother had warned her that the terrible twos didn't necessarily stop at two. Indeed.

Reagan glanced in the other room. Tommy had moved to the couch. He was lying on his stomach crying into a pillow. *I'm a terrible mother,* she thought. *I can't even get through a normal hour with these two.*

Malin lifted her head, held out her hand again, and let out a long wail. "Poppy!" She held out the middle of the word at a piercing decibel for a record amount of time.

"I know, sweetie." Reagan picked up her pace, frantically searching the kitchen. The pacifier had to be here. Every time anyone in the family saw it on the floor it was washed and set aside right here so they could find it in a moment like this. She blew at her bangs and kept looking. The silverware drawer, the glass cupboard, the bread box. Nothing.

The problem was, sometimes Tommy found it on the counter where it was supposed to be, or in the basket, and he'd hide it. "Tommy hide Mali's poppy!" he would exclaim joyfully.

The Tupperware cupboard, the plastic-wrap drawer, the space where her mother kept the pot holders. Still nothing. *Please, God . . . help me.* Reagan bounced Malin as she moved. "It's okay, honey. Shhh. Mommy's looking for the poppy."

She moved down the counter a ways and opened the place-mat drawer and the utensil drawer. Finally, in the last possible place, she opened the junk drawer and there it was. Hidden treasure. She grabbed the pacifier and placed it in Malin's mouth.

Malin sucked on it as if her life depended on the action. Then she rested her head on Reagan's shoulder and made much quieter whimpers.

Reagan braced herself against the counter with her free hand and caught her breath. As she did, her eyes fell on the contents of the drawer. Rubber bands and receipts and batteries and a pair of broken sunglasses, but on the left side, right on top, was a pile of what looked like unopened mail. Tommy hadn't announced that he was hiding mail in addition to Malin's pacifiers, but Reagan was suddenly suspicious.

With Malin settling down a little more and Tommy's cries reduced to a low moan in the next room, she picked up the stack and spread the envelopes on the counter. Sure enough, nothing had been opened. She sighed and sorted through it. A cell phone bill, advertising for a credit card, their Visa bill, and . . . Reagan made a face. Strange. The last envelope was addressed by hand to Luke and her. She turned it over, and on the back flap was Luke's father's address. Once Malin was down, she'd read it.

John had called a few times since the night he'd caught her crying on the phone. At first Reagan expected the conversations with his father to make a change in Luke. But there had been none. Whatever was going on inside him, he wasn't giving her or anyone else a window.

Malin was asleep now. Reagan carried her to her crib and laid her down. She looked at her little girl for a moment longer. She was so precious when she was sleeping. The social worker who handled her adoption had told them the adjustment could take time. Reagan wasn't sure if the difficulties they were having with her were due to adjustment or ear infections or her own inability to handle two children. Either way she was grateful for what she hoped would be at least an hour of peace.

She shuffled back to the kitchen, weary and lonely and frustrated with Luke. He didn't understand what she went through every day. Yesterday Malin had fought against her noon dose of ear drops. Reagan had been late to work again, and her boss wrote her up. They paid her so little that she wasn't sure if it was worth being upset over.

When she reached the kitchen, she remembered the letter. A quick look at the living room told her that Tommy was okay. He'd rolled onto his side, his hair sticking out every which way. Both kids napping at the same time! She picked up the envelope, clicked a few buttons on the in-wall stereo, and waited until soft instrumental music filled the apartment. Then she moved to the recliner in the front sitting room and opened the envelope.

Inside were two pieces of paper. On the first was a handwritten letter from Luke's father dated more than a week ago. She gritted her teeth. They'd have to talk to Tommy about hiding the mail. She found the first line and began to read.

Dear Luke and Reagan,

   I found one of your mother's old letters, and inside was something she'd written and copies for each of you kids. I wanted you to have it as soon as possible. Read this and ask God if there's anything either of you could do to come more in line with this sort of love.

Reagan's heart melted. He had sorted through Elizabeth's letters and found something that could help them survive? She touched her fingers to her lips. No one took time for this kind of thing anymore. She thought about Luke, probably at his desk, face downcast, less than enthusiastic about coming home to her and the kids. If only he were more like his father. She kept reading.

Anyway, Luke, I think your mother really has something here. The whole world would do well to read it. But I think it would make her smile just to know that in this tough time, God brought it to the surface for you. I wish she were here to send it to you. Let's talk soon.

                                   I love you.

                                       Dad

Again Reagan was touched. The man was so open, so involved in his kids' lives. Her mother was involved that same way. She gave advice like she'd done a few weeks ago—reminding Reagan to look for ways to encourage Luke. But she kept her distance much of the time, so Reagan had assumed, as Luke had, that she was disappointed in the time it was taking them to find their own place.

Most of the time the fact that Reagan's mom kept her distance was probably a good thing, especially since they all lived together. She and her mom were close, and her mother was always quick to help with the kids. If she gave advice only once in a while, then that was okay.

Reagan lowered the first page to her lap and opened the second. It was a copy of something Elizabeth had written. At the top it said *Ten Secrets to a Happy Marriage—from Mom*.

Her eyes clouded with tears. Reading the words made her long for her father. Between her parents, he had been the more emotional one, the one she could go to when a boy broke her heart or when she had a misunderstanding with a friend. But he hadn't been a writer. He had left behind no priceless treasures like the one she was holding.

She read the list slowly.

1. *God has you here to serve one another. Love acted out is serving.*
2. *Women need respect and nurturing. Love your wife so she knows you'd lay your life down for her. Continue to date her and admire her. Share a hobby—find something you can do to have fun together.*
3. *Laugh often.*

Reagan stopped there and wiped her eyes. If she was keeping score, Luke would be batting zero. He rarely helped with the kids, and they hadn't gone on a date since before he started studying for the bar. Months ago. There was nothing funny anymore, and the only thing they did together was make the bed each morning. If Elizabeth was right—and clearly she was—no wonder their marriage was in trouble.

She dabbed at her eyes again and kept reading.

4. *Be patient. Love crumbles quickly under the weight of unmet expectations.*

Reagan stared at the line. Conviction poked pins at her conscience. Okay, so maybe she had to take some of the responsibility.

5. *Spend more time trying to fix yourself than your spouse.*
6. *Keep short accounts. The Bible says, "Do not let the sun go down while you are angry." Make it a habit to forgive.*

7. *Determine up front that divorce is not an option.*
8. *Learn about love languages. Not all people show love or receive it the same way. You want a back rub and your spouse wants a clean kitchen. The love languages are fairly simple: acts of service, time, physical touch, gifts, and words of affirmation. Learn them. Love is better received when it's in the language that person speaks.*
9. *Words of affirmation are a love language for all men.*
10. *Men are born to be leaders. He cannot lead unless she gives him the confidence to do so. If you love your husband, build him up. Confident men do not seek love outside the home.*

Reagan reread the list. Tears streamed down her face as remorse settled like a heavy blanket around her. Those last two were the exact things her own mom had been telling her. But she'd ignored her advice completely. Now, though, Reagan was seeing the suggestions in a new light.

Sure, she'd been thinking herself a terrible wife. But not really, not in the way of changing. More because it made her a victim, a martyr.

No matter how hard her mother had tried to convince her of the same thing, not until she read Elizabeth's words did she realize all the ways she truly had let Luke down. In her mind, she didn't need fixing. Luke had the bad attitude. Luke was the one who had changed.

She moved the paper back toward her knees so her tears wouldn't get it wet. She'd kept long accounts, if she was honest with herself, and when they talked about a separation, she could almost see herself divorced and moving on to someone better, someone kinder with a gentler attitude. And love languages? Reagan had never even considered such a thing.

The tears slowed, and she dried her cheeks. What was her love language? Not gifts. She didn't care about material things. Sentimental things, yes. But not enough to consider that her way of loving. She read through the list again. If she had to pick one, it would be physical touch. She loved holding hands with Luke and cuddling with him, feeling close to him. It was what had led to their rocky beginning in the first place. And next would be time—having Luke beside her when it came to working with the kids or taking a walk and having him listen to her. Knowing he was there for her.

But according to Elizabeth, it was more important to know Luke's love language. If his mother was right, then Reagan had never made a conscious effort to love Luke the way he was made to be loved. Words of affirmation? The exact thing her mother had told her weeks ago. She handled things the opposite way, asking questions much of the time. She could hear herself. *"Why are you late? When are they going to give you a raise? Why can't you help more?"*

Another layer of tears covered her eyes. Statements like that would only serve to bring a guy down. But why hadn't she listened to her mother? Why had it taken until now to click in her heart?

Reagan blinked, clearing her eyes so she could see through her tears. What else for Luke? The answer came to her almost immediately. Acts of service, of course. Luke loved it when she ironed his shirts or typed a brief for him when he had to bring his work home.

Something else came to mind. Just last week Reagan had snapped at him for being distant and insensitive. Her mother was out, and Reagan's day had been rougher than usual. There was no dinner ready when he came home. He didn't get mad, but after he changed clothes he spent the next hour making chicken and rice and then cleaning it up. He went so far as to take apart the stove-top burners and wash each individual part.

By then she had the kids in bed. She found him in the kitchen and stared at him. "Thanks a lot."

Luke turned, his expression baffled. "What's that supposed to mean?"

She scowled at him. "It means I've spent the whole night with the kids, same as I spent most of the day with them. And where are you?" She motioned to the kitchen. "In here by yourself."

Her heart sank at the memory. If Luke enjoyed being served, then cleaning the kitchen might've been his way of loving her. Maybe they were falling apart because they were speaking to each other in foreign languages.

But it was the last one on Elizabeth's list that made her throat thick with sorrow. Luke had been scrambling toward solid footing since they got back together. He was the guy who had gotten her pregnant, the one who had bolted into the arms of another woman after her greatest loss. Much of that had been her fault, of course. He'd tried to call, but she wouldn't answer, too panicked over the loss of her father and the realization that she was pregnant.

Still, she had found no reason to compliment him back then. Rather she'd been more reluctant. *Sure, okay . . . we can give it a try.* That sort of thing. And after they were married, he was automatically behind a lap in the race of life. A full-time student, married with a baby, and living with his wife's mother. How often had she asked him when he would graduate or how long before he could take the bar or when he'd become a full-fledged attorney? He kept running and trying, but he couldn't catch up to save his life. Not by her standards. That was something else. She let Luke blame her mother for thinking he wasn't living up to their expectations. But really they'd been Reagan's expectations all along. What had her expectations and criticisms done to Luke?

She placed the pages one on top of the other, the way they'd been in the envelope. Then she set them down on the table beside her and drew her knees close to her chest. Marriage was so hard, so much work. Lately she didn't even like Luke. So putting Elizabeth's secrets into practice would be tougher than if she'd known about them from the beginning.

But she loved Luke, and she believed that God had a plan for them, plans for a beautiful marriage and a wonderful life in which every day was better than the last. Change could come only if she acted out of love for Christ, believing that in the process He would give her the marriage she dreamed about.

She took a mental inventory of the life they'd been living and the pressures Luke had been under. All without any real encouragement from her. No wonder he was frustrated about the discovery that Dayne was his brother. He had worked hard for the past few years with only a rare bit of approval from Reagan. And now here came news that his biological brother was a multimillionaire movie star.

A memory ran through her mind. She and Luke visiting her father at the top of the World Trade Center that long-ago day. Luke had been so sure they'd do everything right, so confident. He wanted to have an office just like her father's someday, he told her. Maybe right next door.

Oh, Luke . . . you had such high aspirations, such a positive outlook for the future. What happened to you?

And like that, the answer was clear. Sin happened to him. Not just to him but to both of them. They had gone against God's plan, and at least some of what they were dealing with was a result of their poor actions. That could be why she struggled with giving him praise. Secretly she might still be blaming him for derailing her plans—plans to finish college as an all-star athlete. Plans to date and travel and get married later when the timing was right.

Reagan sniffed and stood, carrying the letter back to the kitchen. They would live a lifetime with the consequences of their choices. But God had a better future for them than the one they were living. She surveyed the situation. It was three o'clock, and the kids were still sleeping. Luke wouldn't be home for two hours. That meant there was time to take action now. Today.

Before the weight of her unmet expectations caused love to crumble completely.

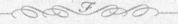

CHAPTER TWENTY-FOUR

LUKE COULDN'T CONCENTRATE.

He was still getting flak from the guys in the office about his newfound fame. Admiring women from other floors of the office had heard that he was Dayne's brother, and two of them had sent interoffice mail his way asking if he was interested. Word got around, and the guys couldn't resist poking fun at him.

"Can I have your autograph, Dayne . . . er, I mean, Luke?" Then they'd burst into laughter as if the whole situation was beyond funny.

Luke's boss, Joe Morris, was the only one not laughing. The moment he saw the story, he called Luke into his office and smacked the magazine down on the desk between them. "What's this?"

Luke had to think quickly. He tried for a casual tone. "The guy chased me down." He leaned back and shrugged. "Blew the whole thing out of proportion."

"So what's it mean, your comment?" Joe wasn't angry, but he was on the verge. "I don't care if Dayne's your brother. He's one of this firm's top clients."

"Obviously I realize that." Luke tried a lighthearted laugh, but it fell flat. "What I meant was I can't give any information about Dayne. He didn't grow up with the rest of us, you know?"

The lines around Joe's eyes eased some. "That makes sense, I guess."

"That part about being a Baxter—" he gestured toward the magazine—"only means that finding a brother this late in life doesn't give you a whole lot in common."

Joe nodded thoughtfully. Then he took the magazine and shoved it in a file. "Let's just be a little more careful what we say to the press from now on."

That was four days ago. Things were fine with Joe, but the incident clearly wasn't going away and neither was the dilemma Luke faced with his family. In the past week Luke had seen the same photographer again, and this time he handled it better. If the guy wanted his picture, fine. He could take it. He would take it anyway. Luke put up nothing to block the way and didn't turn toward the sounds of questions and a clicking lens. Instead he ignored the man and kept walking, staring straight ahead. The photographer wouldn't catch Luke Baxter making a fool of himself again; that much was certain.

Luke studied the file on his desk. It was a corporate takeover case, and he was supposed to find a truckload of varying precedents for the petitioner, who was a big client. He was working with the client's corporate lawyer, but progress was tediously slow.

His call to Reagan earlier hadn't lightened his mood any. Seemed like all the kids did lately was scream and cry. And Reagan wasn't much better. He pushed his chair back from his desk. Maybe if he got a coffee he'd have a better chance of getting through the afternoon. He was about to stand up when Joe opened his door and stepped inside.

"Luke—" his boss was smiling—"we need to talk."

"All right." Luke sat back and gestured to the chair across from him. The man didn't look nearly so ominous when he was in a good mood.

Joe ignored the offer of a chair. He came closer and leaned his free hand on the desk. With the other, he held up an envelope. "You aren't going to believe this."

Luke blinked. He had absolutely no idea what Joe was talking about or what could make him look so pleased. He waited for him to continue.

"So I'm sitting in my office yesterday wondering how we can take on the ten clients knocking on the door without hiring another attorney, and I get a call." Joe chuckled. "Guess who it is?"

The question made him lower his brow. "No idea."

"Dayne Matthews' agent! The guy tells me I'll be getting an overnight package from him, so keep an eye out for it."

Luke had no idea how the story might involve him. He crossed his arms and tried to look appropriately interested.

"Anyway, it gets delivered to my office a few minutes ago, and I open it. Inside's this letter." He waved it at Luke. "It's a written request made by Dayne before his accident. You ready for this?"

"Uh, I think so." Luke gulped. Back then Dayne couldn't possibly have thought Luke felt any ill will toward him.

"Okay, listen." He searched Luke's face. "Once you pass the bar, he wants you to consider moving to our Indianapolis office and working exclusively on his contracts and holdings." He straightened and slapped the letter on Luke's desk. "It's all in here. He wants the firm backing you, but he wants exclusive access to your services." He chuckled again. "And get this. He wants your salary at about twice where we would've started you. He'll pay it." He let his arms hang at his sides in a way that said he was too shocked to say anything else.

Luke's world tilted hard and began spinning out of control. He must be daydreaming, right? The Friday afternoon doldrums had finally gotten to him. Joe Morris couldn't possibly have just said that. Luke squinted at his boss. "He wants me to think about transferring to Indiana?"

"Exactly. Isn't that what you've been saying for the last year? That you'd like to get back there?"

"Yes, I . . ." Luke rubbed the back of his neck and tried to find a modicum of clarity. Dayne wanted to increase the rate he paid the firm so that Luke would net twice the standard starting salary? He searched Joe's eyes. "Are you serious?"

"Of course." Joe's laugh came easily. He took a step back and propped himself up against the wall. "We'll miss you around here, but it allows us to keep a top client happy and justify hiring two attorneys full-time to help with the workload around here." He tossed his hands in the air. "Everyone wins."

Joe picked up the letter. "I'll make a copy for your file. It's legal verbiage, something his agent drafted." He took a few steps back toward the door and paused. "Now that Dayne's out of the coma and making a recovery, I'll need you to let me know as soon as possible. Dayne's willing to start paying your salary November 1, which means you could wrap things up here in the next few weeks and spend November with your family—waiting for results on the bar exam."

Spend November in Bloomington with his family? Leave the city and have the salary to buy a house less than an hour from his dad and sisters? The news was beyond anything Luke could've imagined.

Joe moved toward the door. "Hey, Baxter . . ."

"Yes, sir?"

He grinned at Luke over his shoulder. "Good thing you didn't mean those things in the tabloids. Sounds like Dayne's taking the whole brother thing pretty seriously."

The words hit Luke like a machete. Joe closed the door behind him, and Luke sat back in his chair, dazed. What about the tabloids? Dayne was awake, so he was bound to see them. Luke hadn't talked to Ashley or his dad about Dayne's progress. For all he knew the offer was already pulled off the table.

But even if it was, that wasn't the point. Here was Dayne, reaching out to him the only way he knew how—by offering him his dream job on a platter. Dayne, who hadn't lived a Christian life until lately, had shown himself to be the better man by far.

Luke considered the spread in the tabloids. What had made him so mean, so ready to lash out? Dayne had done nothing to earn his spite and venom. Shame filled him, suffocated him. He'd been raised to believe that love was always the answer, that the people sitting around the dining room table would always be his closest friends. How could he have behaved so badly?

Ten minutes passed while he beat himself up, blow after blow after well-deserved blow. Then, like the crack of dawn, gradually he began to see things differently. No one had called to tell him Dayne's offer had been pulled. So maybe he hadn't seen the magazines, or maybe someone had explained them to him in a way that didn't upset him. Either way, it might not be too late. He could call Dayne and apologize about the tabloids, try to make him understand that it wasn't anything personal. And they could talk about Dayne's offer.

He called the hospital on his way home, but a nurse informed him that Dayne had requested no phone calls while he was in rehab. She took a message and promised to get it to him.

Luke snapped his phone shut, disappointed. He would fly to LA if it meant clearing things up with Dayne. He'd acted horribly, and the strange bitterness and jealousy he'd been feeling weren't Dayne's fault.

Luke was still sorting through the possible scenarios when he walked through the door of his apartment that evening. "Reagan, I'm—"

She walked around the corner, and the sight of her made him weak at the knees. She'd been wearing sweatpants and T-shirts lately, and more often than not she looked like she'd been through a marathon by the time he came home. Not tonight. She wore black slacks and a tan silky blouse. Her hair and makeup were done.

Her expression wasn't suggestive. Rather it was contrite and deep and full of a longing he hadn't seen in months. She came to him and slid her arms around his waist, never taking her eyes off his. "I'm sorry."

"Sorry?" What was happening to him? Someone must've been praying; that's all he could figure. He ran his thumb beneath her blonde bangs. "Honey, for what?"

Her eyes sparkled with tears. She took a step back and pulled a letter from her pocket. "Here." She handed it to him. "My mom's reading to the kids so I could have this time with you." She nodded to the letter. "Read it. Then you'll understand."

He took it and studied it. "From my dad?"

She smiled, but her eyes filled a little more. "And your mom."

Luke wasn't sure he could take any more surprises today, but he opened the letter anyway. Reagan led him to the sofa near the window—the place where they'd had a number of recent fights—and they sat down together.

The first page made the contents clear, and the effort touched Luke's heart. His dad cared so much. He moved to the second page and began working his way down the list. If his heart had become as hard as concrete, each of his mother's secrets chiseled away another piece of cement.

His parents had always been the picture of married love, and now his mother had shared her wisdom at a time when he needed it most. Every single point she'd made was something he'd known deep in his heart that he was supposed to do. He'd watched his parents all his life, after all. But he hadn't been doing a single one.

No wonder his marriage felt like it was falling apart.

Luke folded the letter and held it to his heart. Only then did the tears come, tears that had been building inside him since he first heard the news about Dayne. He missed her so much, his mother. She had always loved him in a special way, complimenting him and encouraging him to follow his dreams. Living out the things she'd listed on this page. But missing her wasn't an excuse for him to treat Reagan poorly.

Next to him, Reagan was looking at her wedding ring, twisting it, waiting for him to finish reading.

He set the letter down and turned to her. "Reagan—" he took

her hand and wove his fingers gently between hers—"how can you ever forgive me?"

"You?" She laughed, but it came out like a quiet sob. "It's my fault. I've . . . I haven't loved you like you deserve. Not for a minute. And I've had expectations that were all wrong."

He slid closer to her and pulled her into his arms. "That's crazy. I've been moody and mean and . . ." He kissed her forehead and kept his face close to hers. "I watched my parents model those ten methods of love all my life, but these last few months it's like . . . I don't know." He touched his lips to hers. "It's like I forgot how to love at all."

"We both did."

"Can you forgive me? Let me make it up to you." He kissed her again, with more passion this time. "I've missed you so much. None of this, whatever I'm going through . . . none of it's about you."

"I know. But I haven't been very supportive." She drew back and looked him straight in the eyes. "Luke, if I haven't said it before, let me say it now. I'm so proud of you." Her lips curved into a smile. "You're doing everything you can to build us a future, and I don't know if I've ever thanked you." Her voice was thick with regret. "I'm so sorry."

For the next half hour they cuddled and kissed and talked about time together and love languages. Luke smiled when she said that besides words of affirmation, his was acts of service.

"I finally figured out that when you stay in the kitchen cleaning, you're trying to tell me you love me, right?" She ran her fingers along his jawline.

"Right." He felt like a fool. "But all you wanted was this."

"Mmm-hmm. Exactly."

When they were finished talking, she grinned at him. "I have a surprise for you."

"A surprise?" Luke wasn't sure he could take much more. He still hadn't told her about Dayne's offer.

"Come on." She led him into the kitchen, and there—like

something from a magazine spread—was the table done up with linens, china, and candles. The smell of grilled fish filled the kitchen, and on the stove were two covered pans full of rice and vegetables.

He was about to say that she shouldn't have, that the work was more than she needed to do, but he stopped himself. "Acts of service?"

She held his eyes and took both his hands in hers. "I love you, Luke. I'll say it in whatever language you want to hear it."

Reagan's mother came around the corner with Malin in her arms and Tommy tagging along beside her. "The kids are starved." She smiled tentatively at them. "Is it time for dinner?"

"It's time for a lot of things." Luke put his arm around Reagan. Then he squatted down and held out his hands to Tommy.

"Daddy!" Tommy ran and put his arms around his neck. "Tommy hungry."

"Yes." Luke swept their son into his arms. He shared a look with Reagan that told her he would forever be grateful for this night, for her willingness to work on their marriage. Her determination to give love another chance. Luke rubbed noses with Tommy. "That's because most of all it's time for dinner."

The meal was the way Luke remembered dinnertime from his childhood. Good food, great conversation, and a feeling of love so strong Luke felt energized by it.

They were at the end of the meal when Tommy began banging his spoon on his plate. "Drum, drum, drum," he said. He grinned at Malin and hit his spoon on his plate again, a little harder this time. "Look, Mali. Drum, drum, drum!"

Luke was about to say something, but Reagan's mother was closest to the child. She put her hand over his and gave him a stern look. "Tommy, your plate is not a drum." She took the spoon from him and set it near his plate, neat and orderly. "You need to eat like a gentleman."

Tommy looked at his grandma and then down at his plate. His

brow lowered, and he pursed his lips into an angry face. Then, in slow motion, he turned his hand into a gun and slowly pointed it at his grandma. He even closed one eye as he took careful aim. Luke knew what was coming, but before he could do anything to stop him, Tommy made a loud firing sound.

Then, with great drama, Tommy looked at Reagan across the table. "Tommy shoot her." He nodded as if to say Grandma would no longer be a problem.

"Well . . ." Reagan's mother inhaled sharply. Even so, there was a twinkle in her eye. "That's not very nice behavior, Tommy."

Luke looked at Reagan. The corners of her mouth were quivering, same as his. Her mother was right. Tommy's behavior was completely inappropriate. Luke and Reagan had a lot of work to do, figuring out how to parent two children while learning how to love each other. But in that moment, as if their hearts had finally fallen into alignment, they chose to participate in one of his mother's secrets to a happy marriage.

Loud, sidesplitting, heart-cleansing laughter.

CHAPTER TWENTY-FIVE

DAYNE STEADIED the bar on his shoulders and willed his back to stay straight as he bent his knees. He lowered three, maybe four inches. *A little more . . . just a little more.* His body shook as if he were the heroin addict he'd played once in a movie. But he pushed himself another inch. Then with what was left of his strength he rose to a fully straight position. "Ten." He blew the air from his lungs and sucked in a series of breaths.

Katy helped him lift the bar over his head and set it back on the rack. "That's your best yet."

"Thanks." He smiled at her, but he could feel it fall short of his eyes. "It has to be better."

She seemed to hold her breath for a moment, as if she wasn't sure she should speak her mind. Then she exhaled in a defeated sort of way. "Maybe you're pushing too hard."

"I'm not." He limped to the nearest bench, grabbed his towel from the floor, and dabbed at his face. Sweat streamed down his forehead. He'd never known so much pain in his entire life. He dropped his towel and reached for his water bottle. When he'd downed half of it, he looked at Katy. "I want to get out of this place."

"I know." Katy looked worried. "Just be careful. Healing is a process, remember? That's what the physical therapist told you."

"The process has to be faster." He closed his water bottle, dropped it on the floor, and stared at his legs. They still didn't move right, though he'd been told by several doctors that they would in time. He was fully awake now, his voice and mind and thoughts working clearly and keenly the way they had before the accident.

His doctors had moved him to a rehab facility, where Katy had kept her promise. As much as possible she stayed by him, encouraging him, pushing him. They were a little more than a week into the rehab process, and he had a much better understanding of Dr. Deming's original assessment. Even with the way he was pushing himself, the process was unbelievably slow.

"Crunches next." He lay back on the bench and used his hands to pull his right leg up until his foot was on the black bench top. The effort left him out of breath, and he paused until he found another reserve of strength. Then he did the same thing with his left leg, so his feet were together, knees bent.

"Want me to help?" Katy sounded tentative.

"Not this time." He hesitated long enough to reach for her hand. His tone softened. "But thanks. I couldn't do this without you."

She narrowed her eyes, concern coloring her expression. She sat down in a chair opposite him. "I'll count."

Dayne focused his energy on his midsection. At first he had needed her to help lift his legs, and then after a few days she helped hold his knees together while he did the exercises. Now he could do them without her help.

He pressed upward, again shaking so hard he could barely stay on the bench. He was supposed to blow out with every exertion, but sometimes it was impossible to breathe and work all at once. This was one of those times. He held his breath as he lifted himself higher . . . higher . . . until his elbows brushed against his knees.

"One." Katy shifted in her chair. "You're sure you're okay?"

He lowered himself, his sides heaving from the exertion. "Yes." He looked at her. "Please, Katy . . . push me. Don't talk me into giving up."

She bit her lip and nodded. "Okay. I'll try."

Once more he steadied himself. Then with all his energy directed at his abdominal muscles, he lifted up.

"Two." Katy sounded more encouraging. "You can do it, Dayne. Come on."

It was better during these sets if he thought about something else, if Katy's counting in the background was nothing more than a distant marker. This time his mind made its way back to the beginning of this journey. In the first few days after he came out of the coma, he'd had trouble remembering simple things. Even so he was able to piece together what happened. By the third day, he talked Katy into showing him photographs of the accident, the ones that had appeared in the tabloids.

"Three."

His heart and soul filled with fury at the price he'd paid for the paparazzi madness. His agent had discussed the possibility of suing them, but since criminal charges had been brought against two of them, Dayne decided he'd let the law take its course. He had too much to be joyful about to waste his time thinking about the tabloids.

"Four. Come on. . . ."

The accident had been horrific. Everyone considered it against the odds that he had survived, and the lack of brain damage was a miracle. Nothing less. He had talked to John and thanked him for bringing Katy and Ashley to see him. When he didn't feel he could move another muscle, the picture of his family reaching out to him that way was enough to keep him going.

"Five." There was determination in Katy's tone. "You're halfway there, baby. Keep going."

He knew about Randi's confession that she had been interested in him, but maybe now she was more interested in Dayne's faith. Prayers had been answered in every area of his life, and there remained just one that mattered. He wanted out of the rehab facility in time to get to Bloomington by Thanksgiving.

"Six."

He was driven to make the goal. At least twice a day his therapist told him it wouldn't happen. "You're making amazing progress, Dayne, but you have to understand. Every muscle in your body has been atrophying for a month. We've assessed your physical condition, and I'd have to stick with the original plan. Three weeks of rehab for every week you were in a coma."

"Seven. You can do it, Dayne."

He caught a glimpse of himself in the mirror, and it knocked him back for a few seconds. His face was fiery red, the veins near his temple pulsing from the effort. His left leg was severely scarred above the knee, and his entire body looked like a skeletal version of his old self. He was grateful the facility was guarded 24-7 from paparazzi. The last thing he needed was for them to snap pictures of him looking like this.

"Eight."

The most amazing thing about his recovery was that Katy had stayed with him. That she had literally kept by his side hour by hour, praying for him to wake up. How had he been blessed with a woman who could give him that kind of love? She could've stayed for a week, then kissed him good-bye and prayed for him from a distance. There had been no way to tell if his coma would last a month or three months or a year. But according to Dr. Deming, she never once wavered. She stayed with Dayne until someone made her leave.

"Nine." Katy was on her feet. "Come on, one more."

He had a picture in his head. Him and Katy, hand in hand,

walking into the Baxter house and being greeted by his entire family—Kari and Ryan and their kids, Brooke and Peter and their girls, Ashley and Landon and their boys, Erin and Sam and their four little girls, and Luke and Reagan and their two. At the head of the table would be John Baxter, and for that one moment he could imagine how it might've been growing up with these people. Sharing Thanksgivings and Christmases and every other special occasion with them. That single moment would make every grueling day of rehab more than worth the effort.

"Ten!" Katy put her hand on his shoulder. "Dayne, that's a record."

He was breathing too hard to speak. She reached out to help him up from the bench, but he gave a slight shake of his head. Everything he did on his own would be one more step toward a complete recovery. With a strength he didn't know he had, he sat up, swung his feet onto the floor, and braced his hands on his knees.

The therapist approached him. "I was watching." He gave a quietly incredulous laugh. "I work with a lot of clients. I've never seen anyone with your tenacity. I mean that."

Katy breathed out, as if no matter how encouraging she'd tried to sound, she'd been anxious all the same. "He's not pushing himself too hard, is he?"

"Not really." The therapist was a young guy with barely any body fat and a fanatical understanding of the human body and how to make it work again. "These exercises can't hurt him." He bent his knees and leaned over, looking at Dayne's leg. "We're strengthening his core first, and after that we'll work the finer motor movements. Running, zigzagging through cones—that sort of thing."

Dayne nodded and tried not to feel discouraged. "See? It's not too much."

The therapist shook his head. "I have to say, your progress is amazing so far." He had a chart with him, and he checked it.

"I don't want to promise anything, but right now you're a week ahead of schedule. We'll have a stretching session in a few hours if you're up to it."

"I will be."

The therapist grinned. "I like your attitude. See you in a little while." He nodded to Katy before heading back through the gym and into his office.

Defeat rattled Dayne's nerves. A week? He'd cut only a week from his rehab? He needed more than that. He wanted to finish *six* weeks early, and he was willing to work around the clock to do it. But he needed to start gaining ground a lot more quickly than he had been. He reached for his towel and flung it around his neck. "I need a shower."

Katy took the cue. "I'll be in your room."

"Hey." He suddenly realized how callous he sounded. He stopped and caught her hand. The look on her face melted him. "Thank you."

She met his eyes and held them. "I can't believe I have you back, Dayne." Her eyes told him all the things there wasn't time to say. "I'll be waiting for you."

He smiled. "I'll hurry. I want to talk about your last call with Ashley."

"Okay." She no longer asked him if he needed help to the shower room.

Neither did the therapist.

He still limped, but that was better than using a walker—which was what Dr. Deming and the therapist had expected of him for the first four weeks.

Katy left through the side door, and Dayne slowly made his way toward the showers.

Half an hour later he was dressed and fresh but exhausted from the morning workout. He limped through the private waiting room to the hall that led to his room. But as he went, a magazine on the coffee table caught his attention.

There was a photo of him and a headline about the war he was waging for his life. But in the upper right corner was a headline that said "Family Feud? Dayne's Brother Lashes Out."

Dayne felt the blood leave his face. Spots danced before his eyes, and sweat broke out on his forehead. What was this, and how come no one had told him? He didn't have enough strength to be angry, not when it took everything he had just to keep from passing out. He made it to the closest chair before he dropped. The workout and the shower had pushed him to the brink, and now this. He put his head between his knees and concentrated on staying conscious.

When the spots disappeared, he sat up slowly and took hold of the magazine. It was dated ten days ago. *What's going on?* He read the headline again, but it felt like a cruel joke. The story had to be about Luke, but Dayne had talked to him since coming out of the coma. He'd also spent a week with him and he'd been great. And that was before he learned the truth about their connection. So what could the rag possibly have found?

He rested for a moment and then flipped the pages until he saw an angry photo of Luke. There it was for the whole world to see. "Luke Baxter wants nothing to do with his famous brother." The caption sliced at Dayne's heart and made it hard to breathe. Katy must've known about this, so why hadn't she said anything?

Against every bit of his will, he read the rest of the story, the paragraph about his birth family, and Luke's quotes and the dirt they'd found on each of his siblings. He felt sick and weak. The news detonated inside his heart like a roadside bomb. *Why? All the time and energy and effort between all of us . . . and now what? It was all for nothing?*

His heart pounded and he felt faint again. He concentrated on the classical music playing over the ceiling speakers and the hum of an aquarium a few feet away so he wouldn't black out. As he did, a Bible verse whispered to his breaking heart. *"In all things God works for the good of those who love him."*

He squeezed his eyes shut. *Not this, Lord. This can never work to Your good.*

Yes, son. All things . . . I have promised this.

Dayne's breath caught in his throat. Only rarely had he ever heard such a clear response from God, but this was one of those times. He opened his eyes. *Okay, steady. Breathe out.* He obeyed his own orders, and after a few out breaths the faint feeling lifted.

He needed to think rationally about the story. Katy hadn't mentioned it and neither had John. That had to mean something. If the tabloid story had devastated the Baxters, someone would've told him. And what about Luke? He looked at the magazine spread again and his mind raced. The paparazzi were insidious, bent on getting their story at any cost. He was proof of that. So maybe they'd badgered Luke into saying something, and maybe they'd misquoted him.

Katy and John had probably avoided saying anything so Dayne wouldn't get even angrier at the tabs. Anger wouldn't help him find the strength he needed to tackle rehabilitation. Katy had reminded him of that every time he brought up the accident, every time he talked about how he hoped the photographers who caused the crash would serve jail time.

He breathed out again, and the slightest bit of peace took root inside him. But just as quickly it died off. Everything was different now. No matter how the press had twisted the story, the picture didn't lie. Luke looked like a different person from the guy Dayne had spent time with in Los Angeles. He was angry, no question. Maybe the anger was directed at the photographer, but what about his quotes? Blood didn't make him a Baxter?

After all this time, after all the ways he'd longed for a family, Dayne had known best all along. Hadn't he warned John and Ashley? The Baxters were private people. Living in the glare of the spotlight, having their photos splashed across magazines in grocery checkouts all over the nation would be more than they could handle. And here was proof.

"In all things God works for the good"?

Maybe God meant that this find, this magazine, was proof that Dayne shouldn't move to Bloomington after all. Maybe the good would be that all of them would be spared further damage if he canceled his plans completely. No Thanksgiving together, no house on the lake. And what about Katy? She didn't want to live in Malibu. He could feel his heart crumbling, feel it landing in a heap near his knees.

Before he could make himself stand and finish the journey to his room, he heard footsteps in the hall coming closer, closer. Then Katy rounded the corner, her face tight with concern. She came to a sudden stop. "Dayne . . ." Her gaze fell to the magazine in his hands.

In that moment he didn't have to ask whether the Baxters were suffering from their newfound visibility or whether the quotes from Luke were true.

The answers were right there in Katy's eyes.

CHAPTER TWENTY-SIX

KATY WAS WORRIED about Dayne. It was two days after he found the tabloids and read the remarks from Luke, and he seemed to have lost his will to move forward. He had barely made an effort in his workouts, and his therapist warned him that if he didn't start working harder, he'd lose the week he'd gained.

Dayne was sitting up in bed, finishing his dinner. "Luke's right."

"About what?" Katy had never seen him so shut down, so uncommunicative. She had begun to wonder if even their engagement might be in jeopardy.

"We're not brothers. Blood doesn't make me a Baxter." He pushed his food table and struggled to lift his legs onto the bed. With painfully small movements, he slid back against the headboard. He was out of breath when he spoke again. "I need to call and cancel Thanksgiving." He flexed the muscles in his jaw, his anger controlled but palpable. "This is my home, here in Southern California."

Katy was seized with panic. This was *his* home? Meaning he no longer saw a future for the two of them? And wasn't his marriage proposal based on the fact that he was willing to move to Bloomington, that he wouldn't expose her to the insane life of having their comings and goings constantly followed by paparazzi?

Her mind and heart raced at breakneck speeds, but before she opened her mouth, she prayed. The Lord had brought Dayne from the brink of death, but why? So they could have another painful good-bye? a final ending? She stared at Dayne, trembling. *What's happening to him? How come it's all falling apart?*

And in the quiet of the room, with therapists moving up and down the hallway outside, God spoke to her more clearly than He ever had in her life.

Wait on Me, My daughter. Be still, and know that I am God.

The response filled her senses and brought a swift dose of hope and peace and strength. Be still and wait? Was that what God wanted from her? Was she supposed to step aside and let the Lord handle Dayne while she did nothing more than stand her ground, helping Dayne, encouraging him, waiting for the hurt to wear off?

She had the deep and certain sense that the answer was yes.

The next day Dayne's determination tripled. He attacked every task he was given, and not until later did he explain himself. "I'm an actor. Maybe it's time I stop fighting the tabloids and embrace that fact." He was squeezing a soft ball, working on his grip. "If I don't find my way back, I'll lose even that."

Understanding came over Katy like a cold rain. He was no longer fighting for his place in the Baxter family. He was running from it. If he focused all his energy on acting and embracing the celebrity life, maybe he could numb the pain in his heart, find a way to live with it. Again she had no idea where she fit into his thinking.

But she'd heard God last night, and until she felt Him leading her another way, she would be still and wait. She would love Dayne even when he was unlovable, stand by him even when he didn't need her help, and believe that somehow God would give them forever even when their future seemed less likely all the time.

🌿

Bailey had finished her Algebra II homework and was researching internment camps after the attack on Pearl Harbor. Her history teacher was very big on Pearl Harbor. Her dad and the boys were at the park with the dog, and her mom was sitting next to her at one of the other computers, talking to Ashley on the phone.

"I can find out what type of windows our builder used for this house," her mom said.

Bailey knew what they were talking about. Katy and Dayne's house and how much work needed to be done. Bailey added another three facts about the internment camps to her index cards. There. Now she was done.

She switched screens and called up MySpace.com. The beginning of the school year had been so busy, she hadn't had time to look through MySpace in more than a month.

This morning's rehearsal for *Cinderella* had been hard. Bailey was one of the wicked stepsisters, a part that stretched her acting skills and gave her a chance to be funny onstage. Connor was a coachman, and overall the rehearsals were going smoothly.

But it wasn't the same without Katy Hart.

Bailey missed her so much—way more than she thought she would. Katy wasn't only the greatest director ever—she was like an older sister. Even with all the activity in the Flanigan home, it somehow felt empty without Katy coming and going.

The Web site came up, and Bailey clicked through the photos on several of her friends' pages. Some of them were so dumb. Girls who had been sweet and innocent in middle school were posting pictures of themselves drinking at parties and making out with their boyfriends. It was disgusting really.

She clicked back out of them and went to Tanner's page. He didn't care about MySpace much, so he hardly ever posted comments or pictures. But every now and then she liked to look at it anyway. In the profile section people had a choice to say whether they were in a relationship or not. It made her smile when she looked at that part of Tanner's page and saw the words *in a relationship*.

Bryan Smythe—the player from CKT—was still making attempts at getting her attention. He said all the right things, but every time she talked to her friends or her parents about him, she had the same feeling. That she was working too hard to convince herself that he was a good guy when in fact he was probably nothing more than a smooth talker. Bryan wasn't in *Cinderella*. He was on his school's golf team, and that took up much of his time. But he showed up after practice now and then. Always he had something sweet to say. "I couldn't fall asleep last night, Bailey. Every time I closed my eyes you were there." Or "The stars are nothing next to your eyes, Bailey."

Most of the time Bailey was glad she had Tanner. He was busy with football, and three weeks into the season he'd won the starting job. He was the team star, no doubt, and she was proud of him. More than that, she loved the way he gave her space. No jealousies or pressures from Tanner Williams.

Next to her, the conversation sounded more emotional. "Ashley, we'll think of something." Her mother's voice was calm, the way it always was when someone was upset. The way it was when Bailey was upset. She loved that about her mother—the fact that she could look at things rationally even when the world felt like it was falling apart.

She turned to her mom and whispered, "Is this about the house?"

Her mother nodded and covered the receiver. "Ashley doesn't think she'll have enough people to help her. She still wants it done by Thanksgiving."

An idea hit Bailey, and she jumped to her feet. "I know!"

"Shhh." Her mother's eyes grew wide. She motioned for Bailey to sit back down.

When she did, she dropped her voice to a whisper. "It's perfect! We'll have the CKT kids help out! We could get dozens of kids and parents over there, and the work would happen super fast."

Her mother smiled and gave her a thumbs-up. Then she stood and took the phone into the next room. "So Bailey has an idea. . . ." The sound of the conversation faded.

Bailey turned back to Tanner's MySpace. There were always comments from girls, the sleazy types who would drop a line the way fishermen dropped a hook full of bait. Rarely did Tanner ever answer them, though. Once in a while Bailey looked, and every time she came away satisfied that Tanner was the real deal. A great friend first and a loyal boyfriend second.

She looked through his comments, each one accompanied by the MySpace picture of the person who left it. They were all pretty harmless. *Hey, Tanner, great game Friday. You rock!* and *Northlake is shaking in their boots, buddy. Way to keep the mojo going.* There were a few comments from girls, reiterating what a great job he was doing leading the team.

Halfway down there was a comment from a girl Bailey didn't recognize. *Last night was amazing, Tanner Williams. And, yes, I'll hang out with you again sometime soon! Let's make it a plan. lol. Remember this? Wait for it . . . wait for it . . . ha-ha. You make me laugh. ttyl.*

Bailey felt a shiver run down her back. What in the world was the girl talking about? The football team had played away last night, and Bailey had been at CKT rehearsal. So who was the girl, and how had she managed to hang out with Tanner? He was supposed to be hanging out at Alex's house. Bailey leaned forward. Her stomach hurt. The girl's ID was *Maybe Tonight*, and she had the cheap photo to match. Bailey stared at her picture and clicked it.

Instantly she was on the girl's MySpace. Whoever she was, she had pictures of herself all over her page. In a few of them she was wearing only a bikini. Bailey scanned her profile. Her real name was nowhere in sight, but she was eighteen and lived north of Bloomington, which meant she didn't attend Clear Creek High.

"Okay, so what about you and Tanner?" Bailey asked. She felt like she did when she was called on to answer a pop-quiz question in front of the class. Clammy and cold and scared to death. Tanner wouldn't have done anything behind her back, would he? Not Tanner.

She scrolled down the page until she saw Tanner's picture. The date was yesterday, and his comment said, *I didn't know you knew Alex! And, ya, about the waiting. Sometimes that makes things more interesting. You never know.*

"What?" Bailey was on her feet again. She turned and paced into the kitchen and then back. She pulled her cell phone from her pocket and fired off a text to Tanner. *So what'd you do last night?*

She hit Send just as her mother came back from the family room and hung up the phone. "Poor Ashley; she has so much work to do."

Bailey stared at her mother and pointed to the computer screen. "Tanner hung out with some other girl last night. Read it."

Immediately her mother's expression changed. Ashley's concerns were important, but Bailey's took precedence.

Bailey clicked to the comment on Tanner's MySpace, then back to the one on the girl's.

"Hmm." Her mother looked at Bailey. "Doesn't look real good."

This was another thing Bailey loved about her mother. Both her parents liked Tanner, but they always told Bailey not to get too attached. She was too young for a serious relationship. But here—when it felt like her world was falling in around her—Bailey could count on her mom to take things seriously. She didn't roll her eyes and make some snappy remark about it being for the best or cluck her tongue against the roof of her mouth and mention something about having told her so.

Instead she did the one thing Bailey wanted her to do. She held out her arms. "Come here, honey."

Bailey fell into the hug and willed herself not to cry. She was too mad anyway. How dare Tanner go to Alex's and hang out with some other girl. She didn't even want to imagine what Tanner must've told her to wait for. Him? His kiss? Or something even more serious?

Her phone beeped three times. She pulled back and flipped it open. Tanner's message was short. *I hung out with the guys at Alex's house. You had practice, right?*

Her anger became a rage. She clenched her teeth and let out a furious cry. "How dare he lie to me?" She looked at her mother and shook her head. "All this time I trusted him." Hurt took the edge in her tone. "All this time."

The calm was there in her mother's face. "There might be more to the story, Bailey. You should call him."

"I should, but I won't." She was too mad. If he couldn't tell her the truth, then forget him. She could spend her junior year without a boyfriend. She opened her phone and punched a series of buttons as fast and hard as she could. *Hey, I've been thinking . . . maybe we should take some time away from each other. You know, see other people.*

"What are you—?"

She hit Send before her mother finished her sentence. Bailey snapped the phone shut and looked up. "There. I broke up with him."

"Bailey!" Her mother couldn't have looked more astonished if Bailey had sprouted a tail. "You can't break up with a boy over text messages."

"Well, I just did." She was still mad, but tears were filling her eyes anyway. "He lied to me, Mom. All the guys at Alex's know he was talking to some—" she gestured toward the computer screen—"some girl. And then he goes and lies to me."

"Okay, so you call him up and ask him over. You take a walk and talk about things." She ran her hand down Bailey's arm. "Tanner's been a very good friend. He deserves more than that."

"And I deserve more than *that*." She jerked her thumb at the screen. Her tone was sounding a little rude. She made her voice get quieter. "I'm sorry. It's not your fault."

"It's okay." Her mother put her hands on Bailey's shoulders. "Listen, sweetie. You have to call Tanner. We're friends with his family, and his mother would never understand why I let you break up with him over texting."

Before Bailey could try to explain herself again, her phone beeped. A part of her didn't want to open it. Her mother was right about Tanner. He deserved a phone call at least. She stared at her phone. She never should've checked Tanner's MySpace, never should've sent that last text message.

Her heart skipped a beat as she opened the phone. His message read, *Uh . . . okay. So is that it? We're finished?*

She blinked back her tears. For a few seconds she considered calling him and telling him everything her mother had suggested. That he should come over and the two of them should talk. But pride consumed her, filled her heart and soul, and before she could stop herself she tapped at the buttons again. *I guess I just don't want a boyfriend right now.*

Her mother tilted her head. "Bailey . . . call him."

"I will later." She brushed her fingers beneath her eyes. Everything had been going so good until now. That's why she hated MySpace. It always made a mess of everything.

Once more her phone beeped. She flipped it open and read his response three times. *Okay then . . . wish I knew what I did. Guess I'll see you around.*

Wait . . . what had she done? Had she really just broken up with Tanner Williams? In five minutes flat? The guy she'd had a crush on since fourth grade, the one her friends thought would be her boyfriend all through high school? Was it that easy to rip a friendship in half?

She looked at her mom. "What just happened?"

"It might take a while to figure that out." Her mom hugged her for a long time. "Promise me you'll call him, Bailey. Please."

"I will eventually." She wiped her tears and tried to put the incident out of her mind. She poured herself a glass of juice and sat at the kitchen bar. "It's okay. We'll still be friends." But even as she said the words she wasn't completely sure. "Let's talk about Katy and Dayne."

And they did for the next fifteen minutes. They dreamed about getting a group of kids over to the lake house and hauling away every piece of debris in the yard. But all the while Bailey couldn't take her mind off the strange feeling inside her, a feeling she'd never known before.

It wasn't until that night—after never getting up the nerve to call Tanner—that she finally realized what she was feeling.

Her heart was breaking.

The first boy she ever liked was out of her life. Whatever had happened and whatever had gone wrong didn't really matter. It was over with him. And she would never, ever be the same again.

CHAPTER TWENTY-SEVEN

JOHN BAXTER enjoyed the drive to Indianapolis—especially when he was picking up one of his kids at the airport the way he was this early afternoon. Luke and Reagan and the kids were coming and would be staying in Luke's old room at the Baxter house for the next five weeks. It would be wonderful—a little wild, maybe, but John could hardly wait to have the sound of children in the house morning and night.

John relaxed in his seat and settled into the middle lane. The skies were blue across Indiana this October day, and the fall figured to be milder than usual. But that wasn't necessarily true for the relationships between his children.

The radio was on, a song playing from an oldies station. John flipped it off and sorted through the events of the past three weeks. Much had been worked out between Luke and Reagan, so that wasn't a worry. At least not for now.

The problem was Luke and Dayne and how they'd get along if Dayne made it home for Thanksgiving. The magazine article had stirred up quite a mess throughout the family. For a few weeks,

Ashley and the other girls had been angry with Luke, wondering how he could say such a thing about Dayne.

But then Luke passed around an explanation. He'd been caught off guard, and though he meant what he said, he didn't mean it definitively. Just in the moment. The trouble was, John didn't know if he believed that story entirely. He'd talked to Luke more than anyone else, and the quotes seemed like more than an off moment. They seemed perfectly in line with the way Luke had been feeling.

Up until he learned about the offer from Dayne, anyway. The opportunity was amazing for Luke and his family. For all of them really. Move to Indianapolis or even a suburb south of the city. Live within an hour of his family and have a high-paying job with only one primary client—his brother, Dayne. What could be better?

Luke and Dayne had spoken once since Dayne came out of the coma, and Dayne had reassured him that the offer was good. Whether Dayne moved to Bloomington or not. Luke didn't mention the tabloid story and neither did Dayne. Luke seemed to think that everything was okay between them, but John wasn't sure.

Since then Dayne had stumbled onto one of the tabloids, and now he knew about Luke's quotes. Luke had tried to call and apologize, but Dayne wasn't taking calls. Apparently Dayne's job offer to Luke was still good—Luke hadn't heard otherwise. But everything else about the future seemed tentative.

John passed a slow-moving trailer and then slipped back into the middle lane. He had a feeling about the coming months. If Dayne felt any hesitancy from Luke, he would walk away and never look back. Dayne wouldn't come between them; he'd said that from the beginning. Dayne had been mostly worried about how his connection to the Baxters would hurt them. But his desire to know them had won out. At least until now.

John couldn't help but worry about the relationship between

Luke and Dayne, especially in light of what Dayne had told him yesterday. He was getting better, working as hard as he could.

"I have to be honest, though. I'm not sure we're going through with our plans to move there." Dayne's words had been almost matter-of-fact. But hidden in his tone was a hurt that John could do nothing about.

John reached the airport and left his car in short-term parking. Inside he joined a small group waiting to meet passengers. He found a place away from the crowd, and as he did, he noticed a young man in an army uniform walking toward them.

Only one person was there to greet the soldier—a man who must've been his father. When they spotted each other, the soldier heaved his bag over his shoulder and took the last steps running. They grabbed onto each other hard and didn't let go for half a minute. From where John was standing he could hear what they were saying.

The older man was crying openly. "I prayed for you every day, Son. I'm so proud of you."

In return, the soldier beamed. As if every dusty mile, every dangerous mission, every sandy sleeping bunk was worth it all to hear those five powerful words. *I'm so proud of you.*

The older man took the soldier's bag, and the two walked off.

But the scene made John think. How long had it been since he'd told Luke he was proud of him? A month? Two? Longer, even? All the talk lately had been about Dayne, and John was unapologetically proud of his oldest son. Dayne had followed his dreams, and despite wild success, he'd found his way home—in every way that mattered.

Still, he was proud of Luke too. Very proud.

He was making a mental note to tell him so when he saw the four of them. Luke was carrying Malin, and Tommy was holding Reagan's hand. They looked tired. Even so, as soon as their eyes met, John could tell something about his youngest son. There was humility and sorrow and pain in his expression.

Luke was hurting too. And that meant—whatever Luke's past mistakes—John could only hope that his trek here was about one thing and one thing only.

Making amends.

※

Ashley pulled into the driveway of the lakeside home, drove up close to the front, and parked. What a day. Practice for *Cinderella* had been crazier than ever before. They needed Katy so badly that she and Rhonda were considering talking to Bethany about postponing the performances—moving them into December maybe.

The trouble was the prince. Connor Flanigan almost got the part, except Rhonda noted that the prince should be someone old enough to shave. Ideally, anyway. The guy who landed the role was skinny and awkward and the only one tall enough to wear the costume. He didn't have a romantic bone in his body. He knew his lines, but every time he spoke Ashley had the desire to yawn.

Ashley gripped the steering wheel with both hands and let her head fall forward. She needed to put CKT out of her mind. They still had several weeks before opening night. God had been working miracles left and right—first with Dayne, then with her family's willingness to help on the house, even if it looked impossible that they'd finish it before Thanksgiving. The play could turn out all right. It could happen.

She lifted her head and stared at the old structure. *Okay, God . . . help me figure this out.*

Landon and Kari's husband, Ryan, had taken the kids fishing. It was Ryan Junior's first time, and the men were excited about the chance to indoctrinate another of the kids in the joy of angling.

Her plan today was to make a list. An extensive list. She had lined up a contractor to do the counters and floors. But otherwise, they were on their own. She stepped out of the van and looked around. On a pad of paper she wrote:

1. *Mow yard, front and back.*
2. *Pull weeds, front and back.*

She wanted to start at the back of the house, the area where Dayne and Katy would spend most of their time. The minute she rounded the corner and looked at the deck she let her notepad hang at her side.

It was never going to happen. Not unless she could get half of Bloomington out here to help. She toyed with the idea of chucking the whole project. But then gradually she remembered the television show. Slowly she felt her determination rise. They pulled off jobs like this in just a week on TV. If God brought the right people, it could still happen.

She lifted her pad and started writing.

3. *Clear debris.*
4. *Rebuild decks.*

The back door was broken, so she had no trouble getting in. She worked her way through the downstairs and up into every room on the second floor. Finally she returned to the backyard, where she was scrutinizing the windows when she felt a hand on her shoulder. She screamed and spun around.

"Sorry." It was Luke, and he was by himself. He laughed and made the same face he used to make when he was a kid. "I couldn't resist."

"Thanks." She bent over and willed her heart to remember how to beat. "You scared me." She caught her breath and stood straight again. "Hey . . . what are you doing here?" Now that the shock had worn off, she squealed and flung her arms around his neck. "You're a month early."

He laughed and put his arms around her waist. "Dad's good. I asked him to keep it a secret." His expression fell, and he searched her face. "I have to talk to you, Ash. I've messed things up with a lot of people. I want to start changing that." He released her and slipped his hands in his pockets, his eyes on the back of the house. "It has potential."

"It does. I made a list of what needs to be done." Ashley handed it to him. "It's ten pages."

Luke let out a low whistle. "Dad says you're working with a contractor?"

"I was. He's doing the counters and floors." She studied her brother, and joy lifted her mood. Luke had been her best friend when they were kids. She had to spend only a few minutes with him to remember why. "So what brings you? Work?"

A grin lightened Luke's expression. "Yep. All month." He pointed at the old house. "Working right here next to you."

Ashley's mouth opened, and she sucked in a slow breath. "Are you serious? That's why you're here?"

"It is." The teasing left his eyes. "I figured something out."

She wandered to the old, broken-down picnic table and sat on top. He followed and took the spot next to her. "What?"

"I figured out why I was so mad all the time." He put his hands behind him and leaned back against his arms. "You know, with the whole Dayne situation."

"Why?" Ashley had wanted this moment for a long time—the chance to sit next to her brother and try to decipher his heart.

He looked out toward the lake. "All my life I wanted a brother." He grinned at her. "You were a good substitute, Ash. But I still wanted a brother." He turned his attention back to the lake. "It wasn't something I talked about."

A glimmer of understanding flickered in her soul.

"Anyway, so here I am all grown up with a family of my own, and I get word that hey, what do you know? I *do* have a brother. Only he's a famous movie star and he's moving to Bloomington.

Strange as it sounds, I think I was mad at everyone. Mad at Mom and Dad for never telling us and mad at Dayne for not being there all those years. And maybe mad that he turned out to be so famous. Because now—even if I did find a way to connect with him—he wouldn't have time for me."

Ashley didn't have to state the obvious. That none of what had happened to their family was Dayne's fault. Instead she slipped her arm around Luke's shoulders. "I can see that."

"Even hearing myself tell you makes me mad. What right do I have to be so selfish? It's like you said. None of us can change the facts. We have a brother. He has a very public life. And right now he has more than that—he has hurdles to overcome that I know nothing about." He narrowed his eyes, and his expression grew determined. "That's why I'm here. My brother needs me."

Ashley rested her head on his shoulder. "You're right. And I need you too." She took her arm from his shoulders and studied her list. "There's so much to do."

"Let's see." Luke looked at the first page. "You have people lined up to help, right?"

"On the weekends, yes." She felt the doubts rising inside her again. "If Dayne gets through rehab in record time, we have just four weeks and two days to get the job finished."

"Well, then." He rolled up his sleeves. "Let's see what we can get done right now."

And with that, they headed into the house and spent the next few hours dragging out broken bookcases and old blinds and other damaged items.

By the end of the afternoon, they were tired and dirty. But Luke looked happier than he'd been since last spring. Ashley knew him well enough to understand why.

He wasn't only talking about having a brother. He was loving him.

In the best way he knew how.

CHAPTER TWENTY-EIGHT

NO ONE COULD BELIEVE the progress Dayne was making. Not Dr. Deming or Dayne's therapist or anyone at the rehab center. Not anyone involved in conventional understanding of traumatic brain injuries and the recovery time after a month-long coma. No one who heard about his progress or saw it detailed in a file or witnessed it firsthand could believe it.

No one except Katy.

Dayne looked at her. She was sitting across from him, the same place she always sat while he did his four daily workouts. He had the bar across his shoulders, about to do another series of knee bends. The therapist had already laid out the routine for this session, and now he was in his office. Katy and Dayne were alone—just the two of them and the clank of the weights balanced on either end of the bar.

"Want me to count?"

"No." He clenched his teeth and stared across the room, as if he could tangibly see the goal in front of him. "Hit Play."

Katy hit the Play button on the CD player. The pulsing beat of something by The Fray filled the space. A week into his rehab, Katy had brought Dayne his MacBook from home. He used iTunes to create four CDs, each one loaded with music that helped drive him. There were movie themes and megahits and Christian songs, all with the same message—don't stop trying; don't ever give up.

When they weren't talking about his progress or working toward his progress, they watched inspirational movies or took turns reading the Bible. He posted Scriptures on the walls and nightstand. *Nothing is impossible with God . . . I can do everything through him who gives me strength . . . the battle is the Lord's . . .* and many others. His efforts were singly focused. He wanted to be surrounded by whatever drove him emotionally and spiritually.

The transformation was amazing. Dayne's first day of rehab had been so taxing that they'd both been sick. Dayne's body shook just shuffling with a walker three feet down the hallway. Back then he was thin and pasty, and he broke into a sweat getting out of bed.

"Four." Dayne pushed out the word and then bent again. He didn't make eye contact. No distractions. Not until he marked another notch on his chart, finished another session.

His form was perfect now—a complete knee bend with more weight on the bar than a rehab patient almost ever used. Strength wasn't the issue anymore, though he still walked with a slight limp. The goal was his fine motor skills. In fact, the therapist had told him that most patients in Dayne's condition would be discharged by now. A person could receive help with fine-motor-skill rehabilitation on an outpatient basis.

"If I stay," Dayne asked a few days ago, "will my progress be faster?"

"The way you attack rehab?" The therapist laughed. "No question about it."

"Okay." He felt steely determination. "Then I stay."

So Dayne split his time between the intense physical workouts—like the one he was starting now—and sessions on improving his hand-eye coordination and other routine movements. He worked on eating without a spill and using a pen or tapping out numbers on a cell phone.

Time in the workout room helped, of course. The stronger his core muscles, the more likely every nerve and muscle in his body would respond. That's why Dayne hadn't let up. Not one day. Not one session.

"Push me harder," he would say at the beginning of each meeting with his therapist. "It's not enough."

It was the same way with his meals. He wanted high protein and fresh vegetables and complex carbohydrates. In large quantities. As of this morning, he'd gained back all but five pounds of the weight he'd lost while in the coma.

"I've never seen anything like it." Dr. Deming stopped in after his weigh-in. "You're a walking precedent, Dayne. Whatever's driving you, stay with it." The doctor flipped through Dayne's chart. "I never would've said this before, but I believe you'll make a complete recovery." She patted her rounded abdomen. "Before this little one comes around Christmastime."

There was only one problem. The thing that was driving him had changed. At first it had been his Thanksgiving goal. He wanted out of Los Angeles, away from the paparazzi, and he wanted it without a change in the original plan. For the first week or so, his determination to heal had everything to do with the Baxters and his move to Bloomington. If he stayed on schedule, he could meet his entire birth family in one setting and know that he wasn't a visitor.

He was home.

If he missed Thanksgiving, he might not have a chance to visit with his entire family in one setting until his wedding. So he worked. To the point of passing out or throwing up or falling exhausted into bed each night, he worked. And for that first week, nothing looked like it would get in the way of his goal.

But then he found the magazine. At first he'd been angry at

Katy for not saying something, angry with John for pretending everything was okay.

"Ten." His face was sweating, his shirt damp.

Katy stood and took a step toward him. "Want help with the—?"

"No." He didn't look at her. "I'm fine."

She sat back down.

He didn't mean to snap at her, but he'd been doing it more often lately. Maybe because he'd become more of a machine or maybe because he was shutting himself off from feeling anything.

Whatever the reason, he knew his sharp answers and cold attitude weren't good for either of them.

Even still, he could do nothing to stop himself.

Dayne was doing the bench press now, still driven, still focused. The song on the player was from the pop charts, and again the beat was fast, driving.

Katy sighed. The hurt was still there, every bit of it. She heard it in his short, clipped answers, saw it in the dark shadows on his face. But there was no question he'd found purpose again.

Forty-five minutes into his workout, he turned the music off, dropped to the bench closest to her, and wiped his face with his towel. "You talked to Ashley this morning."

"I did." She felt herself tense. She tried to take the calls in the hallway or at her hotel at night. Not that she liked keeping her conversations from him, but whenever she talked to one of the Baxters lately, Dayne withdrew. That would explain his attitude this morning.

He was out of breath, his sides and chest working hard. He dug his elbows into his thighs and stared at the rubber mat.

"Are you mad?"

The towel was draped over his neck, creating a sort of curtain around his face. "What do you think?"

"I don't know." She twisted the engagement ring on her left hand. For weeks she'd been careful with her words, guarded in her responses. None of this was her fault, so why was he treating her like the enemy? And how come he wouldn't talk to her? She'd be better off at home, working with her CKT kids and praying for yet another miracle where she and Dayne Matthews were concerned. She was willing to be still and wait, but she wasn't sure how much more she could take.

He put his hands on his knees and straightened a little. "Okay." He sounded fed up. "Just tell me what she said."

Katy lifted her hands. "Same thing she always says, Dayne." Her heart was a dam ready to burst. "She's trying to find people to work on the house, but it isn't really coming together. Everyone's hoping and praying you'll be well enough to move to Bloomington in time for Thanksgiving. And Luke is sorry for the things he said."

Dayne stretched his neck one way and then the other. The pain in his eyes was so raw that it hurt to look at him. Katy knew he had talked to his father a few times since reading the article. But always the conversations were short. Yes, he forgave Luke. No, he wasn't upset.

Finally Dayne raised his brow in her direction. "And you said . . . ?"

"I said what you've asked me to say." She heard a catch in her voice. The edges of the dam were crumbling. "You aren't sure about anything, right? That's still how you feel?"

"I don't want to talk about it." He threw his towel on the floor, started the music, and moved to the butterfly machine. He added weight near the back, ten pounds more than he'd used during rehabilitation. Moving with less of a limp, he thrust himself onto the seat, raised his arms, and hooked his elbows behind the padded bar. After drawing a deep breath, he tightened his features and pushed the bars slowly, slowly, until his elbows met in front of him. Then in a concentrated move, he resisted the bars as he eased them back to the starting position. "One." His voice was gruff and angry.

In a rush, the dam inside Katy broke wide open, crumbled to a million pieces. He wouldn't treat her this way, wouldn't talk to her like this. And she couldn't stand by and watch while he gave up on everything they'd planned for their future. She stood, flipped off the music, and stormed over to him. "Stop!"

His elbows were almost back to center again. He ignored her, shaking as he completed the rep. "Two."

"Dayne!" she shrieked. Never mind if the therapist could hear her in his office. God never could've meant for her to be still and wait this long. "I said stop!"

He let the weights crash back into place. "What, Katy? What do you want from me?"

She grabbed the frame of the machine, her voice still loud, intense. "I want you to fight." Everything else in the room faded from view. "The Baxters are your family, and there's nothing you can do to change that." She paced a few steps, then turned to face him. "Maybe Luke didn't handle the whole thing very well. Maybe their privacy's compromised." She lifted her hands. "So what?"

"So what?" He slid to the end of the bench and stood inches from her. "So maybe the whole thing's just too hard, okay?" he shouted at her. In the background there was the sound of someone shutting the office door. Dayne's anger flashed in his eyes. "Maybe I never should've looked for them in the first place."

She clenched her jaw. "Then you never would've found me."

"And maybe that would've been better too." He stood his ground but turned his face from her.

"No." She gripped his shoulder. "Don't look away."

He looked at her, and for a few seconds it seemed he might break free from her and leave. But he stayed. "It would've been better, Katy." He lowered his voice, but every word was a seething blast of tangled hurt and rage. "I could stay in my own little world, and no one would ever get hurt."

"You would!" Her words were part cry, part scream. She was more out of control than ever in her life. Because the stakes were the highest they'd ever been. "You would get hurt, because God put us together, and God brought you to the Baxters. Okay?" She let go of his shoulder and put her hands on her hips. "Yeah, it's been rough. All of life is rough, Dayne. But this . . ." Her voice broke.

He turned away again.

"Look at me, please." She was breathing as hard as he was now.

"I can't." Reluctantly, as if he had nothing left to give, his eyes met hers. "I can't do this to you anymore. Go home and—" his chin trembled—"I don't know, take some time. It's not working."

"No!" Her tone was strong, determined. The tears stayed somewhere deep in her heart, waiting for permission. "No, I won't go home and I won't give up. The life we can have in Bloomington, your place in the Baxter family—they're worth trying for."

"What if they're not?" His words were quick, knifelike. "What if all I get in the end is more of this?" He waved at the equipment around him. "More anger and pain and heartache? What then?"

"You won't know if you don't try." She was still yelling. "Please, Dayne! Listen to me."

"Why?" He stiffened, his eyes blazing. "When I was a kid all I wanted was a family, Katy. A mom and dad waiting at home, someone in the audience when I won a part in a play. People to laugh with and cry with and learn from. Someone to tell me they loved me before I fell asleep each night." He grabbed hold of the frames of the machines on either side of him. "So I found them. And I was crazy enough to think I might finally belong after all. But it didn't work out, okay?" He did an exaggerated laugh. "It's a big mess, and everyone—" he shook harder than before, and he held his hands up—"everyone loses unless I just walk away."

"You're wrong." There was fire in her tone. "What you felt when you met Ashley and Kari and Brooke . . . that feeling of family, of knowing you belong. It's worth fighting for. Even if you have to fight until your dying breath." She took a few steps back. Suddenly the fight and the tension and the bitterness toward the paparazzi left her. And all that remained was the two of them. Her and Dayne. This time when she spoke, her tone was full of a quiet, burning passion. "It's worth everything, Dayne. You can't tell me it's not."

Slowly, like the subtly fading sky at sunset, Dayne's expression changed. The hurt he'd been carrying since he saw the magazine story burst to the surface, and it reminded her of something. Katy had witnessed a Southern California phenomenon since she'd been there these past two months. The Santa Ana winds. Los Angeles skies, typically thick with a mix of fog and smoke and smog, were swept clean by the warm, constant winds every October without fail.

That's what it looked like was happening inside Dayne now. As though the pain in his soul was suddenly so all-consuming it had the strength to rid his heart of every other emotion. The barriers he'd put up fell with a crash, and his eyes filled with tears. He held up his fingers to her, so the palm of his hand faced her. "Katy . . . please."

She hesitated. These last few weeks he'd hurt her more than she'd admitted even to herself. But the look in his eyes said he wasn't running now. She raised her hand until their two hands met, palm to palm, fingers to fingers. She realized something. Even his touch had been angry lately. Hard and cold and unfeeling.

But not anymore.

A single tear dropped onto his cheek and trickled down his face. "Search your heart, Katy. Your soul." He swallowed, and another tear slid from his eyes. "Am I there?"

Her tears came then. "Yes, Dayne. You're there. A part of me."

"I need to ask you something." He brought up his other hand, and she did the same, so both their hands were touching.

She took a step closer. "What?"

"Us." His voice was much quieter now, a painful whisper colored with tears. "Are we worth fighting for too?"

She slid her hands up around his neck, and he worked his around her waist. They stayed that way, crying in each other's arms, deep silent sobs because of all they could've lost.

"I'm sorry." He never broke eye contact. "I shut out everything I was feeling, but I . . . I shut you out too."

It was the first time since the accident that they'd held each other and cried. Dayne had been in too much of a rush to get better, and she in a hurry to help. But now every bit of sorrow came at them at once. Silent tears streamed down his face and hers, but they didn't look away. He had almost died. Almost. And she never would've had the chance to hold him this way. But over the weeks she had almost lost him again.

Finally Katy willed the sea of emotion to part long enough so she could speak. "Yes, we're worth fighting for."

"Even if we have to live here . . . the rest of our lives?"

Her heart dropped. Leave everything she loved in Bloomington and take on the full-time life of a celebrity? She swallowed, but she didn't waver another moment. "Yes. Even then." Now she searched his face. "Answer me this."

He wiped his cheek on his shoulder. "Okay."

"Promise me you'll go for Thanksgiving if you're cleared to leave." Her heart pounded. Their future depended on his answer. She believed with every breath that if they could only get there, God and the Baxters would take care of the rest. Then Dayne would see that he was wrong, that his family did care about him. That they were willing to fight for him the same way she wanted him to fight for them. A skirmish played out in his eyes, pride and futility versus a promise bright enough to expel any darkness. "I want it so badly." He clenched his teeth, and his whispered words barely made it through. "What if everyone walks away more hurt than before?"

"Then . . ." A lump formed in her throat. She waited, her eyes locked on his. "Then at least you fought. Please, Dayne . . . promise me."

New tears pooled in his eyes. Whatever he was about to say, the words would be coming from the deepest place in his heart. "I'm afraid. . . . It already hurts so much."

She would've done anything in that instant to love away his pain, but she did the only thing she could. She pulled him close and held him, pressing her head to his chest. "I'll never leave you."

"I know." He sheltered her head with his hand. After a while he stepped back, and his eyes told her what he was about to say before he voiced it. "I'll go. I'll pray and I'll trust and I'll fight. And if it doesn't work—" he kissed her brow—"then we come back here and never look back."

A shiver ran down her arms. What if it didn't work out? What if Luke was cold or distant and the tension made Dayne feel like running?

Before Katy could work herself into a frenzy of fear, the full and clear voice of God spoke straight to her soul again. *Wait on Me, daughter. Be still, and know that I am God.*

Suddenly the light in Dayne's eyes shone in her heart as well, and she had a clearer understanding. God wasn't asking her to wait on Dayne, to sit quietly by and let things fester in silence. He was asking her to wait on Him, on His power, the power He would use to bring everyone together once and for all—without misunderstanding or jealousy or bitterness or fear.

He was asking her to wait for Thanksgiving.

CHAPTER TWENTY-NINE

LUKE WAS ON THE ROOF, pounding in the last of a section of shingles. With every swing of his hammer, every drop of sweat, he felt his angry heart healing, felt it growing and filling him with love, joy, peace, and patience, with goodness, kindness, gentleness, and thoughtfulness.

The fruits of living every day for Christ. The very things his mother had spent her life trying to teach them. And it was happening because he was completely focused on helping the one person who seemed to have his act together, the person he'd assumed would never need him at all.

His brother, Dayne.

The house was coming along, no question, but they had just two weeks left.

Kari was watching Ashley's kids so Ashley and Landon—when he wasn't working—could spend every spare minute working at the house. Luke and Reagan had driven to Indianapolis and brought back a U-Haul truck full of windows and doors. Brooke's husband, Peter, and Jim Flanigan had experience in construction, so they had taken time off work to put in the windows and hang the doors. Stunning granite counters, tile flooring, and custom walnut cabinets had been installed in the kitchen, and the bathrooms had been renovated. The new appliances wouldn't be delivered until the Friday before Thanksgiving. None of them had any idea how they'd have time to get them in place before Thanksgiving, but they kept working.

Luke positioned a nail, raised his hammer, and drove it into place. The roof was beautiful. Once it was inspected, it had only a few sections that had needed replacing. A few more nails and that part of Luke's job would be done.

Luke examined the property. They still needed a few heavy-duty workdays, lots of muscle, half a dozen pickup trucks, and a landscaping crew. So far the weather had cooperated. It was the sixth of November. The temperature had dropped, but the sky was clear. The problem was that everyone was busy. Ryan's football team had games every weekend and school during the week. The CKT kids were between weekend performances for *Cinderella*. And everyone they knew had their own holiday plans to pull together.

Ashley wasn't panicking, but she was close. Part of every day's progress was a morning prayer time. Whoever was available, whoever could make it out to the house would meet with her in the backyard, form a circle, and pray. One thing they'd been praying for had already happened.

Dayne and Katy had committed to coming.

Provided his doctor signed off—and at this point that looked likely—the two of them would be here for Thanksgiving. The question was whether they would stay. Ashley had told Luke everything, so he knew how badly his comments had hurt Dayne. He knew too that if his brother sensed tension or conflict or that he was causing any trouble for the Baxters, he would bolt.

And that would be that.

Luke swung his hammer again. There would be no trouble.

Luke would see to it. The one thing Ashley was keeping secret was the progress on the house. She'd been intentionally vague with Katy, telling her that she was making calls and trying to schedule workers since the contractors were too busy before springtime.

The last time they talked, Katy even told Ashley she wasn't sure it mattered. They might hold on to the house for a year and sell it.

Luke reached for another nail. That wouldn't happen. Not after they saw what was waiting for them in Bloomington.

The day disappeared in a haze of sanding and prepping the exterior walls of the house. They were made of rough-hewn logs, but no one had treated them in decades.

At five o'clock Luke saw his dad, Ryan, and Landon pull up. They each wore tool belts with hammers and pliers, and between them they had two buckets of nails.

"Where do we start?" John looked past Luke to the side of the house. "Every log needs to be checked, right?"

"Right." Luke led the way, and as they worked along one side of the house, a stream of vehicles began driving up. A few had ladders sticking out the back.

"I forgot to tell you." Ryan grinned at them. "The football team wanted to put in a few hours."

Thirty-seven guys piled out of the cars and vans, each of them carrying a hammer. They carried a total of five more ladders, and by the time nightfall came, the entire exterior had been sanded and nailed back into place. The next step would be painting it with a heavy stain and sealing it. Then it would look brand-new.

As the days wore on, Luke could sense something big happening. The family was coming together as quickly and beautifully as the house.

"You know what it feels like?" Ashley asked him one day.

"What?" They were unloading a pile of fresh-cut boards, the ones they would use to rebuild the porch and deck out back.

Ashley stopped and wiped her dusty work gloves over her forehead. "It feels like Mom's here. Like this—all of what we're doing here—is our way of showing her that her legacy lives on." She had a smear of dirt on her cheek. "You know?"

"Yeah." Luke felt his heart swell a little more. "I definitely feel her here."

With every passing hour there seemed to be another piece of good news. Erin arrived a week early and set up at their dad's house. She proclaimed herself full-time day care operator, taking on all the kids so her siblings and their spouses could work on the renovation.

Brooke and two of her friends painted most of the inside. Ryan and a few of his coaching buddies built an outdoor island with a built-in barbecue and cabinets. More items crossed off the list.

Finally they received word from Katy. Dayne was officially finished with rehab and had been given permission to travel. The paparazzi would be hot for pictures of the new and improved Dayne Matthews, so he would give them what they wanted. He would stage a press conference midweek and make himself available for interviews over the next few days. After that he and Katy would travel by private jet to Bloomington on Saturday—five days before Thanksgiving.

One night the family had dinner at their dad's house, and Luke watched his father break down during the blessing. "Thank You, God. After the accident . . ." His voice gave out. He waited a few moments. "Lord, we know how great You are, but even we are stunned by the gift You've given Dayne." He wiped at his eyes. "The gift You've given us."

With the knowledge of a time and date, everything about the project kicked into high gear. They had a hard-and-fast goal now. Get the house done by Saturday morning. At first they almost gave way to panic. There was still so much more to do: trim and

staining and ceilings and cleaning up. But an unearthly peace settled over the entire group and their work. Luke felt it and so did
Ashley and their dad. If God could heal Dayne, He could bring
together the pieces of this remodel.

Luke worked with growing excitement. He could hardly wait
to see Dayne, to see the look in his brother's eyes when he realized
just how much they really did love him. Everything would come
together—the house, their relationships, the entire family.

Even if they needed every single hour between now and Saturday to make it happen.

Ashley was torn about how to use her time. It was closing weekend for *Cinderella*, and with the renovation needing her efforts,
Rhonda and Bethany had filled in and worked with the kids for
the performances. Ashley had seen the show opening night with
her sisters and their families. Luke and their dad kept working on
the house, sanding and painting ceilings throughout the upstairs.
They'd rented floodlights so they could work inside or outside as
late as they needed to.

Now it was Saturday morning, a week before Dayne and Katy's
arrival, and Ashley wished she could see the last performance
that evening at five. The problem was, today had been set aside
for removal of debris. They had some of Ryan's football players
lined up and all the Baxters working on the project, but still they
needed more help.

Jenny Flanigan had called last night and expressed her frustration. "Bailey has two dozen CKT kids ready to help. If only this
weren't the last night of the show."

"It's okay. Tell the kids I wish I were there." Ashley checked her
watch. She was always checking her watch these days. "I have to
run. Maybe you can stop by this week sometime."

Ashley arrived at the house at seven, just as Luke and her dad and Ryan were pulling in. Each of them was driving a pickup. The local dump was open until five, and the goal was to haul away every piece of debris before then. Ashley opened her van door and grabbed her checklist off the dashboard. There were still eighteen items unfinished. Clearing away the trash was one of them.

The guys walked by, and Luke smiled at her. "Ready for a big day?"

"Definitely." Ashley watched them, but her father didn't turn around. "Dad?"

"Oh?" He stopped and looked at her over his shoulder. "Hi, honey."

Excitement stirred her sleepy soul. She had a surprise for her dad, something he wouldn't find out until later today. The idea had come to her a few days ago after she'd spent time talking and praying with Landon. God had taught her something important. There was no time for angry feelings, no room for grudges or bitterness or unresolved issues. Luke had learned that and so had Reagan. Katy had figured that out when it came to the paparazzi and so had Dayne.

Love required sacrifice—all the way around. Ashley could hardly wait to see her dad's face when he learned of his surprise. He was waiting for her, and she smiled at him. "You doing okay?"

"Sure." His answer was quick, but he looked tired. "Fine."

The guys moved on, and the work party began. During the next hour, four more men came, doctors from Peter's office. Two of them drove pickups. The group descended on the old, broken-down porch and deck across the back of the house. One board at a time, they ripped out the old wood and hauled it to one of the trucks, careful not to damage the new barbecue and island adjacent to the deck. When a truck would fill up, someone would leave and take the load to the dump. Much of the wood was biodegradable, so it would go in a special section, where it would eventually be sold off as mulch.

Ashley was dragging rickety patio furniture to one of the trucks when she heard the noise. She stopped and looked up, and it took a moment for her to comprehend what she was seeing. When she understood, she had to blink back tears. A stream of CKT kids and their parents began pulling into the nearby field. Ashley lost count at fifteen cars.

Some of them pulled trailers, and as they unloaded their gear, Ashley saw three riding mowers. Before she could make her way over, the dads of three kids in *Cinderella* hopped on the machines and began a methodical mowing of the property.

Tim Reed and Bailey walked up together. "We couldn't stay away." Tim had a rake in his hands. "Katy deserves this."

"What . . . what about your show?" Ashley's head was spinning. More cars were pulling in. There had to be fifty people working fast and hard on clearing the land.

"It doesn't start till five." Bailey smiled. She looked comfortable at Tim's side, but Jenny had said that her daughter was struggling over a broken relationship and that she and Tim Reed were friends, nothing more.

When the craziness of the house project was finished, Ashley wanted to catch up with how the show had brought everyone closer. The way CKT shows always did. Maybe she would have a chance to catch up with Bailey too.

Tim pulled a pair of work gloves from his back pocket and slipped them on. "As long as we leave by two thirty, we'll be fine." He grinned at her and raised the rake. "We have work to do."

In the distance, Ashley saw the Flanigans pull up; then one of the men asked everyone to move their cars back onto the road. The clearing was happening that fast. Ashley could barely remember to breathe as she watched the group. Women carried potted shrubs from their vans, and kids pulled weeds from around the front porch area.

"It's happening, Ash." Luke's face was smeared with grime, and his clothes were filthy. But his eyes shone brighter than the sun. "This is why Bloomington's such a great place."

"Yep, you're right about that." Ashley drew a long breath and stretched her back. Then she and Luke worked together to clear away the patio furniture. The whole time she was thinking about what Luke said. How Bloomington was such a great place to live. It was true, and she was forever grateful that Landon had been willing to leave New York City to fight fires here in their hometown.

Bloomington was about raising kids and church potlucks and drawing close as one season rolled into the next. It was about faith and family and building a future together. And it was what Dayne and Katy were going to love most about living here.

Even if they didn't know it yet.

John was watching his grandchildren clear out the flower beds around the front porch. He wasn't tired; he was simply missing Elizabeth. The buildup of excitement over the house project was unlike anything his family had ever been a part of.

Elizabeth should've been here. She would've overseen the roses, making sure the right colors and mixes were planted along the front of the house and in special areas accenting the backyard. She had been brilliant at homemaking, and this would've been her finest hour—putting together a home for the child she had spent a lifetime missing.

"Papa, can we build a fishpond here in the front yard?" Cole's pile of weeds was bigger than any pile made by the other grandkids.

"Someday, Coley. I think Dayne and Katy would like that a lot."

Tommy was helping, but his attention span was brief. John watched him wander a few feet away, aim his finger at a patch of nothingness, and make a loud shooting sound. "Ha!" he cried.

"Whatcha doing, Tommy?" John walked over and directed the child back to the group.

"Tommy shoot dinosaurs." He looked over his shoulder and

took careful aim again. Once more he made the shooting sound. "Tommy shoot bees."

"Whew, thank you." John smiled to himself. Reagan and Luke had been working with Tommy, convincing him that it was never nice to shoot people. The training seemed to be working. "We don't want any bees or dinosaurs hurting us while we work."

"Tommy shoot tigers, too."

John was about to express his gratitude once more when a familiar car pulled into the drive. He took a few steps in that direction. It was his friend Elaine. The two of them hadn't seen each other since the talk they'd had on the porch swing weeks ago. When she'd asked him why they never talked about their relationship.

He'd had time to think her question over. Two lonely months, to be exact.

But why would she come now in the middle of the work party? And what about Ashley and the others? The last thing they needed was hurt feelings or tension on a day when everything and everyone was coming together. He watched Elaine climb out of the car. She wore jeans and a sweatshirt. In her hand were yellow work gloves and a box of what looked like gardening tools.

As she came closer, her eyes met his and held. She stopped a few feet from him and smiled. "Where do you want me?"

"Elaine . . ." He looked back at the kids, but Cole was busy pointing out areas they'd missed, assigning various weeds to specific children. John faced his friend once more. Never mind that his grown kids might be watching. He set down his shovel and closed the distance between them. Then he hugged her for a long while. When he let go, he let himself get lost in her eyes. "I missed you."

Her smile was shy, not in the least bit suggestive. "I missed you too." She took a long breath. "Maybe you don't know what you want, John. I think I'm okay with that. Life's too short to walk away from a friend, and that's what I did." She paused. "Can you forgive me?"

"Of course."

"Well then." She set her box of tools on the porch and grinned at him. "Looks like we've got some work to do."

He was still baffled. "How did you know we'd be here?"

"Simple." Her smile was filled with meaning. "Ashley called me."

CHAPTER THIRTY

THE PROJECT CAME TOGETHER just before midnight.

By then, all that was left was the cleaning. Otherwise, every item on Ashley's ten-page list had been crossed off. The finished house was stunning, better than anything any of them had dreamed. Thankfully Katy had been too busy with Dayne to ask many questions about it. Ashley had worked with Dayne's agent, getting the okay from him anytime they needed more funds. In that way they'd managed to keep the entire renovation a surprise.

The yard looked like something from a magazine cover. It was green and lush and neatly mowed. Big maple trees had been planted along the driveway, their leaves already decked out in brilliant reds and yellows. Bark dust had been spread along the perimeter of the property, and in the front flower beds Elaine and several other women had planted rosebushes and tulip bulbs that would come up right around the time of Katy and Dayne's wedding.

Maybe the most dramatic change was the log siding—which looked brand-new—and the improvements to the backyard. The new wooden deck was stained and cleaned, and the view from it was breathtaking. It was twice the size of the old one, large enough for big gatherings and barbecues overlooking Lake Monroe.

The inside of the house looked like a different place altogether. Brooke had picked warm colors for the painted rooms, and Kari had taken care to have wooden blinds hung over every new window. The appliances had arrived on schedule and were installed in the modernized kitchen. The ceiling beams were stained and looked warm against the earthy tile and taupe-colored carpeting, which had been laid by a local contractor who got wind of the project. It was the one piece Ashley had fretted about, but by Friday night the installation was completed and the carpet freshly vacuumed.

The final touches were made yesterday. Ashley had hung one of her paintings in the living room. It was the one that showed the back of a man standing in the foreground, looking at the Baxter house all warm and lit up and in the middle of a field that seemed to go on for miles. It was the one she'd painted when her older brother had been only some unknown guy out there, someone who was afraid to make contact with them. Now that she knew him, there was no question the man in the painting was Dayne Matthews. How could it not be him?

She'd patterned the man in her painting after Luke.

The painting wasn't the only personal touch that happened at the end. While watching the kids, Erin had framed some family pictures—Elizabeth and John at different stages of their marriage and collages of the Baxter kids and grandkids through the years. When the cleaning was finished late last night, Ashley and her sisters had worked together distributing the photographs, placing them around the kitchen counter and hanging them on the walls throughout the house.

The project reminded Ashley of dear, sweet Irvel, the woman she had cared for at Sunset Hills Adult Care Home. Irvel wasn't really at peace until Ashley found old pictures of her husband,

Hank. Once the framed photos hung on Irvel's walls, everything about her countenance had changed.

When Dayne saw the family pictures in every room, Ashley hoped the change in him would be the same. She could hardly wait.

When they finished, Ashley and her sisters and Luke and their father formed a spontaneous group hug, and for a few minutes the tears came for all of them. Tears because God had brought together every piece and because they had actually finished. Tears because their mother would've cherished this moment maybe more than any of them. Most of all tears because together they had become greater than the sum of their individual parts.

"Look what we can do when love pulls us together." Ashley sniffed. She glanced at Luke. "Can you believe it?"

None of them could. They were worn-out by the time they left.

Now it was Saturday morning, just ten hours later, and they were back again, anxious and excited and ready to give God the glory for what had taken place on this piece of ground.

Word of mouth spread through their various circles, and this morning everyone who had helped with the renovation was invited. Dayne and Katy would arrive around one o'clock, but the people came at eleven. They brought cards and gifts and flowers, and together they filled the dining room table with the outpouring of their love.

By noon, her dad asked everyone to gather outside.

It took a few minutes for the crowd to make their way out back for an informal worship service. Everyone held hands and formed an enormous circle. Ashley looked from one face to the next, and there was nothing she could do to stop her tears. It was like a snapshot of every season of her life, everything that had ever mattered. She smiled at them as she made eye contact. Kari and Brooke and Erin and Luke and their spouses and children. The Flanigans with their six kids and a couple dozen other CKT kids and their parents. Ashley grinned at Jenny Flanigan, then let her gaze move on around the circle.

Her father was there, of course, and next to him his friend Elaine. Ashley no longer felt threatened by her. God had used Landon to help her see that her dad deserved a friend. And if somewhere down the road that friend became something more, the Lord would meet them in that place. For now it was enough that there were no hard feelings, none whatsoever.

Around the circle were Brooke and Peter's doctor friends, coaches from Clear Creek High, and a crew of carpet layers from downtown Bloomington. There were Rhonda and Bethany and the lady who ran the art gallery near the university. She'd contributed a frame for Ashley's painting, and she wanted to be part of the surprise.

Ashley didn't mind. The more people who could welcome Katy and Dayne, the better.

Her father raised his hand, and the group quieted. "God has met us in this place." His voice was strong, steady. The way they would always see their father, no matter how the coming years might take their toll. "Now we are privileged to give Him thanks." Her father prayed, loud and clear. There would be time for tears later, but this moment was marked by smiles and gratitude and a satisfaction that ran deeper than any of them had ever known.

After the prayer, Tim Reed took his guitar from its case and led them in a few songs. He ended with "Great Is Thy Faithfulness." From the tough football players to the educated doctors to little Hayley holding Brooke's hand, they raised their voices to the clear blue skies as the song came to an end. "'All I have needed Thy hand hath provided—great is Thy faithfulness, Lord, unto me!'"

Ashley savored the moment. As long as she lived she would remember how it felt to see nearly a hundred people circled in her brother's backyard, their hearts joined as one as they gave praise to the Creator, their Father. Savior of all.

Then her dad talked about love. By then he had given all of his children except Dayne the letter from their mother—the one with the secrets to a happy marriage. "A long time ago, my wife,

Elizabeth, wrote down what she believed were the secrets to love."
He smiled. Next to him, Elaine didn't falter even for a moment.
"When we think of love, we think of marriage. But the truth is, the
secret to love works for all of us, whatever relationship we're in."

Ashley saw Bailey look down and lean in closer to her mother.

He went through a few of the points, talking about time, love,
laughter, and forgiveness. Lessons they'd learned that fall. But
he focused most of all on the first point—the one that Ashley
wouldn't have thought much about before taking on this project.
Her mother's wisdom was this:

God had them here to serve one another. Love acted out is
serving.

It was a truth they had played out in every possible way leading
up to this moment. Which was why, as the service came to an end,
Ashley was convinced that after today Dayne would finally know
that he was loved by his family, both now and forever.

Now all they had to do was wait.

CHAPTER THIRTY-ONE

THE MUSCLES in Dayne's stomach tightened as he and Katy neared the Bloomington airport. A part of him wanted to stay on the plane and beg the pilot to take them back to Los Angeles. The whole thing felt like the final scene in a movie, the kind so heart-rending, so gut-wrenching, that the sadness takes the wind out of people and afterwards they sit in the dark theater watching the credits because they don't want anyone to see their tears.

Bloomington lay spread out below as the plane circled low. The university and downtown area, the neighborhoods and sprawling farmlands. The lake.

The flight attendant approached them. "We'll be on the ground in a few minutes. Can I get you anything before we land?"

Katy shook her head. "We're fine, thanks."

"Very well." She smiled. "Let me know if you need anything." She returned to the back of the plane.

Next to him, Dayne felt Katy reach over and take his hand. "It'll be okay," she whispered.

Dayne didn't answer, but he ran his thumb against her hand,

drawing strength from her touch. He looked out the window. Every other time he'd arrived in Bloomington, it had been with a sense of hope and belonging, a feeling that this town, with its rolling green hills and lakeside picnics and close-knit people, was where he would spend forever if he had a chance. Not anymore. This time he saw it as a place he was letting go, a dream that never quite found a way to work itself out.

Dayne turned to Katy and searched her eyes. "I need you. Have I told you that today?"

She smiled. "You're worrying about nothing."

Since they were alone in the cabin, he leaned in and kissed her, the slow, sensual sort of kiss they could only take in small doses. At least until after the wedding. Then, with a lingering look at her, he turned back to the window.

A few years ago he'd starred in a movie based on a best-selling novel. The author showed up on the set during filming, and she and Dayne had shared several fascinating conversations. The whole writing process was beyond his understanding—how a person could sit at a computer, start typing, and create a story as long and complex as a novel.

"Do you ever struggle?" he asked her. "Is there a time when you try to write and the words won't come?"

Her eyes grew distant. "At the end of a book." A hint of sorrow colored her smile. "When it's a story I really love, one I've poured my heart and soul into, I'll sit down to write the last chapter and for a long time I'll just stare at the empty screen. Because deep inside me I don't really want it to end."

That's how Dayne felt now.

He sighed, and Katy leaned her head on his shoulder. That he was even here, with her by his side, was more than he could fully fathom, more than he could get his mind around. By God's mercy alone, Dayne had cut his recovery time in half and come out stronger in the end.

"Listen, man," the therapist had told him on their last day, when

Dayne checked out of the facility, "you're the toughest person I know. I mean that. I've never seen anyone work so hard."

Dayne thanked the guy, but the therapist was wrong. Katy had worked harder than he had. Katy—his friend, his future, his love. He rested his head on hers. She had always believed they would reach this moment. She'd put her own life on hold and had believed with every breath that he would wake up. Even when conventional wisdom said it was time to let go. She pushed him and encouraged him, no matter his mood or frustration. And when he closed her out entirely, she found a way to bring down the walls.

He loved her with his whole life, and nothing could change that. No matter what happened over the next few days.

The plane landed, then came to a stop. Lately he'd been reading the Gospels. He discovered that even with faith the size of a mustard seed, it was possible to say to a mountain, "Move," and the mountain would move. It had been that way with his pursuit of Katy, and certainly it had been that way with his recovery from near death. Though his faith was sometimes less than anything he could see or feel, for the past few months mountains had crumbled to the ground.

But not this mountain.

Coming to Bloomington for Thanksgiving, proving to Katy that his presence really was too much of a disruption for his family, was only his way of keeping a promise. Otherwise he would've avoided the heartache and stayed in Malibu—the place where he and Katy would most likely live once they were married, at least until he was finished with his current movie contract. Then maybe they'd find something along the West Coast—Oregon perhaps. Some small town like Medford, where they could raise a family and be close enough to Hollywood for Dayne to be involved in an occasional picture.

A black Pathfinder SUV from a local rental company was waiting for them as they exited the plane. Once their bags were loaded in the back, Dayne took the wheel. When Katy was buckled in beside him, he started the engine and was about to slip the car into gear when he stopped. He turned to her. "Tell me again. Why are we going by our house first?"

"Dayne—" her eyes filled with a gentle patience—"you're doing it again."

"What?" He pretended to be in the dark.

"Worrying." She put her hand on his knee and gave him a crooked grin. "Everything's going to be fine. I know it."

"Okay, you're right."

It was hard to hear over the sound of jet engines coming from a commuter plane forty yards away. She leaned closer, surprised. "I am?"

"Yes. You got me." He covered her hand with his. "I *am* worried." He searched her soul. "About you." He put the vehicle in gear and drove through the parking lot and onto the main road.

"Me?" She turned her back to the door so she could see him better.

"Yes." They were coming up on a red light. He waited until they were at a complete stop. They'd been trying hard to keep the mood light. But there were no lighthearted words for what he was about to say. He felt the teasing leave his eyes. "I'm worried you'll never forgive me if it doesn't work out. If this is the last time we do this."

For an instant, a ripple of fear passed over her face. But immediately she found her confidence again. Her unrelenting, limitless joy. "It's not the last." She looked straight ahead as the light turned green. "It's only the beginning."

"What if it's not?"

She smiled at him, her brows slightly raised. "Please. You promised."

She was right. As his rehab had progressed he promised not only to go to Bloomington if his therapist gave him clearance but to believe one more time that it was possible—that finding a place in the Baxter family really might work. Only here was the problem: the more he believed, the greater he would hurt when he felt Luke's coolness, sensed the resentment in his other siblings for the embarrassment they'd suffered merely by being related to him.

Still, Katy was right. He glanced at her. "I did, didn't I?"

"Yes." She faced the windshield. "God hasn't brought you this far only to have you lose it all."

They drove in silence. But when they were a few minutes from the house, Dayne remembered his original question. "You didn't answer me."

"About what?"

"The lake house. Why do we have to go there first?"

"Oh, that." Katy folded her arms and studied him. "I guess because it's on the way." She shrugged. "Ashley said it worked better for her schedule. She wants to point out the places the contractor thought needed the most work."

The knots in his stomach were tighter than before. But it wasn't fair to Katy to let them show. Not when she seemed so optimistic about what lay ahead. "That shouldn't take long. The whole place needs work. She can pretty much wave her hand in the general direction of the house and that should cover it."

"True. But we owe it to Ashley to meet her here. She's put in a lot of time making phone calls." She hesitated. "Even if nothing's actually finished yet."

Dayne was about to say something about that, about whether Ashley would be willing to oversee the process of remodeling once he returned to LA. But he stopped himself. He'd rained enough on Katy's parade for one day. Time would show them what lay ahead, even if once in a while he had to close his eyes to bear it.

"We're almost there." Katy put on lip gloss and checked her look in the mirror. "It'll be good to see Ashley again."

Dayne tried not to feel cut to the heart by her blithe comment. Later that week, when things didn't work out and they said their final good-byes, he would miss Ashley and John most of all. Ashley was the one who had fought for his place in their family, the one who had called him on her own that day. He kept his eyes on the road; the house was just ahead.

They saw cars and trucks as they rounded the final bend. In front of the lake house, along the road, and in a nearby field were thirty or so vehicles.

"What in the world?" Katy leaned forward and looked at the surrounding fields.

Dayne felt the same way. That many cars meant that many people. And where was the run-down old lake house?

He was about to pass the driveway of a stunning new home when he brought the vehicle to a screeching stop. "Wait."

Katy was staring at the place. "No way. There's no possible way."

Magically and completely, their lake house had been transformed. Dayne pulled into the drive and stopped again. The grass and shrubs, the landscaping and trees. None of it had been there before.

"How did she do it?" The color drained from Katy's face. She sounded as if she didn't know whether to laugh or cry. "Ashley said the subcontractors were booked until spring."

"I can't believe it." Dayne drove slowly up the driveway. "It isn't just the yard." He nodded to the house. "Look at that."

"It's gorgeous."

The outside of the house looked brand-new. If Dayne wasn't sure of the location, he would never have believed it was the same building. When he reached the house, he parked and looked at Katy. "You knew about this."

"No!" She laughed. "Ashley told me she couldn't get a single person out here to start working. I had absolutely no idea."

Dayne studied the place, the planted gardens and refurbished front porch, the stained logs and the striking windows. "She obviously found the best in the business. It looks amazing."

They climbed out of the car, and Katy came around to his side. As he took her hand, he remembered the vehicles parked along the road. One of them had to belong to Ashley, since she planned to meet them here. But what about the rest? The house was too quiet to have that many people inside.

They reached the side of the house and followed it around to the backyard. From every angle the home was breathtaking, and Dayne felt overwhelmed. How kind of Ashley to see that the work got done. It must've taken hours to call builders and keep searching until she could find the right people. He chuckled. "Ashley never gives up, does she?"

Katy smiled. She couldn't take her eyes off the house. "No. Not since I've known her."

They kept walking, the lake spread out before them like a glistening blanket of blue. Then, in what felt like slow motion, the backyard came into view and with it a sea of people, all of them grinning.

"Welcome home!" A chorus of voices broke the silence. And then all at once, a round of hoots and cheers and laughter burst from the group.

Dayne and Katy stopped and leaned on each other so they wouldn't fall flat on their backs from the shock.

Ashley pulled away from the crowd and ran up to them. She hugged Dayne first and then Katy, and by the time she drew back they could both see she had tears on her cheeks. "Well . . . what do you think?"

The pieces spun like fragments in Dayne's mind. It was like a scene from a reality TV show, only this was so far beyond reality he could hardly breathe. In as much time as it took him to blink, he surveyed the people, made a note of the faces around them. The Baxters were front and center, their kids bouncing up and down around them. To one side were the Flanigans along with bunches of CKT kids and their families. On the other side were football players with *Clear Creek High* emblazoned on their jerseys and beyond them a dozen people he didn't recognize.

Before Dayne's world could right itself, Luke stepped up. He stared at Dayne, his eyes bright with something like regret. He kept his voice low, between the two of them. "Can we talk later, just us?"

Dayne nodded. This was the most difficult part: facing Luke.

Luke put his hands in his pockets. "I said those words. But I never . . ." He coughed and looked down for a moment. When he lifted his gaze, his sincerity came straight from the center of his heart. "I never meant any of it. I'm sorry, Dayne."

Dayne felt flooded by love for his brother. Was this what he'd been dreading? Was it really happening? He put his hand on Luke's shoulder. "We'll talk later."

The onlookers were still hooting and shouting and celebrating the surprise. Dayne looked at the back of the house before he met Ashley's eyes and tried to recover enough to speak. "You . . . you had all these people come just to welcome us?"

"They all—" Ashley's voice cut out, drowned by the noise of the crowd.

Dayne saw Landon in the background, but he seemed willing to give her this moment.

Ashley came to Dayne again, hugged him, and held on tight. "I thought we'd lost you . . . but look at you. Like it never happened." She let go and turned her attention to Katy. "It's a miracle."

"Definitely." Katy took Ashley's hand. The others were still loud, still celebrating. They moved in closer, making a half circle around them. Katy looked as baffled as he felt. "It's beautiful, Ash. I thought you couldn't get subs out until spring."

More tears filled Ashley's eyes. "I couldn't." She massaged her throat. Then she made a wide sweeping gesture toward the crowd of people.

Luke, still close by, gave Dayne a humble, crooked smile. "What she's trying to say is, we did the work." He gestured toward the group. "All of us."

"What?" After a few heartbeats, Katy gasped. "You mean . . ."

"Yes." Ashley was crying openly now. "Everyone helped. Peter and Jim hung doors and replaced windows and Brooke painted and Luke worked on the roof and the football team sanded and stained the exterior and—" she laughed and tried to breathe at the same time—"Erin watched the kids and the CKT kids cleaned up the yard and Dad and Elaine helped the kids plant bushes and . . . I don't know . . . just come in and see it."

Dayne felt his heart bursting. The realization of what had happened was hitting him slowly, like a dream. He searched Ashley's teary eyes. "Why? Why would you do this?"

"Because . . . you're a Baxter." She wiped her cheeks. "That's what we do."

And there it was . . . the answer he'd been waiting for. Waiting for and dreading.

He stared at Ashley and tried to believe that she had really said the words *You're a Baxter. That's what we do.* With every grueling hour of rehab, every weight he struggled to lift, and every afternoon perfecting the once-ordinary skills of writing and eating and brushing his teeth, he had feared this moment. Going to Bloomington for Thanksgiving meant that for the first time in his life he would be with his entire birth family. No matter what he had promised Katy, he knew—he just knew—he would feel like an outcast, the one upsetting the balance for the rest of them. Every night when he lay in bed at the rehab center he had feared this reunion, dreaded it with his whole heart, because this would be the moment of reckoning.

The time for good-byes.

But maybe . . . just maybe he was wrong.

He stared at the ground and closed his eyes. *God, You knew this all along.*

My son, My precious son . . . welcome home!

The words echoed loudly in his heart. He opened his eyes and there was John. Suddenly Dayne wasn't sure if the response had come from God or from the man standing before him.

"We prayed for this moment." John's eyes were watery too. He wrapped Dayne in a hearty embrace; then he stepped back and put his hand on Dayne's shoulder. "Welcome home, Son."

That was the breaking point. Tears fell from Dayne's eyes, and he put his arm around his father's shoulders. "Let's go see the place." The biggest smile he'd had in a long time filled his face, and he hoped with every heartbeat that this wasn't a dream.

Katy walked beside him as they headed, with the crowd, to the back door. She slipped her arm around his waist, and that's when he noticed that she was crying too. She stopped for a moment, rose on her toes, and whispered near his ear, "Told you so."

Dayne wasn't sure whether to laugh or break down. He gave her a quick kiss and held her eyes, hoping she could read all that he couldn't find the words to say.

Then they made their way inside. It was as spectacular as the outside. As they reached the dining room table, Dayne and Katy stopped at the same time.

"What's . . . ?" Katy put one hand over her mouth and pointed with the other.

The entire table was filled with cards and flowers and gifts to welcome Dayne to Bloomington. But it wasn't until they turned as a group and went into the oversize kitchen, where the Baxters were, that Dayne realized how fully, how completely his prayers and questions about today had been answered.

"Dayne." Ashley squeezed her way in beside them. She had a young woman with her who looked familiar. Ashley's cheeks were still tearstained, but she glowed from the inside out. She motioned to the woman beside her. "This is Erin, our youngest sister."

Dayne smiled at Erin, and the last bit of his awkwardness faded entirely. He hugged her. "Hi, Erin." He took Katy's hand. "This is my fiancée, Katy."

"Hi, Erin." Two more tears slid down Katy's cheeks. She sniffed and laughed at the same time. "I can't wait to meet the rest of your family."

Erin seemed shyer than the others. She pointed at something

behind him. "I framed those for you. But everyone helped put them around the house."

Dayne and Katy turned and there on the counters were framed photographs of the Baxter family. The crowd of people stayed outside for the most part; only the Baxters were inside now.

Cole rushed around the counter and began describing each picture. "This one's Grandma and Papa before Grandma went to heaven." Then he moved on to the next one. "This is me and little Devin and Mommy and Daddy. Here's Aunt Erin and Uncle Sam and the girls, and Aunt Brookie and Uncle Peter and . . ." The explanation went on for several minutes. But the last frame in the line was empty. "You forgot one, Aunt Erin," Cole announced, reaching for the empty frame.

A pretty young woman stepped forward. She had an Asian baby in one arm and a mischievous-looking little boy by the hand. "It's okay, Coley." She smiled at Ashley's son. "You can leave that one there." Then she turned her little group toward Dayne and Katy. "That one's for you and Luke." She motioned to Luke and he joined her, putting his arm around her and the baby.

Luke's eyes were damp. "Dayne, I'd like you to meet my wife, Reagan, and our kids, Malin and Tommy."

"Nice to meet you." Dayne's heart pounded. If Luke could say what he'd said in the tabloids, Dayne figured his wife felt the same way. But now he could see that he was wrong. As wrong as could be.

He could live ten thousand years and never forget one detail about this surprise, the house and the yard and the people and most of all the family. He was touched by this moment, changed by it.

Even in the midst of introductions, Dayne realized what was happening. He and Katy were home—the place where he'd always wanted to be, with the people he'd long dreamed about knowing. They were survivors, all of them, and he could see life clearly now for the first time since his accident.

This was only the beginning.

Luke turned to his wife. "Honey, I'd like you to meet Katy Hart, Dayne's fiancée."

The two women shook hands and exchanged hellos. Luke hesitated. He hung his head and gave it a single shake. Briefly he touched his fingertips to his eyes. Then he lifted his head and looked at Dayne. "I've wanted to say this for a long time."

Dayne blinked twice, clearing the tears so he could make out Luke's face.

"Reagan—" Luke looked from his wife back to Dayne—"I'd like you to meet my brother."

Around the room, no one said a word. No one could. Dayne took Reagan's hand, but in the same moment, he turned to Luke and everything about the past faded. Dayne made the first move, and they came together in the kind of intense hug usually reserved for teammates in the moments after winning a championship. They stayed that way a long time, clinging to each other and all they'd almost lost.

And standing there in the kitchen of a house that would soon be home, there was an overwhelming sense that instead of losing everything they had defied the odds. Because in the end they had both won. And now Dayne and Luke had what neither of them had ever had before.

A brother.

CHAPTER THIRTY-TWO

THE TURKEY was in the oven, and the Baxter house was alive with the love and laughter and quiet conversations that Ashley looked forward to around the holidays. She was coming back from the garage with another pound of butter, but halfway to the kitchen she ducked into the living room and marveled. All twelve cousins were together, which meant sometime before the day was over Kari would line them up near the fireplace for the annual cousin photo. It was tradition.

Ashley stayed in her spot, unnoticed by the kids. Their laughter and the football game playing on TV and the smell of turkey wafting into every room were what Thanksgiving was supposed to be. That and their dad's prayer. Each year it was a specific praise time to their God and Savior and a chance for their father to ask a blessing for each of his kids present.

This year that would be *all* his kids.

The scene before Ashley was so alive it would be almost impossible to paint. But someday she'd like to try. Cole and Maddie were sitting at a card table her dad had put in the room for the older kids. They were trying to start a game of Yahtzee, but they seemed to be involved in a lengthy discussion about who would go first.

Cole was easily the loudest. "I go first 'cause I won last time." His tone of voice left no room for discussion.

"No! That's not how." Maddie was quick with her retort. "Girls go first. That's the rules."

Cole stood up and crossed his arms. "The rules don't say that, Maddie, because I read them. You're just trying to be the boss of me."

"No, I'm not." Her tone rose to a whine. With exaggerated movements, she put her hands on her hips. "Girls go first in Yahtzee. Otherwise girls don't play."

"That's not fair! You said you'd play, and now we have the papers out and we put our names on 'em, and that means no one else could use 'em later, so I'll just go first so we can move on."

Ashley stifled a giggle and rolled her eyes at the same time. Cole might have a future as a salesman, but he definitely needed help on his approach. Rudeness wasn't tolerated. She would talk to him about it later.

Malin was out of her playpen, darting about the room on her hands and knees and generally causing an uproar wherever she went. Erin's girls—Clarisse, Chloe, Heidi Jo, and Amy—were playing dolls on the floor with Kari's daughter, Jessie, and Brooke's Hayley. Erin's daughters were making an effort at being polite, but they kept sending the baby bits of instruction. "Stay out of here, Malin." "Go over there, Malin." "Don't touch our dollies, Malin."

Hayley's voice lifted above the others. "Hi, Mali!" She was talking much better, so improved that someone who didn't know she'd been in a near-drowning accident might think she just spoke a little slower than other children. Her tone was happy and earnest. "Mali . . . play with my dolly. Come on."

Malin crawled to Hayley and sat next to her new friend. At the same time, Jessie broke into a song about sunshine and rainbows.

A few words into it she stood up and faced the others. The song wasn't quite in tune, but it was happy and fitting for Thanksgiving.

Tommy was rolling a ball to RJ, which was what Kari and Ryan had started calling their son, who until then had been Ryan Junior. The little boys were a living example of testosterone in action. With every push of the ball, either Tommy or RJ would make a loud grunting sound, followed by a proclamation. "Catch it" or "Mine!"

Malin noticed the action and crawled, lightning fast, toward the two boys.

As she did, Tommy spotted her. He lowered his chin and glared at her. "No, Mali."

Reagan had asked if they would all help Tommy break his fascination with guns. "If you see him raise his finger toward someone, remind him that whatever we do, we don't shoot people."

Ashley wondered if this might be one of those moments.

Sure enough, as Malin came closer, Tommy slowly, methodically, raised his finger at her.

He was about to pull the imaginary trigger when Ashley stepped into the room and put her hand on his shoulder. "Tommy . . . we don't shoot people."

He jerked his hand so that now the trigger was facing the ceiling. Then he made a shooting sound and cast dancing eyes in her direction. "Tommy shoot bees." He followed up the announcement with a big grin.

Ashley was pretty certain he hadn't been aiming for the bees. But the idea that he knew right from wrong was a step, anyway. She praised him and headed back to her sisters and Reagan and Katy in the kitchen. The potatoes were peeled, cut in pieces, and on the stove. A dozen pies had been made the night before, and the Jell-O salads were in the refrigerator.

They had a few hours before dinner, time for coffee and catching up. Ashley had something she wanted to share with them. She had invited Elaine Denning for dessert. So far she and Elaine hadn't spoken much, hadn't developed a friendship or a connection yet. Ashley had simply decided to make her feel welcome. She was their father's friend, and friends were welcome to come for dessert. The way her mom had always made them feel welcome.

So that was tradition too.

The Flanigans were coming for dessert this year and with them Tim Reed. Elaine would feel comfortable, especially if people made a point of talking to her. Ashley was trying to answer God's call to love and let go of bitterness the way Katy and Dayne and Luke had let go of it these past few weeks. Her father didn't need her approval. Besides, he was entitled to a friend. It was that simple.

When Ashley reached the kitchen, the women were discussing Aunt Teresa, their dad's younger sister from Battle Creek, Michigan. She was in Indianapolis visiting one of her kids for dinner, so she might stop by for an hour tonight.

"I love Aunt Teresa." Kari giggled and looked at the others around the room. She stopped at Brooke. "Remember the time she and Dad and Mom were playing some card game and she started laughing?"

"Laughed so hard she developed chest pains. Everyone thought she was having a heart attack, so Dad took her to the emergency room." Brooke looked at Katy and Reagan, the only two who hadn't heard the story—though Ashley and Erin were too young to remember it.

"Right, so there she is in the ER explaining how she was playing cards and laughing, and the doctor presses on her chest, asks her if it hurts there."

Everyone in the circle was giggling now.

Brooke put her hand over her heart. "Most people don't know you have a muscle right here. If you laugh hard enough, you can actually pull it."

"Really?" Katy laughed harder.

"It's true." Ashley was standing next to Katy. "I wouldn't believe it if I hadn't heard this story so many times."

"So the doctor tells Aunt Teresa she'll probably be the laughing-stock of everyone back home, because she isn't having a heart attack. She just pulled her laughing muscle."

"The rest of her visit, if things got a little too silly, she'd go for a walk and tell everyone she needed to rest her laughing muscle."

"Yeah, and later on Dad asked her how come her laughing muscle was out of shape in the first place."

The six of them standing around the kitchen continued to laugh, and Ashley savored the sound. Whatever the future held, for now it was only important to be there together—all of them, including Dayne.

Because togetherness was the greatest tradition of all.

Thanksgiving dinner was about to begin, and Dayne was trying to memorize every moment.

He and Luke had talked outside on the front porch for an hour, and the outcome was better than anything Dayne could've imagined. What Dayne learned from Luke was surprising—nothing like what he had been worried about. Luke wanted a brother in the worst way; he always had. But at first everything had conspired to make him feel jealous instead of joyous. Now that those issues were resolved, Dayne couldn't wait for the future to unfold before them.

They had also talked about Dayne's offer of a law position in Indianapolis. "It's what I'd like—" Dayne felt more comfortable with every passing bit of conversation—"if you're interested."

"Interested?" Luke shoved his hands into his pockets and shrugged. "It's a dream come true."

All of it was really. Everything about today. He and Katy had sat on the floor with the kids for nearly an hour, getting to know his nieces and nephews. He and the guys had watched some football together. They were a remarkable family, the Baxters.

As they gathered around the table, Dayne was drawn back to a scene almost two and a half years earlier. He was in Bloomington for the first time, parked in the hospital parking lot trying to get up the nerve to go in and see his birth mother before she died. And out of the hospital came a group of people. One of the guys looked familiar, and Dayne realized he was watching Luke Baxter and his siblings. Dayne's siblings.

In that moment he wanted more than anything to jump out of the car and run to them, tell them he'd always wondered about them, and ask them a hundred questions. But the click of the paparazzi cameras kept him from making a move. Even when he felt physically ill watching them climb in their cars and drive away, Dayne knew his decision was for the best.

And now God had brought them together.

After some humorous commotion between Tommy and RJ, everyone was seated around two long dining tables.

Taking the spot next to Dayne, Katy grinned and leaned closer. "Told you so." She met his eyes, and he saw his future there. And the teasing glow she'd had all week whenever she reminded him that she had been right and he had definitely been wrong about the Baxters.

John sat at the head of the table, looking around the room. "We are so blessed to be together." His gaze settled on Dayne. "All of us."

Luke and Reagan whispered something, and Luke stood up. "I have an announcement."

Dayne leaned back in his chair and took Katy's hand. Luke had been fairly low-key until now. But the Baxters weren't formal. Whatever Luke had to say, sharing it now seemed like a good idea. Despite all Dayne's fears, these people had a way of making him feel everything he'd wanted to feel in a family. Love and belonging and friendship and common ground. And that was in one week together. He could only imagine what it felt like to be a part of them all his life.

Luke grinned at the faces around the table. "Reagan wants me to tell you—" he flashed a smile at her—"that yesterday I received news that I passed the bar exam. Also . . ." He glanced at Dayne and his smile faded. "I received an offer to represent Dayne exclusively from my firm's office in Indianapolis." He exchanged a look with Reagan. "We'll make the move after Christmas." He found Dayne again. "Thanks to my brother."

There was a round of congratulations, and then John began praying. "Dear God, we come before You with humble, grateful hearts. You have led us through many paths and valleys to get to this moment, but we're here. Together in one place, our hearts in unison as we look to You."

He prayed then for Brooke and her family and the continued healing of little Hayley; for Kari and Ryan and their children, that they would be blessed in their involvement in ministry at church; for Erin and Sam and their four girls, that adjustment would continue as their family came together. He prayed for Ashley and Landon and their boys and for Luke and Reagan and Tommy and Malin.

"Give Luke the strength to stay close to You daily, Lord. Help him be the father and husband . . . and brother he's always wanted to be."

Then he prayed for Dayne. "Father, Elizabeth and I have our lost son back, something that never could've happened without You. We have him back from the accident, of course, but we have him back from a place where we never expected to find him again. I pray that You let him know how much we love him and Katy, how much we're looking forward to a lifetime of days like this."

Suddenly the sum of moments overwhelmed Dayne, surrounding him and making him certain, once again, that this was the moment, the single instant that God had spent the last few years calling him toward. All of it—his trip to Bloomington, the chance moment of witnessing Katy Hart onstage, his decision to let go of his anger toward his adoptive parents, and his near involvement in Kabbalah. And not just those times, but his empty days with Kelly Parker and the pain that followed the abortion, even the terrible situations with the paparazzi—God had used all of it to lead him here.

The words Katy had heard from the Lord during his time in rehab came rushing back: *Wait on the Lord. Be still, and know that I am God.*

He gently tightened his hold on Katy's hand. God was a promise keeper. That much was evident even yesterday, when Randi Wells called and told him she'd bought a Bible. How amazing was that? He smiled, his eyes still closed.

His fame would always be an issue, an aspect of his life, but he was forgiven, and now that he had found his place in the family he longed for, he couldn't wait to start working on forever. Because now that his questions had been answered, now that the lake house was completed, it was time to start on the next project.

Planning a wedding.

A WORD FROM KAREN KINGSBURY

I have a confession to make.

I'm the author Dayne Matthews was talking about, the one he met on the set of one of his movies. I figured I could give myself a cameo appearance after so many books with these characters. My husband thinks I'm a little too close to the whole situation, and we both laugh about how the Baxter family and Dayne and Katy and the Flanigans feel like friends.

But it's also the truth—writer's block comes for me only when I procrastinate at the very end of a book I love. It was that way for the Firstborn series. I remember writing *Fame* and thinking how fun it would be following Dayne Matthews and the struggles he faced as a major celebrity. And now, his story is in many ways resolved. That made the final chapters of this book especially sad and difficult for me.

From the beginning, from the first time Dayne Matthews was introduced as the Baxters' oldest son, I've dreamed about this day—when the entire Baxter family could be together, knowing that they were committed to accepting Dayne as one of their own. And I can only say that God certainly met me at every turn in the road. Always, with each installment of the Firstborn series, there was a message that applied to all of us. For a season, I wasn't sure what God wanted us to take away from the story in *Forever*.

But I see it now.

The lesson is one God gives us throughout the Bible. Love one another. Love through forgiveness and love through service. Keep short accounts and don't let a bitter root grow. If we're going to love the way Jesus wants us to love, then we need to let go of the hurts from our past and let God bring about healing. In many ways, *Forever* was about healing. Dayne was healed from his horrific accident, and Katy was healed of her fear of leaving Bloomington. Luke was healed of his jealousy and bitterness toward Dayne, and Ashley was healed of her distrust toward her father's friend Elaine. Healing took place between many people, in many ways.

Which is exactly what God wants to see in our lives.

It's at the end of any story that we must all ask how it applies to us, what we can take away from it. So what about you? Are you struggling with a broken relationship? The Bible says, "As far as it depends on you, live at peace with everyone." Is God calling you to make a phone call or write a letter? Is He asking you to offer an apology or extend forgiveness? We can't begin to think about forever without ridding ourselves and our lives of the baggage of bitterness and broken relationships.

At the same time, there are situations in which the other person is unwilling to receive an apology or forgiveness. That's how it is with a situation in my life. A long time ago I had a friend whose laughter and love for God helped me in the early days of my walk with Christ. Honestly, I'm not sure how things went south between us, but they did. All attempts I've made toward reconciliation—e-mails, phone calls, gifts—have been met with silence and a painfully locked door.

So what do we do in this situation?

For me, I've had to let go. I continue to pray and believe God that all things work for the good of those who love Him. I've gently placed this relationship into the hands of our Father, and I continue to give the struggle to God whenever the pain returns, whenever the memories push me to want to pick up the phone and call her.

Through writing *Forever*, God taught me what He taught Katy and Dayne. We are always better to be patient and still, waiting on God. I'll be trying to live that way in regards to my lost friend until my dying day. Praying, hoping, believing, letting go, and waiting.

I pray you'll do the same if you're struggling with a broken relationship that feels unfixable. Because most times, the people in our lives *will* listen and they will respond. In that case, as far as it depends on you, live at peace with everyone. Love the way God loves. The rest is up to Him.

So, yes, this final piece of the Firstborn series was special for me. But don't worry. There are still many dilemmas facing Katy and Dayne. They have a wedding to plan and the possibility of Katy starring in a movie with her man. Any of you who read the covers of tabloids know the difficulties of a celebrity marriage. Those challenges will be explored, as will the many situations facing the Flanigans and the Baxters.

By now you know the story that began with the Redemption series and spun into the Firstborn series isn't coming to an end. Not yet, anyway. There are still many trials and triumphs ahead for John Baxter and his family, for Katy Hart and Dayne Matthews, and for the Flanigan family.

My next Baxter book will be *Sunrise*, the first in the Sunrise series. After Sunrise will come *Summer*, *Someday*, and *Sunset*. It's hard to imagine letting go of these characters after that. So I won't think about it yet. Not when there are still so many pages to write, so many hills and valleys to explore together.

As I write, please continue to pray that God will give me story lines that He'll use in your lives and the lives of all who read these books. That He would be glorified, that lives would be changed—that's what matters. If this book helped you understand Jesus better, or if you want to know how you could have a relationship with Him, please contact a Bible-believing church in your area. Get involved in a Sunday school class or a weekly Bible study. There are so many options, and with the Internet, it's very quick and easy to do a check of local churches.

The Christian life is a day-by-day relationship with Christ. Day by day and minute by minute. If you haven't found that lifesaving relationship, there is no time like now to begin. A reader recently wrote and told me that she was fascinated by Jesus and interested in following Him. But she wondered if maybe it was too late for her. Hopefully the story of Katy and Dayne has shown you that it is never, ever too late to take the hand of Jesus and begin the greatest walk of all.

As always, stop by my Web site at www.KarenKingsbury.com and see what's coming up or use it as a place to connect with other readers and book clubs. You can leave prayer requests or take on the responsibility of praying for people. People often tell me they haven't found a purpose or meaning to their faith.

Maybe they're on the go a lot or their circumstances keep them homebound. Remember, prayer is a very important ministry. It was prayer that turned things around for Dayne and Luke, prayer that made the difference time and again in this series. Your prayers—either in the midst of a busy day or as the main focus of a homebound one—could be crucial in the life of someone else, someone God wants you to pray for. Visit the prayer link on my Web site and make a commitment to pray for the hundreds of hurting people who have left requests there.

My family is doing well, about to begin a second year of home-schooling together. It's a wonderful adventure full of laughter and precious memories. Kelsey is a high school junior, talking about colleges. Austin, nine, rarely wakes up in the middle of the night wanting to climb in the middle between Donald and me. Yes, I can feel the days moving too fast, and there's nothing I can do to slow the ride. But I am enjoying every minute all the same, trying to remember the lessons from *Forever*—love one another through forgiveness and service. Always and forever.

Thanks so much for sharing in this journey, the journey of the Baxter family. I pray that God is using the power of story to touch and change your life, the way He uses it in mine.

Until next time, blessings in His amazing light and grace,

Karen Kingsbury

DISCUSSION QUESTIONS

Use these questions for individual reflection or for discussion with a book club or other small group.

1. Why do you think our culture is fascinated by celebrity? How has this fascination affected you personally?
2. What are the dangers of being so caught up in the lives of celebrities? Have you seen this cause a problem for you or someone you know?
3. What messages are indirectly being given to young people from the celebrities written about in gossip magazines?
4. What was the Baxter family's immediate response to Dayne's accident? What were the risks of John and Ashley's trip to Los Angeles?
5. Tell of a time when your family showed you great support in a time of need. What do you believe motivated them? How did that support affect you?
6. What was Katy's response to the accident? As Dayne's coma continued, what did Katy's actions say about her faith?
7. Talk about Luke's struggles with Dayne before the accident. What did you think of Luke's attitude in the early part of the story?
8. What do you think motivated Ashley to get Dayne and Katy's lake house fixed up? How has Ashley grown through this series and the last?
9. Have you ever undertaken a project—a party, a task, etc.— as a labor of love? Explain the project. What were the results of it?
10. Why do you think Elaine left John's house frustrated that day? Do you have a relationship that seems to be on hold? Explain and discuss what you believe is holding that relationship back.

11. Katy found strength in the Bible verse "Be still, and know that I am God" (Psalm 46:10). What do you think this verse means? How does it apply to your life?

12. What happened to the people in Bloomington as they began to pull together and help the Baxters with the lake house? Have you seen a project bring people together? Explain.

13. List three things wrong with Luke and Reagan's marriage and discuss. Do you know people who struggle with these issues?

14. How important was communication to Luke and Reagan? How important is it in your relationships? Give examples.

15. Dayne found strength in this Bible verse: "We know that in all things God works for the good of those who love him, who have been called according to his purpose" (Romans 8:28). What did this mean to Dayne? What does it mean to you?

16. Discuss the timing of Dayne waking up from his coma. Tell about a time when it seemed as though God waited until the last minute to answer your prayers. Why do you think He sometimes has us wait?

17. What was Dayne's reaction when he read the magazine with the quotes from Luke Baxter? Tell about a time when someone you love hurt you for reasons you didn't understand.

18. How did Dayne express his hurt and anger? How do you express your hurt and anger? How does God want us to handle these feelings?

19. Why was it so important to Luke that he take part in the renovation of the lake house? Describe a time when you were able to do something for someone else. How did it make you feel?

20. Explain why Dayne was dreading the Thanksgiving visit to Bloomington. What were the best moments of his homecoming? Describe a homecoming that was special to you.

Please turn the page for an exciting preview of

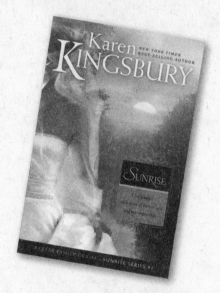

the first book in the

SUNRISE SERIES

by Karen Kingsbury

CP0494

From

S U N R I S E

by Karen Kingsbury

CHAPTER ONE

A WINTRY WIND BLEW across Bloomington the day after Thanksgiving, and it reminded Katy Hart that the seasons had changed. Not just in the air around town but in her life as well. After all they'd been through, after every good-bye they'd ever told each other, this time Dayne Matthews wasn't going back home.

He *was* home.

The walk around Lake Monroe was Dayne's idea—returning to the place where their hearts first connected, the place where they could always find their own world no matter what paparazzi or media circus waited for them on the other end of the wooded path.

They held hands, their pace slow and easy. The shock of the past week's events wasn't wearing off, but it was sinking in. For the first time in his life, Dayne had a family waiting for him around the corner, people he could visit after Sunday church services or invite over for a barbecue. Sisters and a brother and a father who would welcome him and listen to him and laugh with him. People who saw him not as Dayne Matthews, Hollywood star, but as Dayne, the missing member of the Baxter family.

Katy breathed deep and looked up through the barren branches to the bright blue sky beyond. "We're dreaming, right?"

Dayne chuckled. His arm brushed against hers as they walked. "I keep asking myself the same thing." He tightened his hold on her hand. "I thought we'd be on a plane back to LA this morning."

Katy smiled. "I hate to say it."

"I know." He laughed again. "You told me so."

A burst of wind swept in along the path, and Katy moved closer to Dayne. He was warm and strong, and the hint of his cologne mixed with the smell of distant burning leaves. The feel of him against her filled her senses. Even in the darkest days, when Dayne's accident looked as if it would kill him or leave him permanently injured, Katy always believed that somehow, someway, they would wind up here.

When Dayne woke up from his coma, when God's miraculous powers became brilliantly obvious in Dayne's recovery, his doctor and therapist had never thought for a minute that today he would be well enough to walk around Lake Monroe.

But here they were.

Dayne released Katy's hand and put his arm around her shoulders. "We need to shop."

"For the house?"

"Yes." He stopped and faced her. "Every room. You can pick out what you want, and we can have a designer do the rest." He grinned and framed her face with his hands. "As long as it's ready before the wedding."

Katy felt suddenly light-headed. This was the part of being engaged to Dayne that she rarely thought about. The lifestyle change. She would go from her apartment above the garage at the Flanigan house to a beautiful estate on a bluff overlooking Lake Monroe. Whatever furniture, whatever bedding and linens and dishes and entertainment systems she wanted would be hers. The thought was overwhelming, more than she could comprehend. Not that she would change because of it. Her tastes would remain simple; she was sure of that. But still, her new budget was something she'd have to get used to.

"The house could stay empty for all I care." She eased her arms around his waist. "I only need you."

"Mmmm." He came closer, his breath warm on her face. He worked his fingers into her hair, cradling her head with both hands. Smoldering desire filled his tone. Slowly, with a restraint that didn't show in his face, he kissed her. Then he pulled back enough to see her eyes. "You and a big bed with down comforters and satin sheets—" he kissed her again, longer this time—"and a dozen pillows."

"Dayne . . ."

He chuckled low in his throat and swayed with her, dancing to the sound of an occasional passing flock of geese and the whisper of the breeze around them. He pressed his face lightly against hers. "Maybe we should change the wedding date."

She felt dizzy with the nearness of him. "Okay."

His lips met hers. "Let's get married this afternoon."

Katy's body reacted to his, and she almost dropped the teasing and told him yes. But she kissed him instead. Long and slow, a kiss that told him he wasn't the only one looking forward to the honeymoon, dreaming about every day that followed. She could feel him trembling. How easy it would be to get into trouble between now and then. She ran her hands up the small of his back. "We have to be careful."

Dayne kissed her again. When he pulled back, his breathing had changed. "Very . . . very careful." His eyes were smoky, filled with passion and a longing that was more about love than lust. He moved a strand of her hair and looked deep into her eyes. When he spoke again, there was control in his tone once more. "And we *will* be careful." He smiled. "The wedding's going to be beautiful, Katy."

She put her hands on his shoulders. A cool wind blew through the space between them. "I was sort of looking forward to your other idea."

"The courthouse this afternoon?"

"Exactly."

He laughed. "I love you." He kissed her again, but this time he was the one who stepped back. "For now, though, this—" he gave her a pointed look and exhaled hard—"will have to happen in small doses."

Katy laughed and fell into place beside him. For a while it was all they could do to keep walking. She ached to kiss him again, to stay lost in his embrace for an hour. But Dayne was right. They'd made a promise to God and to each other to wait until they were married—a promise that was bound to be more difficult for Dayne, whose past had robbed him of the innocence Katy still cherished. In her private moments with God, she had vowed not to tempt Dayne. For that reason, their tender, intimate moments needed to be brief.

"So . . ." Dayne raised his brows. His expression told her that he was still cooling off. "About the wedding . . ."

She smiled and turned her gaze toward the water. "The real one?"

"Right." He slipped his arm around her shoulders. Their strides were casual and in perfect unison.

"You really think we can keep the media away if we have it at the country club?"

"I'd like to try."

She'd been thinking about the logistics. They wanted a beautiful, traditional ceremony without the chaos of circling helicopters and paparazzi jumping out of the bushes. Especially now, when the chase of media had nearly cost Dayne his life.

Even so, Katy had no idea how they were going to keep the wedding a secret. She looked at him. "I guess I can't get past the impossibility of it."

"I've got someone working on it." His voice was deep, soothing. "I guess the rule of thumb is fifty people. Invite fifty or fewer, and the press usually doesn't find out. Invite more . . ." He shrugged. "It's just about unheard of."

"Fifty?" Katy winced. "CKT alone has more than twice that." She wanted her ailing parents from Chicago, the Flanigans, the Baxters, and everyone involved with her Christian Kids Theater group. Then there were a few dozen Hollywood friends and business associates Dayne hoped to invite.

"I know. We need to plan on a hundred and fifty." Dayne narrowed his eyes and glanced at the path ahead of them. "That's why we need to talk." He stopped and drew a long breath. "I have an idea."

Katy looked into his eyes, and her heart soared. Dayne wasn't willing to settle in any way, not when it came to her. "Tell me."

"Okay." His eyes danced. "Here's what I was thinking. . . ."

John Baxter didn't usually jump into Christmas shopping the day after Thanksgiving. But Elaine had suggested the idea. Now it was Friday morning, and he was waiting for her to pick him up so they could drive to Circle Centre mall in the heart of Indianapolis. Elaine told him the trip could take most of the day. They had fifteen grandkids between them to shop for.

John wandered into the living room and looked out the front window. She would be here any minute. Elaine Denning was never late. He leaned against the sill and thought about last night.

Elaine's visit with him and his kids over pumpkin pie marked the first time he'd included her around any of them. The outcome had been dramatically better than he'd ever hoped. The entire family had accepted Elaine with kindness and grace, making conversation with her and helping smooth over any awkward moments—like the time Maddie walked up, took Elaine's hand, and said, "Are you Papa's girlfriend?"

Rather than looks of shock or disapproval, everyone chuckled and Ashley walked up to her niece. "Yes, Maddie." She smiled at Elaine. "She's Papa's friend and she's a girl. So that makes her a girlfriend." She cast an unthreatened smile at John and Elaine.

"See." Maddie looked at Cole, satisfied. "I thought so."

As his granddaughter walked off, John had looked at Ashley, awed. The animosity she had always expressed about Elaine seemed to have been totally replaced by warmth and acceptance. Her hospitality toward Elaine had been one more way the Baxters' Thanksgiving was marked by God's presence.

After Maddie's innocent remark, the topic of Elaine and him hadn't come up again. Everyone was busy connecting with Dayne and Katy and the Flanigans, who had also joined them for dessert. Elaine's presence felt natural, and John believed they'd found a new level of friendship because of it.

Late last night, when she was ready to leave, he had walked her to her car. Their conversation replayed in his mind.

"I felt welcome tonight, John." Elaine seemed careful to keep some distance between them.

John pulled his jacket tighter around himself and looked at the half-moon hanging over the Baxter house. "I guess they're ready for me to have friends."

Her expression changed but only slightly. She smiled. "I'm ready for that too."

"Good." He reached out and gave her hand a single squeeze. They'd avoided each other for two months because John was determined to give Elaine the space she seemed to want. If she was looking for more than friendship, he was the wrong man. He wasn't ready to love again, and he had a strong sense he might never be.

The memory dissolved as Elaine's car pulled into the drive. A slight thrill passed through him. He was looking forward to the day more than he'd expected. Elaine made him laugh with her subtle sense of humor. Spending a day with her would get him out of the house, away from the memories of a lifetime of Thanksgivings past.

John took a last look at the house before he stepped outside. This was the day each year when Elizabeth would haul out the

Christmas decorations and turn the Baxter house into a wonderland of red and green and twinkling lights.

Since her death, the banister had gone without garland, the mantel without pine branches and bows, and three decades of decorations had stayed in boxes. Last year this had been one of the hardest days of all. He'd spent most of it sitting in his recliner—the one next to her rocker—looking through photo albums of smiles and laughter and loving moments lost forever to yesterday.

He would not spend the day that way this year, though. He turned and closed the door. As he did, he left behind the trace of cologne he hadn't worn in years. Today he would find another kind of smiling and laughter, shopping and joking and enjoying time with a woman he couldn't wait to spend the day with—Elaine Denning.

His friend.

⚜

Someone was knocking at the door, but Bailey Flanigan could barely open her eyes.

"Bailey . . . get up. Come on!" The voice was Connor's.

"Please . . ." She groaned and turned over. "Let me sleep."

She had stayed up late Thanksgiving night, going over audition songs with Connor and texting Tim Reed. It was three in the morning when she'd turned off the lights and finally fallen asleep.

The door opened and Connor leaned in. "Bryan Smythe's here. I'm serious, Bailey. You have to see this."

Bryan Smythe? Bailey sat up. It took only a few seconds before her body responded. She jumped up and ran into her bathroom. "What in the world?" She looked over her shoulder at her brother. "Why?"

Connor grinned. "You need to see for yourself."

"Ugh. I can't go down looking like this." She ran her fingers through her hair and splashed cold water on her face. The mirror told her she still looked half-asleep. There were pillow creases across her right cheek.

"It doesn't matter." Connor's tone was almost frantic. "He's waiting. Come on."

After Connor left, Bailey darted into her closet, water still dripping from her face. She pulled off the T-shirt and flannel leggings she'd been sleeping in and slipped into a sweatshirt and the first pair of jeans she could find. Ever since she and Tanner Williams broke up, her social life had been one extreme or the other. Meanwhile, Tanner had been seeing a senior girl with a reputation for sleeping with her boyfriends. Bailey and Tanner rarely looked at each other when they passed in the halls, and many weeks Bailey could come home form school five days straight without so much as a single call or text from any guy.

On those days, Cody Coleman, the senior football player who lived with them, would pat her on the shoulder and smile at her as if she were a child. "Don't worry, Bailey. They'll be lined up one day."

Her attraction to Cody had cooled a lot since he moved in with them. He dated a different girl every few weeks, and he treated Bailey like she was thirteen instead of sixteen. Sometimes she couldn't wait for next year, when he'd leave for college and they could be finished with him.

Bailey pulled her hair back in a ponytail and hurried out her bedroom door. The text messages from Tim the day before ran through her head. *Do you ever think about the future, Bailey? . . . How things might wind up?* She had kept her answers short. Tim Reed was rarely in such a pensive mood, and she wanted to know what he was thinking. A few texts later he wrote, *Let's go to the park Friday. You and I need to catch up.*

What was this with Bryan? She rounded the corner and headed down the hallway. Sure, he'd acted interested a few months ago. But he'd been out of the picture for a while. Rumors around CKT had him seeing someone at his high school. So why was he here this morning?

She made it to the entryway, and there, standing just inside the front door, was Bryan. He held an enormous bouquet of roses— red and yellow and white. A small note card was tucked in near the middle.

Bailey gasped softly and looked from the flowers to Bryan. "What . . . what's going on?".

He shrugged. "I finally had a morning to myself." He took a step toward her and held out the bouquet. As he handed it to her, he grinned. "I might not call every day, Bailey, but I'm thinking about you." Bryan hesitated; then he moved back toward the door. "I wanted you to know."

She wasn't sure what to do next. "For no reason?" She lifted the flowers close and smelled them. "You brought me roses for no reason?"

His eyes answered her question before he did. In them she could see confidence and determination directed entirely at her. "You're reason enough." He gave her one last smile and raised his hand. "Bye. See you around."

Then, before she could hug him or thank him or get any more information than that, he turned and jogged down her walkway.

Bailey went to the door, stepped outside, and raised her voice so he could hear her. "Thanks. They're beautiful."

He waved and flashed a grin that said he enjoyed this—being mysterious and unexpected and beyond romantic. He was in his car and back down their driveway before she could catch her breath.

What was he up to? And why this morning? She pulled the card from the bouquet and opened it.

> White because I will always treasure your innocence, yellow because we were friends before anything else . . . and red for all that I hope lies ahead.
>
> Always,
> Bryan

343

Chills passed down Bailey's neck and spine. "Okay, Bryan," she whispered as she smelled the flowers again. "Could you be any more amazing?"

She was heading back inside, still trying to make sense of it, when from the far left side of the house she heard her mother scream.

"Mom?" Bailey set the flowers down and raced toward the sound. She heard her father and the boys running behind her.

They arrived at the guest room door at the same time, and Bailey covered her mouth. Her mother was kneeling on the floor, her eyes wide and scared. "Call 911. Hurry. He's barely breathing."

Connor jumped into action, racing past their mom and grabbing the phone.

Her dad rushed into the room and knelt near her mother. "Does he have a pulse?"

"Barely."

Her dad looked like he was going to cry. He moved in closer. "How could he?"

"Pray, Jim." Tears spilled onto her mother's face. She looked at the rest of them. "Pray!"

"Is he . . . ?" Bailey couldn't finish her sentence. She stayed frozen near the doorway.

Cody Coleman was sprawled on his back, his face and arms gray. The entire room was filled with a pungent smell. That's when Bailey spotted it. Only then did she have a clue what had happened. Lying next to Cody was a bottle of liquor—hard liquor.

The bottle lay on its side, and from what Bailey could see, it was no longer full.

It was completely empty.

Three great series
One amazing drama

From the start of the Redemption series, *New York Times* best-selling author Karen Kingsbury captured readers' hearts. The gripping Baxter Family Drama, which has sold more than 4 million copies, begins with *Redemption,* continues through the Firstborn series, and reaches a dramatic conclusion in the Sunrise series. Pick up the next book today to discover why so many have fallen in love with the Baxters.

Available now at bookstores and online.

Other Life-Changing Fiction by

KAREN KINGSBURY

REDEMPTION SERIES
Redemption
Remember
Return
Rejoice
Reunion

FIRSTBORN SERIES
Fame
Forgiven
Found
Family
Forever

SUNRISE SERIES
Sunrise
Summer
Someday
Sunset

RED GLOVE SERIES
Gideon's Gift
Maggie's Miracle
Sarah's Song
Hannah's Hope

SEPTEMBER 11 SERIES
One Tuesday Morning
Beyond Tuesday Morning
Every Now and Then

ABOVE THE LINE SERIES
Take One
Take Two
Take Three
Take Four

BAILEY FLANIGAN SERIES
Leaving
Learning
Longing

FOREVER FAITHFUL SERIES
Waiting for Morning
A Moment of Weakness
Halfway to Forever

WOMEN OF FAITH FICTION SERIES
A Time to Dance
A Time to Embrace

LOST LOVE SERIES
Even Now
Ever After

CODY GUNNER SERIES
A Thousand Tomorrows
Just Beyond the Clouds

STAND-ALONE TITLES
Oceans Apart
Where Yesterday Lives
When Joy Came to Stay
On Every Side
Divine
Like Dandelion Dust
Between Sundays
Unlocked
Shade's of Blue
This Side of Heaven

CHILDREN'S TITLES
Let Me Hold You Longer
Let's Go on a Mommy Date
Let's Have a Daddy Day
We Believe in Christmas
The Princess and the Three Knights
Brave Young Knight

MIRACLE COLLECTIONS
A Treasury of Christmas Miracles
A Treasury of Miracles for Women
A Treasury of Miracles for Teens
A Treasury of Miracles for Friends
A Treasury of Adoption Miracles
Miracles: A 52 Week Devotional

GIFT BOOKS
Stay Close Little Girl
Be Safe Little Boy
Forever Young: Ten Gifts of Faith for the Graduate

www.KarenKingsbury.com

CP0038